Goodbye Charlie Tango

By

John Sutton

In memory of Keith Gardiner

Chapter One

The fifteen men, formed roughly in all round defence, crouched on the side of the hill waiting for first light that would be almost two hours in coming. Their sweat had already turned cold and the mosquitoes were active and in aggravation mode. There was nothing to do but sit and stare at the dark and swat at the whine of the impending mosquito attacks.

For some it was a welcome time to rest and clear their befuddled brains for only four hours earlier they had been sampling the numerous bars and dance halls of the state capitol, Ipoh. On return to camp, some of them the worse for drink, they had barely crawled under their mosquito nets when the second in command of the camp guard was shaking them with the unpleasant news that the tracking team was on call out. The team was permanently on a two-hour stand by so their kit was always packed and ready, all they had to do was draw weapons and ammunition and then wait to be briefed. The briefing had taken place on the truck en route to the drop off point, a grid reference that was on a minor road just south of the village of Chemor.

'At last light yesterday,' Captain Ben Murphy began, 'the 1st Kiwi's, acting on intelligence, ambushed a bridge on the road just outside Kuala Kangsar. It was thought to be elements of 7 Platoon escorting a body of some importance,' he had to shout to make himself heard above the noise of the Bedford truck as he crouched between the two rows of men, 'At twenty thirty five hours the ambush was sprung and the killing group accounted for three and another two were bagged by a stop group in cultivation north of the road. But the rest, and they are thought to number about twenty, did not attempt to cross the road. It is thought that they took off south and could be on our patch,' he laid out his map on the packs piled between the seats and lit it with a torch. 'We're out to nail them or deny them passage south. We are to search for tracks on the central ridge of the Jelapang range. When we find any we will pass their direction to control and ambushes will be put in place in the relevant areas. We will pursue and do bad things to them if we find them; any questions?'

Nobody spoke, they were cold and tired and it did not seem like the most complex of tasks, they had done similar operations dozens of times in the past.

The tracking team was a quick reaction force of sixteen men made up of the fittest and keenest in the battalion and all were volunteers. It included the best signallers, dog handlers, and trackers, the latter being members of the Sarawak Rangers, Iban tribesmen from Borneo. Ben also had two excellent NCOs, Sergeant 'Boggy' Marsh and Corporal 'Tex' Riley. Their brief was to react quickly to any incident or contact that occurred in the battalion's area.

When Ben considered the light good enough to move, he gave the signal and the team heaved their packs onto their backs and then stood, slightly bowed under the weight, waiting for the order to move off. At a few minutes before 0600 hours the long slow climb up the Jelapang range began, hangovers were about to be sweated out. They were glad to be on the move, the sitting and the cold had made them stiff and they knew that the higher they went the fewer mosquitoes there would be.

*

The young man standing by the ship's rail was, in most respects, nondescript; medium would best describe him. He was of medium height and medium build, his features, though not unpleasant could never be regarded as good-looking, they were even and topped with medium brown and curly hair. If his final school report was to be believed, then he was also of medium intelligence. Two things redressed this impression of mediocrity; his intelligent blue eyes and his attire. As the ships orderly officer he was immaculate in starched tropical service dress complete with gleaming Sam Brown, sword and service cap.

After the claustrophobic atmosphere of his shared cabin the warm night air felt fresh and almost cool. It was three o'clock in the morning and the SS Empire Fowey lay in the calm tropical waters of the Straits of Malacca, six miles off Singapore, the gateway to the East.

A myriad of lights beckoned from the great city offering mystery, excitement and adventure, but despite the appeal of the legendary city's lights they were put to shame by the brilliance and vivacity of the stars overhead, cushioned on the blackest velvet sky. They shone with the cold clarity only to be seen at sea or in a wilderness where there is no contamination by artificial light.

Simon Gates was a newly commissioned second lieutenant in the Royal West Lancashire Regiment, and this was his first trip overseas of any significance. He had shared the odd holiday in France with his parents whilst still at school, but Europe in the early nineteen fifties still carried the horrific scars of the Second World War, and there were few places that offered the facilities of a holiday resort that would exist in the years to come. Most Britons took their holidays in their own fair isle, at seaside resorts of Victorian vintage, or in the newly created holiday camps that had begun to spring up around the coast.

Simon leaned on the rail drinking in the view and the magical aura that reached out across the black shimmering water. He had enjoyed the three-week journey, grateful that he had allowed his father to persuade him from his original intention of undertaking his two years National Service in the ranks.

The former German liner carried one thousand four hundred passengers, about two hundred of them, commissioned officers and their families, in the luxury of first class. A further two hundred, comprising of senior NCOs and WO's and their families, enjoyed the second class, and the female service personnel, and other ranks families made up the third class. All of these classes travelled in some degree of comfort or even luxury, unlike those known as the dormitory personnel. These luckless souls, the soldiery, the bulk of the human cargo, were packed below decks in airless and overcrowded conditions. They slept in bunks stacked three high in rows, so close, that two people could only pass with difficulty. Victoria's soldiers would not have found the living conditions much changed.

Visiting the troop decks was the one thing that Simon had detested during the journey, and it was a job that he would avoid whenever he could, but there were times when a trip to the foetid lower decks could not be avoided, and in his role as orderly officer it was required of him to make a number of visits during his tour of duty. He consulted his watch; there was an early reveille this morning so the next depressing visit was almost due.

He inhaled deeply as if to fill his lungs in preparation and perceived a tinge of exotic, but unidentifiable fragrances, combining with the clean scent of the sea which fired his prevailing sense of excitement. This exhilaration had possessed him since they had sailed from Ceylon on the final leg of the journey five days ago.

So much had happened in the past six months. That he would be called up to do his bit he had accepted, there was no choice, but then some great force had seemed to take over his life and his will. He had approached his service with resignation and an expectancy of two wasted, and uninspiring, years and the first twelve weeks had been worse than he had anticipated, or had been warned of.

The life of a new recruit in the South Staffordshire Regiment was tough by any standard; the food was atrocious and only edible because they were run ragged from six in the morning until ten at night and anything placed on their plates would have been devoured eagerly. The living conditions were appalling, the bull extreme and their treatment by the training staff verged on sadism. But this was the norm for infantry recruits in the early 1950s, few were volunteers, this was the age of

National Service and discipline had to be severe for a conscript army to function.

When his company commander had made the same suggestion as his father that he should apply for a commission, he had gladly taken up the offer and had successfully exposed himself to the War Office Selection Board. The six months spent at Eaton Hall, near Chester, had been a complete revelation in both his attitude and abilities of which he had been oblivious. His approach to the two years of enforced service, changed, from one of disagreeable compliance to a positive determination to develop as a person and gain an experience that could not be realised in any other walk of life. His changed disposition and dedicated desire to learn had won him the Sword of Honour for the best officer cadet of the intake. Eighteen months of excitement and adventure now lay before him.

'Are you ready to do the rounds, sir?'

Simon felt that his feet had literally left the deck, the orderly sergeant had approached without a sound and from the hint of the smile on the NCOs thin lips Simon suspected that the shock had been intentional.

'Bloody hell, Sergeant Thompson, I nearly went over the side,' there was little point in trying to hide his surprise it must have been manifestly obvious.

The grin spread over the Liverpudlian's craggy features as he saluted, 'Sorry about that, sir, didn't mean to startle you.'

'Really,' Simon smiled, 'why do I find that difficult to believe.'

'D'know, sir, must be your suspicious nature,' the grin widened.

Sergeant Peter Thompson was returning to his regiment after two years spent on the regiment's selection staff at Sennybridge. It was the toughest course in the military world that had been devised to select, and train volunteers, for the 22nd Special Air Service Regiment. He was glad to be going back to his regiment; he had served in Malaya in the force that had been the forerunner of the SAS, the Malayan Scouts. He enjoyed jungle warfare, it was the type of combat that suited the skills for which his regiment was famous; it favoured the alert and patient and required a high degree of fitness.

As they reached the second deck the overpowering stench of well-worn damp socks and sweating bodies wafted up to meet them and the ships tannoy blared out reveille.

*

On the northern side of Gunong Besar, overlooking the forty miles long Tasek Temengor, Malay's largest lake, was the training camp and headquarters of the Northern Zone of the Malayan Races Liberation

3

Army, MRLA. The HQ was responsible for the regiments that operated in the states of Kedah, Perak, and Kelantan.

It was well sited, extremely well-constructed, and capable of housing two hundred personnel. It consisted of a cookhouse, a hospital - but there were no doctors and little in the way of medicine or drugs - two lecture huts and accommodation. All of the buildings were constructed from resources supplied by the local flora; mainly atap and bamboo. Around the perimeter were bunkers with overhead cover that were considered capable of offering protection from air attack. There was even a twenty-five yard range, but ammunition could rarely be spared for such luxuries as target practice. In the centre of the camp was the parade ground of bare hard earth over which the Red Flag hung limply in the still mid-morning air.

Lau Fong struggled to stay awake in the soporific heat as a visiting colonel from the Red Chinese Army droned on about the thoughts of Mao Tse Tung and what this hero of the people had achieved for the masses.

Although the lecture hut was no more than a roof of atap without sides, Lau still found it stuffy with forty people sat tightly packed on the hard bamboo benches. It was only the discomfort of the hard bench combined with fear of reprisal that kept him awake. His fatigue was compounded by the fact that he had had very little sleep the previous night.

A week earlier they had set out from their base, which was located in secondary jungle near Kampong Jalong, allowing sufficient time to reach Besar for the conference of state committee members. In the Sungei Lintang valley they had been delayed by a lot of security force activity and had been forced to make a detour west for almost three miles. This had disrupted the journey so much that they had had to, with great difficulty and risk, travel through the previous night in order to make their rendezvous on time.

Lau was one of six comrades who formed the bodyguard of the Perak State Committee Member, Beng Kim, a man feared by the population of Perak, the local home guard and police, but even more by his own men. Beng commanded four hundred and sixty men in North Perak and North Kelantan, and he ruled without mercy. Beatings and food denial were his main form of motivation and executions were not uncommon. His forms of punishment for the locals who failed to comply with his demands and instructions were brutal in the extreme, and invariably resulted in the malefactor's death. It is often said that one should not judge a book by its cover but Beng had the appearance of a cruel and ruthless man. A thick mane of black hair topped a low forehead and below his bushy eyebrows, two, close set, black eyes that were mere slits, radiated malevolence. His squat body was supported by remarkably short legs and this made his thick arms appear too long in comparison.

Lau knew that Beng disliked him, and it was not a circumstance that Beng took any steps to conceal or restrain though the reason for this dislike had never been voiced. He felt that his leader's antagonism could be the consequence of two facts. Firstly, as in China, intellectuals were viewed with some concern and suspicion by the proletariat and although Lau, who had been a teacher on the 'outside', did not consider himself to be an intellectual the uneducated Beng might. However, it was his cousin's treatment of Beng that was probably the main reason for his animosity. May Ling had joined the peoples fight when she was only seventeen and already a member of the Malayan Communist Party. As soon as Beng saw her he had her moved from 15 Platoon's camp near Gopeng to his headquarters. It was common practice by the leaders at all levels to avail themselves of the services of any of the female members despite the fact that it was against party rules.

May had refused all advances and threats from the bombastic state committee member, but her fate would have been inevitable had she not caught the eye of the army's propagandist, Hor Lin. Unlike Beng Kim, he was only interested in her dedication and intelligence, and after conversing at length with her he knew she was wasted as a foot soldier. He had her moved to the party's base in Thailand with the view to putting her to better use in a more important and responsible role.

Beng's ego had been badly mauled, and even though he bragged that he had *used* the bitch and then passed her to the higher echelons as a plaything, everybody knew this to be a lie. Lau had received word that she had been seen recently in Ipoh, but he kept this news to himself.

With Lam Ten and a slow-witted Malay, called Abdul, Lau joined the queue forming at the cookhouse. With their bowls of rice and a few jungle vegetables they squatted in the shade to eat and discussed the lecture with guarded opinions. Candid points of view were not encouraged, and if held never made known if they differed from those of the party.

Lam was something of a father figure to Lau although he was only ten years his senior. He had fought alongside the British against the Japanese, and had been trained by them. Lam had been 'inside' since the start in 1948 and had taken part in the killing of the first imperialist planters to die. Slightly built and sallow from so many years shielded from the sun, he had a haunted ghostlike quality and his black eyes seem to see the soul. Beng treated him with some respect as Lau was on

5

friendly terms with many comrades in the highest ranks of the movement. On the other hand, Abdul was transparent, inexperienced, ignorant and crass. He was greedy, selfish and cruel, especially to other Malay's, but a favourite of Beng's as he shared his penchant for bullying and brutality.

They ate in silence for a while glad of a decent meal and the security afforded by their surroundings. Abdul was the first to empty his bowl; he wiped his mouth with the back of his hand and spat at a procession of ants. Most 'inside' people were spare of build due to long periods on scant rations, but somehow Abdul managed to remain fleshy and his low forehead and heavy eyelids gave him a menacing appearance.

'I need a woman,' he growled scowling.

'You should be used to doing without their company,' Lam stood up and went to wash his bowl.

Abdul watched him go, 'It's alright for him he's an old man.'

'He's not much older than us,' Lau said and got up to follow.

'Here take this,' Abdul handed him his bowl, Lau hesitated before taking it but not wanting an altercation did as he was bid.

*

By 0700 hours the troopship was alongside in the Keppel docks, her deck swarming with Lascar seamen and local coolies. Groups of servicemen assembled, when called, by unit or by their common destination. Senior NCOs and warrant officers succeeded in maintaining order in a scene of total pandemonium, and officers wandered the space trying to look as though they were in control and knew what was going on, when in reality, they had less understanding of the situation than their charges. Throughout this turmoil the band and pipes of 7th Duke of Edinburgh's Own Gurkha Rifles, immaculate in dazzling white No 1 uniforms, played non-stop on the dockside as the passengers disembarked.

Eventually, not really understanding how, Simon found himself sitting in the passenger seat of a Bedford three-ton truck, and in the rear twenty soldiers who were also en route to the Far East Land Forces Jungle Training Centre, among them, a dozen men of his own regiment.

Despite having been exposed to the heat of the tropics for the past week they were completely unprepared for the oppressive conditions that existed away from the cooling sea breeze. The vehicle's movement had no effect on the heavy heat in the cab even though both windows were open and the windscreen tilted to allow air to flow in. In the rear of the truck it was little better, the canopy was rolled up leaving the sides open, but even before they had left the shadow of the dockyard buildings their bush shirts were dappled with black patches of sweat.

Private John Cantrill had been keen to join the battalion, but now he was having second thoughts

'I don't fancy playing soldiers in this bloody heat,' he said removing his beret and wiping his face with it.

The truck's progress did little more than move the hot air; it did nothing to relieve their discomfort. He should have come out with his intake seven months earlier, but he had been kept back because of his skill as a footballer and his ability as a long distance runner. He had pestered to join the regiment until he had become a nuisance, and it was only when the last intake of National Servicemen at the depot had included three professional footballers that his request had been granted.

The contingent of the RWL's comprised of twelve men, some new recruits who had only recently completed their basic training and others who had some service behind them at the regimental depot

Ken Duffy, now a Lance-corporal, had just completed a PTI's course and looked every inch the part; muscular, darkly handsome and glowing with good health. Next to Ken sat Brian Large a quiet friendly man with an easy and tolerant disposition who was effortlessly fit and had been in the cross-country team with John. Then there was Sam Andrews, a jolly red-faced miner from Warrington, who lived life at as fast a pace as he was allowed and finally, big Keith Gardner, John's closest friend, a giant of a man with a quiet and easy going character. They had joined up together and, like John, Keith also had sporting prowess of which the depot commandant had need. Keith had represented the depot as a heavyweight in the Western Command Boxing Championship. His success saw him selected to represent Western Command, but he had declined despite many threats and pressure from the depot RSM. Keith was not a man who was easily intimidated. The remainder of the contingent were new recruits.

John came from a tough area of Liverpool, and looked the part. He had a friendly outgoing nature, but did not suffer fools, and he could deflate the pompous and arrogant with little effort. He was from a large family of limited means where the head of the family worked hard but drank equally hard and was generous with his beatings, freely administered to his three sons. John had been hardened from an early age. His tough life had created a hard young man, but not a bully. If he could talk his way out of a fight then he would, but he rarely came off the worse when violence could not be avoided.

His infectious grin and merry eyes helped soften his craggy and scarred features, but most of his contemporaries gauged his disposition from his broken nose and brash Scouse demeanour. This supposition was not false, but at heart he was a peace-loving individual who got along with most.

John felt more happy and content than he could ever recall. He was set for some excitement and in the company of men that he liked and trusted, even the new recruits that he had become acquainted with during the sea journey seemed to be very sound lads, apart from one. Barry Hayes was a National Serviceman who, like most conscripts, complained about his plight but Barry's complaining was not only constant it was akin to whining. That in itself, John could accept in small measure, but it was the 'barrack-room lawyer' and 'know all' attitude that brought Barry very close to receiving a knuckle sandwich from the normally relaxed Liverpudlian. Barry had been active in the trade union when he first started work in Preston Borough Council but as soon as he had realized that toadying would take him further within the council he gave up agitation and assumed in its place a sycophantic mien. In appearance he was as disagreeable as he was in disposition. He was short, no more than five feet five inches, pink and verging on tubby with a moonlike face. His lank fair hair was already beginning to take its leave of his scalp which shone pinkly through his sparse tresses.

As soon as the small convoy of three trucks, a Land Rover and a Ferret armoured car had cleared the sterile environment of the dockyard the men forgot the suffocating humidity and discomfort. In silence they soaked up the sounds, sights and smells that were the great city of Singapore. The place teemed with colour and noise; trishaws, like a plague of locusts, were everywhere, propelled at incredible speed through the clamour of traffic by diminutive, sinewy, Chinese with up to three people in each trishaw, or large Europeans who filled the space designed for two. Buses, filled beyond prudent capacity, outdid the trishaws in their reckless progress having the right of 'weight' on their side. Taxis, mainly large Mercedes, in their hundreds competed effectively in this mayhem and took no prisoners.

Added to the noise of blaring horns and radios in open-fronted shops playing the music of half a dozen cultures, was the chatter and street calls of the mixed tongues spoken in the great cosmopolitan conurbation. A score of Chinese dialects in addition to Malay, Hindi, Urdu, Tamil and of course English with its varied accents, all of them spoken in the daily life of the city.

Curvaceous Malayan girls in snug fitting and brightly coloured, ankle length, baju's, coy and smiling, mingled with peasant Chinese

8

girls in neat pyjama suits, occupied and intent on their business. But the girls who created the most interest were the exotic and sophisticated wealthier Chinese in figure hugging cheongsams, with thigh length splits, aloof and graceful beyond the capacity of other races and with complexions like porcelain.

The stink of petrol fused with joss sticks, countless different spices, strange foods being cooked by roadside vendors, and open drains, but above all was the cloying and disgusting odour of the Durian fruit. Its putrid stench belied its delectable taste, and was a great delicacy that few Europeans sampled finding its pungency difficult to ignore.

As the city faded they passed through areas of more basic dwellings with covered walkways and wide, open, monsoon drain's that could only be traversed via bridges of hazardous design. Smells and the degree of activity varied depending on the ethnic group that resided there. The commotion and din of the Chinese area, and the spice-laden air and bustle of the Tamil district contrasted starkly with the languid pace of the indigenous Malays.

After crossing, the new and magnificent, Johore Causeway they entered the state capitol, Johore Bahru, a miniature version of Singapore, and it was when they had cleared this small town that the convoy stopped and the sergeant in charge gave the order to load their rifles.

'Do not put one up the spout,' he emphasised.

The trucks moved off again, they were now on active service.

Chapter Two

The Jungle Training Centre for Far East Land Forces was situated two miles north of the small town of Kota Tinggi at the southern end of the State of Johore. Its location had been selected well and offered all four types of country that the army would be called on to live and fight in. A little to the north was an area of low mountainous country rising to almost two thousand feet, not one of the highest ranges but high enough for the trainees to be tested. To the east was a region of primary jungle with trees like cathedral pillars rising to two hundred feet where they formed a canopy dense enough to blot out the potent Malayan sun, creating a perpetual twilit world and preventing abundant undergrowth taking hold. To the west were areas of dense secondary jungle known as belukar. These were areas where the primary jungle had been cleared for cultivation or logging and then neglected. Belukar was a nightmare to patrol, its density made it virtually impenetrable at times and a thousand yards in an hour was considered good going. To add to the problems of life in secondary jungle there was little overhead cover at times and then the blazing sun made the hard going even harder.

Formidable mangrove swamps lay to the south along the Sungei Johore, stinking, energy sapping slime, swarming with mosquitoes, leeches and snakes. The stench of decay was ever present and soldiers could find themselves up to their knees or their chests in the glutinous goo. Regions of stunted trees, like prehistoric landscapes, added the merciless sun to their dilemma.

The JTC was located on each side of a shallow valley. The south was pure utility, row upon row of huts constructed from corrugated metal with sides that could be raised to allow air to circulate. Severe paths of concrete ran up and along the side of the valley separating the hideous metal buildings. At the end of the valley, closest to the main road, was a hangar like construction with low, four feet high, walls of breezeblock and a mighty roof of woven atap that extended three feet beyond the walls. The monstrous construction served as the cookhouse, canteen and occasional cinema. This part of the camp was known as Tin City, and was home to the personnel who attended the JTC for a two week introduction into life in the Malayan jungle.

By contrast the opposite side of the valley had the air of a long established camp that smacked of the Malaya of Somerset Maugham in the pre-war days of Empire. Pleasant atap and wood buildings with verandahs and shuttered windows housed offices and accommodation alike. Larger buildings of similar design housed the officer's and NCO's, messes. It stood among neat lawns of yellowing grass and beds of heavily scented frangipani and red flame of the forest. Bushes, with leaves from pale violet to imperial purple, dotted the areas of lawn and Tualong trees, with brilliant green foliage afforded clumps of shade. This was home to the training and permanent staff of the JTC.

After Simon had been shown to his room, by a friendly Malay syce, and deposited his kit he was led, by the same syce, to the officer's mess.

'The Colonel Tuan, very strict man,' the syce informed him, 'he very angry with officers who late for meals.'

Although the JTC had only been formed in 1949 the officer's mess had an air of having existed for a hundred years. In the hall a tiger's head glared from the panelled wall above a large semi-circular table on which lay a number of hats of varying colours and designs; berets of green, black and fawn, glengarries with checked rims and khaki service caps. Around the wall there hung wooden shields showing the badges of scores of regiments, and gruesome bladed weapons, sabres, swords, kukris, parangs and the vicious looking Malaya Kris.

'That, bar and dining room,' the little Malay indicated a door on the left of the foyer and then departed.

'Must be new in,' a large angular captain entered behind Simon and threw a wide brimmed bush hat onto the table and then grabbed Simons hand in an iron grip, 'Tim Kelly, 2nd Royal Australian.'

'Oh,' Simon recovered quickly from the surprise and assault on his hand, 'Simon Gates, Royal West Lancashire's and yes, I have only just arrived.'

'Welcome to the JTC, Si,' come on, let's get you a drink,' he led the way through to the bar, 'or more importantly let's get me a drink. Listen in you fellahs,' he addressed the dozen or so officers in the bar, 'this 'ere's Simon Gates of the Royal George Formby's.'

'Welcome, Simon,' a short, stocky major, deeply tanned and wearing brass shoulder titles of the RWL, took his elbow and led him to the bar, 'pay no attention to that wild colonial. You must update me on people at the depot; I assume that you've just come from there?'

'Yes, sir.'

'Good we must make time for a chat, I'm Cox, Terry Cox, I'm the training major.'

'Here you are, Si, get that down yer neck,' Tim handed him a glass of cold beer.

'This, would you believe,' Terry explained, 'is our adjutant.'

On the other side of the valley the RWL group left the barn like cookhouse carrying mugs of warmish liquid the colour of dirty putty that ACC cooks were passing off as tea. They seated themselves on a scrubby patch of grass in the narrow shade of their hut.

11

'That was shit,' John flipped the lid from his tin of cigarettes and placed it on the grass, 'Anyone want one,' he drew one from the tin and lit it with the chrome Ronson lighter that his sisters had bought him as a going away present.

'It was just about edible,' Sam leaned forward and took a cigarette.

'Hey Sammy,' John exclaimed as he gave him a light, 'you'd eat dog shit if yer think that mess was edible.'

Kenny leaned back on his elbows, 'Good scoff can make any conditions bearable but if it's this bad all the time...'

'We're gonna starve,' Keith offered as an end to the sentence.

'Hey up,' Brian Large started to get to his feet, 'Pearly's here.'

'Okay, stay as you are,' Simon said as he saw them getting to their feet, 'How was the food?' he asked.

'It was shite,' John said with feeling.

'Well that is certainly direct, Cantrill,' Simon smiled, 'but are you sure you're not being a little hard on the cooks?'

'No, that's British understatement, sir,' Brian added in support.

'Oh, well I'm sorry I couldn't get over before but it would seem the commandant is a bit of a stickler for punctuality at meals so I couldn't get away.'

'He wouldn't be such a stickler if they gave him the shite we had,' John volunteered again.

'Right, yes,' Simon knew that he could not win and changed the subject, 'Well I've got our training programme here for the next two weeks. Is there a notice board in your hut, Corporal Duffy?' he asked as he handed Kenny the programme.

'I'll stick it on my locker door, sir.' Kenny told him.

'Right, good, er, well you'll see that first parade tomorrow is at 0800, it gives the dress on the programme and after muster you'll be kitted out with all that you'll need for your training over the next two weeks,' he tried an encouraging smile, 'any questions?'

'Do we get a chance to go to Singapore, sir?'

'I meant about tomorrows programme, Andrews.'

'Where do we parade, sir?' Kenny asked.

'Here on the road in front of your hut will do, 'he paused, there was an awkward silence, 'I'll pop over at teatime to see what the meal is like for myself but I won't be able to do much, I don't want to step on the toes of the orderly officer,' his promise was met with murmur of doubtful appreciation.

'Haven't we got anything else on this afternoon then, sir?' Ken asked.

'No, just get your kit sorted for the morning,' he turned to go then stopped. 'It might please you to know that the training major here is Major Cox of our regiment, one of our own, anybody bumped into him before?' There was a shaking of heads and silence, 'Right, see you at teatime then,' as he walked away he heard the unmistakable nasal tones of Cantrill.

'I bet Major fucking Cox wouldn't eat the shite were getting.'

*

The fare in the sergeant's mess at Wardiburn Camp left no room for complaint it was well prepared, and plentiful. The mess was typical of messes in the Far East, light, airy, and furnished with local rattan easy chairs and sofas at the lounge end of the bar. The dining room was accessed through folding doors that could be pushed back to form a large room on special mess nights and one exterior wall slid back opening one side of the building to a long verandah.

Peter Thompson and SSM Bill Asher, HQ squadron's sergeant major, shared a table by the open side of the dining room; the only other members present were two REME sergeants, most of the regiment was on either on operations or detachment.

Peter and Bill had known each other since their days in 1 SAS during the war in Italy. They had not met for almost two years, and the meal had been spent in catching up.

'Are you able to have a beer, Bill?'

'Shouldn't really but the old man's got a meeting with the police bosses this afternoon and the CO and RSM have gone to visit B squadron up at Grik so I could risk one.'

As they carried their drinks out onto the verandah Pete asked, 'Have I got a squadron?'

'Yeah, 'D' squadron,' Bill replied.

'Who's the SC?'

'Jack Hooper.'

'Oh, great,' Major Jack Hooper was a legend in the regiment having served with the regiment's founder, David Stirling, 'what troop?'

'Twelve.'

'And who's the boss there?'

'Roger Howard, you should know him he must have done selection while you were on the staff at Sennybridge.'

'Is he a tall dark slim lad, ex-Gloucester?'

'That's him, and he seems to have fitted in well with the troop. Dave Snell was his last troop sergeant and Dave didn't suffer fools. You know Dave, don't you?'

'Dave Snell, yeah great guy?' Peter said, 'Where is he now?'

'His tour finished, but instead of going back to his regiment he opted for the West Lancs so that he could stay out here.'

When they left the mess Bill went back to his office, and Peter went to seek out his new troop. He had been told that they were on recreational training for the afternoon; he knew that meant they were probably in the Galloway Club near the railway station. He was tempted to seek them out but decided against it and instead went looking for the troop commander.

Roger Howard found that his height and greater reach gave him no advantage over his smaller and older opponent. Lieutenant Bo Tang, of the Malayan Police, was not as fit as Roger but that did not matter for he had represented his country at badminton, and his ability compensated for his opponents fitness and height.

'You're letting the regiment down, Howard.'

Roger looked up from retrieving the shuttlecock after losing the point.

'Bloody hell, Staff Thompson I'd been warned to expect you, 'he picked up a towel from a chair at the side of the court and mopped his face, 'I take it I don't have to call you 'staff' now?'

'I'll give it some thought,' Pete took the offered hand, 'Good to see you, sir.'

Chapter Three

Though they had attacked the hill at an angle it had still been a stiff climb and by twelve thirty they were only half way to the top of the ridge. A thick area of bamboo had necessitated a lengthy detour but now they were once more in primary jungle.

Ben signalled for a halt, only the second since they set off six and half-hours earlier, he did not believe in the standard five minutes rest every hour. All symptoms of excessive alcohol consumption had long ago evaporated in the humid and oppressive air. Those affected had maintained the pace on automatic pilot but now were in mental company with the rest of the team. They went into all round defensive positions and removed their packs.

'No brewing up or smoking,' Ben whispered to the men closest to him, the message was passed on and Ben could imagine the internal moans, 'Fifteen minutes,' it was passed on in a like manner. He then tapped his upper arm with three fingers and the act was repeated along the team and in a short time 'Boggy' Marsh picked his way past the resting men, and squatted down next to Ben. 'Boggy' was one of those who had consumed a fair amount of Tiger beer the previous night and it was apparent from his breath.

'I'm cream crackered.'

'Well you were on the booze,' Ben said without any sympathy or looking up from his map. He indicated a point on the map with a twig, 'I reckon we're about here.'

'Boggy' peered at the spot suggested, 'I'm not gonna argue with your map reading, sir, but I reckon we must be getting close to Peking.'

'It's taken us too long to get this far,' Ben went on ignoring his sergeants quip, 'so we're going direct for the top I want to be on the ridge well before last light so that we have some time to cast about for tracks.'

'Is it worth splitting, sir?' 'Boggy' asked, 'We could go up at diverse angles, and might have more chance of spotting something.'

Ben thought for a moment, 'Yeah, but we'll stay together until we get to the ridge and then split.'

As they sat, a strong wind suddenly blew in from the west and the hiss of distant rain in the trees could be heard and ten minutes later the storm slipped down the hill and immersed them in noise and alarming strikes of lightning. Within minutes the hillside was flowing with a thousand tiny streams.

The upward journey was only made possible by hauling themselves up on roots and saplings. Noise was irrelevant now; the pounding rain would have drowned the sound of the regimental band.

Ben's estimation of their position was flawed for within three hours of leaving the place that they had rested the ground levelled out with a slight rise going off to the right, they were on the ridge. By 1600 hours the rain had stopped but water, impeded by the jungle canopy, continued its delayed passage for another ten minutes or so. It was a relief to be able to stay on their feet without the assistance of a stationary object. They paused, crouching, while Ben studied his map.

Again he signalled for 'Boggy', 'We won't split just yet,' he explained, 'we'll go north along the ridge for....' he consulted his watch it was 1620, he gave a hiss of frustration, 'we've only just over an hour of light,' he paused, 'We'd better stay together, I can't see what could be achieved with so little light left.'

'Boggy' nodded he knew they were in for an uncomfortable night, 'Okay.'

'Peter,' Ben addressed the Junior Chinese Liaison Officer, JCLO.

Peter moved closer, 'Yes, sir,' Peter's English had barely a trace of accent.

'My map ends at Sungei Siput, Peter, remind me of the country to the north.'

'There is a minor road that goes to Lasah, and then it is mainly cultivation for about three miles, tapioca and a lot of padi, and then you're onto Bukit Tasek and back into jungle.'

'I thought that was the case,' Ben said, 'So they would be a bit exposed for some distance,' his grey eyes flicked from 'Boggy' to Peter, 'What would you do, Peter, if you were in their shoes? You've been hit on the road and forced onto this range, would you seek sanctuary in the south or try to head back north into your own back yard?'

'I see what you mean,' Peter said thoughtfully, 'we think they're isolated over here and we would not expect them to risk going near where they were ambushed and the cultivation and where they know there's a lot of security force activity..'

'It's a possibility,' 'Boggy' put in, 'but I don't see how it affects our task, we can't go north of the road or we'll be on the Kiwi's patch.'

Ben rubbed his square chin, 'Yeah, but we're a good two miles from the road,' he got to his feet, 'Right we'll stay on the ridge and head north looking for tracks, and once we get to the road we'll swing west and then south again half way down the other side.' He hitched his pack up higher on his shoulders, 'I don't think the dogs are going to be any

16

use after this rain so I'll have the two Ibans up front. Eaton,' he said to his leading scout, 'you come behind me then Corporal Riley then the signaller. Let's go.'

*

As the light began to fail the group of MRLA left the security of the jungle and entered the rubber plantation a mile north of Lasah. Lau led the party, his old Lee Enfield held in readiness. The journey back to their own base would take at least three days and en route the locals would be expected to feed them. The closer they got to the village the greater the danger of meeting security forces became. Fortunately they did not have to go too close; the pickup point was in a tapper's hut just off the main road to Sungei Siput.

At the junction of two footpaths was a small clump of undergrowth, Lau stopped and from the foliage took a length of bamboo and two large square cans, the type used by tappers to collect the latex. He placed the bamboo pole across his shoulder with a can on each end, and dragging his rifle by a string he set off again with the rest of the party fifty paces to his rear. If they should meet security forces now he would drop the string by which he was towing his rifle, and try to pass himself off as a tapper who was late for curfew.

The hut was not difficult to find for they had used it before. The rest of the group lay in the knee high green growth that covered the ground in rubber plantations, and Lau approached the hut alone. For a few minutes he stood at a distance and watched to make sure that there was nobody about, and no signs of an ambush. The hut was small; it was where the tappers returned with their full cans of latex. He could see the interior as the walls were only three feet high screens of atap and it was door-less. Satisfied it was safe, he went to the rear of the hut and pushed back a clump of fern, brushed away the leaves, and revealed the top of an old oil drum that had been sunk into the earth. He removed the wooden lid, and his heart missed a beat. The drum was empty; there would be no food tonight.

Beng looked into the empty drum, his face contorted with rage, 'Those worthless wretches will know suffering they could never have imagined,' his words hissed through gritted teeth, 'cover it,' he snarled at Lau, 'and our tracks; we will wait where we left the forest.'

'Do we not continue with our journey, comrade?'Lau could see no point in returning the way they had come. They would go hungry either way but at least they could get a couple of miles closer to their base.

Beng jabbed him hard on the chest with a finger, 'Never question my orders, dog,' the words were delivered slowly and with unmistakable menace, and his small eyes were hard and blazed with fury.

*

Ben could tell instantly that Emau had seen something of significance, for the thin Iban stopped and stared at the ground, he then moved forward one-step and stopped again, this time he gave the signal to halt and turned round grinning broadly.

The ground cover had thinned since reaching the summit of the ridge and they were now in true primary jungle with visibility of almost ten yards at times. On the stop signal the team had dropped down into a crouch and faced alternate ways. Ben made his way silently forward to where Emau waited. As he approached, the tracker put his finger to his lips and Ben's heart leapt.

Emau indicated a barely discernible scuff on the wet earth and a small smear of mud on a fallen leaf. Pangau, the other tracker, had moved past them and was kneeling down a couple of yards ahead inspecting the ground.

'How long ago?' Ben asked of Emau.

'Ten minutes, maybe, maybe five.'

'They are very close, Tuan,' Pangau informed him and held out his open hand which he appeared to hold a scrap of muddied leaf; he indicated that Ben should smell it. He did so but could smell nothing, he shook his head.

'Tobacco,' Pangau explained as though he were dealing with a slow witted child, 'cigarette.'

'How long ago'? Ben asked again.

Pangau exchanged looks with Emau and grimaced shaking his head, 'Minutes,' he shrugged, 'very close.'

The first shot was the unmistakable bark of a shotgun and Eaton's shout, 'BANDITS FRONT!' A dozen shots rang out punctuated by the savage reply of Eaton's shotgun again.

When the team had stopped and the Ibans had given their attention to the spoor, Ray Eaton had moved to the front to give them cover so that he was now about five yards in the lead and crouched by a tree facing an invisible target to their right.

Followed by the two Ibans Ben moved in the direction that his leading scout was looking. Firing was still coming from that area but none of it seemed to be directed at them.

To the left there was a sudden flash of movement and the sound of somebody moving quickly, but carefully, through the sparse undergrowth. A flash of khaki, Ben raised his Remington and despatched two cartridges of heavy shot and at the same time he sensed Emau and Pangau at his side also firing.

The sound of movement increased and he could hear Tex Riley shouting and then the Bren opening up on their left with short bursts of fire. Ahead of them they could still hear movement, and the three quickened their pace scanning the area to left and right as they went.

Ben was conscious that the Bren had stopped firing, but they could possibly be in its line of fire should it open up again. 'Hold your fire,' he bawled. The incoming fire had also stopped which indicated that the enemy were making good their escape. 'Okay, hold it there,' he stopped the trackers, 'Quickly, we must do a re-org,' he began heading back to where the contact had begun, ''Boggy', check for casualties,' he called, 'nobody else move,' he was aware that the two tracker dogs were barking and realised they had been doing so throughout the contact, 'Keep those bloody dogs quiet,'

'Tuan,' Emau called him.

He went to where the, still grinning, Iban stood looking down at a khaki clad body that lay face down on the floor with its arms thrown forward as if in supplication. There was no need to check if he was dead; there was a gaping wound just below his left shoulder blade from which dark blood bubbled and a bullet entry hole just below the base of the skull with another in his lower back.

Ray was still by the tree where Ben had last seen him, and he looked pale, 'I've been hit, sir.'

'Where?' Ben knelt by the wounded man. Ray put his hand on his side; the dark blood was not easily discernible against the wet jungle shirt, but a small tear just above his belt showed the entry point.

'We don't have any casualty's, sir,' 'Boggy' had finished his check, then he saw Ray, 'Oh bloody hell, is it bad?'

Ben stood up, 'Right, 'Boggy', put Corporal Riley out with two men to do a clearance about fifty yards out and get someone to see to Eaton's wound. Corporal Ackers!'

The signaller came forward, 'Sir.'

'Get on net, when you're in contact let me know. 'Boggy', I'll take two Ibans, a dog, Smeaton, and Corporal Riley, when he gets back, and do a follow up. I'm going to call for a party to....'

'I got one sir,' Ray interrupted and pointed to his right. He had removed his bush shirt and Leo Dawes was applying a field dressing to his wound, 'he ran that way but I got a second on 'im and I saw him go down.'

They found another CT lying on his side, a large hole in his chest and his right arm was shattered, his shallow rasping breath showed that he was still alive.

'He's not got long, give him a shot of morphine,' Ben ordered, 'and search him.'

When Riley returned from his clearance sweep he reported that there was another dead CT a few yards away.

'You've nearly cut the poor bugger in half, Parky,' he grinned at the Bren gunner.

Fifteen minutes later Ben set off on the follow up, his half of the team knowing they were in for a very uncomfortable night. Battalion had been informed of their success and a carrying party were on the way to collect Ray. The wounded CT had died after a few minutes, and after 'Boggy' had photographed the bodies, for special branch to identify, they were buried in shallow graves.

*

Roger had met Linda at the VJ day anniversary ball held in the police social club the previous August. She was an old college friend of Irene, Bo's fiancée, who was a police inspector at the KL police headquarters. Irene had found Linda a job in the administration centre at the HQ when she had moved to KL.

When he arrived at the Cathay cinema he saw her already waiting by the entrance. She was a little over five feet tall, slim and deceivingly fragile looking, her athleticism and stamina on the badminton court gave lie to her fragile appearance.

Roger found oriental women attractive and exceedingly feminine, Linda excelled on both counts. Though slight she had a wonderful figure and moved with the natural grace of a ballet dancer. Her jet black hair almost reached her waist and her skin was as smooth as expensive soap.

'Why are you never late?' he reached down and kissed her on the cheek, he felt her tense, she was not happy about displays of affection in public.

'Because,' she smiled up at him, 'it is bad manners to be late.'

'English women think that it is their prerogative to keep men waiting,' he took her elbow and steered her into the welcome relief of the air-conditioned interior.

'Well they are wrong,' she defended her position, 'you are telling the person who is waiting that you do not care, that their time is less important than yours.'

'That's very profound and very true I suppose,' he looked down into her serious and beautiful almond eyes, 'I wasn't late was I?'

'No,' she smiled and happiness replaced the seriousness in her eyes, 'you're a gentleman.'

'There are many who would give you argument on that point,' he laughed as he paid for the tickets, 'We have time for a drink, 'he said and guided her to the bar.

'I am really looking forward to this film,' she told him as he handed her a glass of Pepsi, 'Doris Day is my favourite singer and she is so very beautiful.'

'She is nice,' he agreed.

'Is it true that men prefer blondes?' the question was serious.

Roger could not resist a glib response, 'Yeah, it's because they get dirty quicker,'

She looked puzzled, 'I don't understand,' she said with puckered brow, 'why do they get dirty.'

With an inward sigh of regret for what he had said he explained as best he could, 'It's just a joke,' he said, 'light coloured things are inclined to get dirty quicker than dark things, so as blondes have light coloured hair it implies that will also get dirty quicker but of course it has a double meaning,' he pulled a face, 'you know, that they…'

'Yes, yes, but it's not very pleasant for blondes,' she emptied her glass, and as she put it down a hint of a smile formed on her shapely lips, 'but I can see why it's amusing.'

The film they saw was Calamity Jane, and in one scene Doris Day fell in a creek and was covered with mud.

Linda leaned towards him and whispered; 'Now she really is dirty.'

Chapter Four

It had been a cold, wet, and uncomfortable night, and because of the suspected close proximity of the enemy they were denied the British soldiers' panacea, a brew of tea. Light was painfully slow in coming the pitch dark had given way to a grey morning with reluctance. Before the light was good enough for the pursuit to resume they breakfasted on cold beans and hard tack biscuits washed down with water that was bitter with the taste of purification tablets.

When darkness had forced them to halt the previous night Pangau had estimated that they were only twenty minutes behind the fleeing CTs. Pangau was the oldest member of the Sarawak Ranger platoon attached to the RWL. He claimed to be forty but had more the appearance of someone approaching sixty. This estimation of age was reinforced by the fact that he had tattoos below his wrist. All Iban's sported numerous ornate, blue, tattoos each one having some significance; those on the throat prevented them being beheaded, and those below the wrist indicated that the individual had actually taken a head. As headhunting had been outlawed three decades earlier Pangau must have taken a head before he was ten, or he had not been very candid about his age on enlistment.

Despite this he was considered one of the best trackers and possessed an uncanny six sense that gave him the power to foresee problems, events, and sense danger, or the presence of the enemy, he possessed powers long since atrophied in modern man. He had a crouching gait and was outstandingly bandy, but he could set a pace that was difficult for any but the very fittest to maintain.

As there were no bashas to take down or campsite to tidy up and as they only had to eliminate obvious signs of their presence, they were ready to move in minutes.

'Okay, Pangau.' Ben nodded; the Iban gave him a golden toothed grin, and followed by Smeaton, set off down the hill with only the occasional glance at the ground. It was obvious that their quarry were in a great hurry, as they were making little attempt to cover their tracks, as was their normal practice. After twenty minutes, Pangau's pace faltered and then he gave the signal to halt and began to cast about as though he had lost the spoor.

'What's wrong?' Ben asked, concerned.

The old Iban shook his head and muttered softly to himself his only failing was that his English was poor even by Iban's standards, and what he did know was virtually unintelligible to those who had not worked with him before.

'*Apa khabar, Pangau*'? (What news) Ben asked. Pangau shook his again and continued to examine the ground. '*Berapa orang*'? Ben asked how many CT had made the track but still Pangau did not answer immediately.

'CT, *jalan, satu hari*, no stop' Pangau eventually said and motioned with his arm.

'Shit.'

'What's up, sir?'Dave Smeaton asked hoping that they had lost the tracks and could call the operation off. They had been successful with three kills and now the boss was just being greedy.

'The bastards kept going through the night,' Ben spat the words out angry that he had not anticipated such action, 'they're about eight hours ahead of us now.'

Much to Dave's disappointment Ben decided to continue the chase in case their quarry had problems, or had been forced to stop for some reason. However, his disappointment was short lived for fifteen minutes later they could hear road traffic which could only mean that they had arrived at the main Taiping/Siput road, and the end of their operational area.

*

The fortnight's jungle training, for Simon and his men, began at 0800 with an intensity that would not ease for two weeks. After being fitted out with 44 pattern webbing, and all the extra items of kit that would be needed to survive in the jungle, they sat on a slope in a nearby rubber plantation and watched the demonstration platoon of the 7th Duke of Edinburgh's Own Gurkha Rifles carry out the drill for setting up a camp and immediate action drills for most eventualities that could occur in jungle warfare, skills, which they themselves would perfect over the next fourteen days.

*

Lau woke with a sense of foreboding which not only sprang from the long hard, and dangerous journey that lay ahead of them, but also from what Beng Kim had in mind for the villagers of Lasah, the villagers who had displeased him by failing to provide food as instructed.

By the time it was light the party of CT was laid up in a patch of fern overlooking the tappers hut awaiting the arrival of the plantation work force. They would have some time to wait for the initial task for the tappers was to visit their allocated trees and cut them allowing the latex to run into small cups that were attached to the trunk just below the angled cut. When this was done the latex, encouraged by the heat of mid-morning, would fill the cups and then the tappers would collect

23

their cans from the various huts throughout the estate and gather the harvest of rubber. After four hours, which seemed like four days to the group of terrorists, being constantly bitten by the multitude of mosquitoes that were always present in rubber, the tappers began arriving at the hut, chattering and laughing, oblivious of the watching men. Men and women came and went but Beng made no move he just watched and waited for his prey. Lau was used to being hungry as they all were, but the pangs seemed intensely sharp as they could smell the food that the tappers were permitted to bring with them into the fields for their own consumption.

Mid-morning two women and a man came to collect their cans from the hut. The tapper women wore the large conical hats, common among the Chinese, which were secured to their heads with coloured scarves that hid most of their faces. From the way the women moved Lau estimated that one was quite young and the other a good deal older. At a signal from Beng they emerged from their hiding place and advanced on the trio by the hut.

As the three turned to face the group Lau could see that his impression had been correct, and the women could have been mother and daughter. They stared at the intruders impassively, but the terror in the man's face was unmistakable. His gaunt cheeks sagged as though the muscles had relinquished their responsibility, and his hands began to shake causing the cans that he had just picked up to knock hollowly against his bony legs.

He tried to speak but his fear was too great he could only produce a feeble croaking sound. He swallowed hard and made a further attempt, but before any words could be formed the muzzle of Beng's heavy Colt pistol smashed into the side of face laying his cheek open to the bone.

'We were hungry because of you,' Beng spoke softly through gritted teeth, 'you failed us.' The man fell to his knees blubbering spittle and blood and still incoherent. Beng glared down at him without any emotion, his anger seemed to have evaporated.

The elder women stepped forward, 'He could not help it, lord the running dogs were everywhere,' she pleaded in a voice as frail as her body.

'Silence crone,' Beng spoke softly, and Lau knew that this was a bad omen. When their squat leader had stopped shouting he was no longer cruel his callousness had reached levels of barbarity that made even the brutal flinch.

'Tie them,' he indicated nearby trees, 'not her,' he pulled the younger women aside.

24

'Do not harm her, lord,' the old women implored, 'she knows nothing of the arrangement.'

Beng slapped her hard and pushed his face close to hers, 'Who is she?'

'Our daug....'

'Quiet woman!' the man regained some of his nerve, a look of defiance had replaced that of anguish, 'she is just a girl from the village.'

Beng grabbed a fist full of the man's lank hair and laughed, 'Then she is of no worth too you, dog.'

'None,' he was struggling to maintain his boldness.

'Good,' he turned to Abdul, 'She's yours,' and then to Lau, 'and yours after he's finished with her.'

The girl had remained silent and more bemused than frightened by events, but as Abdul reached for her with a grin she became suddenly aware of her fate. She screamed once and then accepted her destiny with muted sobs accompanied by howls of horror and cries of pleading from her distraught parents.

Lau could not watch, and the cries of anguish of the man and women punctuated by the carnal grunts of Abdul painted an odious enough picture. Instead, he pretended to be acting as lookout and positioned himself on a slight rise ten feet from the scene of depravity.

From his position Lau could see the main laterite track that led to the main road. He was grateful for Abdul's stamina and control as it delayed his own participation. He grappled to think of an argument to put forward in order to avoid any physical involvement, but knew that none would be accepted. Then, to his unbelievable joy, he spotted something that would have normally frozen his heart with fear; he saw the canvass top of a military truck as it pulled up on the track a hundred yards away.

'Army!' he hissed the word and crouched down beside a tree.

Abdul's pleasure was cut short by a savage kick in the ribs from Beng.

'Get up,' he snarled, and then, 'gag them.'

When the old couple had been silenced with the women's headscarves, Beng picked up a changol that leaned against the wall of the hut, and with a few brutal blows to their throats virtually decapitated them, throwing fountains of blood into the lower branches of the trees to which they were secured. Spattered with the blood of his victims, he calmly crossed to where the girl still lay on the floor half-naked and sobbing. He drew a thin knife from a sheath on his belt and slid it easily between the fourth and fifth ribs into her heart. Her eyes opened wide in surprise and she died instantly, without making a sound as the blood from her dying parents spurted from their mutilated necks.

As they sped off towards the sanctuary of the jungle Lau struggled to prevent himself from vomiting and Abdul hobbled after them still securing his trousers.

Chapter Five

The four men approached the Whirlwind helicopter in line ducking below the slowly turning rotors. They heaved their Bergen's into the rear cabin, and clambered in after them. Pete went forward, tapped the co- pilot's leg, and gave him a thumbs-up sign. The noise level increased, the rotors whirled faster, and thirty seconds later the wheels left the tarmac. Pete was starting his first operation just twenty-four hours after having joined the regiment. So much for acclimatisation, he considered that this must be a record even for the regiment.

It was typical of the army all famine or feast. Wardiburn had been like a ghost town when he had arrived the previous day and just as he was showering for his first night out with some of his new troop Bill Asher had appeared.

'Officially you're not on operational strength yet, Thomo but we're desperate for bodies and a nice little four day op has come up,' he grinned and threw Pete's towel to him, 'your troop's got it, and Roger Howard can't be contacted..'

'Count me in,' Pete said eagerly.

'Are you sure you're up to it, mate?' his grin widened.

'Piss off, Asher,' Pete wrapped the towel round his middle, 'What time's the briefing?'

The intelligence had come from special branch and was therefore treated with higher regard than if it had been supplied by military intelligence. A CEP who had been captured whilst acting as a courier had papers on him that indicated that there existed a large training camp on the Perak/Kelantan state border which was regularly visited by high-ranking members of the MRLA from Thailand. It had been suspected for a number of years that such a camp was located in the mountainous border area and in 1952 Pete had taken part in a major operation in the Bubat valley where the Bukit Bubat mountain range creates part of the border between Kedah and Thailand.

It had been a relatively successful operation where they had expected to engage at least two hundred CT's. Three squadrons had been used, two had walked in from the Kampong Pinang road on the southwest of the valley and B Squadron had parachuted in at the north, directly on the border.

Because of bad visibility and continuous rain the two Beverley's had been forced to complete a couple of circuits to try and locate the designated DZ. Planes flying at five hundred feet in such a remote area were warning enough for the quarry and they had fled by the time the first troops arrived. Not all was lost, and over the following three weeks twenty-seven enemy were tracked down and killed and another seven surrendered, but there was still a slight sense of disappointment as it was evident from signs in the camp, and its size, that a great many more had escaped.

According to the briefing that the troop had received the previous evening from a special branch inspector and the RIO, regimental intelligence officer, there was every possibility that this intelligence could eventually lead to as big an operation as the Bubat Valley episode. Pete smiled to himself; it was a good start to his new tour.

The pilot banked steeply as he turned north and Peter was reminded of the immensity of the Malayan jungle. Eighty per cent of the country was a green wilderness that clothed mountains over 7000 feet high, it hid boundless swamps that could take days to cross, and the great trees, that were beyond the imagination of Europeans, were its magnificence.

It was an environment for which modern man was not suited. It was the place of the hunter and the hunted, and in this world skills and senses were required that the civilised human no longer possessed. Western man was poorly equipped for life in the jungle; his eyesight is poor, his hearing corrupted, and his sense of smell almost atrophied.

Pete knew this to be the case, but he also knew that these senses could be re-kindled. It was fact that men who had been in the jungle only for a few days began to revert and their senses were amplified, the need to survive made this essential, but they never could match those who had been born and raised in this milieu.

They flew with the door of the big Whirlwind open; the noise was too great to hold a conversation without bellowing at each other. Peter studied his command. He had met them all during their selection but did not really know any of them, but the fact that they had all passed selection was in itself almost enough, but not quite. Nevertheless, he was confident in their ability. When a new trooper, or officer, joined the regiment they were never fully accepted until they had proved themselves to the other troop members; their peers had accepted these men and that would have to be good enough for now.

His leading scout, Bob Gill, sat by the door watching the passing scenery, his eyes squinting into the light. He remembered Bob as a tough, humorous northerner from Wigan. He was of medium height with untidy brown hair and green eyes that always gave the impression that he had spotted something funny in whatever the situation was that confronted him. Pete remembered that Bob had been close to being RTU'd on a couple of occasions when staff had read this as an attitude issue, but thankfully he had survived and was now, presumably, a useful member of the unit.

Jim Powell sat on the opposite side of the door and nursed his Bren from which he constantly wiped dust with his jungle hat. Jim was a large Brummy of cheerful disposition and unbelievably chaotic appearance. His existence in any other regiment of the British Army would not have been tolerated, and any self-respecting sergeant major would have hidden him in a spare locker rather than allow him on his parade ground. Jim had come from the Royal Engineers where bull was not highly prized, and he was the bricks explosive expert.

Tom Parnell was the last member of the team. On first meeting he gave the impression of being a glum individual, but his hangdog look hid a very funny man. Tom was a Norfolk man whose good looks were marred, pockmarked, by a severe bout of chicken pox in his youth, as well as being a bush doctor, he was also their signaller.

Peter was happy with his brick the only doubts that he had concerned himself. His three troopers were all at peak fitness and immersed in jungle lore having been on repeated jungle operations for the past year or more, whereas, he had just spent three weeks of relative inactivity with an excess of food and drink. In an effort to retain some degree of fitness he done laps of the ship's deck every day carrying a 50lb pack, but this was modest preparation for the undergrowth, mountains and climate that he was about to face. As it was often said in the regiment; there is only one-way to get fit enough to carry a pack up a hill, and that is carry a pack up a hill.

He turned his attention to his map and the area in which they were to operate. The chopper was going to put them down in a LZ, built six months ago by the Gurkha's on the western slope of Gunong Besar. The rest of the troop was to be dropped off by a truck to operate on the opposite side of the ridge. Roger Howard had returned to camp in time to be briefed for command of one of the bricks.

The pitch of the chopper's engine changed and they felt a lurch as the pilot turned and began to descend towards an almost indiscernible clearing on the side of a steep hill. Lightening lit the mountains to the west and thunder grumbled above the engine's roar. Although the clearing was still uncluttered by large trees the undergrowth had taken command of the ground once more and the clearing was covered in small bushes and saplings. They would have to rope the final twenty feet. Pete, as the last man, placed his hand on the rope to begin his descent and the dark Malayan sky released the first rain of the day in an abrupt and ferocious downpour.

'I volunteered for this,' Pete muttered as he slipped down the rope towards the undergrowth that had already swallowed up his three companions.

Goh Swee had joined the MRLA, the inside people, more in a fit of rage than for his political belief or a desire to liberate his people from the yoke of British Imperialism. He had been passed over for promotion to head chef at the Imperial Hotel in Kuala Lumpur, he had resigned in a fit of pique and when suffering the effects of a massive hangover. Not a day passed without he asked the same questions of himself;

'How did I get into this mess? What am I doing here?'

Goh was a most unlikely soldier, his physique was not that of a warrior, nor was his temperament, but he was rather quick tempered as his present situation proved. He was not a naturally violent man and any form of active soldiering called for a certain degree of ferocity.

When he had first joined, five months ago, he had been with number One Regiment which operated in the northern part of Selangor. To his great relief he had never had to confront the British Army, but security forces constantly harassed the platoon in which he served and they were forever on the move. As most of that part of the state was swamp he had found the life harder than he had ever anticipated.

He was saved from his dilemma the day that he escorted his district committee member to a meeting across the state border in Pahang. The meeting was attended by Osman Chang, Chin Peng's second in command. The man and woman who usually did the cooking in the camp had both been killed in an ambush when they went to a kampong to collect food. Goh volunteered to the fill the vacancy and after Osman Chang had sampled the food he had instantly demanded that Goh accompany him back to his base on the Thai border.

Goh received this information with equal measure of relief and alarm. Relief to be out of the swamps and constantly on the move but alarmed because the border was a hundred and fifty miles away and that was a long walk, a very long walk. What Goh did not know at the time was that men in Osman Chang's position did not walk that sort of distance, in fact, they barely walked more than twenty miles, and the major part of the journey was covered by bus and train.

Although Goh's life was now less strenuous, and a lot less dangerous, he still regretted the fact that he had taken this route, but to show any sign of regret would have been as good as committing suicide, waverers were not tolerated. Goh counted his blessings despite his lack of enthusiasm for he never went short of food and usually managed to keep the choicest pieces for himself, and the most dangerous task he ever had to perform was the one that he was engaged in at that moment; sentry duty.

Through a gap in the trees to his right he could see Lake Temengor flat and blue, stretching into the misty distance and behind him the summit of Gunong Besar ended in limestone crags, but out of sight from where he squatted with his Japanese Nambu carbine leaning against a tree beside him.

He had started his stretch as sentry immediately after the noon meal, and he was to be relieved after four hours so that he could oversee the preparation of the next meal. He was bored and desperate for a cigarette, but it was a craving that he dare not satisfy, the punishment was too severe. He tried to put the longing from his mind by remembering happier times when he prepared food in a huge and modern kitchen for the hotels wealthy guests. He felt for the comfort of the vine that extended along the floor for the fifty yards to the camp which he would tug sharply if danger presented itself and a bamboo rattle would alert his comrades.

Another need now overcame him, the need to urinate, another forbidden activity when acting as sentry. Members were required to have enough self-control or to have relieved themselves before taking up their post, the stench of human urine was distinctive and long lived.

Minutes passed, and neither urge diminished. Goh decided that his bladder could take the strain no longer. He knew that he would have to move away some distance or the next sentry would certainly be able to smell the urine; most of his comrades had been in the jungle since they fought the Japanese, and they had developed animal like senses.

There were many clumps of tall bamboo on this side of the camp and it was beside one such clump that the sentry post was sited, providing natural and effective camouflage. Goh knew that he was limited in which direction he could go to relieve himself. Going closer to the camp was out of the question as was going up the rise to his left. No sentry was ever placed on that side of the camp, instead, the jungle floor was littered with fronds of dry bamboo, which, if stepped on snapped with a crack like a pistol shot.

Taking his rifle and loath to be out of reach of the alarm vine he moved down the slight rise heading for a thicket of atap which would give him cover from most directions. He rested his rifle against a tree and lowered his trousers half way down his thighs. A soft sigh of relief escaped his lips as the pressure on his bladder eased. As he gazed through a small window in the trees at the purpled majesty of the distant mountains, that marked the border with Thailand, his attention was attracted to a slight movement about five yards away, and at an angle to his right. It was a dirty red patch of colour; he stared at it trying to detach its shape from the surrounding foliage. As he gazed the shape

31

suddenly jumped into focus; his heart momentarily stopped, and then began to pound. It was a hat with a dirty red patch on the front, the type of hat that the security forces wore. The wearer was looking down and seemed to be seated. Goh was too petrified to move, he was rooted to the ground. The man spoke quietly and a voice answered him out of sight on Goh's left.

Now the splashing of his urine on the jungle floor sounded like a gushing torrent breaking noisily over rocks, and equalled in volume by the thumping of his heart as it pounded against his rib cage. He tried to halt the flood but he seemed to have lost all control of his body and the flow continued, he was certain that this seemingly endless stream would be heard. He waited, holding his breath, for the man to look in his direction. The torso of another moved into his line of sight blocking out the head of the first. His shirt was black with sweat and he had a shotgun tucked under his arm. The low voices continued and others seemed to join in, Goh was certain that he was living his final moments. It crossed his mind to act first and shoot the man who now had his back to him; there was not the slightest chance that he could miss, but what then? No, if he fired then he was certain to die, they were oblivious to his presence and while that situation prevailed there was a chance that he would not perish. After what seemed an eternity the voices ceased and he was certain that he could hear the sounds of bodies moving carefully through the undergrowth away from him and the camp. Silence descended on the sullen wilderness, and in a distant valley a hornbill called loud and discordant.

Goh considered that it was now safe to move. As he adjusted his trousers he was horrified to discover that it was not only his bladder that had emptied.

*

For four days they had scoured their side of the range for any signs of human activity but without any success, late afternoon of the previous day it was decided to call off the operation. Tracks, unless used regularly, rarely remain visible for more than a few days in the jungle. The frequent and sometimes constant downpours usually eliminated any signs within a matter of hours except to the most expert trackers, and these were invariably Iban's or Aborigines.

The track that had been found were possibly a few days old, but Pete could not be more certain than that, he could not even evaluate the number in the party that had made them. The track went southwest-northeast but in which direction the creators had been travelling was impossible to ascertain in spoor of this age. They split into pairs and

32

checked in both directions but neither direction revealed anything positive. This was the extent of human activity that had been found.

Tom Parnell crouched over his radio like large crow surveying a potential meal and dextrously tapped out the message to control asking for permission to extend the duration of the operation. When he had finished he listened intently through his headset, writing on a message pad as he did so. When he had finished he handed the grubby slip of paper to Pete;

Request denied for operational reasons Stop Keep to planned extraction RV Stop Out

Pete grimaced, 'Were going home.'

Bob Gill grinned at him, 'You've 'ardly 'ad time to become ulu tolerant, boss.'

'Piss off, Gill; I was Ulu tolerant when you were just a twinkle in yer father's eye.' Pete got to his feet, and hauled his Bergen onto his back and indicated the direction of travel with a flat hand. Bob, still grinning led them off towards their RV on the road five thousand yards to the south.

Chapter Six

The five, after a brief argument, agreed not to stay in the Services Club where they had been dropped off earlier that morning, but instead decided to have a look round the seething city before any serious drinking began. It had been Ken Duffy's suggestion.

'You'll all be too pissed by nightfall to enjoy the nightlife,' he pointed out, 'let's see a bit of the town first.'

The only real dissenter was Sam, 'I can pace myself,' he protested, 'I don't wanna waste a single minute; we don't know when we'll get here again,'

'Sod off, Sam,' John dismissed his pleading, 'you'd not make it to tea time if yer started drinking now,' Sam made to object but John continued, 'and yer definitely wouldn't be in a fit state to perform in a knocking shop,'

This caused Sam to reconsider but he still felt obliged to defend the macho image he liked to display, 'Hey, this is Sammy yer talking to, the stud of Sankey,' he called as he followed them away from the club along Beach Road.

The teeming cosmopolitan city was a seething mass of humanity reflecting every aspect of life. Beggars of every colour, creed, and age sought to better their plight at the expense of the scores of Commonwealth servicemen, traders and shoppers that filled the walkways and pavements.

Shrill, strident, Chinese music, mingled with the latest Western hits from Doris Day, Johnny Ray and Frank Sinatra that emanated from open fronted bars and shops. Everywhere there were beautiful girls of every shade of brown, from light skinned Chinese girls to the darkest, black eyed, Tamil's.

The five negotiated the swarming streets soaking up the sights, sounds and smells, exchanging words but not really conversing, each enclosed in their own magical world of sights and sounds.

Keith brought them all back to reality, 'I'm bloody starving,' the aromas of exotic foods were tempting.

'I'm not eating fucking wog food,' John said determinedly.

'Aw, come on, Cantrill,' Brian mocked, 'we're in Singapore and you want bloody fish and chips.'

'I've eaten enough shite over the last two weeks, I'm paying, I'm choosing,' John retorted.

After more discussion and advice from a passing group of sailors they returned to the Services Club where they had a choice of both European and Eastern food at reasonable prices.

'You want to head for Bugis Street and Lavender Street.' a rather superior RAF corporal sat at the next table informed them, 'but you have to be careful; there are a lot of out of bounds clubs and bars.'

'I'm not gonna let that stop me getting a fuck.' Sam scoffed.

'The place is crawling with 'redcaps',' the corporal warned.

Sam snorted with derision, 'Us jungle troops can out outwit the monkeys anytime.'

The NCO smiled, 'Well that's up to you,' he stood up, 'But duty calls I'd better be off,' from the floor by his chair he picked up a white topped service cap, and from inside it he removed an armband bearing the letters SP, and fitted it to his sleeve, 'I hope I don't see you again lads.'

'What you laughing at,' Sam asked Ken as the corporal left them.

'D'you know what he is?'

'Bloody RAF isn't he?'

'Oh aye, but what d'you think his job is?'

The truth dawned on Sam, 'Police?' Ken nodded.

'Aw, he's RAF,' Sam sneered, 'he can't touch us.'

'I think you'll find that he can, Sam,' Brian drained his glass and got to his feet, 'my cousin did his time as a 'snowdrop', that's what the lads call 'em, and I remember him saying that any service police can arrest any serviceman.'

Sam gave another snort of derision and stood up, 'Bloody Brylcreem boys just let 'em try.'

By the time they hit the streets again it was dark and the night air seemed to intensify the noise and the seductiveness of the city. There now appeared to be even more girls filling the pavements and they were all starting to look more beautiful after a few of pints in the Nuffield Club.

They found Bugis Street following the RAF corporals directions and saw that a lot of the seedier looking bars bore the signs informing the world that the particular establishment was; *Out of Bounds to all Service Personnel.*

As they passed a shadowy side street Keith felt a gentle tug on the waistband of his bush shirt. Thinking that he was the target of a pick pocket he spun round with his right fist poised to despatch the purloiner.

'Okay, Johnnie,' the small man stood with his open hands held in an attitude of supplication. He wore a tee shirt, that had once been white, and baggy OG shorts from which his skinny legs emerged like two joss sticks, 'you want nice girl?' he grinned exposing a set of yellow teeth that resembled crazy paving, 'very young, very cheap.'

'Not your bloody mother is it, John?' Brian asked.

The man flashed his deformed and discoloured teeth again, 'Oh no Johnnie,' he chortled, 'my mother no good, dese young girls, you like Johnnie, come see,' he beckoned them to follow him into the gloom.

'How cheap,' Sam homed in on the man.

'You talk with girl,' the man replied.

'Forget it lads,' Brian felt repelled by the man, 'they'll be right old slag's.'

'Oh no, no, Tuan,' the scrawny man persisted, 'lovely young girls only. You come, you come, 'he beckoned and edged towards the alley.

'Come on lads, might be a laugh,' Sam was clearly impressed even though his question on the price of the merchandise had been skilfully side-stepped.

'I'd sooner find good bar,' Brian was uneasy.

'Oh, it very nice bar too,' the man's face lit up as another objection was overcome. Some with reluctance, some with enthusiasm, they followed him into the shadows.

Fearing they would become lost in the labyrinth and being the only NCO present, Ken felt burdened with the responsibility of making sure that no serious mishaps occurred. It was difficult keeping track of the route that they were taking in the cluttered unlit back streets but after a few minutes he was relieved when they emerged onto a brightly lit main street buzzing with life both Oriental and Caucasian. Ken's solace was short lived for they crossed the street and immediately plunged back into the shadows of the side street opposite. Almost straightaway, after only a few paces, they entered a dimly lit doorway and mounted a narrow staircase, lit by a single bulb. Music and loud voices drifted from an open door on the floor above them.

The room was better, in its décor, than Ken had expected but the ambience that it portrayed was everything that he had anticipated, it was a knocking shop. Males, obviously servicemen, and working girls occupied cubicles extended down the length of the room. Other tables were scattered around the room and most were taken. It appeared their scrawny guide was more effective than a large expensive sign, and he was more discreet. The air reeked of cheap perfume, sweat, and spilt beer and a haze of tobacco smoke played around the two slowly turning fans on the ceiling.

'You meet pretty girls, Johnny,' he tried to usher them towards a half a dozen girls sat at the bar.

'Alright mate you got us 'ere leave it at that,' Ken shooed the man away.

'What yer having lads,' John headed to the bar.

'Hey, John, look who's over there,' Brian pointed at a booth in the corner to where Barry Hayes was sat with a generously built girl.

'Hayesee, yer dirty little sod, I thought you were engaged to that big ugly tart on yer locker door,' Sam leaned over the table, 'He'll do you no luv, he's queer,' he gripped Barry's shoulder, 'and he's only got a little dick.'

'D'you mind, Andrews,' Barry tried to get to his feet but Sam forced him back into his chair, 'I'm just having a quiet drink with this young…'

'Quiet drink my arse,' Sam grinned.

'Sammy, come on we've got you a beer,' Keith called.

'I'll be keeping my eye on you, you little randy sod,' Sam called over his shoulder.

Two bottles of Tiger beer later and Sam's thoughts began to return to the subject of sex, 'Are we not getting off with some these birds, lads?'

'Come of it, Sam,' John dismissed the suggestion, 'there's only the roughest ones left, your cock would drop off within a week.'

'Give over, Cantrill,' he got to his feet, 'where's yer sense of adventure.'

'In me pants and I'm keeping it there, anyway it's your round.'

'Right, same again,' Sam did not wait for an answer and took up position at the bar next to the three remaining girls. The noise in the room was too loud for them to hear his conversation with the girls, but he had his arm round the nearest.

'I'm not going on the piss with him again,' Brian observed, 'he's only had four pints what's he going to be like after a couple more,' he shook his head, 'daft bugger.'

'We'll look after 'im,' Keith grinned, 'he's always like this.'

Sam was heading back with a tray bearing their drinks weaving between the crowded tables; he had a small Chinese female of doubtful age in tow.

'Bloody hell'! John cursed, 'he's picked up an old whore and he's bringing her over here.'

Sam put the tray down and selected a pint and a small glass containing a green liquid, 'Me an' this young lady are going to have a discussion in her room upstairs.'

'And how much is that going to cost you,' Brian whispered.

'We still have to discuss that,' he smirked, 'but when she sees what's on offer she'll probably pay me.'

'Don't be all bloody night,' John urged without humour, 'we're having one more here and then we going somewhere else.'

'He'll be back down in less than three minutes,' Keith emptied his glass and grinned.

'Very funny, Gardner,' Sam became concerned, 'Don't piss off and leave me though will you lads?'

'Get a move on you soft sod,' Brian gave him a gentle push, 'and remember what the MO told us last night,' he raised a finger of warning.

As Sam turned to follow the girl a tall Australian on the next table stretched his arms as he spoke to his three equally tall companions.

'I'm fair tuckered out, mate,' he informed them and sat there with outstretched arms.

Sam's turn brought him into contact with the large colonial's right arm knocking the drinks from his hands and depositing their contents over the Australians shoulder.

'Watch it mate,' the sudden, unwelcome cascade caused him to leap to his feet. His exceptional size did not allow that his long legs be extracted from under the table with ease, consequently, his sudden, clumsy movement upended this table spilling the glasses and bottles to the floor and showering his comrades with their contents.

'You clumsy, sod,' was Sam's inappropriate response, 'you can buy me another fucking drink, and one for her,' he added as an afterthought.

'You what, you cheeky Pommey bastard,' and with the usual Australian diplomacy he swung a punch at Sam's head but it never landed.

'No need for that, mate,' Keith grabbed the Aussie's wrist in an iron grip. For a large, heavily built man he had got to his feet with amazing speed. The man was a good head taller but probably weighed less, 'we'll let it pass,' Keith said quietly.

All present felt that the animosity had been subdued, and that there would be an amicable conclusion to what could have been an explosive situation. Sam did not quite see it like that. His drink had been spilt; he had been delayed in his pursuit of carnality and called a bastard.

Just as the semblance of a smile began to appear the Australians thin lips Sam's right boot connected with the his groin turning the smile into a shriek of excruciating pain as he doubled up in agony on the floor.

Australians appeared from every corner of the room. Fists, feet, bottles, chairs and table's flew as the five Royals conducted a fighting withdrawal maintaining the honour of their regiment, but determined in their bid to live and fight another day.

The narrow staircase was easy to defend although backing down a steep flight of stairs with a horde of enraged Antipodeans in violent pursuit created its own problems. They all realised that once they reached the alleyway other difficulties would arise, and the annoyed Aussie's would then have room to manoeuvre.

'When you get to the door leg it,' John bawled above the nasal threats.

Brian, who was the first out of door, turned in confusion not knowing where to run, but his quandary was instantly resolved. In the alleyway crowded a posse of service police. Two Royal Military Policemen in the company of two Australian Military Police and the Royal Air Force Service Police corporal they had met in the Nuffield Club. Brian had never greatly admired the 'monkeys' as the RMP were affectionately known but at that moment he had never been so glad to see anyone in his life.

As the pursuing horde spilt out into the alleyway their wrath quickly evaporated.

'What's going 'ere then?' A huge Australian MP Sergeant enquired pleasantly.

Throughout the two-hour drive back to the FTC Sam lamented the missed opportunity of a night of lust.

'Shut up, Sammy,' John opened his eyes, like everybody, apart from Sam, he was trying to sleep, 'you've probably been saved from getting a dose, so think yourself lucky.' he shut his eyes and dropped his chin on his chest. Sam continued his lamentations in soft undertones.

Chapter Seven

The heat in the office was oppressive and it had only just turned ten o'clock. The louvered window shutters were closed to defend against the morning sun and the ceiling fan was set as slow for anything faster would have scattered the papers across the desk. John Sankey continued the chore of reading the dozens of field reports that landed on his desk every day. Most were routine, but occasionally, once a week on average, there was something to grab his attention, a gem of intelligence that was worth acting on and this was one such day.

He smoothed the small sheet of rice paper that had been rolled and left in a length of bamboo at the 'letterbox'. It was from a very reliable informant known as Yang buta orang, the Blind Man, and only John knew the man's real identity.

The message was written in pencil and was somewhat difficult to de cipher having suffered from a week exposed to the damp. Blind man would have left the note in a letterbox near the jungle edge from where it would have been collected by another agent living on the outside. He, or she, would have then left it in yet another letterbox where a special branch undercover agent would have picked it up, and eventually it arrived onto John's desk. It was an intricate and long-winded method of passing intelligence but it was secure and virtually fool-proof. Nobody in the chain would have known the identity of any of the other couriers.

The contents referred to the brutal murder of three rubber tappers on the Enjol Rubber Estate a month earlier when a family of three had been hacked to death, and the daughter raped before suffering the same fate as her parents. It had been assumed that it was the work Ben Kim; it had his signature of virulent and cold-blooded cruelty, even though it was at the limits of the area over which he ruled. The message confirmed John's suspicion but more importantly it informed him that a meeting of the top brass of the MRLA had taken place a day or so before the murder in North Perak and Chin Peng, the General Secretary of the MCP, Malayan Communist Party, had attended.

The existence of a large camp in the border area was not new information but it did confirm what they already suspected, and justified the continued efforts being made to find it. Unfortunately Blind man did not know the precise location but John was confident that they were looking in the right area. Finding a camp, even a large camp, in vast jungle clad mountains of the northern states really was looking for the proverbial needle in a haystack.

He urgently set about changing his notes for his briefing of the Emergency War Committee that was to take place the following day in Ipoh.

*

The morning was still fresh as Sergeant David Snell entered the magnificent marble hall of Ipoh railway station. He arrived at exactly the same moment as did the train from Singapore, it squealed to a halt in a skirt of swirling steam and disgorged two hundred and fourteen passengers onto platform one.

Dave was pleased with the job he had been given on arrival at the Royal West Lancashire's. As the senior NCO with the battalion's training team it kept his jungle skills honed without the arduous life that accompanied normal jungle operations. Ben Murphy had endeavoured to recruit him into the tracking team, but he had resisted the vigorous offer, he was due to leave the army in three years and had recently married, he desired a quieter life.

As an orphan, and unable to find work or a home, he had enlisted into the Coldstream Guards, and just as he was becoming bored with ceremonial duties Hitler thwarted his intention to leave the army. Having survived Dunkirk his service life took a new turn when he volunteered for the newly formed commando's, and his long association with Special Forces began. He ended the war in Italy as a member of the 2nd SAS. When the SAS were disbanded he transferred to The Gloucestershire Regiment and served in the Korean War. He managed to evade being taken prisoner when the regiment was surrounded and captured. 1952 saw the re-birth of the SAS and Dave was one of the first recruits and he had just completed his three-year tour. His parent regiment was still the Gloucester's, but he had applied to move to the RWL's so that he could continue to serve in Malaya.

In his starched, neatly pressed, OG's and highly polished boots his guardsman's bearing was easily recognised; only the Sabre wings on his right shoulder indicated his time spent as a more unorthodox soldier.

'Mr Gates?' Simon turned to see a tall immaculate sergeant, dark haired and sporting a thin neat moustache. Despite his crispness there was an aura of kindness about him and there was a glint of humour in his black eyes.

'Yes, sergeant, you've come to collect us?'

'I have, sir. Yourself and seven OR's I believe,' he took hold of Simon's largest case.

'Name's Snell, sir, I am with the battalion training platoon. I'll be looking after you for the next two weeks. Are these your chaps? Fall them in corporal,' he said to Ken, 'and follow me.'

'You're about to become involved in one of the most fascinating and challenging activities known to man,' Lieutenant Colonel Jeremy Crawson MC paused for effect, 'a manhunt.'

Simon stood easy before his commanding officers desk on his initial interview, and was feeling a little uncomfortable and unkempt after his long journey. The CO's thin blonde hair was parted in the middle of his head and brushed flat to his tanned scalp. The right side of his face was mask-like due to plastic surgery administered to a severe head wound that he had received during the Normandy landings. His pale blue eyes held Simons, and seemed to be seeking any detectable weakness or indecisiveness apparent in his new subaltern

'And that's what this war's about, Simon, hunting men,' he paused again, 'but don't let the fact that they refuse to become involved in a conventional warfare lead you to believe that they are cowards or ineffective soldiers. That is not the case. Many of the CT fought with us against the Nip's, and damn good fighters they were too, we trained them and armed them and they were loyal and brave allies. This is a guerrilla war and this is what we trained these chaps to do and they do it damn well, but in the final analysis we're better. We're better trained and we're better armed and right is on our side despite what the damned lefty politicians might say on the matter,' he stood up and stretched out his hand. 'Welcome to the regiment, Simon, make the most of your time with us it will stand you in good stead no matter what path you might take when you return to civilian life.'

'Thank you, sir, I will.'

'Now we must get you bedded down before lunch,' he tapped on a hatch on the wall behind him, and called, 'Nigel.'

The adjutant, Captain Nigel Smith-Parr, appeared in the opening, 'Sir!'

'Get young Simon here settled in, Nigel.'

'Sir,' he disappeared and then re appeared in the open doorway and led Simon to his office.

Simon's interview with the adjutant was what he would have expected. Regardless of an officer's natural disposition, once appointed as a regiment's adjutant they were transformed into martinets overnight. Officers renowned for their sense of humour became unsmiling ogres, friendly outgoing types turned into cantankerous demons and young men of nonchalant inclination were transformed into pernickety fiends who demanded attention to the smallest detail no matter how trivial. Captain Smith-Parr was no exception; his instructions to Simon were precise and curt.

'There is no swearing in the mess or discussion of the opposite sex in a derogatory manner, the correct mode of uniform will apply at all times, the details of which are contained in this,' he handed Simon a booklet entitled *Officers Mess Rules*. 'Ignorance of the rules will not be tolerated so I would advise you to read and digest. After lunch you are to report to Captain Haskin in the training office. He stood up and consulted his watch, 'Lunch is in thirty minutes, do not be late.' For a moment he surveyed Simons crumpled uniform, 'I would suggest you smarten yourself up, your turnout requires a lot of improvement.'

Simon was on the verge of protesting that he had just travelled overnight by train but the look in the adjutant's eyes persuaded him otherwise.

Chapter Eight

Headquarters of 28 Commonwealth Brigade occupied a slightly elevated site set in a three-acre Padang overlooking the junction of the Sungei Kinta and one of its tributaries. The camp was composed of the large airy, white painted, two storied buildings with shaded verandahs at both levels. The central structure was a late Victorian house of generous proportions and great elegance. The spacious former ball room was now the HQ's secure operational conference room in which the District War Committee met every week.

A large, highly polished, table of rosewood filled the centre of the room and was surrounded by twenty-four Victorian balloon chairs of which half were occupied by officers from the Army, RAF and Malayan Police. On the only windowless wall was an enormous map of the peninsula and before it a low dais on which Inspector John Sankey of the special branch stood behind a wooden lectern.

'We now have corroboration from a very reliable agent that the murder of Ah Lee and his family, at Lasah in North Perak, was committed, in person, by State Committee Member Beng Kim,' as he spoke he indicated the kampong on the map with a long pointer. 'We had suspected this to be the case. Not that he had personally perpetrated the crime but that he had ordered it …Sir?'

Brigadier Harry Woodhouse the Commander of 28 Commonwealth Brigade had raised his hand. Most senior officers would have simply interrupted but Brigadier Woodhouse was the archetypal Edwardian gentleman. He was a small, slight and wiry man immaculately turned out with greying hair, and his medal ribbons testified to an active war record.

'So sorry to butt in, John, but did your source put forward a reason as to why?'

'He did sir, it was in reprisal for failing to provide food at a certain time, but this is the most interesting part. As you know, sir,' John continued, 'we've suspected for some time that there is a camp of some significance in the area of the mountain range connecting Besar, Chamah and Noring gunong's,' he tapped each gunong in turn, 'and we consider that the only reason that Beng would have been this far north was for a meeting in the border area. This region is too sparsely populated…sir.'

The wing commander ever eager to advance more use of the RAF cupped his hands behind his head, and leaned back in his chair, 'It would seem to me that with an area of jungle of that magnitude my chaps and the Royal Artillery observer aircraft would be the best tools for the job of finding these blighters.'

'Too much aircraft activity in that area would cause them to up sticks, Roger,' the brigadier said, and then nodded to John to continue his briefing.

'Thank you, sir,' John continued, 'we also discovered that Yeong Kwo the SCM of West Pahang, and Loi Tek from Johore travelled together by train to Kemubu in North Kelantan two weeks before this murder. A further indication, that a high powered meeting took place in the north about that time.'

The brigadier turned to young looking major wearing the insignia of the Royal Scots Fusiliers, 'Allen.'

Major Allen Doyle, the brigade major, joined John on the dais. He placed a bundle of papers on the lectern and cleared his throat, 'General Goodier has given 28 Commonwealth Brigade the task of locating this camp, destroying it, and inflicting the heaviest casualties possible on the CT. To assist in this task; one company from 1/10 Gurkha's, one company from 2/2 Gurkha's and one squadron of SAS have been placed directly under brigade command,' he looked up and let the words sink in. 'All other infantry regiments in the brigade will continue to perform their normal patrolling duties as no suspicion must be raised that we are increasing our interest in that particular area, and the easing up of pressure in unit areas would make Charlie suspicious.

The attached units will have sole responsibility for areas allocated and no other operations, either air or ground, will take place in this region until further notice,' he took the pointer and turned to the map. ''D' Squadron SAS will cover the Besar area, 'B' Company 1/10th, Chamah and 'A' Company 2/2 the area of Noring. There will be a detailed briefing of the company commanders of the relevant unit's tomorrow morning at 0830. This, gentlemen, is obviously a covert operation and I don't need to spell out to commanders of your experience the necessity of 'need to know'.' He directed his gaze at Jeremy Crawson, 'You will also be required on the briefing, sir, as it is your regiment that will most certainly become involved once the camp has been located.'

The commanding officer of the RWL's appeared a little startled; the brigadier looked across the table and smiled.

'Hope it's a pleasant surprise, Jeremy, but as the Kiwis are due to leave and be replaced by the 2nd RAR I am going to give you responsibility for the area northwest of Sungei Siput, when the time comes, as there may be need to act before the Aussie's have settled in.

In the meantime, however you will continue to operate in your current area.'

'Aussie's are not going to like that, sir,' Lieutenant Colonel George Elloy, commanding officer of 22 SAS laughed, 'bloody Pom's getting the action in their area.'

'Then they'll have to lump it, George. I'm not having green troops mess this up,' he stood up. 'Now gentleman, let us retire to the bar for a G and T before lunch.'

*

The new campsite was within four hours march of Kampong Rambutan, and about six hours from Tanah Hitam with the Guntong rubber estate just two hours to the south. Sited thus, Beng's new HQ could be easily kept supplied with most of the provisions that would be required.

Beng's decision to move was as surprising as it was welcome, but no one would have dared suggested it even though they all knew it was the safest thing to do following the killings at Lasah. On the eastern side of the main Kampah/Taiping road they had quick and easy access to the great wilderness of Kelantan without exposing themselves to even the smallest settlement. Over two thousand square miles of jungle covered mountains that, apart from a few aborigines, man rarely trod. They had spent three days making the camp as comfortable and as secure as they could. It was a small area of flattish ground on the northern side of a steep valley and to the east the valley rose to the heights of Gunong Korbu. Two hundred feet below, a mountain stream tumbled over rocks on its way to the fertile plains of Perak. The opposite side of the valley had a gentler slope and a good proportion of it was visible from one of the sentry posts, the sentry post that Lau now occupied.

He had spent the previous day and all of that morning gathering palm and bamboo branches to cover the ground on the north and west of the camp. It had been tiring work as they were only collected at some distance from the camp so as not to leave signs of their activities in the immediate vicinity.

Lau had seen a number of atrocities committed during his time with the inside people and a fair amount of engagement with the security forces, but the murders at Lasah haunted him. What concerned him most was the apparent lack of concern that his comrades displayed after the ruthless deed.

'No amount of regret or guilt on your part will change what's happened,' Lam told him when he voiced his anguish, 'you've got to tell yourself that war is terrible and many innocent people get killed, and that the means justifies the end.'

46

Lau shook his head as he recalled the words of his friend knowing there was some truth in what he said, but unable to fully come to terms with the lack of compassion. Abdul's only emotion was one of disappointment and anger that his sexual activity had been abruptly cut short.

The full weight of the oppressive heat gripped the jungle in a sullen, breathless silence. Because of the camp's altitude there was not even the annoying whine of mosquitoes, and the air was almost brittle in the oppressive, ponderous, temperature. Away up on the heights to his left a family of gibbons protested noisily for a few moments at some encroachment of their territory and to the south, in lower hills, some howler monkeys joined in with their mournful lament that began slowly and gradually built up into a long drawn-out wail.

'Comrade's' the voice boomed out across the valley startling Lau out of his unintentional reverie. After the initial shock he realised what was happening, 'you fight for a lost cause,' the disembodied voice went on, 'you suffer unnecessarily,' by now Lau could hear the drone of the 'voice aircraft' that had been masked by the noise of the howler monkeys. It was a common enough occurrence. Surrendered or captured MRLA members were persuaded to record propaganda messages to play to their former comrades still carrying on the fight in the jungle.

The voice continued to relay the message of enticement and Lau knew that although he could not see them, thousands of safe conduct leaflets would be showering down into the trees. The leaflets enforced the message and also served as safe conduct pass to those who wished to imitate the owner of the voice and give themselves up. To be discovered with such a leaflet in one's possession, automatically attracted a sentence of death.

Then they began to flutter into view and Lau watched as scores of bright orange leaflets drifted slowly into the valley below. He decided, much to his own surprise, that when he next visited the water point he would try to find one, if it was safe to do so.

*

At twenty-four Eric Haskin was the youngest captain in the regiment, and one of the youngest in the Army. His unbounded enthusiasm for soldiering, and total dedication to his calling, did not always endear him to others of less ardent nature in particular the National Servicemen that he commanded.

He was known among the troops as Attila because of his Teutonic appearance. Fair skinned and blue eyed with almost white hair, so white that he did not appear to possess eyelashes, he did have the appearance of the ideal Wehrmacht leader. He halted the column, took of his hat and mopped the sweat from his face, 'Where d'you estimate we are, Simon?'

Simon moved forward and crouched beside the training officer. This was a testing time. Eric had set a hard pace and Simon had struggled with fatigue, the effort to keep his sense of direction, and at the same time appear to be in tactical control of the small unit. They were a little over section strength having been joined by four men who had been removed from an earlier course because of sickness. In addition there was a signaller, Sergeant Snell, another training NCO, Lance-corporal 'Ruby' Murray and an Iban tracker with the name of Yau.

It was difficult terrain in which to keep ones bearings being devoid of easily identifiable features, and being composed of belukar and thick patches of bamboo. Progress had been slow and extremely arduous with visibility of no more than a few feet. After debussing at Batu Gajah, a small town two miles south of Ipoh, they had passed through a small rubber estate and into a huge expanse of lalang, elephant grass, ten feet high. The leading scout had to be changed every ten minutes because of the tremendous effort required forcing a passage. It had taken them more than an hour to cross the five hundred yards that separated them from the Sungei Timah. All the time they were exposed to the ferocity of the morning sun, and the lalang seemed to soak up the oxygen creating a feeling of suffocation.

The Timah, when they reached it, was a sluggish river twenty yards wide the colour of strong milky tea. Eric had obviously operated in this area in the past for he entered the water without even pausing to check its depth. It came up their chests and despite an initial apprehension the tepid waters gave some relief after the trial of the lalang. Leaving the river they found themselves in swamp that at times came up to the waist. Mosquitoes, in their thousands, added to their discomfort and roots acted as underwater snares. In less than thirty minutes, much to their relief, they reached firmer ground but faced the turmoil of the vegetation that formed secondary jungle.

Simon studied the map trying to recall the last two hours, the ground that they had covered and any significant features that he could identify on the almost featureless map. Eric was seated on his pack eating a packet of raisins and seemingly oblivious to Simons quandary. He traced their path in his mind. After leaving the trucks they seemed to have kept on a bearing that ran almost due west. He could not recollect if there had been many, if any, deviations from this course. He cursed inwardly that he had not made regular checks on the bearing as he had been advised at the FTC.

'Even if you're not in command,' the squat Maori sergeant warned, 'know where you are in the jungle. Your life and those of your men may depend on it. It don't matter if there are several people senior to you on the patrol, make sure that you know where you are.'

Eventually he screwed up his courage and ventured, 'I reckon we're just here,' he touched a point on the map with a twig.

Eric grinned, 'Are you sure?'

Simon grinned in return, 'Not to the exact yard.'

'Not the exact hundred, I'll lay.'

Simon shook his head, 'I should have kept a closer check on our bearing.'

'Oh, we haven't deviated greatly from our bearing,' Eric assured him, 'the trick here is to try to estimate how far we have actually covered. In this type of country you're lucky to cover a thousand yards an hour, and your indicating that we've done about two and a half when in fact it's nearer to fifteen hundred.'

'Is that all,' Simon was incredulous, 'I'm knackered.'

'It's the lalang,' Eric explained, 'it's a right bastard.'

At the rear of the small column Dave Snell rested his Bergen against a tree without removing it.

'Can we smoke, sarge?' Sam whispered.

'Best not lad,' Dave replied, 'eat something it'll do you more good.'

'I thought we we're supposed to stop every hour,' Barry Hayes voiced his disapproval.

'This is the Army, Hayes, there's no bloody union rules here, just rules that'll will keep you alive and beat the enemy,' Dave had taken a dislike to Barry from the moment he met him, he was the typical barrack room lawyer with uninformed opinions on everything. 'Corporal Duffy' he went on, 'your presence is being requested.'

Ken turned to face the opposite way and saw John Cantrill tapping his left forefinger on his right upper arm.

'Right, Corporal Duffy,' Simon said when Ken reached him, 'I want you to detail another man, and we will take the Iban and recce for a campsite. No need for packs.'

Yau was a short, rather plump, Iban, he led followed by Simon then Hayes with Ken bringing up the rear. After fifteen minutes they broke free of the belukar but were faced with another wall of lalang.

'Tuan,' Yau pointed to a tunnel about three feet high forced through the thick coarse grass.

'CT?' Simon asked breathlessly, fearful of the answer.

Yau shook his head, grinning, 'Pig' he pointed at the tunnel again, 'We go?' Simon hesitated; Yau sensed his doubt and began to try to make his point with his limited English. 'Dis way bery hard,' he made the actions of struggling through the grass and wiped imaginary sweat from his brow. He crouched at the opening, 'here go bery fast, here okay.'

If they did not use the trail already forced by the wild pigs then they would have to force a path and Simon recalled how bad that had been earlier. Although he did not relish the idea of meeting a four hundred pound boar head on neither did he appreciate the thought of another battle with lalang, and after all Yau was the expert and would know how great the risk was of a possible confrontation with a large porker.

He nodded, 'Okay.'

Yau led off on all fours followed closely by Simon and the others. The going was easy and a lot quieter than forcing a passage. He was surprised when he found that they were able to walk almost upright after about fifty yards of crawling. This relief was short lived and a tiny grain of doubt was born in Simon's mind. A doubt that grew with each step but before he could relay his developing suspicion to Yau that something a little larger than a pig may have had something to do with this path, they stepped out into a small clearing with a number of atap basha's, it was a camp, a CT camp.

Simon immediately dropped into fire position and cocked his SMG, but there was no sign of a living soul or the slightest sound of a fleeing enemy. As he gazed intently round the camp he was suddenly hit from behind and a body crashed onto the ground beside him.

'Bloody hell, stay alert, Hayes, you idiot,' he hissed, 'get over there and cover that area,' he indicated the left side of the camp.

'Fucking hell,' was all Ken could manage as he crouched beside Yau.

'Cover our rear, corporal,' Simon was regaining his composure and enjoying the adrenaline rush. He felt a little unsure of the best course of action and he cursed the fact that he did not have a radio. It was obvious that the camp had only just been vacated although they had not heard a sound. The basha's still had personal kit strewn about and a small fire burned in the centre of the camp. There were six basha's which indicated that there had been at least twelve occupants, he did not care for the odds.

'Corporal Duffy,' he whispered once he had settled on a plan.

'Sir,' Ken moved closer.

'Take the tracker,' this had dented his faith in the little Iban, but he was confident that Yau would have no problems returning to where they had left the main party, 'and go back to Captain Haskin and tell him what we've found. Tell him that we'll stay here in case they return.'

'Are you sure, sir?' Ken whispered nervously, 'there'll be about a dozen of 'em if they come and....'

'Just do as I say, corporal,' he interrupted annoyed that his order was being questioned but at the same time reassured that the NCO was only showing concern for his safety, 'we'll be alright,' he added less aggressively, then smiled reassuringly.

As soon as Ken and Yau had left Simon took stock, and quickly came to the conclusion that his predicament would be precarious should the occupants of the camp realise how small his force was and return. The CO's words about the thrill of a manhunt came rushing back to mock him as he now felt like the hunted. Hayes had lost his shiny pink complexion, and had turned a deathly white, his wide staring eyes were fixed on Simon, and his hands shook as he clutched his rifle which pointed down towards the ground.

'Stay alert,' he hissed, 'and cover that area.'

'What we gonna do, sir?' He was on the verge of tears.

'Wait here until the others come,' Simon turned in the opposite direction and watched the silent, deserted camp.

The next minute Hayes was at his side his rifle pointed towards the sector he had been ordered to protect,

'They're here!' he almost screamed the words.

'Where'? Simon spun around bringing his SMG into the aim; there was nothing to be seen, 'where?' Simon demanded.

'I heard em,' tears were running down his chubby cheeks, 'listen.'

'Keep your voice down,' Simon hissed.

All was silent apart from the odd sniff from Hayes,

'There!' he almost shouted in jubilation. Simon heard it, the sound of a body moving carefully over wet ground, there was probably swamp over to the left.

Simon rose slowly to a crouch, 'Follow me.'

After about five yards the ground dropped sharply for five or six feet, and he could see the black water of the swamp. Even to Simon's untrained eye there were evident signs that a body had passed this way. He stooped low trying to see through the tangle of greenery. He listened cocking his head; the sound of slow progress came again and at the same time a rifle crashed close by his head, so close that he felt the blast of heat from the muzzle.

'I can hear 'em,' Hayes bawled as he struggled with the bolt of his rifle, a round had jammed halfway into the breach.

Simon could not see anything, and his ears rang with the concussion of the shot. Silence descended again on the sullen jungle clearing; all that could be heard was the sobbing and belaboured breathing of Hayes as he struggled with the rifle's action.

Simon hoped and prayed that there were no unseen eyes witnessing this debacle.

'Get a bloody grip of yourself man,' he forced Hayes down, and took the rifle from him and cleared the jam. 'Just sit there and get control of yourself,' he thrust the rifle back at him. Simon settled down to watch and wait; to his horror he realised that he was shaking.

Barry's mind was in turmoil he wanted to get up and run, but even in his terrified state he knew that was not an option. The thought of being alone in this uncompromising wilderness with enemy so close at hand kept him rooted to his position. Even so, when he considered the possibility of the camps occupants realising that he and his platoon commander were alone in the camp his racing mind returned to the prospect of taking his chance and trying to get back the main body.

The single consideration that all soldiers derived courage from, whether part time or career men, when thrust into the danger and trepidation of combat, was their standing with their mates and not wanting to be seen to be afraid. This did not enter Barry's churning brain his own survival was all that mattered.

He found himself on his feet and uttering words he had not intended. 'We've gotta get out of here,' his voice was hoarse.

The debilitating fear being exhibited by Hayes gave Simon the courage that he needed, 'Sit down, Hayes,' he growled, 'and shut up.'

The tone of Simon's words, and the look of disdain and anger on his face had the desired effect and Barry sank to the jungle floor sobbing.

'You'll get us killed,' he gasped between sobs.

'For crying out loud shut up and act like a man,' Simon's anger was tempered by the fact that the CT who may not be that far away would hear Hayes protestations and return, though this was becoming less likely.

The heavy heat and silence descended on the small clearing yet again, not a bird or insect called, the small fire had died and no breeze disturbed the limp vegetation. The putrid stench of the nearby swamp hung on the oppressive air like a damp mouldy blanket.

Simon became aware of a movement behind him; he turned quickly bringing his Sterling into the aim. Hayes was on his feet his fleshy features washed in sweat; his eyes were wild and staring, and his movements sluggish.

'You can't make me stay here,' he shook his head slowly as he spoke, 'nobody can, why should I die?' He began to walk back along the track by which they had arrived.

Simon got to his feet and went after him, 'Hayes this is desertion,' he grabbed the frightened man by the shoulder, 'come back and I won't take this any further.'

Hayes shrugged out of his grip and continued along the track.

Simon paused full of doubt as to the best course. The CT could still be in the vicinity, even watching this farce as it unfolded. Should he return to the camp and allow Hayes to go and deal with him later if and when they got back to battalion, or should he make this ineffectual little man do his duty?.

Suddenly he felt very angry at the precarious plight that he had been put in because of this inadequate man, 'Stop now,' he went close behind Hayes.

Hayes spun round anger now mixed with fear on his flabby face, his rifle pointing at Simon's chest.

Simon waited for neither word nor further action, the threat was indisputable. The small amount of unarmed combat that he knew he put to use. Both of his hands were free as his Sterling was carried on a sling around the neck. With his left hand he grabbed the muzzle of the Hayes No 5 carbine and forced the barrel up and to the left and at the same time he punched him in the face with his right fist. But the punch did not land squarely and merely brushed the side of Barry's neck.

The two fell back into the tall coarse grass and the thought of snakes briefly troubled Simon, but his immediate task pushed them from his mind. To his horror Hayes began to shout.

'I'll get you court martialled for this, I'll....'

Simon jammed a hand over his mouth and found it surprisingly easy to restrain the raving private.

'Shut up, Hayes, you're going to get us both killed,' he strove with the burning desire to smash his fist into the podgy face. He could almost smell the man's fear. Hayes stared up at Simon with eyes that were full of tears and dread.

Simon felt the urge to remove his hand from Hayes mouth repulsed that his hand was wet with saliva, mucus, and sweat. The pathetic man had now ceased struggling and was sobbing softly; Simon decided he could now reason with him.

'I'm going to let you go but you've got to be quiet; do you understand?'

Restricted by Simon's grip he nodded slightly. At that moment the unmistakable sound of bodies moving through the undergrowth could be heard.

'Shit,' Simon freed his SMG from around his neck and turned to face the direction from which the noise came. Because of the recent commotion he had lost his bearings and to his great relief he realised that the sounds were coming from the direction that they had approached the camp. He prayed that it was the rest of the patrol but maintained his stance, ready to respond to an enemy appearing.

'Sir,' the word was whispered urgently and the welcome sight of Ken Duffy pushed into view followed closely by David Haskin.

'We heard a shot, have you got one?' David asked eagerly.

'I'm sorry, sir,' Simon explained, 'Hayes lost control.'

'Oh, we'll sort that out later,' he gave Hayes a contemptuous look. 'They knew you were here, Simon, nothing's lost. But let's see what we can find that will be of interest to intelligence.'

David placed the unit into all round defence, told the signaller to set up and then with Simon and Ken began searching the camp while Sergeant Snell did a sweep of the surrounding area with Yau and Lcpl Murray.

Most of what they found were mundane items necessary for day to day survival: cooking pots, a few spare clothes, basic medicine and a few first aid supplies.

'These seem a little incongruous to find in the middle of the Malayan jungle,' Simon held up two expensive Parker fountain pens.

'This looks like it might be something, sir,' Ken drew a sheaf of paper from a waterproof wrap and handed them to David.

'We could have done with a JCLO with us,' David mused as he briefly studied the sheets of paper that were covered in Chinese writing, 'we must get them back quickly,' he explained, 'there may be useful intelligence here but if they have time to change things it will be useless.'

'Through to control, sir,' the signaller looked up at David from where he crouched.

'Give me a quick briefing on what happened, Simon.' David produced a message pad.

As Simon related the events the training officers face darkened, and he shook his head as he wrote. When Sergeant Snell's patrol returned he reported that there were four sets of tracks heading off in different directions.

'How many'? David asked

'Ten, maybe twelve, in groups of three or four,' he replied.

'No signs that any of them returned?'

'Naw.'

'Hayes, get over here,' David ordered as he passed a message to the signaller to be relayed.

'This man is under field arrest,' David told his sergeant, 'he is to carry his weapon, but take all of his ammo from him, and he is to stay with you or one of the other NCO's until we get back to battalion.'

By the time that they completed their search of the camp control had responded to David's message.

'Right, Simon, they've agreed that we should get any intelligence back with the utmost urgency. A Sycamore will be at a nearby DZ before last light. We won't have time to prepare it for a Whirlwind, which could lift us all out, so I will take one man and RV with the chopper. You make camp in the vicinity and tomorrow morning RV with transport at the twenty-third milestone. The tracking team are on their way in even as I speak so keep the net open so that they can contact you if they have any problems. If they have enough hours of daylight left they will start the pursuit tonight, if not then at first light.' David gave Simon a reassuring grin, 'Bit much on your training op, but it's better than being bored.'

'What the bloody hell have you done, Hayes,' 'Ruby' Murray asked as they set up their basha, he had had Hayes put under his jurisdiction for the night.

'It's that stuck up bugger,' Barry retorted nodding towards Simon, his cockiness restored, 'I heard 'em coming back and he didn't want to know.'

'Bollocks, Hayes,' John Cantrill and Keith were building a basha close by, 'Pearly's got more guts than you,' John paused from his task, 'you lost yer bottle didn't yer?'

Barry's flushed faced flushed darker, he wanted to respond belligerently but he knew that John was not to be crossed and he contented himself with a mild denial.

'You're in the shit, pal,' John continued, 'you'll be lucky if you don't get a court martial.'

'He'll be lucky if he does,' 'Ruby' put in, 'if he stays in battalion his life won't be worth living.'

'Well its best we find out now that he's a yellow bastard than when we get into a real fire fight,' Keith added.

'Can't you still be shot for cowardice?' John winked at 'Ruby'

'Only if the CO demands it,' 'Ruby' winked back and they kept their backs to Barry who busied himself with the basha but made no response.

Chapter Nine

Linda lay staring at the slow moving ceiling fan and calmly analysed her feelings. The sun had risen, but the louvered window shutters filtered the morning light to a soft, gentle radiance and threw lines of sunlight onto the teak planked floor. A gecko scuttled silently across the ceiling in a never-ending search for sustenance and the sounds of the hotel gardeners, already about their business, drifted up from the lawns below. The only sound in the room was the tranquil whirr of the fan and Rogers light and even breathing.

Her unwelcome feeling of contentment was tempered by a nagging shard of guilt. On reflection she realised that she had always been conscious that she would have to succumb to Roger's entreaties, she knew that it was required of her. He had never been robust in his efforts to seduce her, but he had been persistent in a gentle and undemanding way. She took solace from the fact that at least she found him physically attractive.

Her previous experience of sex had been brief, disappointing, and some time ago. They had both been young and inexperienced with vastly differing aims and ambitions. She had wanted education and was driven by the desire to improve her position in life. To throw off her peasant background and achieve something in the world of politics in order to help the painfully impoverished that she had been raised among. Yam, on the other hand, had been content with the limited learning given to him at the local school until he was fourteen, and then to work in his father's shop selling cheap imported clothes to the locals. They would have lived as part of Yam's, family and she would be at his parent's beck and call working in the shop, helping in the family kitchen, and bearing numerous children.

When this war was over, the war she was helping to bring to an end, her aspiration was to be one of those aiding the country find its own identity and cast off the trappings of colonial rule. Now that she had a new and more responsible post in special branch her contribution to ending the battle would be much greater; and to be the lover of an officer who was serving in an elite regiment was an added bonus.

The British, despite what many said, had put many good things in place. Their flair for civil administration and their expertise with rail systems plus the establishment of a sound trading position would be of great benefit to the country once Merdeka had been achieved.

Her meditation ended as Roger rolled over and wrapped his strong arms around her slight body.

'Good morning,' he grinned; his breath carried a suggestion of brandy from the previous night, 'we have another eight hours before I must be back; how can we fill all that time?'

*

After only one month in a rifle company, John and Brian had, without any real justification, adopted the air and confidence of seasoned soldiers. As they had expected, at the end of their training, they had all been assigned to different companies within the battalion. With Keith, they had been sent to 'A' Company, and thence to 3 Platoon, whereas Keith had gone to 1 platoon. Simon Gates was 3 platoon's commander and Dave Snell his platoon sergeant. The training company had few trainees and until new replacements arrived from the depot, Dave was on loan to 'A' Company. The company commander, Big Jack Winslow, had allowed Simon to take command of a platoon despite his lack of operational experience, but he knew that a proficient platoon sergeant would be needed and Dave Snell fulfilled that need.

Sam and Ken had been posted to HQ Company; Sam to the MT platoon and Ken as a PTI and coach with the boxing team. He had done his best to persuade Keith to box but the big ex-farmer would not be moved.

'I want a bash at the jungle,' was his firm response.

The section commander of 2 Section, in which John and Brian found themselves, was Corporal Alan Baker, a regular, who came from the same village as Keith and the two were lifelong friends having gone to the same school and lived only a few houses apart.

Alan was an open faced, friendly, twenty-year-old with the fair complexion of a country boy. He was of medium height with a square muscular build and a boundless energy that motivated those he led.

The platoon, on a food denial operation, were making camp a few hundred yards from the jungle edge on a hill, a half a mile north of Kampong Siputeh, a village known to be sympathetic to the CT. Once the clearance patrols had returned and sentries placed the task of building basha's began.

'Only cut wood from areas deeper in and keep the noise level down,' Dave ordered.

In less than twenty minutes fifteen basha's formed a circle around platoon HQ, a perimeter vine had been erected to assist men moving around the camp at night, and a toilet had been dug about thirty yards from the camp.

John and Brian shared a basha next to the one occupied by Alan and his leading scout Andy Barton. They squatted outside their shelters preparing their evening meals over their small cookers, the white hexamine blocks giving of enough heat to boil a mess tin of water in less than five minutes. The smell of cooking food, mostly with added curry powder, drifted through silent camp, only the odd murmur of low voices or the accidental metallic clink of spoon on mess tin disturbed the early evening calm.

'O group at 1700 hundred, Corporal Baker,' Dave Snell slowly toured the camp checking the layout and informing his NCO's of the orders group.

At five minutes before the designated time the three section commanders sat on the ground outside Simon's basha, their maps and notebooks at the ready.

'I'll give two section's orders first,' Simon consulted his notes, 'because you'll be providing tonight's ambush, Corporal Baker.'

'Right, sir,' Alan was both pleased and disappointed at the same time. Pleased that he had been selected but sorry that they had pulled the first night ambush after a busy day.

'I will be coming with you,' Simon added.

'Sir'!

'Get Lance-corporal Steel over and give him the news so that he can be preparing the section.' When this had been done he continued, 'We leave as soon after 1800 as possible, and as we only have one signaller, comms will be via runner, but there will be no movement after the ambush is set until first light, except in the direst emergency. The password will be DASH, Delta Alfa – Sierra Hotel.' Everybody made notes as Simon continued with his briefing, 'Although we do not have intelligence that specifies a date we are told that this village is contacted by the local band of CT at least twice a week so there is a good chance of a contact during this operation.' The gathered NCO's exchanged looks of scepticism; they were all experienced and knew that even so called positive intelligence was never very reliable. Simon went on, 'I will lead off with the first stop group which will comprise of Lance-corporal Steel, Barton and Hall. You will then follow, Corporal Baker, with the killing group, your gun team, Fitch and Hodge and the two new chaps Cantrill and Large, so with you and myself that will make six,' he gave Dave Snell a questioning look.

'That'll be more than enough, sir,' Dave assured his green subaltern, 'Are you taking an Iban?' it was a suggestion more than a question.

'Oh yes we'll take, Lameh,'

'He's the best for this job,' Alan concurred, 'Ngumbek is a bit excitable.'

'The second stop group will consist of the rest of your section, Smith and Wilson and Green will join them.' Wilf Green, Simon's batman, looked up from cleaning his rifle and grimaced. 'Normal ammunition allocations will apply, and in addition NCO's and myself will carry smoke grenades and we will also take a para flare and battery.' Alan nodded without looking up from his note taking, 'On Sergeant Snell's advice there will be no mosquito repellent worn nor will there be a rum issue for the ambush group.'

'Best practice, Al,' Dave explained grinning at Alan's shocked look, 'I don't know why either is allowed on ops, you can smell them yards away.'

'Your chaps can have a tot when we return,' Simon granted, 'We won't have time for a rehearsal of the move in, but we need to do a run through of taking up position and setting the flare just for the sake of the new chaps.'

Lance-corporal 'Stainless' Steel was a competent and experienced soldier who did not carry his rank willingly or comfortably. He was a regular of four years service and a known loner who spent more time with the Iban's when off duty than he did with other platoon members.

'Gather round,' he called the section to his basha, 'we're doing an ambush tonight; Al will brief you when he's finished his briefing. You all know the score ,' he paused, 'belt kit only, woolly pullys, it can get bloody cold, hockey boots and be sure to secure all kit and make sure nothing rattles in yer pouches. Dry clean yer weapons, lightly oil working parts and check mags. Okay?' They all nodded and then dispersed to carry out their tasks.

It was almost dark as the section left the jungle edge and entered the regimented order of the rubber plantation. From their elevated position they could see the lights of Siputeh encircled by the more powerful ring of the security lights. Otherwise the valley below them was a basin of blackness that ran up to the horizon of the mountains that formed the Batu Berinchang range. Brilliant stars and a sickle moon lit their way along the wide logging track. They made good progress and in less the fifteen minutes they shrugged off the shadows of the trees and emerged into the low bushes of the tapioca fields. They were close enough to the village now to discern the inimical, discordant strains of Chinese music carried on the soft southerly breeze.

'Sounds like a cat pissing on a tin roof,' John whispered to Brian as they crouched at the side of track, he was urgently hushed by Alan.

The progress was more cautious now as they approached the ambush position. At a bend in the track the first stop group was sited on a slight rise about six feet from the track. The rest of them continued to a track junction about fifty yards further on and in a slight depression, where a fragile bridge crossed a small stream, this was the killing group's position.

Alan gave them brisk whispered orders, 'Brian, go with Mr Gates as escort, he's taking the other stop group to their position, and you come back with him.'

When Simon and Brian returned ten minutes later Alan, with Hodge as cover, crossed the track carrying the para flare and paying out wires. Behind a stake that supported a tapioca bush he forced the point of the flare into the ground and then taped the electric detonator to the top and attached the wires. As they returned he brushed leaves and dirt over the wires, and once he entered the ambush position he touched Fitch's head and whispered, 'Ambush ready.'

Anything that came into the killing area from this moment forward would be blasted into oblivion, hopefully. The Bren gun team, plus Simon with his 9mm Sterling and Brian with the newly issued, semi-automatic FN, faced the killing ground. John and Alan covered the flanks and rear of the position and no matter what mayhem took place behind them they would not let their attention deviate from their arcs; that was the theory.

The initial excitement began to melt away by 2200 hours; John's grip on his rifle relaxed and he gave up straining his senses at every sound, and every slight motion of leaf or fragile bough. No longer was the nocturnal racket of cricket and cicada feared to be masking the stealthy approach of the enemy. Gradually, the distant sounds from the village became less frequent and the cold more intense, he was glad that he taken Stainless' advice and donned his lightweight pullover. On the move in he had cursed having listened to the gangling NCO, the sweat had poured of him.

Now the slightest movement that any of the ambush group made, as they eased cramped and cold limbs, sounded loud enough for anyone in the distant village to hear. By midnight the moon had sunk below the horizon and staying awake became the main priority. The cold was now of secondary importance, in fact it was now a positive element. John's arc was to the rear and right of the killing group a fact that disappointed him for if the ambush was sprung his involvement would not be required. He lay in the shadow of a tapioca bush with Alan to his left their feet in touching distance so that could give a warning to each other without moving their positions.

John started, he realised his head had dropped forward onto his hands, he had fallen asleep. Guiltily he looked round to see if his transgression had been noticed. Alan was motionless with his face turned away facing his arc and main group had their backs to him. Relieved he turned back to face his area of responsibility.

At first he thought that he was hallucinating, the shape seemed to emerge from the distant gloom like an ethereal imprint, it seemed to float soundless over the uneven ground. He blinked rapidly wanting to rub his eyes but reluctant to take his hands from the comfort of his FN.
It could not be the expected CT; the ambush was facing in the opposite direction – towards the track. Was somebody from one of the other groups coming to report some problem? Was it really a human form?
If it continued on the course that it seemed to be taking it would pass to his right but so close that he would be able to touch it.

He dared not take his eyes of it to ascertain if Alan was aware of the presence. He gently tapped his jungle boot against Alan's and slowly, very slowly, he began to raise the sights of his rifle. As he did so he was aware that to his right another ghost like figure had materialised. At that moment all decision was taken from him as the vicious crash of the Bren blasted the silence, and the night was miraculously transformed from darkness to glaring daylight as the para flare ignited with a muted bang.

When Alan's screams of, 'Cease firing, cease firing,' eventually restored silence to the tropical night John found that he was in the kneeling position but could not recall moving from the prone. The flare began to lose its power and gradually the night regained control of the scene.

'Stay in your positions,' Alan's voice rang authoritatively, 'do not move and stay alert,' no sooner than the words were out of his mouth than a rattle of gunfire split the night again as the stop group, closest to the jungle edge, opened up briefly. Silence again.

'Sir,' Alan hissed for Simon's attention.

'Yes.'

'It's normal practice to fire at any noises now that the ambush is sprung. Some may have gone to ground and be trying to sneak away,' he explained.

'Good idea, did you all hear that?'

The remaining five hours to dawn proved uneventful but the intense few minutes of electrifying excitement and danger expelled any further desire to sleep. Simon could not believe his good fortune. He had heard the statistics regarding operational hours in the jungle for every kill made, and here he was on his fourth operation and he had just experienced his second contact and this time, hopefully, there was a successful outcome.

He had seen the man step onto the path from only a few feet from their left, and had gently nudged Fitch who was already slowly shifting his position so that his Bren was directed towards the figure. Hodge had his hand poised over the torch switch, the torch that was attached to the LMG and zeroed to ten feet.

Even now Simon was not certain that they had hit the only person that he had seen. After the initial fusillade everybody's night vision had been destroyed, and even under the LMG's powerful light, and the brilliance of the para flare he could not see any targets to engage. He could only hope that the amount of fire that swept the killing ground would have accounted for any living thing unlucky enough to have been there, and that was the basic theory of a night ambush, fill the zone with as much fire as possible.

'D'you think it's light enough to search the area, Corporal Baker?' Simon asked when the dark of the plantation had lightened enough to distinguish individual bushes. He was wise enough to rely on his NCO's experience.

Alan slowly got to his knees and examined the area. He could see a grey shape just on the opposite of the track it was half hidden in a small ditch, 'Yeah, I think it might be alright, sir, he got to his feet, 'we'll take Hodge and Cantrill.'

The shape, half in the ditch, was a tall thin man who had not suffered a lingering death. He must have been no more than five feet from the Bren when the ambush had been sprung and appeared to have sustained at least a dozen shots to his upper body and one of his legs had been almost severed. Covered by the others Simon and Alan made a brief search of his blood soaked pockets, a more thorough search would be made later.

'Make that safe, Jack,' Alan said to Hodge and indicated a Sten gun that lay close to the body.

John was surprised and pleased with his own reaction to the horror that lay in the shallow depression. He had always feared the moment of seeing his first casualty. He knew that he was not particularly squeamish, but had been afraid he might vomit if the sight was too bloody, but this poor sole was just like meat on a butcher's slab. Experience and time would reveal that a dead enemy, whose lifeblood has drained into the dry earth, could not compare with witnessing a wounded comrade in the throes of dying.

For ten minutes or so Lameh searched the area but found no signs that any CT had fled that way. The dead man must have been the leading scout, Simon was a little disappointed, the ambush should not have been sprung that early.

'There was one at the back of us when we opened up, sir.' John pointed out.

'I didn't think he'd come along the track,' Simon looked at Alan.

'I didn't see 'em sir, I just heard something before you fired.'

Ten yards from where John had lain they found the second body. It was a girl whose age was doubtful; in death she looked no more than her early teens and was tiny even by Chinese standards.

With signs, and much pointing, and a few words of English, Lameh explained that even though she had been wounded she had managed to crawl the few yards despite one of her legs having been smashed by a couple 7.62mm rounds.

'She must have bled to death the poor little sod,' Alan said, the pity in his voice genuine.

John felt the elation of his first contact replaced by a feeling of remorse; he could have been the only one who had fired the shots that had led to the poor girls lingering death.

He shook his head sorrowfully, 'She must have lain here all night, and didn't make a sound,' he said in disbelief.

'Don't take it too hard, Johnno,' Alan pulled a .38 Smith and Wesson from her belt, 'if she'd have seen you first she wouldn't have hesitated to use this on yer.'

Later, tracks were found that indicated that there were six in the group, and the two fatalities were in the lead. Stainless' stop group had seen nothing but had opened fire when they had heard movement a few minutes after the main ambush had ceased firing.

'Good result, sir,' Sergeant Snell reassured Simon when he had voiced his concern about number of CT who had escaped, 'people can spend a full tour out here and never have a kill.'

The Tracking Team arrived a little after 10.00 hours as a storm descended on the death scene like an artillery barrage. Thirty minutes earlier a Land Rover of the Malayan Police had departed with the two bodies.

It had been decided, by battalion, not to continue with the operation as not even the most foolhardy CT would visit the village for some time. Trucks were to RV with 3 Platoon at the village main gate as an exercise of intimidation, there was no requirement for secrecy now, publicity was now of a good propaganda ploy.

3 Platoon waited by the small bridge, hunched and disconsolate, under the merciless pounding downpour, but still in tactical attitude covering arcs that gave them all round protection. Some had removed their hats and lay them over the exposed breechblocks of the FN's in a futile effort to keep them dry.

'At least we'll have a dry bed tonight, pal,' Brian leaned across and offered John a cigarette shielding the tin with his hand, 'not like the poor buggers in the tracking team.'

'No thanks mate,' John shook his head and he turned his attention back to the track.

'Hey come on, Johnno, you couldn't have known it was a girl. Anyway she was tooled up, and I bet she's done her share of killing in the past.'

John nodded his head slightly keeping his face turned away, 'She was only a kid, Bri; she didn't look any older than our Joan, and she's still at school.'

Brian detected a catch in his friend's voice and moved closer placing a hand on his shoulder, 'Even so you couldn't have known pal...'

'All right, Cantrill?' Sergeant Snell had approached unnoticed and crouched in front of John, 'Just face it lad, it'll take you a bit of time but you were doing the job that's been asked of you, and you were protecting your mates.' John sniffed hoping that the rain running down his face would mask any tears. Dave went on, 'I hope it never happens to you, son, but when you see a mate slowly dying and you can do nothing about it you'll be ready to kill the next Chink you see whether it's a kid or someone's granny.'

'She died on her own, sarge, completely alone lying out there, shit scared,' John shook his head.

'I know, but this is a war, Cantrill,' Dave explained needlessly, 'you just have to get used to it. When you see what they can do to prisoners they get hold off you won't feel so bad.' But his platoon sergeants words did nothing to ease Johns sorrow and guilt.

The torrential rain had turned to a depressing drizzle by the time that Simon, Ben and his team returned.

'Tell your chaps they can brew up, Sergeant Snell.' Ben said and while this moral boosting activity took place he had Corporal Ackers go on net to seek permission to call off the chase as tracks were non-existent after the heavy rain.

*

'Well done Simon,' Colonel Crawson released Simon's hand and indicated a chair, 'a well-executed ambush, first class.' Simon mumbled an embarrassed thanks and pointed out that his NCO's had got him through it. The CO went on, 'Captain Murphy tells me that you were disappointed that you hadn't accounted for more,' he shook his head and smiled as he offered Simon a cigarette, 'you were damn lucky to get any, from all accounts they almost walked onto your position and when they arrive from a direction other than what you anticipated it's just a tad difficult to get them all in the killing area. Always remember, Simon, the enemy are rarely considerate enough to follow your plans they always seem to prefer their own. And it is also worth remembering that a battle is won with ten per cent tactics and ninety per cent luck. You had some good chaps with you. Corporal Baker is a first class NCO, but had there been a cock up you would have carried the can and rightly so, for you were in command. But by the same token you should also receive the praise for a very successful operation.' He smiled warmly, 'Anyway, before you go off to get debriefed by the RIO let me hear the facts from your own lips.'

Simon took the CO through the events of the previous night and ended by telling him of John Cantrill's regret over the death of the CT girl.

Jeremy looked his watch, 'After lunch get all of you platoon together and I'll have a word with them.'

Moral soared after the platoons talk by the CO. He had arrived in their lines accompanied by the formidable form of the RSM. RSM Colin Matthews, known throughout the battalion as Matty the Bull, a man who was both feared and respected as much by junior officers as by the other ranks. It was rumoured that he changed his starched OG's twice every day, and his immaculate appearance at all hours gave credence to the story. Squarely formed with none of his ginger hair visible beneath his SD cap, and his upper lip hidden under a thick but neatly clipped moustache, he had entered the basha four paces ahead of his colonel and growled them to attention.

The third member of the group was the Regimental Intelligence Officer, a tall bespectacled and angular lieutenant by the name Linaker, who showed them photographs of unspeakable atrocities that had been carried out by the CT in the battalion area. Men and women tied to trees with their stomachs slit open and then left to die slowly, rape victims, people beheaded, and whole families hacked to death.

After the CO had praised them for a well-executed ambush he asked, 'Which of you is Cantrill?'

John raised his hand, 'Me sir'!

'Stand up, lad,' the RSM snapped.

'I believe that you're somewhat concerned about the death of the young women, Cantrill?'

'A bit sir,' John replied self-consciously.

'Tony,' the CO spoke to the RIO.

Tony Linaker produced a piece of paper and read from it, 'Special branch has identified the female killed in last night's ambush as Lee Swee, who despite her youthful appearance, was twenty four years old and had been a member of 15 platoon of the MRLA for five years. 15 Platoon have been responsible for dozens of murders in the Batu Gajah and Pusing area long before we arrived here. They have carried out countless attacks on the local home guard and police…'

'Though we don't know for certain, Cantrill,' the CO cut in, 'it is more than a possibility that this female has taken a few lives herself and most of these would have been innocent lives. So please cast off your remorse, you only did your duty, you killed an enemy soldier,' he raised his eyebrows questioningly.

'Yes sir,' John answered, his moral improved.

'The ambush was a successful operation of which you should all be very proud, well done,' the CO turned to Simon, 'Carry on, Simon.'

*

Lau had met both of the comrades on a number of occasions the most recent being the great gathering at Besar, but at first he had recognised neither, for they were covered in mud and aged by exhaustion.

When Lau returned to the camp after his stint as sentry, Siti Maideen, a Malay women in her thirties, seemed to be in a state of shock and sat shivering by the fire with a piece parachute canopy, that afforded little warmth, around her thin shoulders. Goh Ling the branch committee member from 15 Platoon was in deep conversation with Beng Kim in the latter's basha.

'There's been an ambush at Siputeh,' Lam told him as he handed him a bowl of rice and a small amount of fish, 'two of our comrades were taken, probably killed,'

'Who were they?' Lau asked.

'I don't know.'

Lau sat on the log beside the woman and offered her his bowl; she looked at him with blank unseeing eyes and shook her head. 'Was it bad?' he asked and immediately felt foolish, what else could it be. She nodded but it was plain that she was unable to communicate further so he asked no further questions.

'She's in a bad way,' Lam attempted to persuade her to take his mug of weak tea but again she refused.

'You should try to eat and drink,' Lau advised, 'you're going to need your strength.' He wanted to touch her as a way of showing his concern but he knew that Malay women were rather sensitive on such matters, more so than Chinese.

'She must be worn out,' Lam said, 'they've come over twelve miles in less than twelve hours, and nearly half of it through cultivation, they were lucky to make it.'

Before darkness fell Siti was induced to eat but had still not spoken.

'Surely she has been in contact with the running dogs in the past,' Lau said to Goh.

'She has, but only with police or home guard, these were British or maybe Gurkha's. There must have been fifty of them at least,' Goh exaggerated, 'and her friend Lee Swee was either killed or taken.'

'We will avenge our comrades,' Ben Kim joined the group around the dead fire, 'I already have a plan, and the revenge will be taken out on the British and not their lackey's.'

Lau's heart sank, attacking the home guard or police carried a degree of risk but taking on the British or Gurkha's in a set piece confrontation took risk and danger to a new level. The home guard in particular were not enthusiastic fighters, they had to live in the villages and many of them had friends and relatives with the inside people. They were also a good source of supply for weapons and ammunition. The Malay Police also preferred a quiet life but many of their officers were British and fought with more vigour than the home guard when thus led. But the British and Gurkha's had no local attachment and were in the country with the sole object of defeating the MRLA, furthermore they were trained to a much higher standard than the indigenous forces.

Chapter Ten

That morning Linda had arrived early at the offices of special branch. She was staying in the married quarter of one of Roger's married contemporaries who was currently in England on extended sick leave because of an injury that he had sustained parachuting.

The quarter was a modern bungalow that offered views over the Kuala Lumpur racecourse. To Linda it was sheer luxury, and the family's amah still came every day to carry out her duties; having a servant did not sit easily with Linda. At the moment she had the bungalow to herself as Roger was on operations somewhere in the north, but exactly where she did not know. Guiltily she pushed the idea from her head that she might be becoming attracted to the life of a Mem Tuan.

The main reason for her feeling of joy was that the previous day she had received notification that her security status had been upgraded, had it not; she would have not been able to continue in her new position within special branch.

It would be at least another hour before the rest of the staff arrived it was only seven thirty, quiet and still wonderfully cool. She addressed herself to John Sankey's mail.

Even with her up rated security clearance she was not allowed to open mail marked as *top secret,* but the general communication between the military and special branch was within the sphere of her responsibility.

The first letter that she opened was from Malayan Command informing the police of unit movements, and changes in areas of responsibility. It transpired that the 2nd Bn the New Zealand Regiment would be leaving their base at Taiping at the end of the week, and returning home. They would be replaced by the 3rd Bn the Royal Australian Regiment who were currently stationed at Kota Tinggi undergoing their jungle training. This was pretty common knowledge but the surprising paragraph was the second, in which it stated that the current area covered by the New Zealanders would now become the responsibility of the Royal West Lancashire's for the period leading up to Operation Clive. It went on to give details of other minor unit changes but in the final paragraph it referred to other attachments to 28 Commonwealth Brigade for Operation Clive; that name again, included were two companies of Gurkha's and D Squadron Special Air Service. All attached units would move to Ipoh for the duration.

The elation that she had experienced dissolved. Roger had not mentioned his temporary posting; she thought that he was on routine jungle operation but this indicated that something more important was afoot.

'You look as though you've just lost a dollar and found a cent.'
Linda started, she had not been aware that John Sankey had entered the office.

'Oh,' she forced a smile, 'I didn't hear you come in.'

'You look very crestfallen, what's the matter?' he looked pointedly at the letter in her hand, 'is it bad news?'

'No, oh, no' she handed him the letter, 'it's just from Malay HQ, nothing special,'

He sat down at his desk and read, 'Isn't your friend in the SAS?'

It irritated her the way he used the word 'friend' as though he did not approve.

She nodded, 'Yes,' she said without looking up from the letters that she was grading.

'And is he in 'D' squadron?'

Again she nodded without meeting his gaze, 'I think so.'

'And I assume that you were aware that he was away for an undefined period?'

'Well I knew he was going away,' she looked up from her task.

'They're a secretive bunch,' he continued to address his mail. 'Is it serious?'

'Well from that letter it seems...' she began.

'I didn't mean that, I meant you, and this chap.'

She looked at him for a moment before replying, he seemed interested but was trying to give the impression that it was no more than small talk, 'Not really,' she replied.

'And what about you is marriage what you'd want?'

'Not at the moment, I have too much to achieve in life.'

He stopped what he was doing, 'Such as'?

She hesitated; careful of what she revealed, 'You're asking a lot of questions, sir,' she bent over her task hoping the subject would be dropped.

'He could be gone for some time,' he insisted, 'I know something of this operation.'

She looked expectantly hoping he would enlighten her but he busied himself at his desk but continued, in what seemed to her to be, baiting.

'And as I said earlier, the SAS are as tight as clams,' he met her gaze, 'or should be.'

Linda felt that the words were almost an interrogation, was he trying to find out how much she had been told, 'Well, you're right about Roger, he tells me nothing,' she answered quickly.

'Apart from the fact that he was going on operations for a period?'

'Yes.'

'In the north'?

'Yes, I think he may have mentioned that but I can't see that he told me anything top secret, troops are constantly…'

'No, no of course he hasn't, 'John cut her short, and 'I wasn't suggesting that your friend would be indiscreet.'

Linda found this difficult to believe, but let it pass and for a little while they worked in silence.

'You'll have seen in the letter that Ipoh is to be their base for the foreseeable future, that's your home town isn't?'

Linda smiled, 'I have just been security checked, sir, I'm sure you know everything there is to know about me; my schools, my friends…'

'True, but I can't remember every detail about all of my staff but I thought I recalled that Ipoh was your home town.'

'It is,' she passed him a pile of correspondence.

'Do you still have family there?'

'You don't recall the fact that I was orphaned at the age of ten?'

'Yes I do recall that,' he paused in his task and fixed her with a penetrating look, 'but I meant other relatives; uncles, aunts or cousins even.'

'None,' she continued to open the mail with a beating heart.

*

The narrow road that joined Lasah to Kuala Jenera, in the state of Kelantan, wound for eighty miles through some of the most forbidding territory in the entire country. For fifteen miles it climbed up and over the Gunong Besar range before the long, ten-mile, descent to the southern shore of Lake Temengor which it then followed for almost five miles before another extended climb over the even higher Chamah range. The road then descended into the fertile Jenera valley, where it ran alongside the River Nenggiri and through lush cultivation. To this point its entire length had been shaded by the oppressing green twilight of towering, primary, jungle which crowded almost to the very edge of the metalled surface of the highway, stopped short by a narrow fringe of belukar. It was a road that only the foolhardy would travel unless well-armed and in company of others similarly equipped and of steady nerve. It was dappled with small patches of sunlight which infiltrated through tiny gaps in the thick canopy that extended across the man-made gap.

As darkness rapidly fell, deepening the gloom, and rousing the nocturnal chorus of insects, the four men moved forward to relieve the four who spent the hours of daylight in the OP. The position was elevated about ten feet above the road, and situated on a sharp bend of a steep hill. It was an ideal spot for a vehicle ambush but the half troop had only been tasked with the tedious role of gathering intelligence.

Roger's team quickly and silently took over the position and he had a brief, whispered, sitrep from Corporal Jerry Singleton. There was nothing untoward to report and with the hand over complete Jerry departed with his brick to their base a hundred yards back in the jungle.

So dark was it that the road below was merely a band of grey in the ink black that surrounded them and only became discernible as they gained their night vision. Hearing was of greater importance than sight but for the next hour or so even that would be almost obsolete as the nightly, nocturnal, refrain gathered momentum.

The mere effort of getting into position caused them to perspire freely even though the air was a little less oppressive at this altitude, for they all wore extra clothing in anticipation of the cold that was inevitable in the early hours of the morning.

Roger and Dan Cullis, a stocky Manchunian, covered the road, while the flanks and rear were taken care of by Rob Coupe a tall, quiet man from Stafford and Dick Holt another Manchunian with a bad complexion, boundless energy, and enthusiasm for every task that he undertook.

No flares had been set for they had orders not to engage unless they were compromised. Extra effort had been made throughout the operation to cover all signs of their presence, an activity that was always performed, but now with extra care.

'It is essential that your presence is of the utmost secrecy,' the IO had emphasised at the O group, 'nobody, and I mean nobody must know that you have been in the area.'

Rogers half of the troop was to gather details of all movement along the road be it vehicular or pedestrian, be it security forces, or civilian.

'We do have our doubts about some of the local home guard,' the IO had added.

Sergeant Thompson's half troop were scouring the jungle north of the road for any signs of human activity but with the same orders of non-engagement. Because of the secrecy of the operation they had been forced to undertake a four-mile jungle trek carrying seven days rations. It had taken them a backbreaking two days.

As the night dragged slowly by and the boredom set in Roger envied his sergeant his task, which was a more physically demanding, but a good deal more interesting. His mind drifted back to the blissful few days that he shared with Linda in Alex's quarter. He had only ever seen her in European clothes except when she occasionally wore a cheongsam, but each evening she had arrived back from work, put on a samfu, and her whole persona had changed. The way she walked, the food she chose to prepare, the radio station she listened to, were pure Chinese. He smiled to himself in the dark at the memory of the complete reversion to Western ways when she dressed for work, or to dine out. It had been a remarkable and sudden transformation, and he found it difficult to decide which, if either, of these dissimilar personalities, was the real Linda. Was one an act, or was she able to completely transform from one culture to the other without any apparent difficulty.

He wondered what she would be doing at this late hour. He checked his watch, it was a little after midnight, and he guessed she would be in Chinese attire, and fast asleep in the large king size bed.

Chapter Eleven

May Ling boarded the third class carriage and settled herself on the hard wooden seat opposite a shrunken old man of great maturity who was already beginning to doze in the early morning heat.

May had selected the seat purposely it was near the door that opened onto the verandah, and she did not want conversation, she wanted to follow the old man's example and relax. She was very tired and the journey to Sungei Siput would take at least two hours providing there were no hold ups, so it was a good opportunity to catch up on some sleep.

The old man opened his yellowing eyes and smiled, he flicked open a fan and waved it in front of his puckered face. May willed him not to speak and her will proved strong enough, for he closed his eyes again and soon his chin dropped onto his thin chest.

Although the journey had come at an inconvenient time it was very important and furthermore, her duty. She still retained a sense of guilt over the comfortable life that had been thrust upon her. Her time inside had been the most satisfying period of her adult life; it was only Hor Lin's insistence that she was of greater use to the cause in what she was doing now, rather than living a fighter's hard life inside, the thought eased her mind.

The basket on the seat beside her contained sufficient food for the journey, Emergency Regulations forbade people from carrying more food than they required for their own needs, the police and army had the power to check for illicit food at any time. The carriage was filling up and May was forced to put her basket on the luggage rack so that a fat, perspiring, Tamil man, who reeked of stale sweat, could sit down; she kept her red parasol on her lap.

*

The garrison church, St Mary's, was almost a hundred old and had originally been built by Stamford Raffles for the British administrators in the state of Perak. A larger and more impressive structure had replaced the original building in 1879 and now the army paid for the upkeep of St Mary's as the garrison church. Despite there being no fans it was cool inside its dim interior, providing the main double doors and vestry door were left open permitting a gentle, almost imperceptible breeze, free passage along the nave.

When Simon arrived the church was almost full and he had little choice of where he could sit. Self-consciously he made his way up the main aisle to a side pew where there appeared to be space, but the apparent gap contained a small child. He turned, his embarrassment increasing, he could see the CO sitting near the back observing his plight with folded arms, and just the hint of a smile on his thin lips.

'There's room here,' the voice was as soft as the touch on his arm.

She appeared to be in her late twenties to early thirties, of medium height, and everything about her had an aura of softness. Her eyes were large and dark and seemed to smile. Her oval face was framed by a mass of chestnut curls and her simple pale green dress did nothing to hide the sensuality of her body. Unlike most women present she did not wear a hat, but instead a white silk scarf was tied loosely over her hair.

'Thank you,' he gratefully edged in beside her.

Her scent was faint, but both fresh and erotic, he noticed that she wore a wedding ring, and on her right was a middle-aged man of generous build whom he took to be her husband.

Throughout the service he was conscious of her closeness and the odd touch of her arm on his as they shifted position from kneeling to standing, to sitting. When they sat, through what in normal circumstances would have been a long sermon, he could feel the heat from her thigh on his and he willed the padre to find more and more to say in guidance of his congregation so that the moment would be prolonged.

Never before had he been so disappointed when the parting blessing was given. He stood back to let the woman and her husband out and then followed them into the bright glaring sunlight. To his amazement, and delight the man turned left onto Colombo Road and she remained by the church gate removing her headscarf.

As Simon walked past her he heard himself say, 'Jolly warm isn't it?' It was as though somebody else had said the words.

She turned and smiled the warmest smile that had ever blessed him, 'I'm pretty well used to it by now.'

Simon noticed a slight turn in her left eye but this defect only added to her charm. 'Oh yes of course. Err. I've um, been here a few months myself but I don't think that I shall ever get thoroughly accustomed to the heat.'

'You will,' she placed a slim brown hand on his arm that sent a shiver through him. She went on, 'Are you army?'

'Yes, West Lancs. Are you...I mean is your husband army.'

She smiled at him, 'I am with the WVS, and my husband was army.'

'Was?'

'David, my husband,' she explained, 'died at Arnhem.'

'Oh, I'm so sorry, I didn't mean to pry and upset...'

She cut him short with a wave of her hand, 'It's quite alright, and I came to terms with my loss many years ago.'

'You don't look old…'

'Please,' she laughed shortly, 'don't tell me I appear too young to have had a husband that served in the war; that's an overused line.'

Simon was shocked that she should think he was flirting, but then why had he spoken to her, it was because he was attracted to her. He felt himself beginning to blush a problem that he had suffered since he could remember, 'I wasn't… it wasn't meant as a line…'

She touched his arm again, 'I'm sorry, I've embarrassed you,' she offered her hand, 'my names Susan, Susan Blackburn.'

'Simon Gates.'

They had left the churchyard, and she stopped by an open topped cream coloured MG TD Midget.

'Can I offer you a lift, Simon; I am going your way, I have a bungalow at the top the hill behind your camp.'

'That's very kind, thank you,' Simon slid into the passenger seat pleased that he could remain in her company for a little while longer.

They drove out past the garrison medical reception station and dental centre onto the Guntong road that would take them to Colombo Camp. Although Simon was quite used to travelling in open vehicles there was something altogether different about being in an open topped sports car in the company of a lovely woman. He felt reluctant to speak for fear of breaking the spell of the moment; Susan had no such reservation.

'Do you have to be back in camp at any particular time or would you have time for a drink?' she shouted above the noise of the engine and rushing air.

Simon could not believe his astounding good fortune. When he had left the mess after breakfast, he saw before him the usual boring Sunday in camp and would have possibly preferred a duty orderly officer in preference to the monotony that lay ahead. Not that he been forced to spend many weekends in camp, duty and operations took care of most, but those that he had experienced had been insufferable.

'Where did you have in mind?' he leaned towards her so that she would hear more easily and her scent was once again apparent.

'Well I don't think it would be appropriate to use the Garrison mess or yours, do you, how about the Swiss Hotel?'

He had heard of it as a bastion of old Empire, frequented mainly by European planters, tin miners, and some of the more senior officers. Under normal circumstances he would have quailed at the thought of entering an establishment where it was rumoured that a whiskey cost $3, but on Friday he had received £20 from his maternal grandmother in anticipation of his birthday the following Tuesday, so he now he felt relatively wealthy, he had $240 in his wallet.

'Fine,' he shouted, 'that is if they let mere subalterns in.'

She grinned and mouthed, 'They will, trust me.'

*

Yang, Blind Man, was feeling the effects of the long trek. He had left the camp early the previous morning with a message sewn into the flap of his shirt pocket. It was to be delivered to a 'letterbox' by the twenty seventh mile stone on the Lasah – Gua Musang road. He travelled alone as most couriers did and he estimated that he had covered at least ten miles, most of it along the jungle edge or through cultivation, and should be very close to Kampong Jalong where he should be able to acquire some food.

Yang possessed a legitimate ID card that he kept in a secret pocket down the inside of his trousers. It would be difficult to explain its existence to other members of the platoon as ID cards had only been issued when the New Villages, with all of their security, had been formed.

The two home guard personnel, who were manning the gate, were as slack as he had expected. The thin, one who smelt of beer, examined his ID casually and handed it back to him without speaking, and waved him through. In less than fifteen minutes Yang was leaving the village again having eaten an austere, but welcome, meal and this time neither of guards left the shade of their atap shelter and he passed by unmolested.

Half a mile along the road, and out of sight of the village, he left the road where a laterite track dropped down from the rubber plantations that clothed both sides of the wide valley. He sat down in the shade a large sign that bore the words *Simpang Rubber Estate,* in black letters on a red background. He took a crumpled packet of tobacco from his pocket and rolled himself a cigarette. As he smoked he casually surveyed the area and saw no indication of any other human presence.

The sign was supported by two vertical posts that were set into pillars formed of brick. Without moving from his relaxed position Yang eased out one of the bricks, and in the space he placed a small sheet of paper, and then returned the brick.

Five minutes later he continued his journey to the twenty seventh mile stone, another day's travel away. Early the next morning, before the village gates had opened to release the scores of rubber tappers into the fields, a postman stopped to urinate by the same sign, and Yang's message was retrieved.

*

It was mid-afternoon and May Ling was now on an airless, overcrowded, bus but took comfort from the fact that this part of the journey was almost at an end. She did not know exactly where it would

76

end or how contact would be made, but she was familiar with this road from her childhood and there were only a couple of places where 'an event' could safely take place. The road from Sungei Siput to Lasah was narrow and although it wound its way through mainly cultivated regions it was very isolated.

The driver crashed the gears noisily as the ancient vehicle attacked the steep climb that heralded their approach to the highest point of the journey. Inwardly May tensed herself for some calamity that would indicate a contact. A burst of gunfire, a shout, an explosion, but nothing happened, and they reached the summit without incident. She was a little disappointed as she would now have to prepare herself again, her nerves were taut, and she was beginning to perspire.

The open windows gave little relief from the overpowering heat, and stench of unwashed bodies. The old lady sat next to her was contributing generously to the pungent bouquet, and her breath, when she leaned sideways to speak, was equally repugnant.

'Are you from these parts, daughter?' she hissed through yellow, crooked, teeth,

May tried not to recoil, 'I lived not far from here when I was a child, mother.'

The old lady nodded and turned her attention back to the view out of the window and appeared, to Mays relief, to fall asleep.

When the time came it was anything but dramatic, no shouting, no shooting, no squealing of tyres as the bus braked sharply to a sudden halt to avoid an obstruction placed purposely in the road to stop it. May felt something touch her thigh, when she looked down the old lady, who still seemed to be dozing, was clutching what appeared to be Mays red parasol in her claw like hand, and she was pushing it against May's leg.

May assumed the parasol had fallen from her lap, and the old women was giving it back to her, but when she tried to take it the claw held it in a tight, vice-like, grip. Her eyes snapped open, and fixed May with an intense, meaningful, look. It was then that May realised that her parasol was still in her basket between her feet, and she understood. Quickly she plucked her parasol from the basket and exchanged it with the crone.

*

The Swiss Hotel lived up to everything that Simon had heard about it. It was sumptuous in its decor, and abundantly manned by obsequious staff whose whole purpose, and pleasure in life was to serve the wealthy customers and residents who could afford the exorbitant prices. The reception hall was a lofty cool area with a marbled floor and walls and a staircase rising in a sweeping curve to the upper floors.

A smiling Malaya syce led them out onto the large verandah that overlooked the Padang where a sedate game of croquet was taking place.

'A game of cricket is always nice to watch on lazy days,' Susan said as they occupied the easy chairs indicated by the syce, 'but until a couple of months ago even croquet was considered too rowdy for the Sabbath,' she placed a silver cigarette case and lighter on the low table as she sat down. 'This is one luxury that I permit myself,' she said when the syce had left with their order of two Singapore slings. She wrinkled her nose, 'Well maybe there are a few others,' and she laughed.

'Like what? He asked feeling uncomfortable with the question but at the same time suspecting that he was expected to ask it.

'Nothing too extravagant, just little treats I spoil myself with occasionally,' she leant forward and picked up the cigarette case, 'Cigarette?'

'What are these extravagancies you mentioned,' he said when he had lit their cigarettes.

'Perhaps when we know each other better,' she changed the subject. 'I don't want to appear forward, but would you like to come to my bungalow for lunch, my Amah lives in so you're quite, safe and she's a wonderful cook.'

'I would love to,' Simon replied without hesitation. He felt that he was on a roller coaster over which he had no control of the speed or direction. Never had he met a woman so unconventionally forward without seeming in the least brazen.

Her bungalow was an officers married quarter and of a style that was common throughout the Far East. The outer lounge wall was a folding metal grating that opened onto a large covered verandah running the length of the building. Next to the lounge was a modern, well-equipped, kitchen and behind this a bathroom and two or three bedrooms depending on the size of the family.

They ate on the verandah, a meal of a fragrant fish curry with rice followed by exotic fruit salad. Didi, Susan's Amah, had cooked the meal and served them, and she also ate with them. Simon was impressed that although Didi spoke acceptable English Susan communicated with her in what seemed, to him, fairly fluent Malay

'You speak Malay?'

'Why so surprised, I've lived here for almost two years,' she took a cigarette from the packet he offered, 'haven't you tried to learn?'

'Not really,' he replied a little shamefaced, 'we usually have a JCLO or the Iban's can speak a little English.'

'You must have learned a few words.'

'I can count up to ten, say 'come here', 'halt', and 'how many', just the usual essentials'

'Shame on you, Simon, you are just like most of our countrymen, and how we've been for generations. We always expect everybody we meet to be able to speak English,' she tutted in feigned dismay and poured him a whiskey. 'Where would our great Empire have been if people like Clive and Brooke had relied solely on interpreters?'

'I suppose that you're right in a way.'

'Only in a way?'

'Yes, well, they set out to build an Empire and if they wanted to communicate with the natives they had to learn their language as none of them would have then spoken English. I'm here very much against my will, just doing the job I've been asked to do,' he excused himself lamely.

'Oh come on, Simon' she sat on the sofa next to him, the view they had was out to the purpled hills of the Batu Berenchang mountain range. 'Don't waste your time out here, it's a unique experience. These days will pass, the Empire will pass and you will be able to look back on singular events that very few will be able match,' she patted his hand. 'I pity those who go through life content with their mundane existences, look what they're missing.'

A tropical storm was lighting the distant mountains with extended blue flashes of lightening against slate grey clouds that were marching steadily in their direction, and the distant thunder sounded like a creeping artillery barrage. Simon was grateful that he was not preparing to sleep under a basha in those hills.

'I can't believe I'm here,' he said as he stared out at the approaching storm, 'I went to church this morning with no idea of what the day held other than boredom.'

She looked up at him and smiled, 'And are you glad that you are here?'

'Yes, very much.'

'Good.'

They sat quietly and watched the colossal exhibition being performed by Mother Nature.

Chapter Twelve

The road made a long sweep to the left and then a sharper one to the right. On the convex part of the bend, steep jungle covered hills swept up to the mountain's six thousand feet summit. On the concave side it dropped to a small tributary of the River Perak, a hundred feet below. At this point the road was also beginning a long ascent as it headed to the state border with Kelantan.

It was here that Beng Kim had set up a large, well-prepared ambush to avenge the deaths of Lee Swee and Tang Loh. In his usual uncompromising way he had, in the last two weeks, gathered all of the most effective weapons from other units regardless of their own commitments, and had formed a formidable armoury including a PIAT anti-tank rifle and most importantly for an ambush, two Bren guns.

He was not acting with any certainty of when or who would pass this way. He was, however, sure that eventually security forces would pass by and he was prepared to wait even if it took a month. This in itself was not a problem it made little difference where they lived; be it in deep jungle or on the edges of civilisation, the only thing that changed was the degree of safety. Providing they were not betrayed by a passing local they could stay on the site indefinitely. This was a very remote area, the nearest new village was more than twenty miles away and aboriginals had not been seen in the region for some weeks. So the possibility of discovery was insignificant no matter how long they had to stay to execute their plan. The only chink in the armour was the possibility of being spotted from the air. If the ambush was set back in the cover of the trees it restricted their field of fire, too far forward in the low belukar to gain the best cover of the road, and they would be exposed to passing spotter aircraft who regularly sought out signs of camps or jungle cultivation.

They had dug shallow trenches where natural overhead cover existed, and afforded good fields of overlapping fire. The tell-tale displaced soil had been removed into the undergrowth. Two hundred yards up the hill a camp had been constructed to house over forty comrades, twenty five comrades would occupy the position day and night so there had to be relief's and porters to keep them supplied.

Beng surveyed the completed site from every angle and moved positions until he was satisfied that not even the sharpest eyed running dog's from Borneo would spot anything to give the smallest hint of the danger that lay in wait. Who would come? The police and home guard would be the easiest prey to deal with followed by any of the Malay or

Federation regiments. Although the danger was greater, he wanted the British to be the victims, for not only would it be the greatest coup and boost to the morale of the entire movement but it was they on whom he wanted vengeance. If everything went exactly to plan he knew that his men would spring and end the ambush successfully. The biggest problem was that there was no single plan, as he had no clear picture of who would come, or how. A number of alternative plans had to be made to include the most likely types and numbers of enemy.

The main plan centred on vehicles as in such a remote place it was unlikely that there would be troops on foot, but it was still a possibility. Then there was the question of numbers, what types, would they be armoured or soft vehicles, how many and in what formation, the possibilities were endless. Beng was certain he had allowed for all of the most feasible eventualities. To guard against taking on too powerful an adversary he had two reliable lieutenants, each a hundred yards on either side of the position, who would give warning should the approaching force be too powerful. After making a final check of the area he returned to the camp content in knowledge that he had prepared as well as he could.

*

On the road that ran alongside Lake Temengor a, high-sided, tin mining truck pulled over and stopped. The noisy engine coughed a couple times and cut out. The drivers mate got down from the cab and lifted the hatch that gave access to the five-litre engine, and spent a few minutes inspecting various pipes and cables as if searching for a fault.

Only the sharpest-eyed observer would have spotted the Browning 9mm in the shoulder holster under his grimy checked shirt, or have noticed the Sterling SMG on the floor of the cab beside the drivers left foot.

The truck was close to a high bank and as the mate continued to seek the imaginary problem in the engine, he saw, from the corner of his eye, an abrupt flurry of movement and the canvass that covered the cargo area moved slightly a few times.

The driver leaned out of his window and called, '*Moh.*' (Come on)

The mate closed the hatch, climbed back into the cab and the truck set of on the sixty-mile journey to Sungei Siput. The SAS half troop had been picked up successfully without being seen.

*

Company sergeant major Raven looked up from the hated paper work as the company clerk entered the office.

'Gardner's outside, sir,' he said.

Jimmy Raven was a kind man who cared for his men like a mother hen but this was a quality few recognised until many years later when they were older and wiser and could reflect from the comfort and safety of middle age.

'Gardner,' he screamed.

Keith appeared in the doorway, 'Sah!' he replied with equal volume.

'The OC wants a word in your shell-like, Gardner, what 'ave you been up to?' He got up from his desk and put on his beret, 'A likely fucking tale,' he snapped without waiting for a reply, 'Wait there.'

'What's up?' Keith asked the clerk when the CSM had gone.

The clerk shrugged the shrug used by company clerks throughout the army and down through history. The shrug that says -I probably know but you don't know if I know and I'm not letting on if I know or not, and he said, 'Dunno.'

Further discussion was brought to an end by the CSM, 'Gardner!'

Keith was wheeled into the OC's office with the alacrity and din that only the army is capable of when a soldier is attending an interview.

Major Jack Winslow DSO, Big Jack to the rank and file of 'A' company, was a big placid man with a very relaxed attitude to the running of his company and did not particularly approve of a lot of the unnecessary bull and military ceremony whilst on active service. But he would have been the last man to interfere in areas that were the responsibility of his company sergeant major and he knew that his CSM would not have permitted interference anyway.

'Stand easy, Gardner,' he said when the CSM had completed the rigmarole for bringing a soldier before his OC, 'we haven't had a face to face since you joined the company have we?' Keith shook his head.

'Ave you been struck dumb, Gardner? Jimmy intervened ear-splittingly, 'answer the OC.'

'Err...No sir,' Keith heeded the advice.

'How are you settling in?'

'Fine, sir,' he replied.

Big Jack examined a sheet of paper on his desk, 'I see you had a great deal of success with the depot boxing team.'

'A bit, sir,' Keith now realised the reason for the interview.

'You are being very modest, Gardner, in light of the fact that you won all of your contests with knockouts or technical knockouts,' he paused for a moment and continued to stare at the paper. He looked up, 'The RSM tells me that he tried to persuade you to represent the battalion in the coming FARELF championships in Singapore?'

'Yes, sir.'

'And you declined.'

'Sir'!

'I would have thought that somebody with your unquestionable ability would have been glad of the opportunity…'

'I could 'ave….' Keith interrupted.

'Quiet!' the CSM almost had seizure 'don't you dare interrupt, you 'orrible man,' he screamed.

The major half raised a hand, 'It's all right sa'rnt major, carry on Gardner.'

Keith shot a sideways glance at the puce WO2, and then went on, 'I packed in the boxing so I could come out here and do a bit of soldiering, sir, it's a chance I don't want to miss.'

'Good,' the OC smiled, 'never let it be said that I stood in the way of a young man wanting to soldier,' he nodded, 'March him out sa'rnt major.'

When the clamour of the exit faded Big Jack picked up his phone. 'Give me the RSM,' he waited a moment. 'Mr Matthew's, Major Winslow, I've spoken with young Gardner and the answer's the same. In his words he wants to do a bit of soldiering,' he listened for a moment and then said, 'My sentiments precisely, we could do with more like him.'

Chapter Thirteen

Throughout the British army, no matter where it was serving, Wednesday afternoon was given over to sport whether any was organised or not. This tradition even applied to units on active service when conditions allowed. Some of the members of 3 Platoon were indulging in a spot of 'Egyptian PT' as no other activity had been organised and the crushing afternoon heat did nothing to encourage violent movement.

Of the dozen or so men in the hut half dozed catching up on missed sleep as only the British soldier can, and the remainder lay on their beds reading or carried out chores that required little effort. Alan Baker sat at the wooden table in the middle of the hut writing letters home when Keith entered the basha.

'Hi ya lads!' he ruffled Alan's hair vigorously and went and sat on John's bed.

'Sod off yer big daft bugger,' Alan protested smoothing down his damp mane. 'I've had a letter from old man Jolly,' Alan continued holding out an envelope.

Keith leant forward and took it, 'Can I read it?' he removed the single lined sheet of paper from the envelope, 'He's a farmer we used to work for,' he told John, 'I didn't know the old bugger could write.'

'I think it must have been their Joan,' Alan said without looking up from his task.

'She fancied you didn't she, Al?' Keith grinned.

'She fancied every bugger,' Alan responded.

'She never showed any signs of fancying me,' Keith said a little sadly as he read.

'Who'd fancy you, you big ugly bastard,' John said and put a foot against the big man's back and tried to push him off the bed but Keith's bulk hardly moved and he grabbed his assailants big toe and twisted it drawing forth a shout of pain.

'Mary's had a foal,' Keith looked up and smiled.

'Is that Joan's sister?' John asked keeping feet out of reach.

'She's a Shire, yer daft Scouse sod, a horse.'

'How d'you, tell the difference,' John retorted remaining at a safe distance.

'Yer want to see the knockers Joan Jolly, Cantrill, put yer skinny Scouse birds to shame,' Keith made a half-hearted attempt to grab John again but he got off the bed and picked up his towel.

'Can yer hear these bloody woolly backs, Largy?'

Brian looked up from his paper, 'Don't drag me into your war of words, Cantrill, it's too hot even to argue'

'Yer right I'm off for a shower,' John headed for the door.

'Are we going to the Naafi tonight,' Keith called after him.

John stopped at the door, 'I've no money, pal.'

'I've enough for a few jars,' Keith held up a ten dollar note. 'What about you, Brian?'

'I was gonna go to the AKC, there's a John Wayne western on, Red River.'

'Saw it in Blighty years ago,' Keith replied, 'wasn't that good.'

John nodded at Keith, 'He's showing off now, Largy, he's been to the moving pictures....' his sentence was cut short as Keith's massive frame left the bed with a speed that would not have disgraced a gazelle pursued by a lion, and John left the hut with equal alacrity. Seconds later shouts of pain echoed from the corrugated iron structure that housed the showers, and after a few minutes Keith returned, wet, but grinning and carrying John's shorts and towel followed by jeers and catcalls from the surrounding huts as John sprinted, naked, for the shelter of his billet.

'You bastard, Gardner,' he grinned grabbing his towel and wrapping it round his middle, 'people could see me from the main road.'

'You've got bugger all to see,' Keith retorted.

'You wouldn't like it on yer nose for a wart,' John called over his shoulder as he returned to the shower block.

'Weren't you on OC's orders today?' Alan looked up from his writing.

'Yeah,' Keith admitted, 'bloody boxing team again.'

'D'you, tell the old man to get stuffed?' Alan asked.

'Not exactly like that.'

'Good man,' Alan seemed pleased, 'I've had a word with Pearly about getting you moved to 3 Platoon.'

'What did he say?'

'Said, he'd have a word with Big Jack.'

'That's me knackered then, in' it?'

*

Linda had been ill at ease all day she had not seen Inspector Sankey for five days, nor had there been any communication from him. It would not have been considered appropriate to ask of his whereabouts of his contemporaries or even from her fellow workers. Special branch officers often went missing for days, and even weeks, on sensitive operations and anyone making enquiries would have been viewed with deep suspicion.

She had access to his office but when she endeavoured to put some files away, she discovered that all of the cabinets were locked. Instead she placed them on his desk that was strangely devoid of any paperwork; it was usually strewn with non-sensitive documents and scraps of paper bearing hastily scribbled notes.

A little after noon Irene breezed into the office wearing civilian clothes, 'Fancy popping out to at lunch time?'

'I have something with me,' Linda replied apologetically, it was clear that Irene was in good spirits.

'Come on,' she urged, 'my treat, a celebration.'

'A celebration?'

Irene twirled and spread her hands, 'I've started six months' probation with CID.'

*

Double doors led directly from the wide Colombo road into the Garrison Naafi canteen, forgoing the trappings of a porch or foyer. It was a large, lofty room with a long bar down one wall, and the only furniture comprised of tubular metal chairs and tables of basic design. At one end of the bar was the juke, box safe in a cage and beside it a green door bearing the sign *WVS*. This door led to a haven of peace that had a reading room full of books and out of date British newspapers and magazines. Next door was a lounge full of rattan easy chairs and low tables where tea, coffee and non-alcoholic drinks could be purchased at subsidised prices. It was a place that soldiers of a more sensitive disposition frequented as well as those, and there were a few, who had fallen in love with the two WVS ladies or merely lusted after them.

Susan tidied the piles of magazines and opened the shutters that offered a view over the garrison sports fields that also served as a helicopter LZ. She knew that there would be few visitors this early but there would be the odd soldier who had a day off or was excused duties through some injury or illness. And then there would be the odd individual from the medical centre across the road whose members sometimes spent for their Naafi break there.

Joe, her Chinese assistant, rushed in breathless and grinning the grin that rarely left his broad face, 'So sowwy I wate Mrs Bwackburn,' he scurried into the small kitchen and reappeared at the serving hatch still grinning, 'You so kind, you switch on urn.'

She smiled at her dishevelled assistant, 'You're a disaster Joe, you know that.'

He busied himself and grinned even more broadly, 'I know Mrs Bwackburn, Joe bwoody disaster. Aways wate a bwoody disaster,' he crashed cutlery.

'Morning, Susan' the first visitor was, as usual, Ken Ribby from the MRS. Ken was a thin man of twenty-two who had been a late NS entrant on compassionate grounds because of a sick mother. It was a story that Susan had had to suffer more times than she could recall. 'Usual please, Joe,' he turned to Susan who continued to tidy that which did not require tidying just to avoid getting into a conversation with Ken, 'Would you like a cup of tea, Susan?' he asked in his broad Lancashire accent.

'Not at the moment thank you, Ken,' she smiled sweetly, 'I have a lot of paper work to do,' she lied.

'Never mind I'll pop over this evening,' he pushed his glasses up on his overlarge nose.

'That would be nice,' she lied again.

More people began to drift in and someone put a record of Tuxedo Junction on the radiogram. Joe was having a short busy session so she went and helped him to serve.

At first she did not recognise Simon; he was in full uniform complete with Sam Brown. It was only when he removed his cap that the penny dropped.

'Good morning, sir,' she came from behind the counter.

'Good morning,' Simon looked a little taken back at her greeting.

'I take it you're the orderly officer?'

He nodded, confused at her welcome, 'Err...Yes.'

'You'll want to see the books, I'm afraid they are not fully completed,' she turned and led him to her small office.

'What books?' he asked, 'I didn't know that...'

'It's just a ruse,' she smiled, 'I have an admirer out there who I want to avoid and in any case we can talk with a degree of privacy in here. Would you like a cup of tea?'

'Thank you that would be most welcome.'

'I'm glad you came in,' she said when she brought him his tea, 'Keely Smith is on at the community centre next week, you've heard of her?'

Simon nodded, 'Of course.'

'D'you fancy going to see her?'

'I'd love to,' he replied less than eagerly, 'but there's a possibility we could be on op's by then.'

'Don't they give you warning?'

'Sometimes, but then at other times we're reacting to incidents.'

'Yes of course, how stupid of me.'

'I could get the tickets,' he said seeing her disappointment, 'and then if we are out on ops' you could take a friend.'

'I've already got the tickets,' she said, 'so we can do that, if you want to.'

'Great! Now I'd like to see your admirer.'

'Oh Simon, I must sound so cruel but he is such a boring little man and he tries to act so suave but sadly falls well short. He worked for a bus company somewhere in Lancashire and his part in reorganising and improving the timetable is his main subject of conversation, apart that is, from his mother's assorted ailments. If I hear the story, one more time, of how he improved the passenger level on the Preston to Blackpool route by merely changing the times by fifteen minutes, I'll scream.'

'Sounds riveting stuff to me,' Simon mocked.

'Well I'll introduce you to him.'

'Is he an RWL?'

'No he's a clerk in the MRS, medical corps.'

'Come on, show me,' he grinned, 'by the way,' he added as they left the office, 'We have big mess night on Saturday, Kimberley Day, would you come as my guest?'

She stopped and turned and looked up at him, 'Simon I like your company, I like it very much but I've been a long time around the services and I think that it is best that we are not seen together at official military functions. I am not being arrogant when I tell you that I sometimes have to fight off the attention of some men, in particular senior officers, and that could cause problems for my escort if he were junior to the pest. I'm not being conceited; it's just the shortage of European females that causes it.'

'No its not,' he said gallantly, 'it's because you're so lovely.'

'Thank you kind, sir,' she pecked him on the cheek. 'We can see each other, and I'm not saying it should be a secret, but we would have to keep it on a non-military footing for the time being, okay?'

He smiled and nodded, 'Sure, for the minute I thought that I was getting the brush off.'

'Since I lost David I have only had one relationship. I know that women in my situation, widows, are considered to be easily available, and we should be grateful of the attention that we are given. I am neither and I will only befriend those who want a serious relationship and not those hoping to have latched on to a randy widow.'

He was a little taken aback by her frankness, 'If you don't want me to tell anyone that…'

'No, no, in a community like this it would be impossible to keep it secret and I don't care, we just don't meet at military functions and flaunt our friendship. If we're both invited individually, fine, but we don't go as a couple,' she suddenly looked uncomfortable. 'Am I being premature, am I taking this friendship for granted, do you not see it as being...'

'No, Susan,' he shook his head, 'it's not premature, I like you very much and I think what you say is very wise,' he kissed her on the cheek, 'Now let's see the competition.'

*

Headquarters of 28 Commonwealth Brigade was now the control centre for Operation Clive and as a consequence a section of military police kept the immediate area of the building free from any intruders and checked the identity of all those attending the briefings. The current briefing comprised of about thirty officers from the units that were involved in the operation. The CO and all company commanders of the RWL's plus two majors of the Gurkha's, a major from the SAS and representatives from the Royal Signals, RASC, Artillery and RAF.

'Welcome gentlemen to the first of our monthly briefings for Operation Clive. Let's hope that there are not too many and that we can get this camp located and destroyed before many moons pass.' Brigadier Woodhouse surveyed his audience with his piercing grey eyes as if expecting some dissension. He continued, 'To date we have not had a great deal of success, though that does not mean there has been a lack of determination and effort. Hundreds, nay, probably thousands of jungle hours have been endured in the search for evidence as to its whereabouts but without a great deal of success.' Again he paused for a moment, 'To quote the greatest general of the last unpleasantness, Bill Slim. *Winning a battle is ten per cent tactics and ninety per cent luck.*' He thumped the lectern, 'We need some of the ninety per cent and I think we may have had a small amount, not much, but a small amount, Inspector Sankey!'

John stepped forward and stood before the lectern with the nagging feeling that the brigadier had overegged the contribution he was about to make, 'As the brigadier said,' he began trying to play down the significance of his intelligence without contradicting the brigadier's enthusiastic take on it, 'we have received some new intelligence that confirms our suspicion as to the site of this camp,' he drew breath and shot a quick glance at Harry Thompson who was busy examining the large map on the wall behind them. He continued, 'Our source is of the highest reliability and we have been using him for a number of years. He not only confirms the approximate area, but its size and importance to the MRLA... 'Yes major.'

Major Hooper, 'D' Squadron commander, raised his hand but before he could make his point the brigadier cut in.

'Let's keep questions to the end, Jack,' he smiled. Jack Hooper nodded.

John continued, 'We have also learned that time is on our side, for the moment, as the camp does not currently house significant numbers of personnel or anyone of significant status. And obviously the ideal time to attack would be when there are large numbers CT and high-ranking official's present...'

'We've got to find the bloody thing first,' Jack Hooper muttered out of the side of his mouth.

'..but either circumstance will suffice,' John turned and indicated an area on the map with a pointer. 'We are searching in the right area,' he continued, 'but I am afraid I can't narrow this area down. We are sure that the camp is on the north or northeast side of the Besar Range. However, we will still have to have a more extended search, as by doing so we are more likely to find tracks leading to it, as the camp itself'.

'Thank you, John,' the brigadier got to his feet ending John's speech regardless of whether or not he had finished, 'Does anyone have any questions for the inspector? I think you wanted to ask something Jack.'

'Well my first question was actually covered, but I would like to know just how reliable this informant is and if he has been to this camp why he cannot be a little more specific as to its position?. It seems rather strange that we are left to flounder about on that entire range.'

'Firstly,' John began, 'this informant is rated very highly; we have used him for the last three years and to date he has supplied us with very reliable information. On this occasion, although I believe that what he has told us is correct, I suspect that he is not telling us everything that he knows..'

'Excuse me,' Colonel Crawson politely intervened, 'why then do we not wait until he gives us more complete intelligence. I don't know how you reward these chaps but it would seem to me that a generous payment might loosen his tongue.'

Harry Woodhouse laid a restraining hand on John's arm as he was about to reply, then stood up, and picked up the pointer.

'I understand your frustration, Jeremy, but this chap will have his own agenda. He has to be ever alert and considered in what intelligence he passes to us, and when, and how.' He held the pointer like shepherd in contemplation with his hands clasped over the end and his chin resting on them, 'The slightest mistake and he's a dead man. Too much information at the wrong time could mark him as the traitor. We just have to be patient, each small piece of intelligence is analysed and put into the pot and he has confirmed much of what we already know, the picture is becoming clearer by the day. He will always have to know when it is safe for him to pass on his intelligence,' he allowed one of his calculated pauses, 'Anymore questions before the IO takes over.'

*

The well-concealed trench that Lau occupied, with two others, was protected from view in all directions, but the thin overhead cover did little to protect the occupants from the blistering heat of the late morning sun. The two men with whom he shared the position were virtual strangers having been brought in on loan from 17 Platoon, and although talking was forbidden, Lau would have felt a lot more comfortable with members of his own platoon. Lam had been away acting as a courier and had only returned early the previous morning so their usual pairing had been by passed and now Lau was with two people whose dependability was an unknown quantity.

By normal MRLA standards they were well armed, Lau with his Lee Enfield, Sardin, the tall Tamil, had a Sten and the squat, pock scarred Au Kok manned one of the two Bren's. More ammunition would have made them all the more formidable but they only had enough rounds for about twenty minutes of active engagement and then they would be forced to disengage if there was still an effective opposition.

The trench was slightly angled to the road so that they had a field of fire that allowed them to fire across the face of the main position. This enabled them to give cover to their comrades and at the same time cut off an escape route for anyone fortunate enough to have survived the initial onslaught.

Flies buzzed annoyingly round their heads alighting briefly, and frequently, to taste the sweat that streamed down their faces. They could not be slapped away as any movement, especially sudden movement, was forbidden. The pests had to be tolerated even when they crawled part way into a nostril or corner of an eye or mouth.

Lau allowed his mind to drift in order to bear the aggravation of the unyielding sun and relentless attention of the flies. His shirt was stuck to him with sweat and he knew that the surrender leaflet in his shirt pocket, which he had not touched since the day he had tentatively picked it up, would have almost disintegrated by now.

Surrender was an activity that was rarely out of his thoughts, and it frightened him. On occasion, when he saw Beng looking at him, he experienced waves of terror; certain that those small, black, evil eyes were reading his very thoughts. He desperately wanted to discuss his growing appetite to yield to the seduction of a return to normal life, of regular meals, of shelter from the elements, of being without fear, of laughter and speaking in normal voice.

It wasn't just the ease of life outside that called him he was also being driven by disillusion and the barbarity and ruthlessness of some of their leaders. Some of them, like Beng, seemed to have lost sight of the original aims. No longer was it a battle to free the people from British rule; the fight had become a personal struggle for power and position within the movement. He shuddered to think of such people holding positions of authority if the battle was won. Most of Beng's torture and abuse had been against the very people on whose behalf the struggle was supposedly being fought. But it was a problem he would have to struggle with alone, to trust even Lam with knowledge of the path he was contemplating was too great a risk. In the event that Lam was having similar thoughts he would not have dared admit it even to Lau as snares had been used many times in the past to test peoples commitment.

Suddenly all the physical discomfort was forgotten and his attention was wrenched back to the task in hand as the signal vine jerked on his upper arm to warn of an approaching victim. Immediately the whining growl of a powerful engine, as it laboured on the steep incline, disturbed the heavy stillness of the jungle and sent adrenaline coursing through thirty tense bodies.

Sergeant Ahmed bin Wazir, of the Malay police, was feeling very frustrated with the WS-19 pattern radio-set in the Dingo armoured car. He had been like a child with a new toy when two of the squat armoured vehicles had been allocated to the Lasah police detachment to afford them some protection when moving around their division. He had been only too eager to volunteer when Inspector Masters had suggested that both vehicles be given an extended test run to familiarise themselves with the new addition to their armoury. The Inspector had taken one on a run up to Lake Temengor, and Ahmed was to patrol as far as the Tangi Rata road.

Two miles from the station he had lost contact with the inspector and in the last ten minutes he had also lost contact with the station, he was becoming worried. The Dingo was not the most invincible armoured car available, in fact, as armoured cars went; it was probably one of the least protected. Its 20mm armour was defence against small arms fire but both driver and gunner were vulnerable from above, as there was no turret. The crew of two sat side by side, the driver on the right and the gunner on the left with his Bren gun mounted through a slit. To fire in any direction other than forward meant the gun had to be withdrawn from its aperture and fired out of the wide-open top. As there were three in the vehicle Sergeant Wazir stood behind the crew with his head and shoulders exposed.

Ahmed took the decision that as he had lost all communication he would be perfectly justified in returning to base. He ducked down and tapped the driver on the shoulder and shouted.

'Find a place to turn round we're going back.'

The chubby police sergeant, unknowingly, was the luckiest man on the Malayan peninsula that day. Thirty armed men, set on revenge, watched as the little green, armour plated, vehicle passed through their killing zone, reversed into a space that was the opening of a logging track, and then return enticingly through the sights of thirty guns.

Beng Kim had decided the lone vehicle, with only three people on board, was not worthy of the effort and planning, nor were there sufficient of the enemy to avenge the death of his comrade's four weeks earlier. He had been briefly tempted to spring the ambush and capture the armoured car but resisted as his preferred target were the hated British, regardless of the risk, and they could make little use of such military hardware as an armoured car.

Chapter Fourteen

Feeling extremely content and just a little smug Simon sat on the verandah of the officer's mess waiting for his taxi. He was picking Susan up from her quarter at seven and then they were going on to the Keely Smith concert followed by a meal at the Chinese Palace.

Mobs of nameless flying insects threw themselves, with total abandon, at the exterior lights that lit the verandah and pathways dissecting the parched lawns. Across the shallow, jet black, valley the battalion lines, comfortingly lit, emitted the equally reassuring sound of dozens of radios playing popular Western music. In contrast, the strident, discordant noise of Chinese and Indian music competed faintly and ineffectively from the camp contractors lines a little further up the hill.

'Your lager, sir'! Simon was snatched from his reverie by a mess waiter offering a tray bearing a tall glass.

'Thank you, Larkin,' he took the ice cold glass, 'put it on my tab will you?'

'I've already done so, sir.'

Alone again he took a mouthful of the refreshing beverage and returned to his blissful anticipation of the coming evening.

To the right of the mess was the row of single storied offices that housed battalion headquarters, illuminated by a single bulb at each end of the verandah. Simon was surprised when one of the doors opened washing the dark lawn with yellow light. Three figures, no more than silhouettes, emerged and headed towards the mess. As they mounted the steps to the front door Simon recognised his company commander Major Winslow, who was accompanied by the adjutant and RIO. From their manner and the urgency of their step Simon knew that something was afoot, and somehow, he also knew that it was going to affect him.

'Ha, Simon' the big major spotted him, 'briefing in half an hour in the company office.'

'Tonight, sir'? Simon asked disappointed.

'Yes, tonight sir.' the adjutant snapped.

After phoning Susan from the mess foyer and giving her the bad news which she took, as he expected she would, with calm resignation, Simon went up to the platoon lines. Most of the men were out but he was fortunate enough to find Green, his batman, writing letters home.

'Green, I'm glad I caught you, standby for ops in the morning'

'You're lucky you caught me, sir, I was going t'Naafi when I'd finished these,' he put the letters in his locker, 'how long are we out for?'

'I don't know yet I'm just on my way to a briefing but....'

The appearance of Dave Snell cut short his sentence and lifted his spirits, 'Evening, sir.'

Simon acknowledged his sergeant's salute, 'You're a sight for sore eyes, Sergeant Snell.'

Dave raised his eyebrows and stroked his moustache, 'Nice of you to say so, sir, not something I hear every day.'

'We're out tomorrow.'

'Yeah, I heard from the RSM, that's why I came up,' he looked around the room, 'I suppose they're all out on the piss.'

'I haven't got a clue what's happening yet,' Simon admitted glancing at his watch, 'I've got a briefing in ten minutes.'

'We're out for five days in the new area, sir,' Dave informed him, 'doing blocking ambushes on a road north of Gunong Korbu.'

Simon looked the NCO in awe, 'How come the WO's and sergeants always get to know things before the officers?'

The tall sergeant winked, 'Cos we run the army, sir, we just let the commissioned ranks come along to blame when things go tit's up.'

Simon smiled, 'I think there's some truth in that.'

Dave just grinned, 'I'd better get up to the Naafi and see if I can round any of the lads up before they get leg-less.'

*

Simon was glad of the protection of the three tonner's cab, it had been raining when they left a little after 0400 hours and the early morning air was chill. Sergeant Snell had been able to round up the entire platoon apart for one. Owen, a Liverpudlian, had arrived back at camp as the two trucks were being loaded. He was not in a fit state to take on operations even though Dave had suggested he would have sobered up by the time they reached the drop of point. Simon had overruled his platoon sergeant with some reluctance not wanting to risk having an armed drunk in their midst.

'The sergeant major will keep the little waster busy,' Dave pointed out, 'he'll wish he'd come with us before the day's out.'

As ever, the information coming out of the WO's and sergeant's mess was of the highest grade. 2 and 3 platoons were to set up blocks of section strength each a hundred yards apart on the only road that skirted the north of Gunong Korbu. Simons platoon would be almost at the Kelantan state border. As they would not arrive until daylight each platoon would give the impression that they were intending a normal operation. They were to set off into the ulu but halt after a thousand yards or so and then rest up until early afternoon when they would return, undercover of the jungle, and set up their ambushes by section. Platoon HQ would set up a base camp a hundred yards to the rear.

The stimulus for these stops had resulted from a patrol of the 6th Gurkha's finding a camp two miles east of Tanjong Rambutan. The camp was for about thirty men but the occupants had fled minutes before the Gurkha's had found it, and all of tracks left by the fleeing bandits had headed north.

*

The four Whirlwind helicopters crouched on the camp square, like giant grey mosquitoes, in the early morning mist their 53 feet rotors turning slowly. Two troops, of sixteen men each, piled into the aircraft, eight fully kitted troopers to each chopper. The pilots received twin thumbs up from the ground staff stationed in front of each aircraft and as one, the pitches of all four engines rose, the fuselages shuddered with anticipation, and then one by one they rose into the damp morning air.

Major Jack Hooper stood by the MT sheds and watched half of his command turn north, and like four heavily laden bumblebee's head for the mountainous region that straddled the Perak/Kelantan border. Jack looked at his watch; it was a little after 0600 hours. He knew the officers mess cooks would only just be getting their act together so he walked across to the OR's cookhouse certain of a mug of strong tea.

*

The glare of the sun, as it crept over the horizon, caused Simon to turn his gaze to his left and rest his eyes on the luxuriant green expanse that enfolded them. He checked the map for the umpteenth time and estimated they would have about another mile to go after they had crested the hill.

The day was warming fast and he wound down his window. The morning air still retained some freshness and the utter silence was only disturbed by the noise of the trucks engine. Simon still suffered a little from the uncertainty and nervousness of someone new to command. Dave Snell, he knew, would always protect him from serious error but he could not be seen as being too reliant on his platoon sergeant as the men would never have confidence in his ability.

The disappointment of breaking his date with Susan had now slipped from his mind, and he concentrated on the task in hand but it did little to lessen his trepidation. They were in a true wilderness many miles from the nearest friendly force and in territory that was new to them all. The inclusion of Corporal Terito, who was on loan from the Kiwi's, and who had operated in this area for the past two years, provided a degree

96

of assurance. Tel Terito was a Maori about 5'9" tall and of a similar width, he had only joined the company a week ago to help them to familiarise themselves with the area, along with another half dozen of his countrymen and he was already accepted and liked by all members of 'A' company.

In the brief moment between the PIAT firing, to initiate the ambush, and the stunning fusillade which followed, Simon thought the discharge of the anti-tank gun was the truck back-firing. Then he saw the slow moving rocket strike the road a yard in front of the three tonner and then noise, concussion and darkness overwhelmed him.

*

John had been dozing for most of the journey but he had always remained aware of conversations among those who stayed awake and of the speed and exertion of the truck. He thought that he experienced periods when he had actually slept and feeling warmth on his face he opened his eyes to find that he had indeed been asleep, for the last time he had opened his eyes it had still been dark. Although the sun was still only just peering over the eastern hills it was already warming the damp air.

'Back from the dead, Cantrill,' Brian grinned.

'Are we still in bloody Malaya?' John asked, he adjusted himself to a more upright position and looked at his watch, 'Half past six we've been on the go for two bloody hours we must be in sodding Thailand by now.' He looked around his travelling companions, all seemed to be asleep apart from Alan Baker and the two sentries one of whom was Brian, the other being, Roger Powell, a thin Boltonian with features that resembled Mr Punch.

Brian was seated just behind the cab on the nearside of the vehicle; he was not feeling very conversational and continued scanning the area to the front and left as they travelled slowly up a long hill. They had lost sight of the leading truck momentarily but he expected to get a visual on it again as they rounded the long left-hand bend they had just begun to negotiate.

'Did you hear that?' Roger Powell asked looking across at Brian anxiously.

Brian concentrated his senses; it was hard to hear anything above the guttural grind of the truck's engine as it laboured up the incline. Alan got up and moved to the front of the truck.

'What was it?' he asked screwing up his eyes at the low sun.

'I thought I heard shots,' Roger replied lifting his rifle onto the roof of the cab, 'Did you hear owt?'

Brian shook his head.

97

They rounded the bend and on the road ahead the leading truck was now visible, it appeared to have come to a standstill.

Fifty yards away the truck could be seen, and the firing, no longer masked by the thick blanket of jungle, could be clearly heard and its effects seen, as sparks marked the strike of bullets on the road sending screaming ricochets over their heads.

'There they are!' Brian cocked his rifle.

The truck seemed to shake under the impact of the devastating fire. A number of troops had gained the fragile cover of the vegetation at the side of the road opposite the screen of dust and smoke that marked the ambush position, and they were returning steady fire. A number of bodies could be seen on the road and in the rear of the truck.

Travelling in the cab, Dave spotted the ambush as soon as those in the back of the vehicle, he screamed for the driver to stop the truck, 'Debus left, debus left,' Dave shouted as he leapt from the cab.

As they scrambled from the rear of the truck they heard savage zip and crack of rounds passing close by as the enemy spotted them and fire was turned in their direction.

'Leave yer pack,' Alan yelled as Powell dragged his Bergen from the pile of kit.

'Follow me,' Dave dived into the undergrowth fifty yards below the ambush.

There was no need for orders or briefing; they had all practised the IA drill for ambushes until their reactions became second nature. As John went into the vegetation closely following Brian he threw a last quick look at the scene of destruction. He saw the devastated three tonner, leaking smoke and oil slowly begin to roll back down the road towards them. An eruption of gunfire close by dragged his attention back to his own situation.

Dave had half expected the man to be there, it was a likely spot for a lookout to be posted. The man had displayed the posture of somebody hiding, hoping they would pass him by unnoticed, and when he realised this was not to be he tried to flee instead of taking aggressive action. Dave emptied half a magazine of 9mm rounds into his upper body before he was fully standing and then another two into his head as he crumpled, twitching in his death throes. Quickly Dave replaced the magazine with a full one.

*

The fact that the truck was hit at all by the rocket was something of a miracle as the individual detailed to fire the PIAT was selected purely on the grounds that he had seen one fired as far back as 1942 when he was fighting alongside the British against the Japanese. As he had only been given two rounds he did not even have the luxury of a practise shoot to familiarise himself with the weapon and zero the sights.

Beng had instructed him to aim at the cab, as a strike there would certainly bring the truck to a halt and kill the unit commander as they always made sure that the comfort of the cab was theirs. Although the round had gone low it had luckily ricocheted off the tarmac and struck the front wheel. He was luckier with the second, and it hit the grill demolishing the engine and spraying oil over the shattered windscreen.

Lau could not see how anybody could survive the volume of fire that hammered into the stranded truck. He could not make out the detail of the horror on the road as a curtain of haze covered their position due to the expenditure of ammunition. He did find it surprising that there was some incoming fire; but this was largely ineffective, as their positions were so well prepared and camouflaged. Even so it was a little unnerving to know that some had survived and were making efforts to fight back.

His uneasiness was increased greatly when one his companions pointed out that there was another truck fifty yards down the hill and most of its occupants had already alighted and were disappearing into the undergrowth on their side of the road. He was already down to his last two clips of ammunition and knew they would be incapable of withstanding a determined attack. He left his trench and crawled to where he knew Beng was watching the effects of his plan and as he expected his leader was furious at him having left his position.

'You have deserted your comrades,' he screamed above the cacophony, 'get back to your place.'

Lau knew that he had to be defiant, 'There's another truck further down the road and I think they are preparing to attack.'

'How many'?

'I didn't see for sure but at least ten.'

'Fool,' Beng punched him in the face and blood spurted from his nose.

*

The thick undergrowth that they had entered soon gave way to more passable jungle, but with enough cover to conceal their approach, yet open enough for them to advance in extended line and still remain in contact.

Dave stopped and told his group to close in close enough to hear his orders. There had been half of the platoon on each truck so he had fifteen men and the driver.

'Corporal Chester.' he spoke quickly and softly, 'take the driver and one other and go back to guard the truck and deter anybody coming down the road to get behind us.' When the three had left he went on, 'You know the form.'

They automatically moved into extended line, making sure that they were in touch with their comrades left and right. They would hit the enemy's flank and roll up the ambush; it was something that they had done scores of times in training. As they prepared to advance the rate of fire from the ambush seemed to lessen.

'Chances are their short of ammo,' Dave shouted, 'and will soon disengage but don't take anything for granted. Everyone got one up the spout?' A solitary FN was cocked, 'Right lets go, good luck.'

With sweat streaming down their faces and their hearts pounding they advanced up through the jungle covered slope.

'I hope I don't come up against any bloody women again,' John muttered to Brian.

'Well, you've no choice, mate,' Brian replied as he pushed through a patch of fern, 'it's them or you.'

*

Simon regained his senses in a bedlam of noise and thick smoke filling the cab. All of the windows were gone and the acrid smoke, black with oil, floated out into the morning sunshine. The firing was coming from his side and it passed through his mind that he could not possibly be alive under such intense fire. He knew that the only way out was via the driver's door.

He grabbed his SMG, 'Get out, Knowles,' he yelled turning to the driver. There was no time to be shocked by the state of the young Cumbrian's head wound; he decided in an instant that the man was dead. He scrambled over him and forced open the door falling out onto the road just as the truck began to roll back down the hill. With the lorry giving him some cover he tried to run towards the frail protection of the thick belukar but felt that he was dragging something heavy and the wall of greenery seemed to get no closer. Bullets zipped ferociously in the air around him, some striking sparks on the tar macadam before screaming skyward. He felt that his lungs were bursting as he struggled against the tremendous weight that felt to be holding him back all the time anticipating his body being torn to pieces by the lead filling the air around him. Then, suddenly, he was lying in cool long grass and looking up into a familiar face, grimy and full of concern.

'Okay, sir?' Tony Hall briefly stopped firing.

'Yes, I'm okay,' breathless, he rolled over and fired off a full magazine at nothing that he could see but it made him feel better. It was then that he felt the pain in his legs but it seemed unimportant as he tried to recall the procedures that he should now follow.

'D'you know where everyone is?' He could see somebody on the far side of Hall returning a steady rate of fire; the man's apparent coolness stimulated his confidence.

'Those that got away are all down here somewhere I think,' Hall fired of a couple of rapid shots.

'They may try to rush us under the cover of this smoke,' as the responsibility of his small command became his concern again Simon felt his fears subside and his training take control. First he had to find out how many men were with him. 'Ask along to see how many we are,' he said to Hall and then moved a few feet to his left and found Ambau one of his trackers, 'Okay, Ambau?' he forced a grin but the normally cheery Iban barely gave him a glance and proceeded to return unhurried but deliberate fire.

At that moment the rate of enemy fire seemed to ease and he feared that the CT would suddenly emerge from their position and over run them. He was about to shout orders to expect a charge when there was a sudden great surge of small arms fire, but the sound was quite different.

'They're FN's,' he shouted encouragingly.

'You're right, sir, look,' Hall pointed. Two men knelt on the bank just above where the three ton truck had come to rest, 'It's Cantrill and Large!'

The firing lessened and finally petered out. Only the odd shot rang out in the oppressive silence that slowly fell on the scene. The fauna made not a sound silenced by the fury of the vicious conflict.

*

The five dead lay in a row at the side of the road covered with groundsheets. A defensive ring was in place around the site and the four wounded were being attended. Ron Flowers, the platoon medical orderly finished applying the shell dressings to Keith's chest and back as John knelt and supported his friends head and held his hand

'Soon have you in Taiping, mate....' the words caught in his throat, 'with all those sexy little QARANC nurses looking after yer.' Keith's healthy complexion had become the colour of dirty putty and his lips were pink with blood, blood that John wiped away with his sweat rag. 'And when you've had yer skive we'll get that leave in Singapore we've got coming.'

Keith smiled weakly, 'It doesn't hurt as much now, Johnno' his words were barely audible.

'You've had some morphine, pal.'

'It's bad in' it?'

The exit wound in his chest was the size of golf ball.

101

'I've seen worse at dart matches,' John swallowed hard and fought back the fear that his friend was beyond the limited help that Flowers was capable of administering. Even though he had no medical training, apart from what the army had given him, he feared that Keith's wound was fatal.

Keith coughed as he gave a little laugh and blood bubbled from his mouth, John wiped it away as best he could with the sodden rag. His huge chest heaved as he tried to get his breath, 'Good old, Scouse,' his voice was becoming weaker, 'keeping moral up ay?'

When he spoke again his voice was much stronger, worry spread across his face and there was a little panic in his words, 'I won't see my mum again, Johnno,' his large hand gripped Johns painfully.

'Don't talk soft yer big daft bastard,' John forced a smile.

The big man's body relaxed and his grip on John's hand eased. A smile spread across his blood-smeared face, 'I feel comfortable now, Johnno,' he whispered. He closed his eyes and life left his massive frame.

John felt a hand on his shoulder, he looked up and through the blur of tears saw Dave Snell, 'He's dead, sarge, me best mates fucking dead.'

'That's war, son,' Dave replied trying to balance his response between genuine sympathy and the need to relate to his men that they had to accept this inevitable outcome to combat. 'There's nothing you can do for the big fellah now except to make sure you're doing your job to try and stop it happening to anymore of your mates.'

John remained kneeling staring at Keith's remains; he gave a great sigh and looked up at the tall sergeant, 'You're right, sarge,' he got to his feet, 'and I was upset for shooting that little tart, an' it could have been someone like her that did this to Keith,' he made an effort to smile.

'Go and make a brew for the wounded,' Dave said knowing none of them must be left to sit and brood over these losses.

The five who had died had all been in the leading truck and included the big cheerful Maori who had been shot in the neck and shoulder and then run over by the truck as it rolled back down the hill crushing his head. Ngumbek, one of the Iban's had also died in the initial hail of fire along with the driver, a small dour Cumbrian on his first operation, and the platoon signaller.

The loss of the latter was a great practical loss as his skills had never been more needed. Corporal Rex Chester had been on a signals course some months earlier but had been removed from the course for lack of application and he now struggled to recall what he had learnt so that he could report their predicament to battalion.

Of the wounded Simon was the most serious, for the rest of his life he would never understand how he had managed to escape from the cab, dash five yards across a road saturated with small arms fire, and reach the sanctuary of the undergrowth without knowing that he was wounded, fear and adrenalin were powerful anaesthetics.

He had been hit twice in the thigh and had a few small shrapnel wounds in his hip and left buttock. Less serious, but looking gruesome, there were also a half a dozen cuts to his face caused by glass from the shattered windscreen. His wounds were taking effect and he now lay semi-conscious in a peaceful cocoon of morphine watching the platoon re-grouping and preparing for any further enemy action that might take place.

'How are you feeling, sir?' His platoon sergeant crouched beside him.

'A bit drowsy,' he realised his speech was slurred, 'how bad was it?'

'Bad enough, five dead, four wounded.'

'Oh my God what have I done?'

'Nothing, you've done nothing wrong, sir,' Dave reassured him, 'that was a well sighted and prepared ambush anyone would have suffered the same, no matter how experienced.'

'The colonel will throw a wobbler,' Simon strove to resist the effect of the morphine.

'Don't you worry about the CO he's seen it all, he'll know we were doing everything right.'

'What happened to the bandit's?'

'They, legged it when we went into our IA drill, but we got two of the bastards, and Corporal Baker's got a patrol out now trying to flush any of their wounded or any bugger that didn't get clear.'

'Who are the dead?'

'We'll talk about that later, try to get some rest.'

'No sergeant, I need to know,' but he was talking to himself, Dave had walked away.'

He drifted into intermittent and troubled sleep trying to compose a letter to the mothers of the men he had lost. He no longer felt like a young man.

*

Rex Chester had absorbed sufficient knowledge to make contact with control but only after he had re sited the aerial three times did he succeed, but this was a problem that even trained signallers experienced in such remote and mountainous terrain.

Within an hour of the incident the battalion tracking team was on the road heading for the scene to put their expertise to use. The four helicopters bearing two troops of SAS had aborted their original plan and were discharging their loads in four separate DZ's where they could be called on to intercept any CT known to be heading in their direction and a Sycamore helicopter had been dispatched from BMH Taiping to evacuate the wounded.

*

'When the fuck did you last see him?' the adrenaline that had fired him for the last two hours had drained from his blood and Alan was feeling tired. The morning had been taxing, emotionally and physically, and this patrol had depleted his reserves of patience.

Now he had been told that the patrol had lost one of its members, the last man, the tail-end Charlie, Barry Rushton. Barry was a quiet well-mannered man who had failed his WOSBY because, as his report said; *this man lacks a sense of urgency.* It was an observation that not even Barry would have contradicted.

'I'm not sure,' Marsden replied, an expression of sham concern on his face, 'I kept checking him but then he was just gone.'

Alan did not like Les Marsden, he regarded him as shifty and lazy, and the fact that he had served twenty eight days in the guard house for stealing another man's rations whilst on operations with 'B' Company, endeared him to no one. Nobody in 'A' Company welcomed him when he was transferred after his sentence, and the least pleased was Alan when Marsden was put in his section.

'Why can't we find his bloody tracks if you've only just missed him?' Alan was finding it difficult to maintain his 'jungle voice' and not shout in anger, 'you're supposed to check him every bloody minute.'

'I did,' Marsden protested.

'Don't bullshit me, Marsden, you're an idle bastard,' Alan knew they would have to extend the search but he would also have to let Dave know of the results of his patrol and the additional problem.

'We're gonna have to split, someone's got to go back....'

'I'll go,' Marsden quickly volunteered and then just as quickly qualified it, 'but not on me own.'

'Shut up, Marsden,' Alan said through gritted teeth thrusting a finger at him, 'you're coming with me, that's for sure.'

He untied the lanyard that secured his compass to his shirt epaulette 'Here, Andy, you take Chalky and Arnie and get back to platoon HQ,' Andy was the section's leading scout, 'you've used a compass before?'

Andy looked decidedly worried, 'I'm not too good with 'em, Al.'

Alan's patience was waning, 'It's not fucking brain surgery and you're supposed to have been trained...'

'Here give it me, Al,' Chalky White took the compass, 'if it's just a matter of going on a bearing....'

'Good lad,' Alan had overlooked Chalky in his anger. Bill White had been a lance-corporal at the Depot and had been demoted for absence when his wife had sent him a *'dear John,'* 'it's set on....' he checked the map and adjusted the compass,'...195 degree's, stay on that bearing and you'll hit the road about a quarter of a mile south of the ambush, so you have to turn left and leg it along the road. Okay?'

'Fine,' Chalky took the compass.

'Tell Dave that they seem to have well and truly exited the area. And tell them about Barry going missing. Say that I'm taking Lameh and Marsden and back-tracking to find him,' he looked at his watch, 'so we should be back at our start point, on the road, in about an hour and a half. Okay?'

'Okay.'

'Oh, Chalky,' Alan said as they were about to go their separate ways, 'move tactically down that road, they could still be in the area, so be careful,' and again, 'And another thing, just be careful you don't bump Barry and shoot him up,' he shook his head, 'it's not likely but be careful all the same.'

*

Barry saw Marsden sink to his knees and rightly assumed the patrol had stopped. The fact that Marsden did not give a hand signal did not concern him as the man rarely did anything as they had been taught. He too sank down and faced the way they had come knowing that he would have to stay alert for the patrol moving on. It was the responsibility of every patrol member to ensure the man to his rear saw all signals but he knew that he could not rely on Les. Barry did not dislike Les, in fact he found him quite a likeable chap in many ways but he was selfish, a little untrustworthy and extremely expert in the NS mans favoured art of skiving.

He glanced over his shoulder to make sure he was still in view of Les and could just make out the red recognition band that the regiment wore round their jungle hats. The colour changed about once a month so as to avoid the CT obtaining jungle greens and passing themselves of as security forces.

The jungle, so silent after the storm of the ambush, gradually began to return to normality. In the hills to their right a family of distant gibbons could be faintly heard voicing their disapproval of the disturbance caused by the so called more intelligent species, man. Even the mosquitoes seemed to have been alarmed by events and until now they had not troubled him. A red centipede appeared briefly before disappearing into the greenery seeming to be on a journey of some significance.

The stop seemed longer than normal, either they were taking a break or something of interest had been spotted. Barry slowly stood up to get a better view of Les and try to find out what was happening; slightly annoyed that he was not being kept informed, as he should have been.

To his horror he realised that the smudge of red that he had taken to be a recognition band was in fact a dead bamboo leaf, his heart leapt. He moved forward expecting at any second to spot his careless companion. Three yards, five yards, ten yards, perhaps he had moved in the wrong direction. With his heart pounding he retraced his steps and looked around there was no sign of human presence or of their recent passing.

'Les,' he hissed, 'Les,' and then louder, 'Les, stop fucking about, Les.'

He dared not shout too loud, any of those who had so recently attacked them could be within feet of him and he would not know it. He could feel his heart thumping against his rib cage and he realised that he was totally disorientated.

'Don't panic,' he whispered to himself, 'think.'

He looked up at the sun and trying to remember where the sun had risen but there was no sight of the solar body, the canopy above was too dense to even see a patch of sky.

'Right,' he said sitting on the trunk of a small fallen tree, 'it's no use running around, let's think for a minute,' he found that talking to himself helped.

He was grateful that he was wearing his belt kit and that it had always been his way, as he had been trained, to carry twenty fours food in his pouches. Without opening them he ran through the items that he knew he had packed. Inside his small mess tin were tea bags, sugar and a tube of condensed milk, his folding cooker and a packet of fuel blocks. In the large one was a small tin of sausage and beans, two oatmeal blocks, a packet of raisins, a packet of hard tack and a small tin of processed cheese. He was also carrying, in his bush shirt pocket, a bottle of water sterilising tablets and a packet of energy giving barley sugar that he also used to lessen the foul taste left in the water by the sterilising tablets. This was considered enough food for twenty-four hours but he knew that he would have to plan for it to sustain himself for a longer period than that, he settled on three days. Barry sensed fear crawling through his body; about to overwhelm him, he took a number of deep breaths and told himself that he was well equipped to survive. He was armed, had food, water, and he had the means and knowledge to make himself a shelter.

Now he had to decide on the best course of action, stay where he was? Alan would have a rough idea of when they lost contact and with the skills of Lameh would most certainly find him. Try to retrace the path of the patrol, but now that he was completely disorientated he had no idea where to start and his tracking skills were non-existent. What if Lameh could not differentiate between his tracks and those of the fleeing CT, or if they did not become aware of his absence until they returned to the road? This was a possibility with Les, he was so lax over the essential detail of military procedures, in fact, he was lax over most things military or otherwise.

As he contemplated his predicament he became angrier at Marsden's laziness and complete disregard for the safety of others. It wasn't just his carelessness over things concerning the military, after all he did not want to be in this alien environment suffering the many privations that this war exposed them too, but none of the National Servicemen did. It was his carelessness and laziness that created problems for his fellow, reluctant, soldiers. The extra barrack room tasks they had to carry out when Marsden had skived off on some pretence, the extra duties when he got himself excused duties because he did not administer his prescribed treatment so that his time off sick with jungle sores, tinea or prickly heat was extended.

'You bastard, Marsden'! He put his head in his hands, and as he sat alone in the great primeval forest he began to hear the sounds that, had he been in the company of others, he would have taken for silence. Short quick bursts of almost inaudible scuffling, slow, quiet, deliberate movement as both prey and predator lived out their perilous existences. The fauna had never held any fears for Barry and in his sixteen months of jungle bashing he seen very little of the more dangerous species. On one occasion, when they were carrying out an ambush on a wide logging track near Batu Gajah, a rather unkempt tiger had wandered down the track just as the sun rose. It had paused in the killing area, with every weapon trained on it, and sniffed the air in a disdainful fashion before sedately continuing on his way. He had not been the magnificent creature that Barry had seen at the zoo or in films. His coat was not sleek and healthy with powerful muscles rippling beneath. In fact he was rather a down-at-heel specimen; his head seem too large for his body, and his coat looked second hand, but nonetheless the ambush party had enough respect that they held him in their sights until he disappeared round a bend in the track. Things were now somewhat different and he prayed that such a creature would not cross his path again.

The question now was, should he stay put or try to find his way to the road? If the platoon had moved on he could wait by the wrecked truck for it would definitely be recovered. He decided to attempt finding his way out for if Alan did not find him in the next hour or so he would have to move anyway, as he would eventually need water.

He recalled that at the start of the patrol they were travelling up a fairly steep incline for about fifteen minutes so if he set off and did not descend, or found he was ascending, then he would be pretty sure he was going in the wrong direction. He felt a sense of relief at coming to this conclusion; he could not wander off into the wilderness as the road that they had been on was cutting through a valley so if he found that he was ascending he was going the wrong way.

He was feeling tired and hungry so he did what British soldiers have always done when faced with great discomfort or danger, he brewed up and permitted himself a hard tack biscuit with a piece of cheese. He sat drinking his tea feeling quite smug and surprised at his composure.

*

Lau had made no plan to surrender beyond picking up the safe conduct leaflet all those weeks ago. Although on reflection he probably did have the intent providing an opportunity presented itself and he could summon up the courage. During the ambush he had been too occupied to even give it any thought, and even when the speed and vigour of the counter attack fell upon them his only thought was to escape the vengeance that was inevitable. It was the punch by Beng that triggered the determination and gave him an instant strategy. He did not have to give it any consideration; it was like a sudden flash of light, a revelation.

In situations like this the platoon would now scatter in all directions, in pairs, in small groups or singly and then regroup days later at a pre-arranged rendezvous from where they would return to their previous camps providing they had not been compromised. Lau was resolved to go singly, it was an ideal time to surrender. He would be alone and it would not raise any suspicion, everybody including Beng, would be too concerned with his or her own survival to be interested in watching what anybody else was up to and he would have a few days grace before the alarm was raised.

The only problem that he could see, and it was quite a major one, was that there were troops around to surrender too, which was essential, but they were troops in an extremely belligerent mood. They had just witnessed some of their comrade's killed and were now bent on seeking out the perpetrators and inflicting a similar fate upon them.

It was a chance that he was not prepared to take, he told himself as he brushed over the tracks that he had created as he hid himself under a thick clump of atap. When things had quietened down he would head for Lasah and give himself up to the police post there. He took the safe conduct pass from his pocket and hoped that it would still be recognised for what it was even in its advanced state of disintegration.

*

When Alan and his patrol got back to the scene of the ambush a little after 10.30, the tracking team had arrived and were visibly straining at the leash. Ben Murphy fell upon him like an avenging angel togged out for war.

He thrust a map case at Alan, 'Show me where you lost contact with your man,' he snapped.

Alan removed his hat and wiped the sweat from his face, he studied the map for a moment and then picking a long blade of grass pointed at a spot on the map, 'It must have been around here,'

'And what time was that?'

Alan shrugged, 'Half past seven, eight o'clock.'

'Can't you be more precise than that, man?'

He shook his head, 'I'm sorry, sir, I can't. Marsden, the man who was next to last, is a bit of a waster but I can only go on what he told me.'

'You want to get a grip of your section, corporal.' Ben glared and turned away, 'Sergeant Snell,' he called, 'we're moving out now; you can use our trucks to return to Ipoh.'

Behind his back Alan mouthed, 'Fuck off.'

Dave handed Alan a mug of tea laced with rum, 'Finish this of, Al.'

'Were any of our lads killed?' Alan asked.

'Five,' Dave watched the young NCO's face knowing the worst news was yet to come.

'Five!' he took a swallow of the tea, 'Bloody hell, who?'

'Ngumbek, Knowles the driver, Pratt...'

'Shit, on his first op,' Alan interjected.

Dave went on, 'and the Maori lad.'

'Bloody hell, how many of those bastards did we get.'

'Two.'

'Well that's something. Do we have wounded as well?'

'Four but not bad, Mr Gates was the worse he got two in the leg and his face was badly cut up with glass from the windscreen,' he grinned

109

wickedly, 'and he has shrapnel wounds that will make sitting just a bit uncomfortable.'

Alan laughed, 'Poor Pearly. I'll tell you what though, sarge, if there'd only been the one truck they'd probably have been wiped out.'

'Yeah, no sign of tracks that could have been, Rushton?'

Alan grimaced, 'Lameh said there were too many tracks all about the same age to decide which could have been his, we followed up on a few but Lameh reckoned they were for more than one.' he took another swig of tea. 'He's a sensible lad though, he's only got go south and he'll hit this road somewhere.'

'I just hope Super Spud doesn't shoot fuck out of him first,' Dave nodded towards Ben.

Alan laughed, 'Is that what they called him in the SAS?'

Dave grinned and nodded, 'Don't let on I told you,' he watched Alan drain the mug and then said, 'I've not told you names of all of the dead, Al.'

Alan went through names in his head, 'No, that's, only four in'it?'

'It's bad news, son,' he paused knowing from the look of horror that spread across Alan's face that he did not have to say the name but he did so, 'I'm afraid it's your mate, Keith.'

The five inert figure's lay half hidden on the grass verge covered with their groundsheets. Slowly Alan walked across to the row of covered bodies knowing which Keith's was from his size. He pulled back the ground sheet and Dave watched him sink to his knees and lower his head as in prayer. The young corporals shoulders shook gently as he covertly sobbed for the big man, his friend from childhood.

*

Barry was dreading the approaching night. The unconditional blackness of night in the jungle was bearable in the company of others, where the occasional glow of a cigarette or hushed conversations and the subdued sound of changing sentries confirmed the presence of other humans.

He selected a small clearing in a clump of bamboo as his camp for the night, but was driven out in a matter of minutes by swarms of red ants who took exception at his intended residence; his arms and neck bore evidence of their anger. His second choice was a bare piece of ground sheltered on one side by a mass of wait – awhile – thorn and enclosed on two other sides by atap.

He brewed up from one of his remaining three tea bags, intending to recycle each bag at least twice, and ate one of his oatmeal blocks. After his meagre meal he constructed himself a rough form of shelter between the roots of a huge tree then stripped and cleaned his rifle. This normal military chore boosted his confidence, confidence that surprisingly increased as the light gradually faded until the inky blackness became almost tangible. It seemed to enfold and protect him and the dread he had felt throughout the day departed. If he could not see, then he could not be seen.

Despite his new found confidence sleep did not come easily; the normal nocturnal chorus had never seemed so loud. Cicada, frog and cricket competed with dozens of unidentifiable insects and creatures to create such a racket that it would have cloaked the noise of an approaching elephant. Sat with his back against a tree and his rifle cradled in his arms he sought the comfort and revitalisation of sleep.

His thoughts turned to home and his family in their comfortable house in Woking. It would be around mid-day and his young sister and parents would probably have just returned home from church totally unaware of their only son's hazardous predicament.

His father, now a solicitor, had commanded a squadron of tanks in the 11th Hussars at El Alamein, he had been disappointed when Barry had failed his commission but had done his best to hide his chagrin. It had been extremely difficult for him following so close on the heels of Barry being expelled from Winchester for 'ungentlemanly behaviour' in short, securing females undergarments to the spire of the cathedral.

It was difficult to imagine that those he loved were living their lives in complete normality. Of course he would be in their thoughts and he was certain that he would have been in their prayers less than an hour ago. The thought that he had recently had prayers said for him inspired him to say one on his own behalf. He had talked to God most of the day but it had been more of a conversation than a seriously considered and delivered entreaty.

He woke suddenly, something had disturbed him but he was not sure that he had actually been asleep. He could not see his watch but he was sure some hours had past. He felt cold and the last recall that he had the night air had still been heavy with the day's humidity. Had the cold woken him? Then he smelled a smell that although alien was distantly familiar, something from his childhood. It came to him on a torrent of terror, the zoo, the big cat's enclosure.

'Shit!' the loudness of the word startled him and he was aware of soft movement that was barely audible, dry leaves rustled and he detected a whiff of the rancid breathe of a carnivore.

He was now wide-awake and gripping his rifle that no longer seemed the potent weapon he had cradled prior to falling asleep. Nor did he any longer feel the cold, sweat was coursing down his face and body but he dared not wipe it away because that would have meant releasing his grip on the rifle. What to do?

He could not see the beast, if it were a beast, and if he fired in the direction of the noise he may only wound it then it would probably attack him in rage. However, if he did not take some action it may attack him anyway, it was certain to be aware of his presence, it could presumably see, as well as smell him. But then there were the CT to consider, they had scattered in all directions and it was possible there could some close by.

He did not deliberately take the decision but the crash of the discharge echoed through the still, black, night and the muzzle flash destroyed what night vision he had. He thought he heard a large body moving quickly away through the undergrowth but he could not be sure as his ears were ringing from the shot. He realised that the muzzle was pointing skyward so the beast, whatever it was, was not maimed. His main concern was that he would have to clean his rifle again. He struck a match, and looked at his watch, disappointed to see that it was only a little after mid-night.

The morning was a long time coming and he was not sure whether or not he slept again, but he determined that if he were unfortunate enough to spend another night in the jungle alone, then he would have a fire regardless of the security issues. There was no repeat of the noises but the acrid scent remained until morning.

Just before dawn it began to rain and his atap shelter proved inadequate in the tropical downpour. He watched miserably as great drops of rain splashed into the water in his mess tin as he prepared his pitiable breakfast of tea, made from last night's tea bag, and a couple of hard tack biscuits with a thin slice of tinned cheese. His mood lightened at the thought of the magnificent feast he would have that night, a tin of sausage and beans.

Because of the overcast conditions he was not able to establish where the sun had risen so he was no wiser as to the direction that he should take. As the rain continued he could not see the point in cleaning his rifle again and set off in the direction he thought that he had been travelling the previous day, the direction that he hoped would take him to the road and eventual safety.

*

Lau had woken with a start, his heart beating wildly. It was still dark and he estimated that he had not been asleep for very long. He waited listening. Had he been dreaming? The previous day had been eventful and his present course of action was a great strain on his nerves but he was certain that it was the sound of a gunshot that had woken him. Shortly after going into hiding he had heard sounds of a pursuit and from the direction they seemed to be taking he assumed they had found tracks other than his.

He waited alert, straining all his off senses but after an hour concluded that he had dreamed that he had heard shooting which was not surprising in the circumstances.

Today he would take another irrevocable step towards surrender, give up this life that he had grown to hate. Gone was the sense of martyrdom, the sense that he was freeing the people from the imperial yoke. If men like Beng were going to replace those they were striving to overthrow there would be no improvement, rather the reverse.

When morning came neither the rain nor his raging hunger could repress his feeling of excitement. He decided to go a little further east to ensure that he was a significant distance from the ambush site. He could remain in the cover of the jungle edge and follow the road to Lasah. If he should see security forces along the way he would, taking into account the prevailing circumstance, consider surrendering to them.

The volume of the downpour increased cloaking any sound of movement that he made and he was able to travel at a decent pace without creating any substantial noise and knowing his tracks would be obliterated. At the same time he was aware that it also covered any noise made by others, but the British, in the main, were unable to move without telegraphing their presence with noise and smell.

Just as he was comforting himself with these thoughts he saw the soldier moving towards him from his right. He was about five yards away but had not seen him. Lau sank slowly to his knees, careful not to make a sudden movement that would attract the eye. He looked around for others. Visibility was no more five yards but there were still no others in sight. He knew that the British were properly trained and kept well-spaced but they always remained in contact and the next patrol member should have been obvious, but he could neither see, nor hear anybody.

*

Barry saw the man slowly stand up, he wore the uniform of the CT and had his arms raised in the posture of surrender. He was tall and uncommonly thin, a nervous, uncertain smile did nothing to relieve the fear on his pale gaunt face. Barry swiftly brought his rifle into the aim, pointing it at the man's chest, his eyes darting around seeking out others.

Slowly the man lowered his right arm and extended it towards Barry, in his hand was a sheet of red paper; 'I wish to surrender,' his English was good, 'this is my safe conduct pass which was dropped from an aircraft.'

Barry swallowed hard, his mouth was dry, 'Are you armed?' he croaked.

The man nodded, 'I have a rifle here, on the floor.'

Barry went towards him, 'Move away from it,' he ordered, Lau complied. Barry saw the worn Lee Enfield, 'Pick it up by the barrel and remove the magazine,' he commanded, 'and open the breech, if you make a sudden move I'll fire.'

Lau did as he was bid, 'I have no bullets left,' he showed the empty magazine and opened the breech.

'Are you alone?' Barry asked.

'Yes,' Lau said, 'are you?'

Barry hesitated not wanting to admit his vulnerability but there was something disarming and pathetic about the man, 'Yes' he said after a pause, 'I got split from my patrol yesterday.'

'You were going the wrong way just now if you were heading for the road,' Lau pointed out.

The two men stared at each other in silence, each carefully considering what his next move should be.

It was Lau who broke the silence, 'We can help each other.'

'Yes,' Barry agreed slowly, 'we probably can.'

'Excuse me, but d'you have a cigarette?'

'I don't smoke,' Barry could see the disappointment on Lau's haggard face, 'but you look half starved, I have some food but not very much.'

*

Had the REME recovery team arrived alone to recover the stranded Bedford there could have easily been a serious mishap with grave consequences. As it was the tracking team had requested an RV with transport that morning, a mile and a half further along the road from where the ambush had taken place. The recovery team, therefore, had infantry vehicles and escort in attendance so a calamity was avoided, when, as the small convoy drew to a halt two bedraggled figures, one in CT clothing, emerged from the undergrowth.

Corporal 'Tex' Riley who had only just returned from a tracking course was in charge of the escort. Taking no risks he ordered the other vehicle escort, drivers and REME team into defensive positions at the side of the road and then approached the two men with his sterling's change lever on automatic.

'Put your weapons down!' He ordered, 'Are you the lad that's missing from 'A' Company?'

'Yeah, and am I glad to see you,' Barry grinned placing his FN on the road alongside Lau's rifle, 'this chap has surrendered to me, his rifle is empty.''

'Have you searched him?' Tex kicked the Lee Enfield across the road. 'Clear that,' he called to his fellow escort.

'No,' Barry admitted sheepishly.

'Tex' gave him a look of irritation, 'Daft bugger, first thing you should 'ave, he could be carrying anything.'

'Yeah, sorry,' Barry agreed.

'Can he speak English?'

'I can,' Lau answered for himself, nervous again. The man he had surrendered to was clearly not a professional soldier this stocky man with sandy coloured hair most certainly was.

'Empty your pockets,' Tex snapped.

'I have nothing of worth,' Lau spread his hands that until now he had held aloft.

'I'll be the fucking judge of that, empty them,' he motioned with the barrel of his SMG.

Once that he was satisfied that Lau presented no threat his manner changed and a smile softened the hardness in his narrowed blue eyes.

'Yer both lucky that you met each other aren't yer?' he said offering a pack of cigarettes and Lau took one almost salivating.

Chapter Fifteen

The military cemetery on the outskirts of Taiping was the resting-place of more than a hundred British and Commonwealth soldiers who had died during the 'emergency'. They lay side by side with the eight hundred young men who had fallen fighting alongside the present enemy against the ruthless Japanese a decade earlier.

Like all military cemeteries it combined a pristine disposition with an ordered and composed tranquillity. The neat, precise, rows of white headstones stood out starkly against the dark greenery with distant, misty, hills forming a sinister backdrop. At the end of a wide grassy avenue stood a large cross of white marble on which the names of the missing were inscribed. A road, flanked by low walls, separated the Christian portion from the Muslim and Gurkha graves, randomly placed palm trees softened the rigid lines of headstones.

The sad strains of the regimental slow march, *The Red, Red Rose,* seemed somewhat incongruous in such a tropical setting but this was diluted by the Britishness of the assembly. The white mass of the band in No 3 tropical dress, the crisp starched uniforms of the attendant officers, the firing party and the bearers, and the brilliant colours of the flags that draped the five coffins, each on their separate gun carriage of shining brass and olive green.

A few wives of officers and senior NCO's waited in an orderly group by the five freshly dug graves with husbands who were not on operations or involved in the ceremony.

The RSM had drilled the bearers and firing party for two days solid, it was a drill that the British Army never rehearsed until there was a funeral to perform. As always, the drill was executed with a precision and crispness that could not be bettered despite the newness of the movements to the soldiers involved. This was being done for their friends and comrades and no amount of bull or effort could be too much.

Simon had insisted, as much as a subaltern could insist when faced with a QARANC matron, that he would be at the funeral. He had to be, he needed to face the men and his failure. Matron had agreed after Lt Colonel Crawson had taken responsibility for his platoon commander and sent Private Green to assist the nurse who accompanied Simon in his wheelchair. The BMH was only two miles from the cemetery so he had only been given leave of absence for two hours. It was only two days since that dreadful incident and his morale had not been improved

When he saw Susan in her pale green WVS uniform and wide brimmed hat standing on the opposite of the graves he was not sure whether he was pleased or disappointed. She smiled and discreetly waved a gloved hand.

Green nudged him in the back, 'Your lady friend's waving, sir,' he grinned.

'Thank you, Green,' he snapped, just a touch embarrassed, 'Mrs Blackburn is just a friend.'

'That's what I said, sir,' Green turned his grin to the nurse.

'I know, now shut up and have some decorum,' the wounds on his outstretched leg were beginning to ache but he dared not complain.

The service and internment went with the meticulousness that was to be expected of the military. Even the six volleys were discharged with such precision that they sounded like six single shots, but it was the poignant strains last post that did the damage among the females present and tears flowed. The members of 1 platoon, who made up the bearers, found it difficult not to let their emotions taint their military bearing.

*

Simon had returned to his room feeling even more despondent than he had been before the funeral. In itself, the ceremony had gone some way to lift his spirits as the camaraderie and sense of loyalty and duty assuaged the pain over the loss of his men and comrades. The brevity of the CO's conversation with him compounded his devastating sense of responsibility for the death of the five men. He felt as though he had been discarded, he had not seen anyone from the regiment until the funeral and because of the ritual nobody really had time for anything other than the briefest of conversations. Had he been in a more positive mood he would have admitted that all those who were able to speak with him did so with great compassion and warmth.

The QARANC sister and a Malay orderly helped him onto his bed. The window shutters and the door that led out to the verandah were open and he had a view across the neat gardens to the distant hills.

'How do you feel, Simon?' the sister enquired, 'do you need any pain killer?'

'Just aches a little, I'll be alright for the moment.'

Jeremy Crawson was a commander of great experience and possessed an acute sense of responsibility for those under his command. It was only two days since the ambush in which the regiment had suffered its greatest lose since arriving in Malaya, and he had written letters of genuine sorrow and condolence to the families of the men who had died. The funerals had presented him with the first opportunity to visit Simon and he felt guilty about this unavoidable delay.

Simon heard the rapid click of heels on the concrete path and then Captain Smith – Parr appeared in the doorway, his uniform crisp and unaffected by the humidity.

'Simon, old chap we've shamefully neglected you,' he put his cap and cane on a chair and sat on the bed, 'you must think we're a right load of shits.'

It passed through Simon's mind that he had held that opinion of the adjutant from their very first meeting, 'I realise everyone must be busy,' he replied a little overwhelmed by Smith – Parr's uncharacteristic chumminess.

'That's been the case old chap, just about every company has been out trying to catch the bastards, plus a squadron of SAS, and a company of Gurkha's.' He produced a half bottle of Johnny Walker from the voluminous side pocket of his immaculate bush jacket and slipped it under Simon's pillow. He winked, 'Probably not what the doctor ordered but it'll doubtless come in handy. The Colonel's with the doctor right now and he'll be along shortly. How's the wounds?' he grinned, unnerving Simon even more, he could not recall ever seeing the adjutant even allow the merest smirk crack his stern expression.

'They're not too bad.'

'You're a seasoned, battle scarred old warrior already; I think everyone of your fellow subalterns is green with envy.'

'Why's that?' Simon asked beginning to relax a little.

'Crikey Simon, you haven't been here more than a few months and you've had more brushes with Charlie than some of the chaps who have been here for two years.'

'And handled them like a professional,' the CO entered, 'well done Simon. I must apologise for having neglected you.'

'I lost five men, sir,' he protested, he could hardly believe the CO's compliment.

'So have I,' he sank into a rattan easy chair, 'The fact is, Simon, five men were lost to enemy action, you saved the rest of your platoon.'

The CO and adjutant stayed for half an hour at the end of which Simon's morale was well on the way to recovery.

'If you feel up to it I'll send the IO up to debrief you tomorrow,' the CO said and another half bottle of Scotch was surreptitiously slid under his pillow.

When he was alone again he felt sufficiently encouraged to begin writing letters to the next of kin of those who had died.

*

A tall rangy young officer and another Briton in civilian clothes were already in the room when Lance corporal Conlan and another

118

regimental policeman escorted Lau across square from the guardroom and into the cool shade of the room.

He had never really believed the propaganda that comrades who surrendered were cruelly abused by the British before being hung, but he had felt slightly threatened by the party that had collected him from the jungle earlier that morning. Nobody had been physically threatening but there had been an aura of menace and he felt that it would have taken very little to trigger some form of violence. In the guardroom he had received his first real and satisfying meal for weeks, a plate of stodgy pastry surrounding unidentifiable meat and overcooked vegetables that most Chinese would have found completely unpalatable, but to Lau it was a feast.

'Sit down,' the officer commanded. A light knock on the door of the office checked any further exchange, 'Come in,' the officer said. Peter Wong entered the room a little breathless.

'I got here as quickly as I could, sir,' he explained.

'Thank you for getting here so soon, Peter,' the officer turned to the man in civilian clothes, 'this man is one of our JCLO's. He speaks a number of dialects, I thought it would be useful to have him here...'

'I speak perfectly good English,' Lau pointed out.

The officer gave him a hard look and went on, 'This is Inspector Barrett of Spe...er, the Malaya Police.'

The questioning began and both men wrote down everything that Lau said in reply, the JCLO said nothing but watched him with unblinking eyes.

They were all the questions that he would have expected to be asked; his name, how long had he been a CT, where his home was before he had joined the bandits, how many people were in his group, who was the commander and so on.

After about fifteen minutes they were silenced by the clatter of a helicopter landing on the square a few yards away. For a few moments the scream of the engine settled to a flutter and Lau expected the interrogation to continue but then the engine noise rose with even greater intensity and receded as the machine gained height and eventually died away to a distant flup flup. Voices could be heard outside the door, it opened, and a dark haired man of dishevelled appearance entered the room.

'Have you started?' he asked brusquely.

'We've just begun,' the plain clothes policeman replied.

'D'you mind,' the newcomer dragged a chair round the table and placed it uncomfortably close to Lau. He sat down and stared intently into Lau's eyes.

'My name's Sankey,' he said, 'you're going to join us Lau and give us a lot of help,' he paused, 'aren't you?'

*

The journey back to Ipoh in the three tonner was subdued, each of them alone with their thoughts, the warm rushing air barely relieving the intensity of the afternoon sun. The black patches of sweat on the starched bush shirts had dried leaving whitish smears of salt.

'Keith's mum will know by now,' John said to no one in particular, it was as much a question as statement.

Alan looked at his watch and gave a deep sigh, 'Just about, she'd have probably got a telegram this morning.'

Alan's mind drifted off to the four cottages that stood next to the car park of the Farmers Arms. He pictured the telegram boy leaving his bike at the gate of number four and raising the highly polished brass knocker that, because of its weight, was impossible to knock quietly no matter how careful you were. He pictured the look of horror that Nelly Gardner would have had on her, round, rosy face when she saw the boy; since the end of the war telegrams were not a regular occurrence in Woodlankton. She would have known instantly its appalling content, she had received one in the early summer of 1940 notifying her of the fact that Keith's father was missing believed killed during the evacuation from Dunkirk. Even as a child Alan had been conscious that it had been a number of years before she had regained her jolly disposition. Now, he thought, she would probably never recover.

'I've written to her,' he said quietly remembering how difficult it had been, 'but she won't have had it yet.'

'He had a sister didn't he?' Brian asked.

'He had two,' Alan stared down at his highly polished boots, 'Ann, his eldest, married a right bastard from Preston, and Joyce leaves school this year.' There was silence for a few minutes and when Alan spoke again his voice was full of anger and controlled emotion, 'That bastard Booth beat Ann up once. Keith was only sixteen but he went round and half killed him. I've never seen Keith so angry before. Booth was no softy, in fact he thought he was a bit of a hard man but he didn't know what the fuck had hit him' his face lit momentarily 'it looked like a bloody tractor had.'

'You'll have to write to his sister, Al,' John was moved by Alan's words, 'and tell that if the arsehole starts again I'll go round and take over where Keith left off.'

Alan tried to smile and nodded, 'I'll give you a hand.'

*

120

Inspector Sankey had made Lau nervous. He had begun to develop a sense of safety and well-being but this tall unkempt man had made him feel threatened the moment that they had met. He had found his very first words alarming. But in retrospect he realised that it was what they would expect of him, guiding them to old camps and other sites they may be interested in.

But it wasn't just this demand; the man looked at him during the interrogation as though he knew a lot more about Lau than was possible. He asked questions in a manner that led Lau to believe that he already knew the answers. Lau's uneasiness was increased when during a pause he suddenly looked up from the papers that he was studying and said.

'Where is your cousin now, Lau?'

Lau hesitated, 'I don't know?' he replied honestly.

The inspector leaned back in his chair and stared at him for a moment, a slight smile on his lips, 'Well let me put it this way, is she one of the inside people?'

Lau was as certain as he could be that this was a rhetorical question, 'She was,' he said slowly.

'Was? Has she reformed, has she been killed,' ?He leaned forward and took a quick look at his papers, 'I think I would know if either of these eventualities had occurred.'

'What I mean is, that I have not seen her for almost two years,' he hoped that would be enough but he was disappointed.

'And what were the circumstances of your last meeting?'

Lau decided that providing the full truth on that period need not be a danger, 'When she first joined, she came to our platoon, 15 Platoon...'

'And then?'

'It was recognised that she had more to offer at a higher level.'

'At what level would that be?'

The responses to Lau's answers were rapped out almost before the sentence was completed.

'At a zone, I think.'

'Would that be central or north,' he shook his black unruly mane, 'wouldn't have been the southern would it?'

'I don't know. I've not seen her since that day she left our camp.'

'Could it have been to join the Central Committee, in Thailand?'

It was Lau's turn to shake his head, 'As I said I have not seen her since that day'

'Have you heard from her, or of her?'

Again Lau shook his head.

'Who did she leave your platoon with?'

121

Lau hesitated, he did not want to give too much away at this stage, and he did not want to involve May Ling at all. But he must not be seen to be lying; otherwise he would not be trusted. Again he sensed the answer that was being sought may be already known, and his veracity was being put to the test.

'Hor Lin,' he said the words quietly as if this in some way mitigated what he said.

'Hor Lin! Well he is very high up in the organisation isn't he, Lau?' Lau nodded, 'In fact, if my memory serves me right isn't he a member the MCP Central Committee?' another nod, 'So she could be in Thailand?'

'She could be,' Lau agreed, 'but as I said I've lost ...'

'But then again she might not be,' the inspector cut in, he looked at his watch. 'I think it's time we concluded our little chat and have some refreshment.'

Lau sighed, an inaudible, sigh of relief.

*

Lau's first night in captivity was spent in the guard room of the RWL's, it was his first night spent in a building for more than two years and to his surprise he had not experienced any feeling of claustrophobia.

After the interrogation he was disappointed to be taken to the civilian prison that was situated next to the army camp. It held a large number of CEP's, captured enemy personnel, and SEP's, surrendered enemy personnel. The two types of prisoners were segregated for obvious reasons. SEP's were only held whilst they underwent questioning for most of them would receive their bounties of $10,000 and be deported, if they wished, to Hong Kong and occasionally to mainland China.

There were nine SEP's at varying stages of de brief, and seventy two CEPs twenty six of whom had been sentenced to death and were just awaiting the inevitable. The segregation was total, but threats and insults were shouted across the open space that separated the blocks.

Lau found that he was sharing a cell with a Malay by the name Ahmet, who appeared to be in his mid-twenties. He was a little surly when Lau was placed in the cell late that afternoon, and seemed to resent giving up his solitude.

'How long have you been here?' Lau asked ignoring his companion's reticence.

'Four days,' he lay on his bed reading a book and did not look up to answer.

Lau began changing into the prison clothes that he had been given. 'What regiment were you?'

Ahmet lowered his book, 'You ask a lot of questions friend, you would be wise not be too inquisitive in here.'

'What does it matter,' Lau finished buttoning his shirt, undeterred by his cell mates warning, 'we're all here for the same reason.'

Ahmet lowered his book again and stared at Lau in silence for a moment, 'Even so,' he said at last, 'it is better not to know too much about others, or let them know too much about you,' he paused for a moment and then added, 'I was with 8 regiment, in Kedah.'

Lau resisted asking further questions but later that day when they had eaten their evening meal, Ahmet's attitude changed completely, he became extremely verbose and Lau learned more than he would have ever dreamed of asking. It was not a remarkable story. Ahmet had, like many others, become disaffected after living cheek by jowl with communism, and after two years had taken the huge step. Whilst on a courier mission he had walked into a police post and given himself up.

'I would have done it sooner,' he added, 'but my brother is also inside and it would have been bad for him.'

Lau's thoughts turned guiltily to May Ling, 'What made you change your mind?'

Ahmet shrugged and his reticence returned, he lay down on his bed and picked up his book, 'I don't know,' was his curt reply.

Chapter Sixteen

Until the visit of the RIO, Tony Linaker, Simon did not have a complete picture of the ambush that had savaged his platoon. At the end of the debrief he understood the great Generals Slims assertion that to win a battle required ten percent tactics and ninety percent luck. Of one thing he was sure; Dave Snell had saved the day. Without his quick and effective IA drill, all of those in the leading truck would have probably been wiped out. Tony repeated what Simon had already been told, that it had been a well sited and prepared ambush and certain to succeed regardless of the victims ability.

'The old man's well chuffed with you, Simon.' he said as he put all of his papers carefully away in his battered brief case, 'he's put you forward for an award.'

'That's ridiculous,' Simon was more irritated than surprised, 'it's the chaps on the second truck who should get the awards, without them we'd have all been goners.'

'Ours is not reason why,' Tony stood up, 'When d'you expect to be released?'

'I don't know, I feel pretty good now but sister told me that I will have to spend some time recouping in the Cameron Highlands wherever that is.'

'Well it's not in Scotland, old chum. It's up in the mountains between Kampar and Ipoh. The climate is supposed to be wonderful, bit like a hot English summer. Everyone that I know that's been lucky enough to spend time there loved it.'

'How many were in the ambush?' Simon asked.

'At least thirty and the armoury was pretty comprehensive for the CT. They had at least two Bren's and an anti-tank rifle. Sergeant Snell's party got two of them and another surrendered to your chappie who got lost, what's his name, Rushton. Special branch have got him now and are expecting some good stuff from him, the SEP I mean, not Rushton.' When he got to the door he paused, 'By the way Big Jack will be in to see you, we came up together.'

By the time that Big Jack Winslow, his company commander, had left Simon was beginning to feel a little tired but at least it had relieved the boredom that he had suffered the past days and his stash of scotch had increased.

'Would like you something to drink, sir?' he must have dozed off; the young Irish nurse was stood by his chair with a jug of orange.

'Thank you,' he managed when he had gathered his sleep befuddled wits.

'You have another visitor,' the nurse added, 'A WVS lady.'

'Yes I'm here in my official capacity,' Susan entered the room with an armful of magazines and newspapers which she placed on the floor beside his chair.

'The papers are at least a week old, and the magazines are even older,' she kissed him on the forehead which pleased him.

'That wasn't in my official capacity,' she smiled, 'Shall we sit on the verandah?'

Simon's morale took a great leap, 'You haven't driven up on your own have you?' he asked anxiously.

'Good Heavens no, what sort of fool do you take me for, Simon. Major Askey's wife is visiting the BMH and I came up with her and her armoured escort.'

'Who's Major Askey?'

'HQ Squadron Commander of the Hussars, so I was well protected, sandwiched between two armoured car, plus two armed troopers in our Land Rover,' she tutted, 'Did I drive up on my own, honestly.'

'I'm sorry,' he was truly contrite; 'I didn't think you'd be so reckless.'

'Your forgiven,' she patted his hand. 'Now are you going to offer me a glass of the deliciously cold orange?' Without waiting for an answer she stood up and filled two glasses, the ice cubes clinking invitingly.

'Thank you,' he took the glass she passed to him. 'What time do you have to leave?'

'As soon as she's seen the gynaecologist,' she looked at her watch, 'It would be better if we were back before dark so we'll have to leave no later than five.'

It was almost midday, 'Oh wonderful!' Simon anticipated a pleasant day, 'What will you do for lunch?'

'I shall have it with you if that's alright?

He hesitated, 'Er, yes but...matron...'

'It's all arranged, Simon. Kathy, matron, is an old friend.'

A little after 16.00 hours a trooper from the Hussars appeared at the door, 'Excuse me, sir but the majors wife is ready to leave,' he saluted and left.

'Thank you so much for coming to see me, Susan; it's been a wonderful afternoon.'

She kissed him gently on the mouth, 'It has been nice; I'll come again if I can.'

He watched her cross the lawn and then hobbled to his bed, he was feeling tired and his wounds ached, but he was happy, and the room smelled of her freshness.

*

Early in the morning, two Malay policemen collected Ahmet and took him away for further questioning.

'There's nothing much to tell you, sir,' Sergeant Ahmet said to John Sankey.

They were sat in the back of a two tone Ford Zephyr at the end of the runway at the Ipoh Flying Club. The windows were fully wound down but the morning heat was already uncomfortable.

'Did you play the family card?' John asked.

'Yes sir, but he didn't mention his cousin.'

'Not at all'?

The sergeant shook his head slowly, 'Not a thing.'

'Did he give any sign?'

'Nothing, well nothing that I could detect.'

John stared out of the window in silence and watched a frail looking Auster descend at the far end of the grass runway like a large green and brown mosquito. After a couple of low bounces it settled to its taxi across the uneven surface.

'Bring it up again,' he said at last, 'as subtly as you can.'

They stared at each other not speaking.

'How would you suggest?' Ahmet asked, 'I don't want to make him suspicious.'

'I know, I know, I know.' John pressed a finger and thumb against his forehead and thought. Suddenly he looked up and smiled, 'I have an idea.'

*

'Right lads gather round,' Dave stood at one end of the basha and leaned on the table. The platoon had just returned from company muster parade and a fifteen-minute stint of the favourite military pastime – area cleaning. This diversion involved picking up every scrap of paper, every cigarette end and generally making the place spick and span and fit for military purpose. They were all dressed in tropical fatigue; jungle hats, JG shorts and boots; many were suffering from the effects of the previous night's intake of alcohol.

'I've got a mouth like the sole of a zoo keeper's boot.' John muttered as he squeezed onto a bed on which three other platoon members were already sitting.

126

'You'll be glad to know,' Dave continued when they were all paying attention, 'that the bandit who Rushton here captured single handed...'

'He should've shot the bastard,' John muttered.

'...has given us enough info to enable us to carry out some speculative ambushes.'

A suppressed groan of despair went up from some of the longer serving members of the platoon.

'For how long, sarge?' Rex Chester asked.

'Four days or so, but it depends.'

'On what?' Rex questioned.

'Well you know how things can change, Corporal Chester. You've been doing this long enough,' he handed Alan a mill board, 'List all those available, Al. We'll be manning a killing group, and two stop groups so only those at deaths door will be excused,' he looked at his watch. 'There will a briefing for all NCO's after tea,' he paused, 'at 1800.'

'Where are we having the O Group, sarge?' asked Lance-corporal Owen, a tough little Welshman.

'We'll have it in here, Taff, that's all NCO's,' he surveyed the glum gathering, 'Come on lads cheer up, it may be a chance to have your revenge,' their response was totally without enthusiasm.

At 1800 Dave returned in civilian clothes and carrying a roll of maps, 'Al, send a couple of lads up to the QM's and bring the blackboard that the store man will give them.'

Alan detailed two platoon members just returning from the cookhouse.

'Don't smudge the writing on the board you two,' Dave called after the 'volunteers'.

'Will we be able to get out for a pint, sarge,' Brian called from the other end of the long basha.

'Yeah, you can go and get pissed, Largy, you won't be briefed till tomorrow.'

A murmur of appreciation ran round the room and there was a sudden surge of activity as bodies rose from the incline and headed off towards the shower block.

'If you buggers have smudged that I'll have your guts for garters,' Dave threatened good humouredly as the 'volunteers' entered with the blackboard and set it up. He took a lightweight blanket from the nearest bed and covered it.

'Right lads,' he addressed his six NCO's 'you all got notebooks?

'Is it alright if they stay sarge?' Rex asked indicating half a dozen men still in the billet,

'You don't have to leave,' Dave called, 'but whatever you hear doesn't get repeated outside this billet, savvy? The task is,' he began, 'acting on information received, to carry out a speculative ambush on a logging track just north of Kampong Jalong. It's a track junction at GR 010280,' he paused while the three section leaders found the spot. 'Attachments are two signallers and two trackers. Arms and equipment; normal weapon and ammunition allocations, and each section will carry a para flare and battery. Every man will be issued with three days rations plus four tins of self-heating soup, as there will no hot food for those in position, he halted again to allow pencils to catch up with the spoken word, 'Move out will be 1600 in civilian mining trucks that are being provided by the 'green slime', sometimes known as the Intelligence Corps, and if those buggers are driving we could end up in a knocking shop in Bugis Street Singapore,' he raised a hand to halt the laughter. 'We will work three shifts, one section at a time providing four in the killing group and two, three man stops. We will operate four hours on eight off for twenty-four hours a day. It will be in numerical order starting with 1 section. Questions so far?'

*

Linda had not seen much of Irene since her probationary transfer to CID. Her work was purely criminal now and she was working from an office on the second floor. They occasionally met in the canteen but Irene's enthusiasm for her new role was such that their coffee and lunch breaks were brief and hurried.

Irene was in HQ that morning for an IUM, intelligence update meeting, so they had arranged to meet for coffee. It was immediately clear to Linda, as her friend hustled up to her, as she waited in the queue, that all was not well. The broad smile was absent and her smooth golden forehead was creased in a frown.

'You're not your usual happy self,' Linda gave her a hug.

'Oh, honestly Linda, just when I get this great break, Bo goes and gets posted.'

'Oh no, where to'? Linda sympathised.

'Sungei Siput, to the field-force, it seems that there is a lot of activity around the Thai border and as he was with field-force a couple of years back, they've called on his experience again.'

'When does he go?'

'He went yesterday.'

'That was sudden. What are you going to do?'

'What can I do?'

'Two coffees please,' Linda handed over a dollar bill, 'You could ask for a transfer,'

Irene grimaced, 'How can I this chance with CID is too good to ruin. They may not have any vacancies for CID probationers in Perak. Anyway,' she said as they sat down, 'he doesn't think it will be for long. Bo reckons that they will have found this gang within a couple of months.'

'Oh well that's something,' Linda took a sugar lump and stirred it into her coffee. 'How big is this gang?' she asked.

'Well I think it's a little more than a gang. It seems that there's a large camp in the border area where all of the top CT have their meetings.'

'That's been suspected for ages,' Linda said with dismissive wave of her hand.

'I know but there is suddenly a lot of security force activity up there, well you should know that, your boss is deeply into matters in Perak. He's still away isn't he?'

Linda nodded, 'Yes but exactly where he is I'm not sure,' she changed the subject suddenly, 'Listen, Roger's away again and you're on your own, lets got to the pictures, there's a Dean Martin and Jerry Lewis film on at the Cathay, we could both do with a laugh.'

*

The search had temporarily moved to a range of less demanding hills covering an area of jungle of about seventy-five square miles. The east side was bordered by the river Perak and the west by the road that linked Ayer Kala with Grik. Another range of similar size, north-west of Grik, had proved to be a favoured hiding place for large bodies of CT in previous years.

The troop had set up a series of four OP's overlooking the huge cultivated area that clung to the banks of the river, and extended the five miles to Gunong Besar, where most of the search for the suspected camp had been concentrated thus far.

It was hoped by the planners that signs of those fleeing the recent ambush on the RWL's, or diverse units converging on the secret camp, may be spotted crossing the cultivation, or even using the river as means of travel. It was an almost desperate bid, the month long series of patrols on Gunong Besar by the Gurkha's and SAS had revealed no signs of large bodies of personnel either moving or having occupied the area.

Roger felt that they were wasting their time and during their briefing by a major from the Intelligence Corps, Pete Thompson had undiplomatically given voice to this universal feeling.

'Exactly why are doing this mission and are we acting on info that's reliable?' There was no attempt to hide his contempt for the plan; 'Surely,' he went on without allowing the major to reply, 'some bloody home guard could do this, they'd only be too happy to sit on their arses achieving sod all.'

'Brigade specifically requested SAS for the task,' the major replied a little shell shocked.

'But we're at best a mile from the river and possibly up to three in places; even with the most powerful glasses we'll see nothing in any detail.'

His argument fell on deaf ears and here they were into their third day with aching eyes and thoroughly bored. They had been dropped by truck on the Grik road in the early hours, under the cover of darkness. They had then had a day and a half hike across the ridge to get to their selected OP's.

Roger's site was the most northerly and he was on stag with Dick Holt a congenial red-faced Manchunian who, being very fair-haired, suffered from too much sun; his ruddy face erupted in a mass of unsightly spots at any extended exposure.

Dick was keen to the point of irritation at times but Roger was glad to be with him as he could afford to let his mind wander knowing that his companion would miss nothing. Since he had managed to persuade Linda to succumb, and they had been given the wonderful opportunity of sharing his friends married quarter, he had virtually been on constant operations. He wondered if his absence accounted for the undercurrent of tension that he sensed on the last couple of days they had shared. Her demeanour towards him and the affection she displayed seemed normal enough, but he could not rid himself of the impression that she had to make an effort to act naturally.

It annoyed and puzzled him that this should disturb his equilibrium. Their relationship was no more than an affection that would pass in time so why did it concern him so. In his thoughts he always saw her as fragile and vulnerable but when he was with her this fluffy conception was soon eradicated. Beneath the tender femininity that flourished in most oriental girls, he sensed a core of steel. At times he could see, in her black almond eyes, another life, a secret life where pain and sorrow had played their part. Selfishly he had resisted enquiring; it was not a burden that he desired to share.

'Here, boss, you have a go, my eyes need a rest,' Dick brought him back to the task in hand.

Roger took the field glasses and put Linda from his mind.

*

The high-sided mining trucks captured the late afternoon sun and turned them into virtual ovens. As the trucks negotiated the bends of the narrow road that led to Kampong Jalong the eight foot high metal sides afforded a small amount of shade. The fifteen entombed men shifted from side to side of the vehicle seeking what small relief there they could find.

'What daft bastard thought of this?' John scrambled over the pile of large packs that were stacked down the centre of wagon to get into the shade.

'Try not to drink too much,' Alan warned as he mopped the sweat from his face, 'it's not likely we'll get anymore till we make camp.'

The idea was that this mode of transport meant that the platoon could be conveyed to the drop off point with a degree of secrecy that a military truck would not afford. The idea was that the high metal sides of the mining trucks would hide them from prying eyes and to the local populace it would just be two mining trucks going about their normal business. It had once been observed that no plan withstands contact with the enemy, this plan fell apart before that first hurdle had been reached.

As the Intelligence Corps had come up with the transport plan and provided it they had also assumed responsibility for the drivers and the route. Secrecy had been maintained until they arrived at the village of Chemor.

The sweating, red faced, platoon looked up from their furnace like boxes to see impassive Chinese, in first floor windows, staring down at them without a trace of emotion on their inscrutable, faces.

'By the time we get out of town every fucking CT in Perak will know what we're about,' Dave hissed through gritted teeth.

But there was yet another equally disastrous flaw in the plan. The timing of the journey had been miscalculated and they arrived at the drop off point before curfew fell, so there were still tappers returning home from the plantations. The two large trucks had to park up and tin mining trucks parked on the edge of a rubber estate looked a little out of place.

The Intelligence Corps sergeant who had travelled in the cab of the leading truck seemed completely unaware that anything was flawed in the plan until Dave pointed it out to him in undiplomatic terms.

'I've a bloody good mind to abort the whole fucking mission,' he began.

The sergeant looked startled, 'Why, what's the matter?'

'What's the fucking matter?' he struggled not to shout, 'You brought us through a village where every bugger in first floor windows waved at us, and then you park tin mining trucks in a rubber estate while there are still tappers in the fields and you ask me what's the fucking matter.'

'Hey hang on...' he began but Dave had turned away and was preparing his platoon to move off little knowing that the worst was yet to come.

It was a stiff climb up through the rubber tree's carrying four days rations, their personal kit and the extra items required for the ambush. Speed was also important as they had to establish a base and then set up the ambush. Although it was a relief to be out of the exhausting heat many of them were feeling drained of energy after the furnace like conditions inside the mining trucks and the march in was proving almost as bad.

Tom Fitch attacked every task with thoroughness and enthusiasm and when given any responsibility always responded positively. His tour of National Service was coming to its conclusion, but unlike most NS men he had not adopted the usual attitude of total disinterest.

He had been a leading scout since joining the battalion and was regarded as good as any in the regiment. He had made friends with the Iban's and had tried to acquire as many of their skills as he could. In this he had been successful and his expertise was highly regarded by the rest of the platoon. The position of leading scout was the most arduous and dangerous task in a fighting section and carried with it great responsibility. In many instances the leading man was the only one to see the enemy in a contact.

Tom only had another four months of his service to complete and then he would be able to continue his life as a painter and decorator and marry his fiancée Maureen. Despite his impending demobilisation, Tom still carried out his role in the platoon with all of the keenness and aptitude that he had displayed throughout his service. Tom Fitch was, indeed, a very rare conscript.

He was leading the platoon up the rise with Dave Snell about five yards behind him when Dave saw him give the thumbs-down to signal enemy and then sink to his knees beside a tree. Without turning his attention from what had caused him to pause or lowering his shot gun from his shoulder, he tapped his upper left arm with three fingers and Dave, crouching, moved forward to confer. He had only taken a couple of paces when he heard a shout in Malaya and Tom's shotgun barked twice. He squatted by Tom with his rifle pointing in the direction that Tom was looking as the unseen foe opened fire.

Twigs, pieces of bark and leaves flew about accompanied by the zip and crack of passing rounds, but fortunately the fire was ineffective.

Dave could see people moving to his front and left. Behind him a few of the platoon returned fire and the scurrying figures went to ground. Dave sensed that something was not quite right, there were no CT uniforms visible, and the bodies that he had seen all seemed to be wearing jungle greens. It was not unknown for CT to carry out raids posing as security forces but not common. The fire from both sides was desultory which indicated disciplined troops, as there were no clear targets to engage.

'Cease firing,' he bellowed.

'I saw four of 'em, sarge,' Tom shouted over his shoulder without diverting his attention away from the position they had seen men going to ground.

'Alright, Fitch, just keep your eyes peeled but don't shoot unless....'

He was cut short, 'Hello there!' a voice called from the cover of a slight dip.

The voice was distinctly British. Dave cautiously raised himself onto one knee with the tree as protection, 'Who are you?' he called.

'Police field force,' was the reply.

'Oh shit!' Dave and Tom said in unison.

'We're Army,' Dave shouted and got slowly to his feet but stayed by the tree his rifle still in his shoulder. He raised his voice, 'Number one platoon do not fire,' Alan was last man, 'Corporal Baker did you hear me.'

'Wilco, sarge,' Alan replied.

Leaving their units where they were Inspector Bob Brewster and Dave met between the two forces and shook hands.

'That could have been very bad,' Bob grinned, 'your man took a great chunk out of the tree I was stood by.'

'He'll have to have extra range work,' Dave joked, 'I don't want a leading scout who misses,' he raised his voice, 'D'you hear me, Fitch.'

'Not long enough to do to worry, sarge,' came the reply.

'You get demob happy, you get careless and die,' Dave warned and then to Bob. 'What was your task?'

Bob produced his map and pointed to a point where a logging track left the rubber and entered the jungle, 'We were to ambush a probable pick up here.'

'And we were going to do spec' ambushes for the next four days just there,' Dave indicated a spot on the same logging track, it was less than a hundred yards from the police ambush, 'I think our intelligence people should be talking to yours.'

'We got this info from military intelligence,' Bob pointed out.

Dave gave a snort of derision, 'The word intelligence doesn't apply. If we'd been in close country there'd have been a fucking blood bath, Signaller!'

'Sarge!' Les Reeves stood up.

'Get on net and let control know, that we're aborting the mission.'

'Sarge,' he gleefully swung the heavy radio from his back.

*

When Ahmet returned to the cell it was late and he looked very tired and downcast.

'Have you eaten?' Lau asked, to him, after years of being constantly deprived of sufficient food it was important not to miss out when it was available.

'Yes,' Ahmet sank wearily onto his bed and covered his eyes with his arms.

'Have they questioned you all this time?' Lau was truly concerned not only out of compassion for his cell mate but also over what lay in store for him. Ahmet nodded but kept his face covered.

'Was there any torture?' they had always been told, but he did not fully believe it, that should they fall into the hands of the British then torture and eventual death were inevitable.

'I hope that I've done the right thing,' Ahmet seemed to be speaking more to himself than Lau, 'they told me it was for the best but I'm not sure.' He paused and Lau waited feeling that Ahmet was thinking aloud and he would be privy to more by keeping silent. 'If it all goes to plan and people react the way they're expected to then I suppose I will have nothing to regret,' he dropped his arms from his face and turned to Lau. 'The British are full of confidence their plan will succeed,' he swung his legs over the side of the bed and sat up and leaned forward conspiratorially and lowered his voice, 'They have people inside you know.'

'I've heard that rumour,' Lau replied in equally hushed tones, 'but I'm not sure that I believe it.'

Ahmet became more animated, 'Oh it's true.'

'How can you be so certain?'

'They've promised me that if I can tell them where my brother is one of their people will get in touch with him and give him the chance to surrender before it becomes knowledge that I have.'

'But would he?' Lau was unconvinced.

'He would have no choice, he would be in too much danger if he remained, he would not be trusted and you know what that means.' Lau nodded, the slightest suspicion of a comrade's dependability was as good as a death sentence.

'Once it is known that you have surrendered any relatives still in there will be in the most dreadful danger,' Ahmet watched Lau's reaction keenly but saw no sign of any emotion on the haggard face. Inside Lau's emotions were in turmoil; regret and fear for May's safety, abomination at his own weakness for giving up the struggle, hatred for the comfort he was enjoying.

'I have a cousin inside,' he said at last, 'but I really don't know where she is, so they wouldn't be able to help her,' it was now Lau's turn to cover his face in despair, 'They want me to lead them back to the camp sites I know, everybody will know of my treachery and my dear little cousin will pay the price.'

The enormous burden of guilt was short lived and substituted for one of total mystification. Early the following morning Ahmet was removed from the cell along with all of his possessions. When Lau questioned his cellmate over his departure he just shook his head and claimed to have no idea as to why he was being moved.

Shortly after breakfast Lau was taken to a room where Inspector Sankey sat reading the Straits Times, he looked up when Lau entered and smiled.

'Good news, Lau, you need not have any concerns over your relative, we think we know where she is and she is not in any danger.'

The great weight of his remorse floated away, 'Where is she?' he asked.

'The less people who know, the safer she will be.'

'Can I meet her?'

John shook his head and changed the subject, 'We are happy that we can trust you now, Lau, so on Monday you will be accompanying a party of soldiers on a little jaunt around some your old haunts starting with your last camp on Gunong Korbu.'

Lau was not sure whether he should be pleased or not, but he knew that he was now fully committed, and he must stick to the path he had chosen. His new life began this very day, there was no going back.

Chapter Seventeen

Second Lieutenant Rupert Crompton-Hughes had a crucial failing that not only caused him countless problems but it could also have undesirable effects on those with whom he came into contact. The members of 1 platoon were blissful in their ignorance of this. Confidence comes with knowledge or experience and Rupert had neither, but he did possess and abundance of confidence. His self-assurance arose purely from the fact that he came from an extremely wealthy family and was an only child with a doting mother who saw, in her rather unpleasant off-spring, only perfection.

At Eaton Hall he had been fortunate in that the Commandant, at the time of his course, was his uncle; Colonel Nigel Crompton-Hughes MC, 1st Dragoon Guards. The colonel, who had obviously known Rupert all his life, knew of all his failings and had secretly blocked his entry into his own regiment. He had, however, protected his nephew throughout his time at Eaton Hall and had he not done so it would have probably proved inevitable that Rupert would have failed his commission. He was now being unleashed on the RWL's

Rupert's physical appearance was not at all inspiring or appealing. He was angular, and when he walked his upper body gave the impression that it was travelling faster than his legs, consequently his head and shoulders always seemed to be thrust forward. As John Cantrill was to so descriptively describe Rupert's gait; 'I'm here me arse is coming.'

He was thin faced with a large aquiline nose, slightly receding chin, and hooded eyes that added to his haughty demeanour. Despite his faults he did have one redeeming quality that would be of great benefit to the infantry; he possessed an amazing degree of natural stamina and never seemed to have to train to maintain it.

On his final report from Eaton Hall his uncle Nigel had included the following; '*This officer tries hard, and always gives of one hundred per cent. However, if he were a horse I would not breed from him*', the thoughts of a cavalryman?

Lt Colonel Crawson looked up from the report and examined the bony youth standing before him and wondered if the quality of subalterns coming out of the RMA was steadily getting lower, or was he just acquiring the attitude that all old men acceded to, the belief that standards and behaviour were higher in their youth.

'I have not quite decided which company you'll be going to, Rupert,' he lied, 'I think....'

'I'll fit in anywhere sir, I....'

'Do not interrupt the commanding officer, Mr Crompton-Hughes,' Captain Smith-Parr growled. He stood, in his role as adjutant, by the office door with his cane tucked under his arm and glowering under the peak of his cap.

'As I was saying,' the CO continued, 'at the moment...' he paused mid-sentence, 'Just wait outside a moment if you please, Rupert,' when he had gone, 'What do you think, Nigel?' he asked leaning back in his chair.

'We've had worse, sir but I'll be damned if I can remember who.'

'Well he's definitely unfit to be let loose on a rifle company without a chaperon,' Jeremy mused.

'And he would need to be on a tight rein,' Nigel added.

Jeremy smiled, 'Talking of tight reins just read the last few lines of his personal report from the RMA.'

Nigel handed it back with a grin, 'Ian Pell wouldn't let him get out of control and as he has just been promoted to lieutenant he'd have the rank on him.'

'Trouble is Ian's without his platoon sergeant at the moment so he has his hands full.'

'Alan Morley,' Nigel suggested.

Jeremy shook his head his finger pressed the bridge of his nose in thought. Suddenly he looked up, 'Do you know what I am going to do, Nigel?'

'Sir'?

'I am going to put him with 1 platoon in 'A' company.'

'1 platoon'? Nigel echoed, unable to disguise his horror, 'but with Simon in dock he'd be in charge.'

'In charge?' the CO cocked his head, 'pray, who's the platoon sergeant?'

'Snell...with you sir,' Nigel grinned.

'Send young Rupert away on some pretext, and then send for Sergeant Snell,' and then, as an afterthought, 'And you had better warn Big Jack about his new platoon commander.'

*

Although it was less than two weeks since the ambush Simon's wounds had improved immeasurably, and he was now walking without crutches or the use of a stick. The dozens of small cuts on his face and neck had virtually healed but a two-inch long scar remained on his right cheek, a fact that rather pleased him, it gave him a more mature appearance as well as a piratical air, that made him feel a little more worthy of leading a platoon of fighting men.

Susan had written twice since her last visit and today he had received a third, in which she said she had intended to come up to visit him the following day but had had to cancel because of work pressure. He had hoped to exploit Susan's acquaintance with matron to get leave to go into town for a meal but his pleas had fallen on stony ground.

'You're still a patient, Mr Gates,' she retorted as she made minor, but to her mind, essential adjustments to the folds on the sheet where it was tucked under the mattress, 'and you will behave and be treated like one,' she paused at the door and gave him the look that she reserved for, insubordinate, junior officers, 'This is a British Military Hospital not a prep school,' she departed with a crisp rustle of her heavily starched uniform.

Simon went out onto the verandah and sank into an easy chair in anticipation of another tedious day.

'Hello, Si, old chap,' 'Noddy' Bray breezed onto the verandah, as breezily as someone on crutches could breeze anywhere, and dropped into the chair next to Simon sliding his crutches beneath it. He patted the breast pockets of his bush shirt, 'Got a fag old boy, seem to have left mine in my room.'

Simon threw his tin across to him, 'I don't think your fags have ever left your room since I've been here, Noddy,' he grinned.

'Steady on, old chap; make me sound like a sponger,' he threw the tin back, 'got a light?'

Edward Bray was a Lieutenant in the Lincolnshire Regiment who had broken his ankle when prematurely exiting a hovering helicopter before it descended to the appropriate height. His demob date was fast approaching but he had been told that he would not be returned to the UK until his fracture was fully healed.

'Only five bloody days to do,' he moaned blowing out a cloud of smoke, 'chances are I won't even get a decent piss up in the mess, might be flown direct to Singapore, and then straight back to Blighty,'

'Isn't that what you want?' Simon asked as he absentmindedly flicked through the pages of an old copy of the Picture Post.

'Damn right it is, but I thought I'd get to see all of my old chums in the regiment before I returned to a normal happy life.' They sat in silence for a moment, 'You know Si,' Noddy continued, 'I think I'm going to miss the army and all this,' he waved his arm at the foreboding jungle covered mountains still covered with a flimsy morning mist. 'A solicitor's office is going to be just a little dull after sparring with Charlie Tango these past eighteen months.'

*

A barrage of emotions tormented Lau as he was kitted out with his equipment to re-enter the jungle. They assailed his mind one by one and in combination. Fear, excitement, respect, loathing, envy, regrets, but excitement was the most powerful. He had respect and envy for his new masters, respect for their indisputable professionalism and confidence in their own ability, and envy for the standard of their arms and equipment. He loathed himself for his failure and them for the fact that they were exploiting him. He harboured fear, not for his own safety, his faith in those about him was absolute despite the recent success of the ambush, his fear was for his ex-comrades, he could not now understand how they had evaded death or capture for so long. The regret, which was powerful, was that he had ever got involved in this war at all.

Fully kitted in a new clean uniform and carrying a pack with food for four days, which in his recent existence would have probably had to suffice for two weeks, and armed with rifle and fifty rounds of .303inch ammunition, an amount that he had never seen before, he was ready to re-enter the struggle but now in a different role. Lau's state of mind would have doubtless been different had he known that the well-oiled, and cared for Lee Enfield that he so proudly carried, had had the firing pin removed.

At first he did not recognise Inspector Sankey as he climbed into the rear of the Land Rover; he had never seen him other than in civilian clothes.

'Feeling okay, Lau?' he turned round in his seat to face him.

'Yes,'

'We're going up to an army camp on the other side of town,' he explained, 'where we will attend a briefing this afternoon and then, in the early hours of tomorrow morning, we'll set off with a platoon of soldiers for you to guide to your last camp.'

*

The CO had explained the problem as diplomatically as he could without compromising Rupert's position but still protecting the platoon from the subaltern's inexperience and overconfidence. Even so it had placed Sergeant Snell in an unfortunate and difficult position, and Jeremy was acutely aware of the immense risk that he was taking.

'I think it would be a wiser course to send them out just with Snell,' he said to Jack Winslow as they shared a pre-lunch scotch.

'Well Crompton-Hughes has got to be blooded sometime, Jerry, and he could cause problems for a fellow subaltern,' he emptied his glass and signalled the waiter, 'In fact he could prove a bigger headache for any other young pippy, but David Snell won't tolerate any nonsense, and he's a great diplomat.'

At that very moment the tough sergeant was having a pre briefing chat with the substitute platoon commander in 'A' company office. Like the billets, the offices were constructed of atap on a concrete base and devoid of doors or windows. Three feet of dry brown grass divided the company office and that of the company commander.

'You, sir, will carry the title of platoon commander and as far as the men are concerned you will be in command,' Rupert leaned back against the CSM's desk tapping his silver-topped cane on his calf. 'However,' Dave continued 'you will have to let me take the more important....'

Rupert stood erect, the smug smirk replaced by a look of horrified indignity, 'Have you taken leave of your senses, sergeant?' He tapped the single brass pip on his thin shoulder, 'This was given to me by Her Majesty, and therefore, I am your superior and in command. Do I make myself clear?'

Dave held up a hand to silence the outraged officer, 'Listen to me sir, it's for your own good...'

'I'll be damned if I will,' his face had turned the colour of beetroot, 'the CO advised that I should heed your advice but I am still your superior and don't you forget that. I shall advise the OC of your insubordination this instant and request that I be given another platoon sergeant.' He left the office and crossed to the OC's office, at the open door he knocked on the upright that formed the frame.

'What is it?' The company 2i/c, Captain Whitely, looked up from the papers on his desk. Christopher Whitely, or CW as he was known, was a plumpish man of even temper and irritatingly floppy hair that he constantly had to brush from his face when he was hatless. Despite his rotund and slightly foppish mien he was a very tough man who had spent two years in a North Korean prisoner of war camp causing any amount of trouble for his captors.

'I would like a word with Major Winslow, sir,' Rupert saluted.

CW gave his attention back to the papers on his desk, 'He is not here as you can probably see.'

'Then may I have a word with you, sir,' Rupert persisted.

'What about?' he did not look up from his paper-work.

Rupert gingerly stepped over the threshold and lowered his voice not wanting the offending NCO to hear, 'It's my platoon sergeant, sir, Sergeant Snell, his impertinence is quite out of order and I would request that he be replaced, he's ...'

CW looked up and fixed Rupert with hard look, 'Mr Crompton-Hughes, I was unfortunate enough to overhear your exchange with Sergeant Snell and I am also party to the advice that you were given by

140

the commanding officer. You will have noticed that Sergeant Snell wears the wings of the SAS on his shoulder,' Rupert nodded, 'well in that regiment,' CW continued leaning back in his chair, 'the man commands that possess the skill. So, if a major commands the unit and they are using explosives, then the ordnance expert, even though he may be a trooper, is in command during that part of operation. Do you see the sense in that policy?'

'Well not really, sir a major is a major after all.'

CW drew a deep breath, 'We won't enter into a debate on the matter, Mr Crompton-Hughes, suffice to say that the OC would want you to listen to Sergeant Snell and be guided by him. And furthermore, you will never know as much about soldiering as Sergeant Snell does as long as you've got a hole in your arse. Now go and get briefed by him otherwise you'll spend the rest of your service as the battalion fire officer.'

When his temporary platoon commander returned to the company office Dave felt genuinely sorry for him, it had been impossible not to overhear his conversation with the 2i/c.

'Just be guided by your section commanders and myself, sir, this could be a tricky operation and experience counts for a lot in the jungle,' Dave said as gently as he could.

Rupert was unrepentant, unforgiving, and not astute enough to see the offer of peace that was being extended, 'Thank you for your valuable advice, sergeant,' he snapped disdainfully, 'I don't know what I would have done without it,' he turned sharply and stamped out of the office almost colliding with the CSM.

'Don't forget we have a briefing with the IO at 1400 hours, sir,' Dave called after him.

Rupert spun round his eyes blazing, 'I have a briefing with the IO sergeant and I will brief you after that.'

Dave, undeterred, replied quietly, 'I will see you at the IO's briefing, sir.'

'That one's gonna be a bloody pain in the arse,' Jimmy Raven said as he watched Rupert disappear towards the officers mess.

'Not good form for WO's to criticise young subalterns s'arnt major,' CW's voice boomed from his office.

'Beg pardon sir,' Jimmy replied and grinned at Dave.

'He's just bollocked him,' Dave mouthed returning the grin.

*

Linda had not been aware of John's exact whereabouts, but she knew that there had been a major incident near Sungei Siput in which a number of British soldiers had been killed, and she had read most of the sit-reps that had come in from 28 Commonwealth Brigade. The detail, and the number reported killed in the Straits Times differed considerably with the facts, and usually it was a paper that was not given to exaggeration, so she suspected that they had been fed inaccurate information. This was common practice as it was a reliable method of feeding controlled material to the CT.

According to the Times reporter, ten soldiers had been killed and the perpetrators had escaped unscathed, and although a follow up operation had been mounted within a couple of hours, none of the tracks found had produced any positive results.

The telephone rang startling her. She picked up the receiver, 'Inspector Sankey's office.'

'Linda,' it was John, 'I'm glad I caught you, as I may not get a chance to ring again. I shan't be back much before a week, so if you could ask Inspector Masters to vet any field letters that come in and act at his own discretion if anything needs urgent attention. He's off today and I can't get a reply from his home number. So if you could do that for me it would be a great help.'

'Yes of course, is there anything important you want me to be getting on with,' she asked.

'No, just attend to your normal routine,' there was a pause and then he said, 'I think were onto something big here.'

'Oh!'

'Yes, we have one SEP from the ambush.'

'SEP?'

'Surrendered enemy person,' he explained, 'chap called, Lau,' he paused, 'Lau Fong, and he's taking us back to some of his old camps,' he changed the subject quickly. 'I'll keep in touch and should you want to get an urgent message to me you can do so through the West Lancashire's, the numbers in my book, speak to 'A' Company.'

Linda replaced the handset and stared at the wall feeling more than a little shocked.

*

Sam had jumped instead of waiting to be pushed. He had been up before the MTO twice in a week having been reported by the military police, once for speeding and then again for smoking whilst driving, a contravention of MT fire orders. Going before the motor transport officer was a little different from appearing on OC's orders. As in most regiments the QM and MTO offices were held by quartermaster commissioned officers and Captain Tetlow was the battalions previous RSM. When Sam left the MT office he felt like a bone that had been savaged by a starving dog, a dog with a naturally mean disposition.

142

'Just one more offence, Andrews,' Frank Tetlow growled rather than spoke, his voice box maimed by years of screaming at idle little men, 'and you'll be back in a rifle company so fast that your feet won't touch the bleeding ground,' his voice rose an octave, 'Do I make myself clear?'

'Yes, sir' Sam was rigid; he could feel the sweat running down his bare chest and back.

'Get out of my bleeding office you idle man.'

Sam left cursing the fool who had allowed this psychopathic cockney into a Lancashire regiment. Later that day he submitted his request to transfer to 'A' Company and the following morning his request having been approved. He moved his kit into 1 platoon's basha and the same afternoon he was being kitted out for a four day operation; he was already beginning to regret his rash decision.

'I'd forgotten just how bloody heavy these are,' he moaned as he carried his four ration packs back to the billet.

'You'll be used to it in no time, Sammy lad,' Brian grinned.

'It's alright for you, Largy, you're a fit bastard, I've been used to sitting in a cab and taking you silly buggers to the jungle edge and then driving back to a comfy bed.'

'Well you're one of the silly buggers now, Andrews,' John barged him from behind with his shoulder causing Sam to drop his boxes of rations.

'Sod off, Cantrill yer daft bugger.'

'Come on you lot,' Rex Chester was outside the basha, 'get those rations stuffed in your lockers and then fall in out here.'

'Why?' Brian asked, 'what's going on?'

'Your new platoon commander wants a word.'

'Is Pearly not coming back,' John dropped his boxes on his bed.

'He's having a week's recuperation in the Cameron Highlands,' Rex told them.

'They're sending him home just for a week?' John was amazed at the army's generosity.

'You soft bugger, Cantrill,' Brian mocked; 'the Cameron Highlands are not in Blighty'.

'Well how was I supposed to know that,' John forced the final ration box into his locker, 'it sounds like haggis land - the Cameron Highlands.'

'It's a rest camp in yonder hills,' Rex explained, 'now come on, get a move on and get fell in.'

Rex Chester brought the platoon to attention as Rupert approached between the rows of huts accompanied by Dave.

'He's a fucking gremlin,' John muttered from the rear rank, 'look at the kipper on him, he's got a nose like a cobblers thumb.'

'Shut up, Cantrill,' Rex hissed.

The platoon began shaking with suppressed laughter.

John was not to be easily silenced, 'Look at the way he walks, I'm 'ere me arse is coming.'

'Cantrill,' Alan snapped, struggling to keep a straight face, 'button it.'

Rupert's opening words established the relationship he was to have with his first command, brief though it was to be. It was his idea of being diplomatic and trying to get them on his side from the start as he had been advised in one the lectures he had been given on leadership at Eaton Hall.

'You'll have to be patient with me,' he said after he had stood them easy, 'I have not mixed much with the working class before,' a pace behind him Dave looked at the floor and shook his head in disbelief, 'but I'm sure I'll be able to adapt, and if you can make allowances too then we shall get on like a house on fire.'

'You're fucking basha's the only thing that'll be on fire, pal,' John muttered.

'Did somebody say something?' Rupert adopted a look of authority and strained to see those on the rear rank, 'Understand this from the start,' he tried to look ferocious, 'I will not tolerate insubordination,' he shot a quick look over his shoulder at Dave, 'or bad manners.'

He began to pace along the front rank his hands clasped behind his back and his cane tucked under his arm, 'We are about to embark on our first operation together and I want it to be a successful one. Sergeant Snell and I have been briefed and the prospects of finding the enemy look good. We are taking an SEP out with us...,' he pointed suddenly at Andy Barton. 'What does SEP stand for?' The question took Andy by surprise he was paying little attention, he hesitated. 'Come on man, how long have you been out here?'

'Ten months,' Andy replied sullenly.

'Ten months, what?' Rupert snapped determined to stamp his authority on this rather untidy group.

'Ten months and four days,' Andy replied puzzled that such interest should be taken in his length of service. Barely restrained laughter erupted at Andy's reply which did nothing to improve Rupert's humour.

'Sir, ten months, sir,' he shouted, laying stress on the word, sir. 'ten months, sir.'

'Ten months, sir,' Andy said, even more sullen.

'Quiet,' Dave shouted as the laughter became more audible.

Rupert consulted his watch, 'I shall be back at 1800 hours to inspect the kit that you are taking on this operation. You will have it laid out on your beds,' he turned to Dave, 'Carry on, sergeant.'

'Plattooon shun,' he saluted but Rupert was already ten yards away. 'Carry on, Corporal Baker,' Dave said and with long strides went after Rupert. 'Can I have a word, sir,' he fell in step alongside him, 'When I salute you, Mr Crompton-Hughes I expect the courtesy of an acknowledgement.'

Rupert stopped and turned to face his platoon sergeant at five feet seven he had to look up to Dave's six feet three, 'I did not see your compliment, sergeant, had I done so then I would have paid you the same respect,' he said through gritted teeth.

'I'm not going to bandy words with you, sir, but your decision to inspect the men's kit is crass.'

'How dare you,' Rupert's eyes blazed but then he suddenly curbed his anger. 'Am I not entitled to inspect them as their commander?'

'You are indeed but we are on active service and most of these men of have done dozens of operations, they should not be treated like recruits fresh in ...'

'Sergeant,' Rupert cut in, his anger restored, 'I am entitled to inspect them whenever I feel the need and I shall. Furthermore I expect you to attend with your kit,' he turned and walked quickly away before Dave could reply.

'You've some hope,' Dave retorted as Rupert stormed away.

*

Beng had felt elated during the ambush it had been clear to see, from his position, that serious casualties had been inflicted on the troops and the truck was on fire. Had the second truck not been so far behind then they could entrapped both. If he had put the sentry fifty yards further along the road its presence would have been signalled to him. Even from where the lookout was situated, Beng was certain that he should have heard the second truck but as he had not yet arrived at the agreed RV he had not been 'questioned' on the matter.

The escape had also gone well and only four of those who had taken part were still missing. They could have easily been killed or taken prisoner and if it were the latter he would have to leave the RV within the next twelve hours in case they were persuaded to guide troops to the camp.

The men that he borrowed from other platoons had already left to return to their own camps so now there were just twenty of them, squatting, waiting under their frail atap shelters. The persistent rain added to their discomfort, it had started just before dawn and was still falling. Beng had sought comfort and warmth in the arms of Fang Ying; she had been one of his first mistress's back in 1948 but she had soon been replaced by younger and prettier comrades. But females were now in short supply and despite her age and faded looks he had to make do with her until something better came along.

A large frond of bamboo shook suddenly and everyone grabbed their weapons and packs in preparation to leave quickly. When it shook again the camp relaxed it meant that friends were approaching. Within a couple of minutes Lam Ten and Huang Wu entered the camp. Everybody was pleased to see them, as their packs appeared heavy, indicating that their expedition to collect food from the Hitam Rubber Estate had proved fruitful. The foreman on the estate was a loyal supporter and a leader in the local AWF, and invariably a reliable source of food and other provisions.

'Is Lau back yet? Lam asked as he opened his pack.

'Still four missing,' Beng replied more interested in the food, 'Woman, prepare the rice.'

'I can understand that Kem was probably...'

'Did you go to our last camp?' Beng had almost resigned himself to the fact that the four were dead it was a far preferable conclusion to them having been captured.

'Yes and there were no signs that anybody had been there since we left, but we should not stay here much longer.'

'I know that,' snarled Beng, 'we leave at dawn.'

Chapter Eighteen

They debussed in the dark, just short of the village of Tanjong Rambutan, on a wide logging track that skirted the village to the east, following the edge of the rubber estate and across a wide stream. At the edge of the rubber it was light enough to use the track and the platoon was soon on the move at a brisk pace in order to reach the jungle edge before the villagers were released into the fields. Normally the platoon sergeant brought up the rear but Dave was determined that he was going to control things despite Rupert's belief that he should in spite of the Captain Whitley's advice.

Tom Fitch and Ambau, an Iban with exceptional tracking abilities but some alarming personal qualities, led the way with Dave immediately behind them. Dave had appealed to Rupert's ego and told him that as the commander he should place himself behind the leading section with the SEP and the two minders so that they could communicate easily with him.

The fine rain cooled them and suppressed the mosquitoes and in twenty minutes they covered the mile that brought them to another stream that tumbled noisily from the hills on their right. Here they turned off into the rubber and climbed up through the line of trees for about ten minutes before Dave signalled a halt and ten-minute rest. As he feared Crompton -Hughes picked his way along the line and squatted beside him.

'Why have we stopped?'

'Give the lads a breather,' even in the dark he could sense that Crompton-Hughes wanted to challenge his decision, so he added, 'we enter the ulu here and it's too dark, in ten minutes there'll be enough light to move.'

They sat in silence getting wetter and colder. The sound of somebody moving carefully announced the arrival of John Sankey,

'How's it going?' he crouched between Dave and Rupert.

'Okay, how's your man?' Dave asked.

'He's fine.'

'Not nervous?'

John gave a short laugh, 'No, he's just told me that he has never felt safer.'

'I have resisted raising this matter,' Rupert put in, 'in light of my inexperience…'

'That's rich,' Dave thought to himself and smiled.

Rupert continued, '…but has it crossed anybody's mind that this chappie of yours may be leading us into a trap?'

'That's not very likely, he's been in our hands for over a week now and we've decided where we are taking him, it's not at his suggestion. Anyway he'd be the first to die if we walked into a trap.'

'Well why don't you take them back in immediately they surrender?' Rupert's admission of ignorance seemed to be already forgotten, 'you'd catch the buggers with pants down as it were.'

'I don't think so,' John replied calmly.

'Well if you've never tried it how do you know?' Rupert sounded disdainful.

'We'll have to discuss it some other time,' John got to his feet, 'but we have our reasons and been handling SEP's CEP's and agents for a number of years now so we do have some experience in the matter.'

'Right, let's move,' Dave also got to his feet wanting to avoid Crompton-Hughes giving any more 'advice' to special branch.

It had stopped raining but the saturated jungle canopy continued to drop water on them for the next half-hour. The dampness intensified the rank odour of putrefaction and they all knew that, unseen, in the darkness, the leeches would be homing in on their human prey and would probably not be discovered until they were bloated with their victim's blood.

Individual trees and bushes could now be discerned in the grey light and the platoon, with their guests, began the long climb up the steep hillside that rose to the height of bukit Korbu. To the right they could hear the fast flowing stream that they were following, all the more energetic from the previous night's rain. At times gaps in the jungle allowed them sight of the stream forty or fifty feet below, foaming over rocks and forming the odd inviting pool.

The coldness had gone and their shirts, recently sodden with rain, were now soaked in their own sweat as they slipped and slid along the steep hillside. Fingers of warm sunlight penetrated to the damp jungle floor and the valley, to the left, was filled with the blinding morning sun with trails of fine mist hanging in the tree tops. The sound of the rushing stream helped muffle the muttered curses of men struggling to maintain their balance and the soft thud of bodies on the floor when they failed.

At the next halt Dave held court with John and Lau, Rupert was present but they managed to confer despite him.

'About another hour up here,' Lau said allowing for the tortoise like pace of the troops compared to what he had been used to, 'on the opposite side, there is a good place to camp.'

'Was it used by the CT?' Dave asked.

'No, it could be seen from the air.'

'And how much further from there is the camp you're taking us to?' Rupert put in.

Lau shook his head and grimaced, 'An hour, possibly two, it depends how quickly you go.'

'Well we won't be carrying these,' Dave indicated his Bergen.

'An hour then,' Lau conceded.

'I still don't see why we don't go there directly,' Rupert pouted. He had raised the idea at the briefing and did not appear to have been persuaded by the argument that they did not want to make their approach hindered by their heavy packs. The idea was to gather intelligence and there was the remote possibility that it had been reoccupied and should be approached tactically.

The campsite that Lau had indicated was idyllic. It was a flattish area six feet above the stream where a quiet deep pool had formed. At some time the area must have been cleared for now there was about 200 square yards of belukar that provided plenty of cover on all sides but as Lau had said, not from the air.

Within an hour military order had been imposed on the wilderness; water-point established, latrine dug, vines to both essential points and circumnavigating the camp had been erected and all basha's constructed. Platoon HQ, in the centre of the camp, was bigger than usual having to house special branch and their charge.

When all was completed and clearance patrols returned it was a little after 1500, an hour later Rupert held his O group. He sat on his hammock with the section commanders gathered round armed with note pads and folded maps. Dave and John were near enough to remain under their basha's similarly equipped.

'Patrols will depart this location at 0800 hours,' he began, 'Corporal Baker, you will take your section, plus Lameh, and patrol west along this side of the stream looking for tracks or any other signs of human activity,' he looked up from his notes, 'Okay?' Alan nodded, 'I don't want you back here before 1700. I want a full effective day's work from you, no skiving.'

Alan raised his hand slightly; Rupert spotted the movement, 'You have a question?'

'Do you know me, sir?' the muscles round Alan's mouth were tight.

'Of course not, I only met you for the first time yesterday,' Rupert looked perplexed.

'Well how come you think that I'm likely to skive?'

'Come, come corporal, there is no need to be so sensitive, I just want it to be clear that I will not tolerate any slackness,' he turned his attention back to his notes but then he looked up again and added, 'And I want that message conveyed to the men.'

Dave caught Alan's eye and shook his head slightly warning him not to pursue the matter. Throughout the rest of the O group there was a degree of tension of which Rupert remained unaware.

Rex's section, plus Ambau, was to patrol out on a bearing roughly south-east heading in the direction of the seven thousand feet summit with the same brief as one section, look for signs of recent activity.

'Corporal Murray, you will remain here with your section and the signaller.'

'Sir,' this suited Ruby, he preferred quiet life.

'Sergeant Snell, you can remain with Corporal Murray's section and....' Rupert began.

'I'll be coming with you, sir,' Dave said firmly.

Rupert glanced up from his notes, look irritation on his face, 'Very well. In that case, Inspector Sankey, his sergeant and the SEP will go with me and Sergeant Snell to examine this camp.'

'And the JCLO,' Dave reminded him.

'Ah yes, Mr Wong.'

'Just a word of warning,' Dave said to the two NCO's leading patrols, 'bear in mind that there will be three friendly patrols in the area so be sure of targets before you engage. '

Rupert gave him a sympathetic look, 'They will all be going in different directions, sergeant, what are the chances..?'

'When you've got a few jungle patrols under your belt, sir, you won't be so confident,' Dave said quietly but firmly and everybody nodded.

'Right,' Rupert wore an indignation but resisted responding, 'that's it unless there are any questions?'

'Password for tomorrow, sir,' Ruby asked.

'Oh!' Rupert looked surprised.

'Dick, Dave said, 'Delta India - Charlie Kilo.'

'And what will it be the day after, sarge, 'head?' Rex grinned.

*

Lau found the food rather heavy and stodgy but after years of ceaseless hunger it was something that he could tolerate. The individual ration packs intrigued him as did the cookers, with their smokeless fuel blocks that folded and fitted into the metal dish from which they ate. It was so well thought out and convenient.

And then there were the arms; each man carried almost as much ammunition as a half dozen of his recent unit. If only his past comrades could see what they were up against they would realise the futility of

150

their fight. The single factor that had preserved them this far was the vastness of the jungle in which they hid. He knew now that it was only a matter of time before the MRLA was defeated.

The high spirits of the soldiers was also a shock. Propaganda from the Central Committee gave the impression that the British soldiers were demoralised and a detested the jungle and their leaders equally but the men around him appeared at ease and confident in their surroundings, and although they seemed to complain continuously their morale seemed of a very high order.

When Sankey had told him that the unit he was with was the one they had ambushed a little over a week earlier he had been appalled and had tried to withdraw his assent to co-operate. But the inspector had convinced him that none of the troops would be made aware of the fact, and that the man he had surrendered to was not present.

As he lay in his basha with a full belly and encircled by thirty armed and able men, Lau wallowed in an indescribable feeling of contentment and safety. He realised that he was smiling and could not erase the smile which was causing his face to ache

'You look like a happy man,' Sergeant Rizal the Malay policemen ducked down and looked in the basha.

Lau expelled a big sigh, 'I suppose I am,' he grimaced, 'but I have a little guilt.'

Rizal began to remove his long jungle boots, 'Don't feel bad about betraying that CT scum.'

'I made a few friends in my years, well one,' Lau realised his smile was gone and he did not add that the greatest remorse was over his cousin, May Ling.

*

May Ling entered the station a little before midnight and went to the telephone kiosk by the newspaper stand which at this time was closed. Due to the Emergency only main line trains ran after dark, and these only infrequently with armed troops onboard, consequently there were few people around. May, placed the basket that she was carrying on the shelf provided, picked up the receiver and appeared to dial a number. After a pause she replaced the receiver, picked up her basket and left the kiosk; the sound of her wooden soled clogs on the marble floor reverberated loudly around, the almost empty, vaulted building.

As the clatter of her footfall faded a gaunt Tamil sweeper, who had been squatting by the news-stand smoking a pungent bhidi, rose, and sweeping as he went, approached the kiosk. He opened the door and briefly passed his broom over the floor; a sharp eyed bystander would have seen him remove something from beneath the parcel shelf on which May had rested her basket.

As the great clock, over the station entrance, announced the new day, the sweeper, with his broom across his shoulder, padded his lonely way home. Before he reached the Katong road, and the area of the town occupied by the Tamil's, he turned off the main thoroughfare and paused by a post-box. Just inside the letter opening he secured the item he had taken from the telephone kiosk, and then continued his journey homeward.

*

By the fourth day of the operation Lau had led them to two old camps and an empty food dump.

'He knows of others,' John explained, 'but they're too far from here, it will take a separate operation.'

'Why didn't we head straight for the RV they were using after the ambush,' Dave asked as they both sat on his hammock sharing the remains of the platoon rum issue after the platoon had stood-down.

'According to Lau they would only wait there for twenty four hours and in any case we have another line to pursue with Lau.'

'Well they would have to have somewhere else planned for those who were late to meet up,' Dave persisted.

'Well, as that was their last base I was hoping that they would have considered enough time had elapsed for a safe return to collect any items of importance that had been left behind,' he grimaced to himself in the dark, 'but as you witnessed there was no sign of a return since the camp was evacuated for the ambush.'

'He hasn't been much bloody use as an informant has he?' Dave lowered his voice even lower as Lau was in the next basha.

'That's not quite true,' John corrected him, 'he has given us plenty of useful intelligence even though he doesn't know it.'

'Anything about this big camp, that's believed to exist?'

There was a long pause before John answered, 'A little.'

'As to its location'? Dave asked.

A longer pause followed, Dave sensed his reluctance to reply, 'Here, give me your mug we can squeeze another tot,' Dave took Johns mug and shared the remaining rum.

Rain arrived with the dreary dawn and the platoon stood-to but remained in their basha's. Rupert had feebly insisted they should leave their shelters but Dave's response left him in not doubt that his demand would not be met.

'They've got their dry kit on and it's staying dry,' Dave growled as he and Rupert toured the camp.

'Our dry change is getting wet,' Rupert complained ineffectually.

'That's the cross you have to bear as their leader, sir.'

Once the light began to improve Alan organised the sentries, 'Andy, Sam, sentry.'

Before Sam could form the words of complaint with which he met every command, John Cantrill appeared dressed, armed and wearing his belt kit.

'I'll do the shit-house stag, Al,' he said. Everyone within earshot stopped what they were doing and looked at John. 'What's yer problem,' he asked, wide-eyed with bogus innocence.

'You're either ill or up to no good, Cantrill,' Alan's eyes narrowed, 'Scouser's don't volunteer it's against their religion.'

'Come on, corp,' John's pitifully inferior display of probity continued, 'I'm just trying to do my whack, and straight away the good name of every Scouser is dragged through the shite,' he looked around with a look of indignation, as counterfeit as the innocence he had displayed, 'where's the justice,'

'Cut out the bloody drama, Cantrill,' Alan grinned, he knew there was mischief afoot, 'come on,' as he turned to lead the sentries to their post's John turned to Brian and winked.

After a quick sweep of the area to ensure no CT were lying up close by, Alan posted his two sentries, Andy at the water point and John at the latrine. John's position was a couple of yards further on from the toilet, far enough away to be discreet but close enough to offer protection should the occupant be caught, literally, with his pants down.

The latrine was a simple but effective structure consisting of two diagonal crosses of wood placed on either side of a pit about four feet in depth, and a yard square. The two side structures were joined by a single stout branch which served as the seat and the whole creation was secured by vines.

Once he was alone John drew his parang from its bamboo sheath and gently sawed half way through the vines that held both diagonals together, he then stepped back to where he had been posted and waited straining to hear for the arrival of anyone intent on using the toilet. He was thankful that the rain had stopped as it would have masked the noise of anyone approaching.

Stags as sentry invariably dragged by in what seemed to be endless periods of boredom or equally infinite terms of anxiety. John was finding this bout especially stressful as he had to give his attention to the likelihood of enemy incursion but just as importantly to any members of the platoon coming to make use of the toilet. He knew he could warn them, it was only going to be a problem if Dave Snell appeared or the special branch inspector.

Over the past few days he had observed that Crompton-Hughes attended to his ablutions the instant the camp stood down and sentries had been posted. First he would head out to the latrine and then back through the camp to the water point, so if he kept to his normal routine, he should be the first to make use of the primitive toilet.

Sure enough within minutes he emerged from the wet green foliage with toilet paper in one hand and his FN in the other. With a limp flick of his wrist he motioned John to move further away. John complied but found himself a position where he could see the set trap and remain out of sight of the occupant.

John held his breath as he watched his leader rest his rifle against one of the side cross members and lower his trousers revealing a pure white posterior that showed up like a full moon in the murky light. He carefully wiped the 'seat' with some toilet paper and then, gingerly, he lowered himself onto the pole.

At first John had to clasp his hand over his mouth to stifle the rising laughter, but then disappointment, the structure remained in place, and Rupert completed the task, for which he had come, without mishap. It was as he manoeuvred to employ the toilet paper that the five lengths of sapling parted company and the slight subaltern fell backwards with a shout of alarm, into the four-day collection of faeces and urine. He entered the foetid accumulation with an audible splash and an incomprehensible exclamation that conveyed both horror and rage.

'Sentry,' he bellowed, all thoughts of security abandoned, 'get me out, get me out.' As John reached him, his face wreathed in mirth, Alan Baker and Dave Snell arrived on the scene.

'What the bloody hell's going on?' Dave halted and leaned on his rifle making no attempt to hide his amusement, 'I think it could be said that you're in the shit, sir.'

The manner in which Rupert had entered the cesspool made it virtually impossible to extricate himself without assistance, and there he remained, like a human letter V, a look off disgust and outrage on his face. He strove to haul himself out on exposed roots, none of which would bear his weight, and he slid back into the mire.

Anger replaced his humiliation, anger that swiftly turned to uncontrollable rage, 'Get me out damn you,' another root snapped and he lost the few inches that he gained. 'Someone will be court martialled for this,' he screamed at the top of his voice.

'Were operational, keep your bloody noise down,' Dave hissed, 'Give me your parang, Cantrill.' He cut down a young tree about four inches in diameter and trimmed it to a length of six feet.

'Get over the other side,' he ordered Alan. They stood each side of the pit and placed the pole in front Rupert, 'Put your arms over,' he instructed, and it was thus that Second Lieutenant Crompton-Hughes was removed, stinking and polluted, from the four day collection of human waste.

He stood, his arms hanging loosely at his side with his feet slightly apart, head bowed, his trousers still round his ankles and with his lower regions covered in faeces.

'If anybody laughs,' he said eventually without raising his eyes, 'I will put him on a charge,' he turned and looked at John, 'my rifle's in there, get it.'

'I'm on stag,' John protested and slipped away through the undergrowth expecting to be called back but nothing was said.

Slowly Rupert knelt and drew the rifle from the noisome hole, and then he turned and headed back to the camp holding his trousers up with one hand and his disgusting rifle in the other.

'He's walking as though he's shit his-self,' Alan muttered out of the side of his mouth. Dave shushed him doing his best to subdue a feeling of sympathy.

'Get that built again, Cantrill,' he indicated the destroyed latrine.

John's grin disappeared and he gave Dave a thumbs-up, 'Right away sarge,' the grin returned.

'I'll bloody, right away sarge, you.'

'What?' John put on his tragic look.

Chapter Nineteen

A letter from Susan had preceded his arrival at Frasers Hill; it informed him that she was hitching a ride on a RAF Whirlwind on Friday that was bringing up the Brigadiers wife to convalesce. She went on to say that she would be staying with Mrs Woodhouse in the bungalow that she had been allocated.

Simon was elated; his stay in the BMH been painfully tedious and the tedium had been magnified by his swift recovery. He had expected his time in rehabilitation to be equally dispiriting, as it was even more remote than the BMH.

Now at least he would have a weekend in the company of someone he enjoyed being with and in whose company he felt comfortable. It was something that still confounded him; he had never experienced the normal shyness that he had suffered throughout his puberty and into early manhood. From their first meeting he felt at ease as though in the company of an old and trusted friend.

He sighed deeply, a sigh of contentment, as he gazed out across the lush green lawns to the purple distance of Batu Berenchang that rose to six thousand feet radiating mystery and menace. A twinge of guilt for his good fortune briefly marred his delight. Five young men, whom he had considered his family, would never see their countries of birth again and the families that they had left behind, in tears, would never experience the overwhelming joy of their homecoming, for all their pain and grief, he felt responsible.

He had wanted to be back with the regiment ever since the terrible day that he had arrived at the BMH in a haze of morphine, numbing pain and a crippling sense of failure. The pain was past and the painkillers no longer required but the sense of failure remained, less crippling since the encouragement and praise from the CO and other senior officers of the regiment, but it was still present nevertheless.

In every direction jungle covered mountains flaunted their authority, potency and inscrutability as one of the last great wildernesses. This little pocket of humanity could have contained the only human beings on earth; the high fertile valley was sheer peace and tranquillity. The climate was perfection, seventy to eighty degrees was the norm, and there was an ever-present gentle breeze from one valley or another. Although it rained regularly it never lasted for more than hour and rarely more than once a day. And it was the rain that nourished the magnificent gardens, in which the rest camp was set. Gardens furious with colour and heavy with the scent of frangipani blossom, gardens, where the only sounds were those of nature. A gently sloping waterfall tumbled cautiously over rocks that it had washed smooth over countless years, the far off call of the sambur doe, clear as a silver bell, punctuating the constant singing of dozens of varieties of exotic and more familiar birds.

A gong sounded discreetly and Simon turned and entered the mess leaving behind one utopia and entering another. Although the camp had only been restored after the defeat of the Japanese, nine years earlier, the mess had the air of a gentleman's club that was immersed in tradition and military history, the atmosphere and décor was distinctly Edwardian.

During the day it was cool and serene but once darkness fell, and the staff and convalescents had gathered for pre-dinner drinks, it was a warm and friendly brotherhood, a family home, a closeness and comradeship that only the military can generate.

Compared to the mess of the RWL's the rules here were relaxed, mess dress was never compulsory, and the only two rules that had to be observed, were; shirts had to be worn during the day and ties worn after 1800 hours. Although Simon had only been there for two days he felt very much at home.

The three other platoon members who had been wounded in the ambush had left that morning to return to the regiment. They had been discharged from the BMH a week earlier. It had warmed Simon's heart the way that they had greeted him when he gone to the OR's mess on the day that he had arrived.

'Bloody hell it's, Pearly,' Lance-corporal Brewster had been the first to see him. Eddie Good and Jimmy Eames got to their feet grinning, and the three crowded round him all speaking at once. The enthusiasm of their welcome embarrassed him in front of dozens of other soldiers taking their NAAFI break, but of one thing he was sure, it was genuine. He was disappointed when he found out that they were leaving the following day.

'Get back an' gi' those bloody CT a kicking for what they did tae us,' Jimmy Eames threatened in his thick Geordie accent.

As officer's were not allowed to drink in the OR's mess the four of them sat on the moonlit lawn and consumed large quantities of Anchor beer talking late into the night. Simon felt that he had arrived, he had been accepted. He went to sleep that night happier than he could remember but woke the next morning wishing he were dead with a pounding head .

He entered the mess knowing that he could eat little, but also knowing he needed to eat something to assist his recovery from the night's excess. The smell of spicy food turned his stomach. Buffets were the custom at lunch time as meal times and members had to help themselves, there were no mess waiters on duty for lunch. Simon took a bowl of chicken soup and bread roll and occupied one of the tables by a window that offered a breeze and a wonderful view of distant hills.

'I smell rain on that breeze,' a short tubby, red faced, major with a large moustache sniffed as he deposited a plate piled high with curry and rice, and a pint of lager on the table opposite Simon, 'Don't mind if I join you d'you, old chap?' His brass shoulder titles proclaimed him to be a member of the 10th Gurkha's. He also wore sabre wings on his right shoulder and his medal ribbons indicated hectic wartime service.

'Not at all, sir,' Simon made to stand but the jolly major dismissed the action with a wave of his hand

'Sit, sit,' he offered his hand, 'Willie Ashton, ended up here with a damn snake bite.'

'Simon Gates, but I found out last night that I'm known as Pearly by my platoon.'

The major laughed, 'Damn sight better than Little Willie.'

'Really'! Simon smiled.

'So I'm told,' he filled his mouth with rice, 'and what mob are you with Simon, and what brings you to this enchanting little Garden of Eden?'

'RWL's, I got shot up in an ambush about a month ago.'

'Up near Lasah?'

Simon nodded, 'Yes, they took us apart a bit but I'm told my platoon sergeant saved the day.'

Willie wiped food from his moustache and laughed, 'They usually do, Simon; they usually do,' he half emptied his glass with audible relish, 'Backbone of the British army, and no mistake,' he refilled his mouth with curry and rice again, 'Is that scar on the old fizzog a result of your brush with Charlie?'

Simon nodded, 'Glass from the windscreen of the truck.'

'Badge of honour Simon, badge of honour, bit more glamorous than being bitten on the arse by a bloody bootlace snake,' he laughed and drained his glass. 'None of my little Gurkha's was dashing forward to suck the poison out, what!' He signalled the bar waiter and ordered another pint, Simon declined the offer to join him, 'Last bloody thing I remember before passing out, were all the little buggers rolling around the ulu wetting themselves at my predicament, strides around me ankles etcetera.'

Lunch with the jolly major improved Simon's condition and he returned to his room and fell into a deep sleep.

*

158

Lam was tiring of his role, the physical and mental pressures were beginning to take their toll. He was ever fearful that he was losing his sharpness, the sharpness that was essential to see, hear or sense danger before he was spotted by those presenting the threat. As a trusted courier he had to travel great distances between camps and 'letterboxes'. He was now in his mid forties, not a great age, but the poor diet barely sustained the indolent and he rarely spent more than a couple of days in any one place. Also, he feared that the strain of being an agent maybe starting to show, Beng was shrewd and never really trusted anybody, there had been moments when he had caught his SCM watching him with his cold, reptilian gaze that seemed to be looking into his very soul.

He was tired, he had only spent one night in camp since he and Huang had returned with the food before he had had to set out to collect the message that he now carried, hidden away in the collar of his shirt. His fatigue was confirmed by the fact that the sentry saw him before he saw the sentry, something that had never happened in the five years that he had been a courier.

The youth was surprisingly well covered with flesh as he had only joined them shortly before the ambush; the inadequate diet had not taken full effect on him. He grinned, 'Welcome back comrade, you look tired.'

Lam gave him a disdainful look and went past without speaking. In the camp they were listlessly improving their shelters. Beng lay asleep beneath the most substantial basha and a woman squatted close by repairing an item of clothing. When she saw Lam she nudged Beng who was instantly awake. He took the message without a word and read it in silence. As he read his cruel features became gradually distorted with rage, the sound of his breathing increased and Lam could hear his teeth grinding together.

'The rat,' he hissed as he rummaged in his pack, 'the cunning treacherous snake,' he produced a small note pad of rice paper and a pencil and began to write, all the time inhaling and exhaling noisily. When he had finished he rolled the paper and handed to Lam, 'Take this to the zone letterbox,' he growled. Lam's heart sank; it was almost ten miles away through mountainous country and he would not pass close to any villages where he could beg food.

'I haven't eaten today,' he ventured.

'Then take it with you,' Beng motioned to the woman who wrapped some rice and vegetables in a leaf and handed it to him.

Beng raised his voice and addressed the camp, 'We have lost three comrades to the guns of the running dogs,' he announced and before

159

Lam could ask if Lau was among those killed, he added, 'and we have been betrayed by that dog, Lau Fong, who has sold himself to the British and put our lives at risk.'

*

Jeremy heard the story of Rupert's unfortunate escapade third hand via Nigel. He knew that anger, at the humiliation of one of his officers, should have been his predominant emotion but to his shame he had laughed to the point of tears.

'What on earth am I to do, Nigel?' he eventually gasped, 'what charges can be laid and against whom?'

'I am led to believe that the sentry at the time of this unfortunate event would appear to be the most likely culprit,' Nigel said, 'but it is purely circumstantial, and I doubt whether the Judge Advocate would consider it for one moment.'

Jeremy looked surprised, 'Do you think it could run to a courts martial?'

'Well!' Nigel put on his thoughtful legal expression that has to be mastered on appointment to adjutant, 'if there was an identifiable individual the only charge could be the assault of an officer and that would have to go to courts martial.'

'Yes, but as you say there is really insufficient evidence to charge even the most likely member of the platoon. Perhaps,' the CO said after a short pause, 'we could resort to the old military practice of punishing the entire platoon,' another pause, 'not through official channels, obviously.'

'Obviously,' the adjutant agreed cautiously, 'but 1 platoon has taken a bit....'

'Yes, yes I know, Nigel, it's not a course that I would seriously consider but I have to do something to record my displeasure, the displeasure of the regiment.'

'Displeasure, sir?' Nigel asked with a smile on his lips.

The CO shook his head and bowed it as though to read some papers on his desk but hiding the smile that he could not restrain, 'You can wipe that smirk off your face, Nigel, and send a runner to ask Major Winslow to join us here.'

'It would be quicker to phone him, sir.'

The CO looked up, all humour had gone from his weathered face, 'A runner, Nigel, I want it made public that we are treating this outrage with the all of the seriousness it deserves.'

Suitably chastised the adjutant summoned the Commanding Officers runner and sent him hot foot to 'A' Company with the request that the company commander report to the commanding officer.

'Is this about that silly arse Crompton – Hughes, Colonel?' Big Jack saluted and then removed his cap.

'It's something that we have to address, Jack,' the CO replied handing him a glass of sherry, 'he could make a complaint to brigade if we do nothing, and anyway it would be bad for discipline if we let it pass without some action.'

'Thank you,' Jack took the glass and dropped into the armchair opposite Jeremy, 'Give me ten minutes with him and I'll put the fear of Christ in him,' he drained the glass and placed it on the desk. 'How the stupid bugger could have got their backs up, in so short a space of time, is completely beyond me. It's a damn fine platoon, young Simon had got on with them well enough and all of the NCO's are first class chaps, especially Sergeant Snell, we both thought that he was the best man to control this fool. Didn't like the fellow from the start, pompous little shit, should never...'

'I'm in full sympathy with your feelings on this, Jack,' the CO cut short the big major's rant, 'but if only for the sake of discipline and the morale of the commissioned ranks, I must be seen to act,' he refilled their glasses. 'Brigade will have to know about it and they will want to be informed of the outcome.'

'That's going to be the best course, Jerry,' Big Jack put his empty glass down again.

'What's that?'

'Go and have a chat with Harry Woodhouse, he's an understanding sort....'

'Come on, Jack,' Jeremy cut in a little icily, 'I'm the commanding officer of this regiment and if I have to go running to the brigadier over something like this I don't deserve to be in command.'

'May I make a suggestion, sir,' Nigel had stood quietly by the door throughout the conversation. He now stepped forward and opened a buff coloured folder that he had been holding.

The CO nodded, 'By all means, Nigel, any contribution will be welcome.'

Nigel drew a sheet of paper from the folder, 'I recalled seeing this request from Far East Land Forces Headquarters. It's for units to submit names of any junior officers, with at least twelve months left to serve in area, who would be considered fit to fill the post of Command Fire Officer, after attending a two week course at RAF Changi.'

Nobody spoke for a moment, and then the CO cautiously ventured, 'He would have to be willing for his name to be put forward.'

'Why would he?' Jack asked, 'he can be posted anywhere without his consent.'

'What I mean,' the CO explained, 'is that if he didn't agree to the posting it would appear that he were the one being punished.'

'Well he is,' Jack snorted 'and the silly bugger deserves it.'

The colonel sighed, 'Yes I agree, but it mustn't appear like that for the sake of discipline. Dropping platoon commanders in the shit could develop as a platoon contest. Is there a closing date for names on that order, Nigel?'

Nigel scanned the order, 'By the twenty first, sir,' and he looked at his watch, 'just over a week.'

The CO jumped to his feet, 'Right, Jack,' he looked relieved, 'it's your company so I am going to let you handle it.'

'Only fair, Colonel,' Jack said unconvincingly, 'I take it from your expression that you might be giving some guidance on the matter.'

Jeremy's smile broadened, 'Only with your agreement,' Big Jack signalled his agreement with spread hands and the CO continued, 'I suggest you parade 1 platoon, very publicly, and with Crompton – Hughes in attendance, give them the mother of all bollockings, pointing out that had there been sufficient evidence then charges would have been laid, and those found guilty severely punished. That done you will have to do a damn good selling job on Crompton – Hughes to persuade him that this Singapore posting would be ideal for a man with his great powers of leadership,' he raised his eyebrows.

'As good as done, sir,' big Jack got to his feet.

*

'Hey Baz,' Brian called out as Barry entered the room, 'how was the leave, pal?'

Barry dropped his holdall onto his bed, 'It was great Brian, the food, the people, a lovely peaceful break,' he went down to where Brian lay on his bed and sat down, 'Haven't you got a leave booked?'

Brian laughed and lowered the paper that he was reading, 'Aye, but I'm going with Cantrill and Sam so I don't think it's going to be all that peaceful,' his mood changed, 'Keith was gonna come with us.'

John entered with just a towel wrapped round his waist, 'Hi ya Barry lad, you haven't been visiting all those knocking shops in Penang and caught a dose of clap have you?'

'Shut up, Cantrill,' Brian laughed, 'Barry's a clean living lad.'

'Well I wouldn't go that far,' Barry unzipped his bag and began unpacking a slight smile played about his lips.

'There yer are,' John cried triumphantly, 'yer've been out getting the old jiggy jig haven't yer, yer dirty sod.'

'I take it,' Barry said changing the subject, 'from all the kit outside drying, you've just come back from an op?'

Brian sat up, 'Hey Baz some bloody op.'

'Another contact'?

'Better than that,' Brian went on, 'we've got this right gob-shite of a pippy with us until Pearly gets back,' Brian mimicked an upper class voice,' Rupert Crompton – Hughes....'

'Better known as, 'I'm here me arse is coming,' John butted in.

'Told us all,' Brian took up the story again in the upper class voice, 'we weren't bad chaps for commoners and then had has us empty our packs....'

'Which we'd just packed ready for the op,' John pointed out.

'And then he inspected what we were carrying,' Brian continued, 'Old Snelly was really pissed off with him, Harrison, the company clerk, said he heard them having a right old ding-dong outside the company office. Tell him what happened, Johnno,'

'I didn't hear 'em.'

'I mean on the op you daft sod.'

'Oh aye,' a wicked grin creased John's weathered face and he related to Barry, Rupert's demise in colourful language.

'Bloody hell,' Barry's eyes were wide with disbelief, 'and who sabotaged the shit house?

'That we don't know,' Brian said quickly and gave John a deadpan look, 'do we Johnno?'

'I have me suspicions,' John said seriously and began applying liberal amounts of foot powder to his feet.

'We had an SEP on the op with us, he took us to sites of old camps and food dumps,' Brian offered a tin of cigarettes round.

'Did you find anything,' Barry lit their cigarettes.

'Someone said he used to be a teacher,' John added, 'he spoke good English.'

'A teacher,' Barry's interest intensified, 'was his name Lau?'
John shook his head, 'Dunno.'

'It was something like that,' Brian said, 'I think that's what that special branch fellah called him.'

'Was he about my height, but skinny with long black hair..?

'That narrows it down to about twenty three million Chinese,' John shook his head, 'are you sure you failed your commission, Baz, cos you sound like a pippy at times.'

Barry was undeterred, 'Were his eyes rather prominent for a Chinese, bulging?'

'Yeah,' Brian said thoughtfully, 'they were now you mention it.'

'I think he was the one who surrendered to me,' Barry said with some certainty.

163

'He was one of those bastards who killed Keith?' John shouted with rage, 'he was eating our rations and carrying a fucking gun and less than a month ago he was shooting shit out of our mates,' he hurled the tin of powder across the room, 'I'd have drowned the bastard in the shit pit if I had known, I'd have cut his fucking bollocks off, I'd have blown his fucking head off,' he sat down, suddenly, on his bed with his head bowed and covered his face with his hands.

*

One platoon paraded outside 'A' Company Office before setting off to the Guntong ranges that were situated at the rear of the 6th Gurkha's camp. None of them had ever seen Big Jack in such a filthy temper before. Those, like Les Marsden, who had appeared on orders before the large major, knew he could breathe fire and brimstone when displeased, but the fury that stood, red faced and berating them with choice language, was a spectacle that they never wanted to witness again. Rupert stood behind the raging major trying to appear detached, but it was clear from the smirk that he was struggling to suppress that he was enjoying every minute of the tirade.

When they arrived at the range, still in mild shock from their OC's tongue lashing, Alan noticed that Rupert was not with them.

'Isn't little Lord Fauntleroy coming, sarge?' Alan asked.

'You won't be seeing him again, Al,' Dave told him with a grin, 'this afternoon he is off to Singapore on posting.'

'You're joking.'

Dave shook his head, 'It's pukka.'

Alan turned and shouted across to where the first detail was loading their magazines, 'Hey Cantrill, you can own up now, Crompton – Hughes has been posted,' a cheer greeted the announcement.

'I'm owning up to fuck all,' John shouted.

Chapter Twenty

It was one of those days when the minute he opened his eyes Simon felt an extraordinary surge of joy flood through him without really knowing the source of his ecstasy. It was only when he began to marshal his befuddled thoughts that he recalled the previous day's events that gave rise to his sense of well-being.

Susan's arrival had been cause enough to explain the happiness he was experiencing. He had anticipated, with some apprehension, that he would possibly have to dine with the Brigade Commander's wife, as Susan was travelling down with her and they were probably on quite friendly terms. He was not wrong in his assumption but totally incorrect in expecting it to be a boring and decorous occasion.

The commanding officer of the rehabilitation unit, an RAMC lieutenant colonel who was nearing retirement, was obviously eager to host Jenny Woodhouse, but he had the sense to keep the dinner informal. As there were only four officers on rehabilitation and as many staff, it was a warm and friendly atmosphere with most of the conversation dominated by Jenny and Major Ashton, who were old acquaintances

Jenny Woodhouse was a slim, elegant lady whose refined appearance concealed a robust and somewhat earthy sense of humour.

'Willie Ashton, you old bastard,' she got to her feet as Willie entered the mess and gave him an enthusiastic hug, 'what on earth are you doing here?

'My dear mad, Jenny, has that stuffed shirt let you out on your own?' Willie turned to Simon and Susan, 'The Brig doesn't usually allow our Jen this much free rein, what,' he grinned, 'I take it that you're still hitched to the old sod?'

Jenny grimaced, 'He's still the man of my life, Willie,' she winked, 'but when I tire of him I'll be after you.'

Willie held up a hand of protest, 'Once bitten twice shy old girl.'

'You just picked the wrong woman, Willie,' Jenny sank back into her chair and Simon suspected he saw a brief look of concern pass across the tubby major's ruddy features.

'I say, isn't anybody going to introduce me to this vision?' he leered at Susan,

'Susan Blackburn,' Susan smiled and offered her hand which Willie kissed and bowed graciously.

'No wedding ring on such a lovely hand, perhaps I could be persuaded...' he began.

'She's young enough to be your daughter you old reprobate,' Jenny stood up as a mess waiter approached. 'Shall we dine, I'm starving.'

Dinner was lively and amusing affair and it was only when the meal was over and Jenny and Willie were reminiscing did Simon and Susan get the opportunity to have some private conversation.

'Jenny is only here until the day after tomorrow,' Susan told him, 'and then she is flying down to Singapore to see a specialist.'

'What's wrong with her?' he asked.

'They think cancer.'

Simon looked across at the beautiful refined woman who was laughing unrestrainedly at something Willie had said and found it difficult to believe that this was someone who was facing the possibility that she may have a terminal illness.

But Jenny's departure was one of the reasons for Simon's extraordinary feeling of pleasure; he would have Susan to himself. As he lay watching a flock of green-winged macaw's arguing in the trees opposite his open door, he experienced feelings of both selfishness and guilt.

Another reason for his feeling of euphoria was that he had been given his movement order for his return to the battalion. His regular visits to the physiotherapist was no preparation for jungle operations, and he had been given clearance from the MO to begin a fitness regime that included two visits to the gym every day, an early morning run and an afternoon hike round the immediate hills.

'There's only one way to get fit enough to carry a big pack up a hill and that's carry a big pack up a hill,' the wiry Scots Physical Training Corps WO2 had informed him with a malicious grin as he helped Simon heave a weighted pack onto his back.

After his run he showered, and with a growing sense of achievement went to breakfast. The mess was empty and Susan and Jenny only appeared when he was about to leave.

'I've got physiotherapy at nine,' he explained, 'but perhaps we could have coffee later.'

'I shall be leaving shortly, Simon, as soon as the helicopter arrives.' Jenny gave him her hand, 'It was lovely meeting you,' she smiled. 'When I spoke to the brigadier, on the telephone this morning I mentioned that I had met you,' she lowered her voice conspiratorially, 'and he told me, confidentially of course, that you're CO has put you forward for a decoration.'

'A decoration?' he still felt uncomfortable and annoyed, 'I did nothing.'

'That's not the way it's being seen by those who matter,' she patted his arm.

*

Lau's heart leapt and he had to restrain himself from shouting out. The view that he had of her was both brief and indistinct but he was certain that the girl hurrying along the crowded walkway was May Ling.

He was being conveyed in a police Land Rover through Kuala Lumpur to yet another army camp and a further excursion back into the jungle, but this time the walking would be minimal as there was the added thrill of a helicopter trip. But now the confidence and well-being that he was experiencing fled his soul, to once more be replaced with fear and concern.

The Land Rover drew to a halt in order to allow a group of school children to cross the busy street. With the traffic stationary those on the crowded walkways, who wanted to, seized the opportunity to cross to the other side.

In the mass he caught another glimpse of the girl and was even more convinced that it was she even though she did not have the unhealthy pallor of one who had spent a long period in the damp darkness of the forests and her jet hair was long and sleek, when he had last seen her it had been cropped, much like a mans.

Her lack of height made it impossible to pick her out and he dared not stand up to gain a more advantageous position, he did not want to attract the attention of his escort. He had been questioned regularly about May Ling, both at recognised interrogations, and in 'casual' conversation. It gave him satisfaction that he had so far revealed nothing, or at least nothing that he was aware of. The traffic began to move and the chance of spotting her again was lost.

On reflection, Lau realised that the interrogation he underwent when the subject of May Ling was raised was somehow a little different from the rest of the questioning. There was something in Inspectors Sankey's manner that had changed; it was as though he knew more than he wanted Lau to know. Lau was glad that he had been conscious of this difference from the start and had simply pleaded ignorance so that he would not be caught out in a lie or divulge anything that would be damaging to his cousin.

*

The camp was not full to capacity but there was more than the normal twenty or so skeleton staff that occupied it throughout the year. This suited Goh, security was increased, but his workload in the camp kitchen did not become too arduous, and the extended work level and greater numbers released him from any periods spent as a sentry. Goh

167

loathed being posted as a sentry; he always had, even before his terrifying experience a few weeks previously. It was not only the loneliness and fear of the enemy that made the task so abhorrent; it was his tendency to fall asleep when there was nothing else to occupy his mind. Sometimes, especially in the soporific afternoon heat, he would feel himself succumbing to the desire to sleep despite the terror that he attached to the duty. The punishment for sleeping, when on sentry, was non-negotiable, it was death. On more than one occasion he had woken with a start, alerted by the call of a bird or animal or snapping twig and sweating with fear at the thought that he could have been discovered by one of the camp leaders.

Another plus, when those in high office visited from across the border, was the improvement in the quality and quantity of food. Precious ammunition was made available to shoot a wild boar or mouse deer regardless of the security risk. Long treks were made down to Tasek Temengor and a variety of fish caught and dried. The jungle gardens, that they secretly cultivated, were visited and the best of the crops gathered. The rank and file however, did not benefit fully from the enhanced larder though they did experience an increase in the variety. But Goh and his two assistants made sure that they had a fair share of improved diet.

Osman Chang was in his early thirties, of slight build with delicate features his large eyes, wider than normal for a Chinese, were set beneath a particularly high forehead. He was a quiet thoughtful man and his slowness of speech belied a quick and intelligent mind. Osman was second in command of the MRLA.

His companion, at the split bamboo table where they ate in isolation, was Hor Lin, the army's propagandist. In contrast to Osman's serious demeanour Hor was rarely seen without a smile on his wide face. He was of a similar age to Osman but cut a bigger and more robust figure. The two men emptied their bowls noisily, belched in further gratitude and then rolled themselves fat cigarettes with black, coarse tobacco.

'Did you know him?' Osman asked blowing out a cloud of blue acrid smoke.

'I had met him because of his cousin, May Ling, but I couldn't claim to know him.'

'Beng Kim had nothing good to say about him,' Osman took a sheet of paper from his breast pocket and handed it to his companion, 'that's his letter informing me of the treachery.'

Hor read the letter in silence and then handed it back with a shrug, 'I think that it contains the words of an angry man, knowing Beng Kim he would have disposed of him long ago if they were his true thoughts.

'It matters not, he is beyond our reach for the moment, and the damage is done.' Osman folded the letter and returned it to his pocket, 'My main concern is whether we should vacate this base?'

'It would seem the safest course,' Hor agreed.

'According to Beng Kim he only came here once and he does not think that he could lead the British here.'

Hor shook his head, 'I still don't think that it is a risk worth taking.'

Osman examined the white ash at the end of his cigarette and then blew it off, 'I agree, we will move the base staff out into a number of small camps on the other side of the Lasah road for a few weeks, and leave a few experienced men in a well hidden camp nearby to see if the British find this. If they don't, then we can return after a period,' he gazed around the camp, 'It would be a shame to waste all of this.'

Hor smiled, 'True, I don't think that if they do discover it, they will have the patience to lie here in wait for very long but they may destroy it.'

'May Ling has requested to return inside,' Osman said changing the subject.

'Is she not more use to us where she is?' Hor was a little upset at this news as he had helped to place May Ling where she was.

'I am not sure,' Osman replied, 'I will give it some thought.'

They were silent for a while enjoying the cooling breeze that blew up the valley from the massive lake five miles to the north.

'He has been seen,' Osman said without looking at his companion.

Hor was taken aback, 'Who?'

'Lau Fong.'

'Where'?

'Kuala Lumpur.'

'You said that he was out of reach,' Hor said.

'He is at the moment,' Osman assured him, 'the British are still using him and don't let him stray,' a look of malevolence spread across his normally amiable features, 'but his usefulness will soon be exhausted and then...' he left the sentence unfinished.

Goh collected the dishes with a heavy heart; he had overheard the part of the conversation where the two men had discussed moving them into less comfortable surroundings. As night descended swiftly on the camp Goh squatted by the stream washing the dishes and pans, full of dread at the thought of the possibility of a long trek and weeks of hardship in a more primitive camp.

*

Captain Mike Peters, Royal Artillery, made the decision to return to base at 1702 precisely, just as the northern end of Lake Temengor and the high ridge of mountains that marked the border with Thailand came into view. He tilted the stick to the left and the Auster banked westward towards the setting sun. He kept the stick over and the light reconnaissance plane continued to bank until he was returning south along the lake at 5000 feet. At 1709 he crossed the bridge that carried the Grik road over the narrow channel where it divided into two distinct areas of water. To the left it divided again, and the right expanse continued south for another twelve miles, it was this one that Mike followed.

Ahead he could see black clouds descending over Gunong Besar and he knew a storm was approaching; great flashes of lightning lit the distant hills that were already disappearing into the shadow. Mike pulled back on the stick and the nose of the aircraft rose. Besar stood 5250 feet above sea level and he would normally have increased height and continued on his course but the storm ahead was to be avoided, his plan was to now to head west until he cleared it, flying over it was not really an option in an Auster.

As he turned to head for the Perak valley a sharp gleam of light on the forward slope of Besar caught his eye through a tiny break in the dense foliage. He quickly checked the map that was strapped to his thigh and fixed his position. Mike had been flying reconnaissance and spotting for two years over the vast jungles of the Malayan peninsula and he was in no doubt that he had just seen a fire. It could be an aboriginal village but it could also be the CT camp that was thought to be near the border. Mike was experienced enough not to go back for a closer look and continued on his journey back to base, happy that he was not spending the night by that fire with the storm about to break over them.

*

'Pete!'

Pete Thompson was heading for the camp gate and the taxi that was waiting for him there. He turned to face SSM Asher who was striding purposefully towards him.

'You just off, out?' Bill grinned seeing the look of exasperation on the sergeant's face.

'No, boss I always put on a clean shirt and strides for coal fatigues.'

'Sorry, pal,' the still present grin did not endorse his words, 'bit of a flap on and you're the boy the ol' man wants for the job.'

'I hope you're taking the piss,' Pete fell into step with the SSM, out of habit, as they both headed back towards the op's room, 'What about the standby troop?'

Bill patted Pete's shoulder, 'As I said, the old man wants you.'

'Come on Bill, what's it all about?'

The SSM took pity on his friend, 'You're gonna get briefed, but a spotter plane...Hey where d'you think you're going?'

Bob Gill and Dick Holt stopped when challenged, 'We're off out, boss,' Mick answered knowing full well that this was not now the case.

'Back to your billets,' Bill ordered, 'and catch as many of your troop as you can, you might be onto a good lead. As I was saying,' he continued turning his attention back to Pete, 'the pilot of spotter plane thought he saw a fire in the area where we think the camp is and where you did a search not long back, but Jack Hooper will give you all the gen.'

'I hope that Roger the bloody dodger's been caught for this as well,' Pete said indignantly.

'He's with IO now and he's not a happy man, he was planning a dirty weekend in Singapore with that little Chinese bird,' Bill grinned, 'he won't be getting his oats for a while I'm thinking.'

'This is something good and reliable I take it?' Pete asked, 'not the usual crap the 'green slime' feed us.'

'It's not from Intelligence although it came via them, and the 2i/c is an ex gunner and knows the pilot of the spotter aircraft,' Bill opened the door to the RIO's office, 'Sergeant Thompson sir.'

'Come in Pete,' D Squadron Commander, Johnny Hooper, and Roger were sat at a table facing a large map on the wall and the RIO stood facing the map fixing pins and cotton to represent bearings. Corporal's Jimmy Singleton and Ray Pell sat at another table; both were in civvies having also been prevented from partaking of a night's relaxation.

'You'll find a map on the table, Pete,' Captain Ted Doyle the RIO said, and then launched into his briefing, 'Situation, a little before 1800 today a fire was spotted at GR. 101064,' he pointed to the spot on the map and immediately everybody was interested.

*

Linda was relieved, to some extent, that her weekend in Singapore had been cancelled; it was the late notice that annoyed and disappointed her. She was relieved in that her relationship with Roger was becoming too serious for it was something she knew could not be and the longer it went on then the more difficult the inevitable parting would become.

Her disappointment and anger derived from the lateness of Roger's phone call, not that he could be blamed, and the way that she had received the message via a third person. As she was leaving the Central Police Headquarters, on her way to collect her case from her flat, a

171

young Malaya PC on the information desk where she had to sign out had given her the news.

'Miss Tang?' he enquired.

'Yes.'

'Will you call your office please,' he turned a telephone towards her.

Sergeant Marang answered, 'This is Linda Tang I've been asked to call...'

'Ha, Miss Tang,' the lewdness and pleasure in his voice almost crawled down the line, 'bad news I'm afraid, a Captain Howard has called and I'm afraid your, how do the British say, dirty weekend? Yes, that is what they call it; anyway yours will have to be cancelled due to operational demands.'

Linda put the receiver down without replying, and left the building tight lipped and struggling with her anger. The sergeant's sneering manner and the fact that she had been going away for the weekend with a man would already be common knowledge around headquarters.

*

The psychology of the regiment was to treat all training and every operation with the utmost seriousness, even the most mundane operation was approached with the positive attitude that contact with the enemy would be made and to expect determined resistance. Despite this attitude being held by all ranks there existed, at the troop briefing, an air of greater expectancy than normal as they viewed the large blackboard through a haze of tobacco smoke.

On the board was an unadorned sketch map of the operational area, the call signs of the bricks and their makeup.

'Insertion will be by chopper to a DZ on the Kemudu Estate and from there we will be taken by trucks from 5 Company Gurkha RASC to our drop of point here, our first drop off at GR 102050,' as he spoke the RIO pointed to the relevant spots on the large wall map, 'The three other drop off points along this road are here, here, and here. As you can see they are all sited along a very long incline, the trucks will not stop but will be moving slow enough to debus without indicating that security forces are being left there. At first light each group will then move off to the sites of their OP's'

He looked round the faces of those present and, like the Duke of Wellington surveying his troops over a hundred and years earlier, he was glad that they were on his side, 'You have all operated in this region and will recall that although very hilly it is all primary jungle, and consequently the going is fairly good, so each brick should have arrived at their OP's by last light, as on average you all have about five miles to cover. Any question's so far?' When there were none he continued, 'Seven days rations will be carried and re supply, if required, will be done by the 10ᵗʰ Gurkha's to ensure secrecy as drops by air would obviously alert any CT in the area.'

He went on to give details of the tasks and responsibilities of each brick. They were all to make every effort to avoid contact, the aim of the mission was primarily intelligence gathering and the recent sighting by the RA indicated that the likelihood of finding the camp had increased enormously.

'ETD is 1730 tomorrow evening,' the RIO ended his briefing, 'and at 0830 there will be rehearsals for debussing from a moving three tonner.'

'Weapons,' Pete gave his detailed briefing to his brick, 'Bob, you will carry your Remington with an extra twenty cartridges, the rest FN's with a hundred rounds in five mags and a bandolier of an extra fifty.'

'Am I not taking a Bren?' Jim Powell asked hoping that he had heard right.

Pete shook his head, 'What did I just say?'

'Just checking, boss,' Jim shrugged.

Pete turned to Tom Parnell, 'After rehearsal get your frequency from sigs, normal call sign I think, but double check. Weapon test, at 1100 on the twenty five-yard range, and Powell, as you seem to want to carry extra weight get two spare batteries for the radio and Bob collect a para flare, any questions?'

*

May Ling had fought down the urge to call out when the Land Rover had slowly passed by that morning. At first she had not recognised her cousin. The last time she had seen him, in a camp on the edge of a mosquito infested swamp just north of Kampong Kerung, he had looked pale, emaciated and tired. The man in the rear of the police truck looked a good deal heavier and had lost his jungle pallor.

The pleasure and excitement of seeing him was brief and his notoriety expelled any pleasure from her mind. As she looked quickly away she sensed his eyes fix on her, and she thought that he began to get to his feet but she hurried on hoping that he would not call after her. When she dared risk another look the Land Rover was picking up speed and through the throng around her she could see that he was looking in her direction but she was half concealed by a fat Tamil.

The light was failing as she entered the railway station and the concourse was a mass of humanity. Ten minutes later she was back on the street full of disappointment that there was no response to her request to return 'inside'.

Chapter Twenty One

Simon was not sure if he had ever really believed that he would end up as Susan's lover. He had hoped, in an almost puritanical way, that it would be possible. He had never experienced a great lust when in her presence; in fact he was almost afraid of the prospect, self-conscious of his own lack of experience.

His first experience had been with another Susan. Sue Milton worked as a typist at his father's builder's merchants; she was a Nordic looking blonde of sixteen with large blue eyes and a reputation to make her a target of every healthy youth in the vicinity. Their first coupling had taken place in the office store, one hot August afternoon, when Simon was on school holiday and earning some pocket money doing various tasks around the yard and office. His father thought it a good way to give his eldest son a wide experience of the business; fortunately he never knew just how wide ranging that experience was. The affair only lasted until he returned to school after the holidays. When he came home for Christmas Sue had left the company, and he heard that she had married a driver of one of the firm's suppliers, and had moved to Birmingham.

In the cool of the early morning Susan turned in her sleep and embraced him for warmth. The faint subtle scent of her perfume mingled pleasingly with the pleasant odour of her dried perspiration that had been induced by their recent activity.

Despite his adolescent experiences Simon considered that the previous night he had experienced the sexual act for the first time. There had been a gentle urgency in her lovemaking and although he knew that she was by far the more experienced of the two of them, he felt that he had not been guided but had led regardless of his virtual inexperience.

Susan had woken him gently with kisses on three occasions to renew their passion and now as the tropical morning sun thrust shafts of golden light through the slatted shutters he felt her hand slide down his chest and stomach and come to rest on his loins, she giggled.

*

Having stowed their cases on the luggage rack of the third carriage the four, with Sam in the lead, made their way to the restaurant car and laid claim to a table by the open door.

'Here luv,' Sam waved to the small tubby Chinese waitress, bar service was not permitted, 'Got to get a couple down your neck before the RTO nails you for train guard,' he informed the others.

'Whaa you wan',' the surly waitress stood with her stub of pencil raised over her pad.

'Four bottles of Anchor, sweetheart,' John grinned at her.

'Better make it eight,' Sam advised, 'it'll take ages to get served on here,' the carriage was filling fast.

'You can ony order one drink each,' she fixed Sam with her black sloe eyes, unblinking, daring him to challenge her authority. Sammy accepted the gauntlet by blowing her a kiss; she left shouting their order in shrill Cantonese to the barman.

'She's a sexy little bugger,' Sam leered after her, 'did yer see the tits on it.'

'For crying out loud, Sam let's get there,' Brian stood up, 'anyway she like a bloody barrel.'

'Grab it when yer can,' Sam replied undaunted.

'Give us yer boondocks,' Brian placed their rifles on the luggage rack. When travelling off duty all OR's had to wear uniform and were issued with a No 5 carbine and ten rounds of ammunition which were handed in at their destination.

'Right, corporal, you and your three men are on train guard,' a fat RASC WO2 loomed over them, his bush shirt already soaked with sweat merely from the effort of walking, 'report to me in the guard van,' he glanced at his watch, 'in ten minutes.'

Everybody else in the carriage tried to look sick, drunk or invisible and those at the far end departed swiftly.

'We're on leave, sir,' Ken replied quickly, 'we can't be detailed for....'

'Don't give me any back chat, corporal,' the fat CSM's jowls wobbled in anger causing the beads of sweat to run down his florid face, 'you're on guard, I don't give a fuck if you're going on bloody demob,' he looked at his watch again. 'Ten minutes in the guard van for your stag roster.'

'The fat bastard,' John muttered quietly.

'What did you say?' the fat CSM rounded.

'I said that's a bit of a bastard, sir,' John responded promptly and smiled.

He thrust a podgy finger at them and narrowed his eyes, 'I'll be watching you four,' he threatened.

During this exchange Ken had been considering their position and had recalled something he had seen an old wartime veteran do when he was at the depot. He stood up and took a ballpoint from his shirt pocket 'Excuse me, sir,' he called after the retreating, ungainly shape as the WO continued his search for 'volunteers.'

The fat CSM turned with a look on his face that was meant to deter argument. Ken picked up a beer mat and stepped into the aisle with pen poised, 'As I said we are going on leave...'

'And as I said, I don't give a fuck...' the WO2 began.

'And as we are on leave,' Keith cut in, 'we have been drinking and shouldn't be considered for guard duty, but we have to obey the order you have given us, even though I consider it to be an unlawful command. So I will need your name and unit so that I can report the facts to my commanding officer when we return to our regiment, just in case there's a mishap, and I will also require your signature,' he held out the pen and beer mat, meeting the WO's glare with the calm gaze of someone who is confident of his position.

The carriage had gone quite when the WO2 had revealed his mission, but now the silence was complete and the eyes of everybody were fixed on the two combatants. The train lurched into motion and the fat man had to steady himself by grabbing the back of a seat, his mouth hung open as he surveyed his adversary.

'He's right,' someone shouted from the far end of the carriage.

'Give him your name, fatty,' another voice added from the safety of his anonymity.

The little Chinese waitress pushed past the man's bulk and put the tray, bearing four glasses of beer, on the table, 'Two dollar eighty,' she held her hand out. Tentatively John passed her three one-dollar notes and waved her away.

Still the fat man had not spoken but stood holding onto the seat and staring at the defiant NCO who met his angry and bewildered look unflinchingly. A few more anonymous comments of support for Ken broke the silence.

The CSM gathered his wits and courage and he took a step closer to Ken. He was a man who obviously relied on his size and rank to intimidate, he was almost a head taller than Ken, 'I'll have you before this train arrives in Singapore, sonny,' he hissed, barely audible and with sheer hate in his eyes.

'Any fucking time fat man,' Ken replied at the same volume and indicated the man's medal ribbons with a nod of his head, 'I can see you were a bloody war hero so why don't you have a go now?'

Alongside his GSM for service in Malaya he had only the Defence Medal and 1939/45 Star, which registered a wartime service spent entirely in the United Kingdom. His scarlet hue deepened and he began to shake with suppressed rage and frustration, then suddenly he turned, and with a sprightliness and speed that surprised all present, he raced from the carriage and a loud mocking cheer followed him.

Although Simon was glad to be returning to the battalion he was also greatly disappointed that it had cut short what could have been a wonderful few days with Susan in the beautiful setting and climate of the highlands.

'Well, you seem to be fully recovered, old chap', Captain Connolly of the RAMC observed in his soft Irish brogue, 'and as your regiment are eager to have you back I can see no reason why you can't go today.' He reached across his desk for a pad, 'I'll put you on light duties for the next few days and you can see your own MO if you want it extending or even shortening if you feel the urge to get back to grips with the bandits.'

Susan was spending the rest of her week's leave at Cameron, with Jenny who was due to return the following day.

'It's a pity we couldn't have had another day before Jenny comes back' Susan said over lunch, 'what time do you leave?'

'At 1500,' Simon looked at his watch, it read 1240.

Susan smiled seductively and winked, 'Well if you don't linger too long over your lunch we could say a long goodbye over in the bungalow.'

It was because of Corporal Ray Pell's height, six feet three inches, that he saw the basha which his sharp-eyed leading scout, Dan Cullis, had missed. They were just beginning to descend from a ridgeline down a shallow, now dry, streambed of which the right-hand bank was about four feet high. From there the ground began to rise quite steeply away to the north. It was the straight line of the basha's apex that caught his eye. There are few straight lines in the jungle and it took a few heartbeats for him to discern its shape for sure. He made a clicking sound with his tongue to get Stan's attention and then made the hand signal to indicate that he had seen the basha, and pointed in its direction. The four men sank silently into defensive attitudes.

For five minutes they waited, silent, motionless and alert. Nothing stirred. Ray signalled that he was going to take a closer look. At a crouch, and moving painfully slowly, he noiselessly crept up the bank stopping every two or three steps to listen and sniff the air for the smell of food or scent of humans as he gradually approached the atap shelter.

He knew immediately that this was not a makeshift cover that had been hastily constructed. It was large enough to house four people, and even from a distance of two yards he could see the floor was flat and hardened from use, there was also a sleeping shelf constructed from split bamboo. As he turned and looked over his right shoulder to signal the others to close in he spotted another of equal proportions and between them, the thing that told him he had found a camp of some significance, a bunker with overhead cover. Ray returned to his patrol and led them away for about two hundred yards.

'It looks like we've found what we've been looking for,' he quickly and softly briefed them, 'I've seen two large basha's and a well-constructed bunker but no signs of occupation. Bill and Frank stay here, get on net, Frank and inform control we've found something, and put them on wait and listen. If I'm not back in an hour go off net to save the battery. Stan and me will go back and have a look around.' He wrote a GR on Frank's message pad, 'I think that's where we are but if we have a contact piss off to the last ERV, which is?' He pointed at Bill Cliffe, an earnest and quiet Cornishman.

'The outcrop of rocks about an hour back,' Bill pointed the way they had come.

'Good,' Ray discarded his Bergen and Dan did the same.

'Good luck lads,' Frank said as they left.

*

The adrenaline flowed freely in the RWL Tracking Team, they had been mobilised. Ben cajoled and pestered perfectly capable NCO's to speed up the process of drawing rations, arms and ammunition.

'They can only draw their weapons one at a time, sir,' 'Boggy' pointed out laconically. Sergeant Marsh's relaxed style was not ruffled even by Ben's bellicose exuberance.

'Well get them to do it more quickly,' he turned without waiting for a reply and charged across to the stores to harry those still drawing rations.

'Boggy' raised an eyebrow, 'More haste less speed, Super Spud.' Ben's nickname was now common knowledge in the battalion.

The newly arrived Australians had been involved in a contact, with a group of CT in the jungle north of Kampong Enjol, in which they had lost one man but killed two of the enemy. The platoon commander in question had been surprised by the fight that the CT had put up having been told, whilst undergoing his jungle training at the JTC, that their enemy rarely stood and fought unless they had superior numbers or had the natural advantage, such as a planned ambush. As the Australians had not yet had time or the experience to form their own tracking team they had, with great reluctance, requested the assistance of the Poms; it had been a bitter pill to swallow.

Ben had suggested the Australians fly a couple of sections up to a little known DZ just below the spot height 1324, to act as a cut off party. During his time in the SAS he had used it a couple of times.

Having to request help from the Poms had been humiliation enough but to be given advice, unsought, really did stick in the craw. Fortunately the company commander in question could see the sense in Ben's suggestion, especially has he had no idea that the DZ even existed, and had already decided to send a platoon by road to the plantations well to the north.

By 1130, the men, dogs and Iban's were on the square awaiting the arrival of the two Whirlwind helicopters that would take them their DZ, the Padang in Kampong Enjol.

*

The reason for Sergeant major George Vasey's trip to Singapore was to collect twenty of the new Bedford three tonner's from the huge ordnance depot at Changi. He had been pleased with the assignment, excited even; new vehicles always caused a thrill to run through an RASC company, they were like children receiving toys at Christmas. To carry out his assignment he had with him twenty drivers and another twenty to act as relief drivers and vehicle escorts.

His spirits had been dampened somewhat when he had been detailed as the train's guard commander. It was usually the responsibility of a commissioned officer, but as the only commissioned officer travelling was a captain in the Chaplains Department the RTO had not considered it appropriate to saddle a man of the cloth with what was a combat role.

The bonus, so he thought, of being detailed for this duty was that he could keep his own men free of the onerous task, but despite wanting to save his men the tedium and fatigue of a guard he also wanted the guard to comprise mainly of combat troops, the idea of a gang of clerks and drivers protecting the train filled him with horror, they would be more likely to shoot themselves and other passengers than the enemy. But finding sufficient infantry proved harder than George imagined. Every foot soldier he managed to find already appeared to be three sheets to the wind and having a guard comprised of drunken squaddies was not a good idea.

His confrontation with the four Royal West Lancashire's had warned everyone off and lowered his spirits, the humiliation that he had suffered at the lance-corporals hands called for some form of revenge, and that was still under consideration. George was still not sure that the NCO's argument was valid but he was not confident enough to take a chance. Eventually he had managed to find fourteen troops who were not already under the influence of alcohol or sick but only four were from an infantry regiment. He was surprised how compliant the four men of the South Wales Borderers were, almost eager, and luckily one of them was a corporal so he could leave all of the responsibility in his hands and he would be able to get a good night's sleep.

Among his charges he had Corporal James, a university man, who was normally employed in the transport office. Jack James was built like a beanstalk and was little more than useless when it came too commanding men, he was timid and without a grain of military aptitude. He was coming to the end of his National Service and had only been included in the group, by the OC, so that there was at least one person with a grain of intelligence in the party.

George was grateful of Lance-corporal Hayes inclusion, he had been an infantryman and only been transferred into the RASC three months earlier. From the tales he told he had some experience of fighting the CT. George liked Barry and would not normally have detailed him for the guard but he had no choice.

'Sorry about this, Barry lad,' George laid a fatherly hand on his shoulder, 'but I've only managed to grab one NCO and I can't put that educated idiot James in charge, you're the only man that I've got that I can trust.'

Lance-corporal Barry Hayes glowed, 'You can rely on me, sir,' the single stripe that he had gained had boosted Barry's confidence to a dangerous level. He had successfully put his brief life in the RWL's behind him, and what he did care to recall was a distorted recollection of the true events.

'The CT had put a price on my head,' he had informed his new brothers in arms, when he had been transferred, 'CO said to me, I don't want to lose you Hayes but it wouldn't be fair to put you in such a lot of danger.'

'What price did they put on you, Bas?' a gullible youth, newly arrived at 3 Company, asked.

Barry paused for a moment, '$50, 000,' he said.

The youth whistled in shocked admiration, 'Wow you must have caused them problems, Bas.'

'Look, Rawlings,' Barry donned his chummy NCO demeanour, 'I don't mind you calling me Bas but when the sergeant's around or any of the officers you have to call me corporal.'

The RASC was mainly comprised of misfits who ranged from thugs with lengthy criminal records to frail juveniles who had only just scrapped through the army's medical examination. In addition there were people like Barry who had enlisted in more active units but had failed to live up to the standards. Discipline was of a very low level due to the poor quality of the men and equally low quality of their leaders; it was from this Corps that nearly half of the train guard was formed.

As instructed by CSM Vasey, Corporal Watkin, and his three South Wales Borderers, reported to the guard van which substituted as the guardroom. In their starched, neatly pressed, OG's and their healthy glow that comes from a high degree of fitness, they stood out from the crumpled unwashed look of the RASC drivers.

'I've organised the stags,' Barry handed Jack Watkin a mill board with a smug look, 'I used to be in the infantry,' he added.

Jack studied the list without reply, 'I see your guys are on the early stags and the other units have got them from 2200,' he said at last fixing Barry with a hard look.

'I told him to do that, corporal,' George called from the rear of the van where he was in discussion with the RTO. He came forward, 'My lads are picking up vehicles in Singapore and then driving back up to Ipoh, they'll need their sleep.'

Jack nodded but his agreement was unconvincing, he turned back to Barry, 'And you're my 2i/c?' the disdain in his voice and eyes was undisguised but passed Barry by.

'I am,' he bubbled, 'I used to be in the infantry.'

'So you said,' the laconic Welshman replied, 'I'd have never known.'

*

The Whirlwinds descended one by one onto the Padang in a shower of dust, deposited their human cargoes and then departed into a leaden sky the pilots happy in the knowledge that they were not one of the 'brown jobs' who were about to be immersed in the approaching storm.

As the team organised themselves ready to move off two figures, armed and kitted out in patrol order, emerged from the home guard hut by the main gate.

They were both big men, the eldest of the two spoke; 'Who's in charge?' the accent was clearly antipodean.

'I am,' Ben heaved his pack onto his back, 'Captain Murphy.'

The big man extended his hand, 'Sergeant Murphy 3rd Australian, sir,' he pumped Ben's hand vigorously; 'we must be bloody relatives,' he grinned, 'call me Spud.'

'You're our guides?' Ben asked.

'Sure are, sir. This here's Private Billington; he'll take you to the contact point. Shit hot tracker, part Abo, but we think that that part is just his dick.'

'Very useful,' Ben smiled, 'and what do we have the pleasure of calling you, private?'

'Name's Billy sir, nicknames, Goat.'

*

Thirty miles away, on Gunong Besar, Ray and Dan moved from basha to basha with care making sure they left no sign of their passing. It took them an hour to pace out the camp's dimension's and then make a detailed sketch plan as close to scale as the conditions permitted. Ray then made notes on the surrounding geographical pattern and types of cover. They also found the sentry posts and discovered the carpet of dry bamboo branches that look natural enough but were obviously there to provide audible warning.

'How long d'you reckon they've been gone?' Dan asked offering a handful of raisins to his partner.

Ray shrugged, 'A week?' he shoved the fruit in his mouth.

'No more,' Dan agreed.

When they re-joined the others Ray gave them a quick briefing on what they had discovered, 'They must have found signs that we've been in the area,' Ray mused, 'and the low flying Auster must have put the wind up 'em,' he added.

'Doesn't look as though it's been abandoned though,' Dan said shaking his head.

'Go on net and tell control we'll meet the others at ERV one, we don't want 'em swanning round up here,' Ray undid the straps on his Bergen, 'Let's have a brew'.

Just before dusk the troop met up at the top of the ridge that ran at right angle to the one on which the camp was sited.

'So the pilot was smack on with his reference,' Roger said at the end of Ray's debrief.

'We must have passed pretty close to it last time we were up here,' Pete studied his map, 'we were getting views of the lake and I reckon we moved down this side of the ridge which must have put us within a couple of hundred yards.'

'They couldn't have known you were there or they'd have legged it a while back,' Corporal Jerry Singleton said. Jerry was another Liverpudlian who seemed always to have a permanent smile on his rugged ruddy face. Two years previously, whilst serving with his parent regiment, the Kings, in Korea, he had taken part in the Battle of the Hook.

'That's true, or they would have done then what they've probably done now,' Ray agreed, 'They think that they may have been compromised and they've made themselves scarce intending to return the threat is past. So the chances are they aren't very far away, they'll be keeping an eye on it; we'll have to be very careful.'

'I think you're probably right, Ray,' Pete agreed, 'but if they did know we were here last time and then got spooked by the Auster they'll know we're seriously looking for 'em.'

'You don't think the camp was full last time it was occupied?' Roger asked.

'Naw,' Ray was adamant, 'if there'd have been about two hundred, which is what the full complement would seem to be, we're sure to have picked up some tracks.'

'How many, then?' Pete knew Ray had the experience not to exaggerate.

'Twenty, maybe thirty,' he replied.

'Suggestions,' Roger said.

'We should stake it out,' Pete said without hesitation, Jerry and Ray nodded in agreement, 'if they're gonna return,' Pete continued, 'they'll probably send a couple of good men to lie up and watch for a couple of days so we'll have to be cuter and quieter than them.'

'Where, who, how many, and for how long?' Roger was happy to let his experienced NCO's make the plan.

'Where,' Pete echoed, 'you'll have to decide that, Ray, and I think you're gonna have to be one of the lucky ones who gets the job.'

Ray shrugged, 'I guessed that much.'

'You're best picking the spot also,' Roger said and then wished he hadn't.

'Are you a specialist in stating the fucking obvious, boss?' Jerry asked.

'Sorry,' Roger apologised, 'How long do we need to stay?'

'Well we've got five days rations left so I think the first team should stay up there for four, and then we'll reconsider the situation,' Pete looked at each of them in turn expecting input.

'A full brick'? Ray asked.

'Two would probably be better,' Pete said thoughtfully, 'but you'll need a radio,' he hesitated. 'It's your game, Ray, you've seen the ground what would you prefer?'

'One brick, two's too many. And there can be no other movement in the area of the ridge.'

'We can't all sit here for five bloody days twiddling our thumbs,' Jerry protested.

'Well we can't really be moving about much in the area,' Roger said, 'cos if they have only pulled out with the intention of returning when they know it's safe, they won't have gone too far as Ray said and could have a couple of small units camped up anywhere round here just waiting to recce when they thinks it's safe.'

'Yeah, you're right, boss,' Pete agreed, 'we're gonna have to keep a very low profile.'

'We'll keep busy with some Egyptian PT,' Jerry looked at Roger and grinned, 'Okay Boss?'

*

Simon arrived back at Battalion in the height of the afternoon heat. The camp was quiet and almost deserted. The hustle and bustle of the morning had passed. The band were no longer at rehearsal, the daily flow of the sick the lame and the malingerers to the MI room was over, the MT park was no longer active with REME fitters and drivers attending the scores of trucks, revving and filling the air with their noxious fumes, and the individual company parades were long past.

Although he had only been absent from the regiment for a little over four weeks he felt like a stranger. There was nobody in the mess, not even a waiter, and on his walk to 'A' Company office, a matter of a hundred yards, he passed a half a dozen men and did not recognise any of them.

As he reached the top of the hill, on which all of the company offices stood, he could see a lot of activity on the sports fields beyond the company lines and realised that the absence of bodies in the camp was due to the fact that it was Wednesday, sports day.

CSM Raven was alone in the company office preparing the paper work for the annual range qualification that every soldier in the army had to undergo once a year, 'Welcome back, sir,' he said looking up from his task.

'Thank you, sergeant major,' Simon took the offered hand, 'this camp's like the Marie Celeste.'

'It's sports afternoon, sir.'

'Yes I realised when I saw the sports field. Is the OC about?'

'No, the CO's on a short leave, and Major Winslow is standing in for him at a brigade briefing.'

'Is there something brewing then?' Simon asked eagerly.

'Nothing special apart from Operation Clive, anyway you won't be ready for op's yet, Mr Gates, will you?''

'I feel great,' Simon protested, 'I've been getting some training in over the last week and although the MO has put me on light duties I think I would benefit from a short op just to test myself.'

'Well you're looking fit, sir, but there's nothing down for your platoon at the moment as far as op's go, but they're on the range tomorrow for their classification.'

'Oh well I shall be able to join them on that. Where's Sergeant Snell at the moment?'

184

'Not sure sir, he could either be over on the sports field or in the platoon lines.'

'I'll wander over there's sure to be some of the chaps about, seems ages since I saw them.'

*

Full of his own importance, Barry led his five relief sentries through the carriages, posting a fresh man on each verandah and the man relieved replaced his relief in the file. Barry's gait was unusual and had caused the drill instructors during his training at the depot a great deal of grief and his squad members a lot of extra drill.

'You march like a fucking pregnant penguin, Hayes,' was the common scream of frustrated NCO's. They had not rectified this deficiency and he had therefore not been permitted to take part in the passing out parade.

It was his peculiar gait that caught Sam's eye as the little procession entered the restaurant carriage.

'Hey, it's that little shit, Hayes,' he yelled, 'Bloody hell he's been made up, who the fuck gave you a tape, Hayes?' Sam was on his fourth bottle of Anchor and the entire assembly turned at the sound of his shouted welcome.

Barry knew the voice instantly and he visibly shivered and had to overcome the urge to flee. In an instant he decided that the best form of defence was attack, but this turned out to be flawed strategy.

He turned and put on his new NCO stern face, 'Corporal to you, Andrews,' he tapped the solitary stripe, 'what do you think this is?'

'A piece of bird shite if you've got it on yer arm, Hayes,' John Cantrill joined in, 'I know the RASC are a shower but I didn't know they could be that fucking desperate, and you still look like a sack of diarrhoea with a belt on.'

Four of the relief's were from Barry's unit and he was aware that they were laughing along with the rest of the carriage. For a moment he thought assistance was on the way when he saw CSM Vasey enter the compartment from the other end, but the prospect of aid was quickly dispelled. When George heard the commotion, and then saw the four West Lancashire's baiting his NCO he concluded that Lance-corporal Hayes would find it a character building experience and he turned around and retraced his steps.

George was also to undergo a character building encounter before they reached Singapore that was to leave him a little shell-shocked, a condition that he had never left himself open to throughout his service. Closing the bar had been a task that he had been dreading and it proved more daunting than he could have ever imagined. Corporal Watkin was nowhere to be found when the dreadful moment arrived and he had to enter the baying, singing throng with only Barry as back-up. George knew that he was already a figure of fun from his previous encounter in the carriage and he knew that his back-up would be of little use.

After an hour of merciless ribbing and delaying tactics they finally oversaw the bar closed, all drink consumed, and all glasses removed. By midnight George had gratefully climbed into his bunk in the sleeper compartment. Just as he had finally managed to escape his troubled day and had slipped into the sheltered comfort of sleep, he was dragged back to the torment of his onerous duty.

'We've been ambushed, sir, we've been ambushed,' the little chubby lance-corporal had lost his flushed complexion, and was a deathly shade of grey that was discernible even in the dim safety light.

It took George a few precious moments to gather his reason but it was soon apparent that the train was still in motion, and apart from one or two heads emerging from behind the bunk curtains to enquire, irritably, what was going on, there was nothing to indicate the doom that Barry was reporting.

George rubbed his eyes and sat up banging his head on the bunk above which did little to improve his temper, 'What the fuck d'you mean, we've been ambushed?' he looked around, 'we're still moving.'

'I heard shots,' Barry's panic was unabated, and he kept glancing furtively over his shoulder as if expecting a Chinese horde to come storming into the carriage with guns blazing.

'You heard a fucking shot?' George heaved his bulk to a standing position and tensed against the sway of the train, 'Have you looked out of the window to see if they're galloping alongside on fucking horses?' He put on his bush jacket glaring at Barry the whole while; 'You'd better...' before he could finish his sentence Driver Speight, a dim witted cockney, entered the coach.

'Ere' guv,' he began in his usual manner. George had given up on trying to explain to Speight that, sir, was the correct form of military address when speaking to officers and WO's, 'Yer better come quick those bleeding Welshmen 'ave gone of their 'eads.'

To his horror George saw that Speight's rifle was pointing directly at his ample midriff, 'Watch where you're pointing that fucking rifle, Speight,' he pushed the muzzle away, 'I hope there's not one up the spout?'

'Nah, don't fink so,' he opened the bolt and ejected a live round noisily on to the carriage floor.

As they approached the restaurant car Barry's alarming story was confirmed to some degree, a loud report came from the platform at the

186

far end of the coach and the muzzle flash of a rifle stabbed the darkness. The three of them stopped.

George drew his service revolver and waved Barry and Speight ahead of him. When they were about half way along the carriage they could hear voices, over the clatter of the train's wheels, praising the Land of my Father.

'Sergeant major bloody, Vasey,' Corporal Watkin appeared in the open door with a half empty rum bottle in one hand and his rifle in the other, 'come and join our demob party, boyho.'

George was both relieved and angry, 'Did you just fire that shot?' he could barely believe what he was seeing.

'No,' Watkin grinned drunkenly and swayed, 'that was Dai, I ran out of ammo a while back, they only give you ten rounds you know.'

'You're under arrest corporal, and all those with you.'

Jack Watkin laughed, 'Oh I'm shitting myself, boyho, I've got three bloody weeks to do, and you think I'm worried about your silly little charge,' he lurched towards George. 'Here have a pull of this and join the party.'

'Corporal Hayes, arrest these men,' George ordered. Two more SWB's entered the coach from the balcony and another shot echoed through the night. Barry thought that the end of the world was nigh.

Chapter Twenty Two

Sandes Home was all that they had hoped, and just a little more. The taxi deposited the rumpled, hung over, quartet at the main entrance as a tropical storm ended and the scorching Malayan sun emerged raising steam from the wet roads and walkways.

'I'm gonna get a kip for a couple of hours,' Ken dumped his bag by the reception desk.

'You're on leave with Sam, Duffy, there'll be no time for sleeping,' Sam banged the brass bell on the counter several times.

'Once will be sufficient young man,' the woman appeared from behind a rattan screen. Her grey hair was tied back in a neat bun, she had the air of another age, and although her words of reprimand were telling her eyes were kind and her lined face had an angelic quality. Deftly, like a card sharp, she dealt four cards onto the counter.

'Fill these in please,' the edge had gone from her voice, 'and then Tam will take you to your rooms,' she rang the bell twice and her eyes met Sam's as if challenging him to pass comment, the gauntlet was not taken up.

'You will find the rules of Sandes Home in your rooms but the main ones are; no alcohol in camp or swearing, and no visitors in your rooms. You may have visitors in the public areas, the lounge or the games room and swimming pool,' her voice took on a more severe tone, 'There are no second chances, you will be asked to leave if you break the rules and your unit will be notified.' They completed the cards in silence sensing that here was a lady who was not to be crossed. She continued, 'To your left is the dining room and beyond is the lounge and to the right of that is the games room.'

Sam could not resist, 'Where's the bar?'

She took his card and read it, 'What does the S stand for?'

'Sam.'

'Well Sam, my name is Sally Feltham and I hope that you and I do not cross swords because you will most certainly lose,' she smiled sweetly, 'Tam will show you to your rooms,' a small smiling Malay had appeared at the sound of the bell.

'You do stick your bloody neck out, Andrews,' Brian said when they were outside.

'Miserable old cow,' Sam grumbled, 'we're gonna have a great fucking leave. Whose idea was it to come here?'

'Keith's,' John reminded him.

'It is a Christian organisation,' Ken pointed out.

'Lady Feltham very good person,' Tam informed them over his shoulder as he led them along the open verandah.

'Lady Feltham?' Brian said, surprised, 'the title, lady?'

'Give over,' Sam ridiculed, 'that old bag, a lady.'

Tam stopped and turned, the smile gone, 'You bad man, Lady Feltham not old bag, she wife of General Feltham, good lady, very kind.'

'Trust you Andrew's,' John exploded, 'you've only got up the nose of the GOC FARELF's, wife.'

Their rooms were all next door to each other, and there was a shower block at the end of the verandah with the added luxury of hot water. At the top a shallow rise, in front of the block, was a modern fifty-yard swimming pool, two tennis courts and two badminton courts.

'This place is great,' Ken looked around; his desire to sleep had gone as soon as they had all changed into civilian clothes.

'It's nearly half past twelve,' Brian said, 'shall we have some scoff here before we go into town?'

'Might as well,' John agreed, 'we've paid for it.'

Normally Sam would have dissented; eager to get to the action but the morning's confrontation with Sally Feltham had left him a little subdued.

'You're quiet Sam,' John grinned as they made their way to the dining room, 'anything wrong?' he nudged Brian.

'Oh no, no, just feeling a bit tired.'

Ken turned the knife, 'Oh, this is the Sam who won't have any time for sleeping.'

'I didn't say I wanted to sleep,' he defended, 'I just said I was tired. A couple of beers and I'll be right as rain.'

'It's nothing to do with Sally getting a grip of yer then, Sam?' John grinned, 'You bit off more than you could chew with that one.'

Sam snorted in scorn at the thought of such a thing, a mere woman putting Sam Andrews down.

'We could have a swim first,' Ken suggested checking his watch, 'we've got another half-hour before dinner.'

'Could have had a pint as well,' Sam lamented as they walked back to their rooms to change, 'if it had been a bit more civilised. '

*

Simon regretted, to some degree, the welcome afforded him in the mess the previous night, but his throbbing head was, in a sense, relieved by the genuine pleasure that everybody had expressed at his returned. It was like returning to the bosom of a loving family, even Captain Tetlow, who had little time for National Service subalterns, clapped him on the back with a hand the size a large dinner plate almost dislocating his shoulder.

'You'll have a drink with me young, Gates,' Simon was sure that it was an offer but is sounded more like an order delivered in Alf's best parade ground voice.

Simon felt something of a fraud being treated like a returning hero, the events and a strong desire to live had driven his actions and courage had not featured as far as he was concerned.

The company office was empty but he could hear voices coming from the company commander's office, he knocked a little tentatively on the door-frame upright.

'Welcome back, Simon come in, have a seat,' Big Jack motioned towards the chair against the wall, 'bring it over,' he indicated the spot in front of his desk.

Chris Whitely, the Company 2i/c, sat at a desk on the other side of the office, 'We nearly gave your platoon away, Simon, a new subaltern, but no doubt you've already been informed of Mr Crompton – Hughes's exploits.'

'Don't mention that bloody man's name in my presence,' Big Jack covered his face with both hands and groaned, 'but he is where he belongs now, pushing bits of paper round a bloody desk in Singapore.'

Simon thought it best not to comment on his temporary replacement and changed the subject, 'I'd like to get back onto OP's as soon as I can sir.'

'Straight back into the saddle ay, Simon?' The OC smiled approvingly.

'Yes sir,' Simon said hopefully.

'Well the MO has confirmed that you should be on light duties,' he read a file on his desk and then looked up, 'but I suppose it is how one interprets 'light duties'.'

'The Colonel has asked us to arrange for an overnight patrol for the reporter from the Bolton News, sir, that shouldn't be too arduous,' Captain Whitely suggested.

'Good idea, Chris, a couple of sections would do because a number of your chaps are on leave, Simon. Yes, a little two day jaunt up the back of Tanjong Rambutan would serve both purposes,' he stood up, went over to the Battalions area map on the wall behind Chris's desk, and motioned Simon to join him. With a pencil he indicated a stream that ran down from the ridge between two spurs, 'As I recall that's good primary stuff, and you have to pass through a few hundred yards of belukar to get to it so it will give the paper chappies a good understanding of the sort of country we operate in, plus it's a pretty steep climb.'

'Pity we couldn't have included a swamp,' Captain Whitely observed.

'They're civilians, Chris; don't want to kill the buggers,' he returned to his desk, 'I'll leave it all in your hands, Simon, the planning and the preparation. Go and see the RIO to get area clearance, and then decide how you are going to entertain our friends from the press.'

*

Since his move to KL Lau had not been questioned with same intensity that he had previously and although preparation had been made for another excursion into the jungle it had been cancelled at the last minute for reasons to which he had not been made party. Not that he was in any way troubled by the cancellation, or the reason, Lau was becoming accustomed to the comfortable life that he now lived and was not eager to endure the privations of jungle life again even though it was vastly different with the security forces.

He was now able to enjoy untroubled sleep in a degree of comfort and safety that that he had almost forgotten existed. He had also put on weight, regular meals and reduced exercise had added a little over a stone and he had noticed that his haunted and haggard look had begun to recede.

The sound of the key in the cell door surprised him; he had not heard anyone approaching.

John Sankey entered the cell and the door was shut behind him, 'Sorry about the last minute changes to our plans, Lau,' he sat down on one of the folding chairs, 'There have been some developments in the area that we were going too and the army have denied us any access.'

'This is the area of the state camp?' he asked

Sankey nodded, 'We may not need to use you to find it if the information from the army's as reliable as they believe.'

'I am sorry that I could not have been more helpful, but as I told you I had only been there once,' he said, relieved that he would not have to be instrumental in such a major event where so many of his previous comrades may be killed.

'I am prepared to offer you a greater degree of freedom, Lau, if you feel that you're ready to handle it,' John said watching his reaction closely.

Lau hid the shock well and his expression remained dispassionate as a cold fear radiated through him, 'What degree of freedom?' he asked.

'We would give you a new identity, a safe house in a district where you weren't known, and part of your reward money,' Lau's foreboding began to dispel as the inspector talked, 'We would help you obtain work and after a few months you would be assisted to move to another state or country of your choice, if that is what you wanted,' he paused to give Lau an opportunity to respond.

The pause was long as the one considered all the advantages and disadvantages of the extended latitude and the other scrutinised for any sign that would indicate his true feelings over the offer regardless of the spoken word.

In the end it was Lau who spoke, 'I would still be in some danger could I be armed?' John nodded but remained silent and Lau's thoughts raced, 'could I have a bodyguard?'

John shook his head, 'I don't think that would be a good idea, it could draw attention to you and the safest thing for you is to merge into the population. Moreover, the fewer people who know your true identity the safer you will be,' after another pause he added, 'We would still require some assistance from you so we would be in touch.'

'But what else can I do, I've shown you all the food dumps that I know about, and the camps, except for this big one, but I think you almost have as much idea where it is as I do.'

'Possibly,' John agreed, 'but there still may be ways that you can help and that's the deal.'

'Alright,' Lau said agreed eventually, 'where will it be, my safe house?'

'Here in KL, nobody knows you here.'

*

The camp was perfectly sited and Ray had difficulty in selecting a spot to set up an OP in which he would feel confident that it would not be compromised, and would have some sight of the camp. In the end he decided that the safest place would be by the only stream in the locality. It was almost a hundred yards from the camp but was their closest source of water and they would be forced to use it, he would just have to select the most likely place.

A thick patch of mixed, dense, vegetation concealed the top of a high bank situated on a bend in the stream. The foliage extended down the bank and obscured the stream from view at that point, but to the left, and right it afforded an acceptable view of places that would make ideal water points; low banks and some depth to the water.

Two of them took most of the morning constructing the site, while the other two kept watch. They burrowed into undergrowth from the side opposite from the stream, and had to force a tunnel through twenty yards of thorn, and a thick mass of rotting vegetation before they could form the hide. Because of the density of the undergrowth they were able to create a large area to lie up with sight of both potential water points. They all knew that they had eaten their last hot meal and drunk their last mug of hot tea, for possibly four days. From now on it would be cold beans or stew and water tainted by the bitter taste of purification tablets. They had all managed to exchange, with those not on the OP, their Swifts tinned stew for the nutritious and filling oatmeal blocks that were light to carry, the going rate being three oat blocks for one tin of stew. To avoid any temptation Ray made them leave their cigarettes behind with the Troop.

Although the main purpose was to act as an OP their visibility did not extend beyond the opposite bank of the stream. It had, therefore, been agreed that once a day two of them would move closer to the camp making sure to approach it from a different direction every time, and leave no tracks. It was very possible that the CT may not use that part of the stream for their water supply.

No sooner were they all ensconced in the hide, and had organised their kit than they heard the hiss in the trees that heralded an impending downpour. The first heavy drops fell at 1310 hours and it was still pounding through the leaves as the darkness enveloped them, and the long cold night began.

*

Despite their original plans they had remained at Sandes and after their lunch they had played snooker, lazed around the pool, and slept. At 1800 hours, refreshed, they took a taxi from the waiting line outside the camp gate and headed for the bright lights of Singapore. Without argument they had gone directly to the Nuffield Club to eat.

'Where now?' Sam wiped his mouth with the back of his hand.

'Shall we have a few jars here?' Brian suggested, they were in agreement and went upstairs to the bar that overlooked the pool. The bar was busy without being too crowded and they managed to get a table on the balcony.

'There's some fair looking birds here,' Sam looked around hopefully.

'You've no chance with them,' John said loudly, 'they aren't looking for quick jumps, and they've latched onto fucking blanket stackers and pen pushers that are based here.'

'Hey mate,' a heavily made up girl on a nearby table leaned across, 'are you from Liverpool?' her accent was thick.

'No love,' Ken answered for John, 'he just talks like that to try and sound sophisticated.'

'Piss off,' the girl smiled and her hard look softened, 'yer a Scouser. Where are yer from la'?'

'Aigburth,' John replied, 'where you from, girl?'

'Kirkland.'

'Kirkland,' John echoed, 'they eat their young there don't they?'

'Cheeky bastard, there's nothing wrong with Kirkland.'

'What are drinking,' Brian knew this conversation could go on for a while; Liverpudlian's were rarely short of words.

'I'll have a rum and coke,' the girl held out her glass.

'Do I look as though I'm made of money, love,' Brian said as he turned towards the bar.

'Tight sod,' she called after him.

Sam saw his opportunity to be in the company of the opposite sex, which, apart from the visit to the brothels of Ipoh, was something he had been deprived of since leaving Blighty. There were six men and another three girls sat at the table with the girl.

Sam crouched by her and placed his hand on her bare back, 'I'll buy you a drink sweetheart.'

'It's alright, mate we've a got a kitty going,' the man said who was sitting next to her. He was large, dark haired and was carrying excess fat indicating an inactive life style and he spoke without dialect, upper class possibly but most definitely southern.

'Is he your fellah?' Sam asked the girl ignoring the man.

'We work together,' the man said.

Sam continued to talk to the girl, 'Are you WRAC?'

Again the man responded, 'We're from RAF Changi and were all work mates,' he leant forward as if to add emphasis to his words.

'Your magic,' Sam said looking into the girls eyes.

'Why?' she smiled expecting some flattery.

'You can talk without moving your lips.'

'Go on yer silly bugger,' she gave him push and he fell backwards laughing.

'What's your name?' he asked when he had recovered.

'Deirdre, what's yours?'

Sam felt the excitement of a conquest, regardless of the fact that she was in the company of friends, she was paying attention to his chat up. 'Sam,' he replied, 'usually known as Sam the sex time-bomb,' this brought forth-another squeal of laughter and another push for Sam.

'What's he like?' she directed this remark at John.

'We put up with him,' John replied.

Brian returned with the drinks.

'Where's mine?' Deirdre was clearly not one who took no for an answer. Brian ignored her and placed the tray on the table.

Sam persisted, 'I said I'd buy you drink darling, what are you having?'

'No you're alright, Sam, like Jack said, we've got a kitty and I bet you're a National Serviceman,' Deirdre lit a cigarette that she had been given.

'Bloody right I'm a nashie, I'm not thick enough....' the words tailed away as he remembered that John and Ken had both signed on for the extra year.

'Have you just arrived in Singapore?' another of the men sat at the table asked. Even seated it was apparent that he was exceptionally tall with a prominent nose and same middle class accent.

Brian paused with his glass half way to his lips, 'Just arrived? Do we look like bloody sprogs?'

'None of you seem to be very tanned,' he looked around those at his table as though to confirm his theory by the healthy brown of his companions.

'You don't get a bloody tan in the ulu,' Brian retorted.

'Are you combat troops then?' the first man asked.

Sam preened, 'We've done a bit.'

'What's like in the jungle?' another of the girls asked wide-eyed.

'How long have you got?' Sam prepared to launch into a jungle story.

'Just like the Tarzan films,' Brian grinned, 'exotic birds flitting through the trees, cool gurgling streams, amazing fruit just waiting to be picked; mind' he warned, 'you have to be careful not to stand on the orchids.'

'What about the snakes and spiders?' Deirdre shuddered.

'No problem,' John joined in, 'just stamp on the spiders and bite the heads off the snakes.'

'Are taking the piss?' Deirdre's eyes narrowed.

'Course they are,' the big dark haired man said.

'You're RAF?' Brian confirmed.

'Yes.'

'Well what the bloody hell do you know about it?'

'Well I'm so naïve as to believe that it's anything like you're relating,' he smiled to show that he was not calling them liars and saw their joke.

'Well how about stinking swamps, mosquitoes by the million, and leeches by the thousand,' Sam entered the conversation, 'hills as steep as that wall, covered in creepers and thorn, swamp up to your neck, and just to top it off it pisses down most of the time.'

'Is it true that if you get enough leeches on you they can actually kill you?' the tall man asked.

'Suppose they could,' John replied thoughtfully, until now it had never crossed his mind, 'I heard that bull leeches can take as much as a pint of blood.'

'Well it would only need eight of them of them to take all of your blood, Harold,' a quiet girl sat next to the tall man took his hand, 'I'm glad that you don't have to go into the jungle.'

'Are you serious, Sam,' Deirdre asked soberly, 'do you get many on you?'

Brian answered for him, 'You do but their no big problem, you just touch them with a cigarette and they fall off.'

'What if you don't smoke,' another airman asked.

'Well one of you mates will or you put a bit of salt on 'em.'

'Biggest danger,' Sam leered pointing to his groin, 'is if one gets up your whatsit'

'Actually inside,' the girl with Harold asked, ashen.

'You don't put a lit fag on that,' Ken shook his head.

'Has that ever happened to you?' the girl addressed Sam.

'Naw.'

'There's none little enough for that is there Sam?' Deirdre squealed.

When the laughter had subsided Sam leaned closer to her. 'It did happen to me once, but it turned out to be a python.'

*

Simon checked the luminous face of his watch; it was a little after one. He gently moved Susan's arm from across his chest and slipped out from under the mosquito net but his movement disturbed her.

'What time is it?' she asked sleepily.

'A little after one,' he replied as he pulled on his trousers.

She shivered and pulled a sheet over her nakedness, 'It's gone cold,' she rolled over onto her stomach and watched him dress. The moon washed the bedroom in a soft pearl light, 'Poor Simon,' she lifted the net and stroked his bare back, 'having to get up at this ungodly hour. Get yourself something to eat'.

He took her hand and kissed it, 'No, it's okay, I'll be in time to have breakfast with the men, it's laid on for 0200,' he stood up and slipped his shirt on grateful for the little warmth it afforded, 'At least it's not raining.'

'What time will you be back on Tuesday?' she asked and yawned.

'I can't be sure but I'll ring you from the mess if you're still at work, otherwise I'll come round here if that's alright?'

'I'll be right here waiting and we can carry on where we left off,' she put out her arm and beckoned him, 'come and kiss me goodbye.'

*

Ben was frustrated by the lack of luck they had been having on their recent call outs. The RAR, and it could be excused because of their inexperience, had made it almost impossible for either dogs or Iban's to pick any identifiable tracks at the site of the incident. They had had to cast around for more than an hour before they picked up tracks for two men who they could be certain were CT. By this time it had almost been dark and after less than thirty minutes of pursuit they had been forced to halt. There had not been time to construct shelters so wrapped only in plastic sheets they lay open to what the skies delivered. He had permitted cooking as he was becoming concerned over the moral of his team.

Usually a very positive leader he did not feel that there was a very good chance of having a satisfactory conclusion to this pursuit. It was a cool trail, the dogs had not been able to discern it at all, and it was only down the sharp eyes of Emau that they had picked it up. By then it was five hours old and the hunted revealed speed and endurance only available when survival was under imminent threat. It only needed a heavy fall of rain before morning and the final fragment of hope would be gone.

But despite his pessimism he knew that he would not call the chase off at first light regardless of the evidence and his men's flagging enthusiasm, it was not in his nature to acknowledge defeat even when all of the indications emphasised that the cause was already lost.

Ben decided to follow the tracks as long as the trackers could detect any sign, no matter how faint or old, and once there was nothing left they would cast search until at least midday. Content with his decision he pulled the sheet of plastic over his face in defence against the mosquitoes and as he did so he heard the rain in the trees and seconds later it was pounding noisily on his plastic covering.

*

The group of RAF personnel who had been on the next table had been to the Nuffield as members a Country Western dance club, and were about to leave and return to their base at Changi where a beach party was being held, the four RWL's had been invited along.

They had heard that there was a chasm between life in the army and that in the RAF but Changi RAF base could only be described as sheer luxury compared to the way they lived even when in camp. It was as close to a millionaire life style as any of them could have imagined.

The swimming pool rivalled that of the Nuffield Centre but had the added extravagance of being only two hundred yards from their private beach, which also sported a yacht club, and facilities for water skiing. A little further inland was a large sports field overlooked by the Airman's Club, which would have put any army officer's mess to shame.

It was rather smugly pointed out to them by Corporal Jack Major, the male who had been sat next to Deirdre at the Nuffield Club, that there was also an angling club on the far side of the officer's swimming pool.

'And if you think that this is enviable,' he spread his arms to encompass the beach and pool, 'then you should see the officers little spread.'

'I don't want to, pal,' John piled a plate with a variety of cooked meat from the groaning buffet table, 'this is pissing me off. We're doing the fighting and you buggers have all the goodies.'

'That's life old chap,' Jack grinned and stuffed a small pork pie into his mouth little realising how close he was to receiving a Liverpool kiss.

At two in the morning Ken, Brian and John took the offer of a lift on the camp bus and the Malay driver had been given instructions to take them to the Sandes Home.

'A taxi will cost you at least ten dollars,' Jack had told them.

By this time Sam had made friends with the quiet girl, Ann Davies. Deirdre had passed out around midnight had been carried back to her billet by some her friends. Ann's husband, Harold had gone on duty at ten o'clock, he was a fireman and Sam had gallantly offered to escort Ann back to her married quarter and she had invited him in for a coffee? He had eventually got to sleep about four o'clock and had been horrified to have been woken and hour later.

'You'll have to leave before it gets light,' she had urged, 'Harold comes off duty at six

'Just give me ten minutes,' Sam rolled over.

'No, you've to go now,' she said angrily, 'it's too risky.'

Sam sat up, 'I'm knackered, and it's another hour before....'

She pushed him, 'Just go will you, you got what you wanted.'

He began gathering his clothes, 'Well you weren't complaining.'

She tried to hide a smile, 'I was faking it.'

Sam paused at the door, 'Who are you kidding. Any chance of a coffee...'

The smile disappeared, 'Will you just bugger off, he'll kill us both if he finds you here.'

198

Sam snorted in derision, 'Oh, aye, a bloody Brylcreem boy, I don't think so.'

It was long walk to the camp entrance, 'Can you call me a taxi mate?' he asked the RAF Provost Corporal sat at a desk in the entrance to the guardroom.

The NCO looked up from the book he was reading, 'And who might you be?'

Sam produced his ID card, 'Private Andrews, Royal West Lancashire's, I came to a party last night.'

The corporal examined the ID for a moment and handed it back, 'There's a phone across the road,' he turned his attention back to his book.

'But I don't know a number for a taxi,' Sam pleaded.

The 'Snowdrop' looked up, 'You know what they say in the Russian Army, Andrews,' Sam shook his head, 'Toughsky shitsky,' and once more he gave the book his attention.

Sam struggled to control his anger and won. As he walked away from the guardroom a taxi pulled up and deposited a couple of airmen returning from a night out. Before the taxi drove away, with Sam in it, he rolled down the window.

'Miserable bastard,' he shouted at the Provost NCO and then sat back feeling a little better.

Chapter Twenty Three

The reporter was of an age that should have seen him doing his National Service, but he had failed his medical, and he was accompanied by a grey haired photographer of indeterminate age. The latter had been troublesome from the moment they gathered to mount the vehicles, not only was he still affected from his previous evening's consumption of whiskey in the sergeants mess but he constantly hindered the proceedings by requesting people to pose for photographs.

'I think you'd be better saving your film for when were in the ulu, Bill,' Dave Snell tactfully tried to restrain him, 'if we get a bit of action you'll need all the film you've got.'

'Got you, Dave,' he gave a knowing wink as though he just been passed fragment of secret intelligence that nobody else was privy to. His accent Dave had found difficult to place when the two newspaper men had been handed over to him the previous evening. At first he thought that he detected an Irish lilt but later in the evening he discovered that the irritating man came from the Western Isles and his enormous consumption of whiskey confirmed his origin.

It did not take long for Dave to become isolated at one end of the bar with his two charges. Bill Donald dealt in bull-shit at wholesale level and people of that ilk are soon identified in any sergeant's mess in the British army. Dave spent an excruciating evening listening to more and more outrageous tales. Offers of jobs that he had received with more prestigious national papers but he had turned them down because of his love of the North, tales of hair-raising assignments in outlandish and dangerous places where it was unlikely any regional newspaper would have been called on to visit and the scores of celebrities that he knew.

The reporter, David Baum, was supposedly in charge but the Scot overwhelmed the frail looking youth who stood quietly drinking coke for the entire evening and barely spoke a word.

In the cold early morning mist they shivered in their borrowed jungle greens, their packs causing them obvious discomfort. Neither of them looked as eager for the experience of a jungle operation as the brave words uttered the previous evening.

The journey north to Tanjong Rambutan took a little over an hour, and apart from those designated as sentries, the rest of the platoon dozed as best they could on the hard wooden seats with the cold wind increasing their discomfort. Being only two sections strong they had only required one three-tonner and a Land Rover, Simon made sure, much to his platoon sergeants irritation, that the newspapermen travelled the Bedford.

Half a mile north of the kampong they debussed at the twenty-eighth milestone, went a hundred yards into the rubber and sat down to wait for first light. The mosquitoes fell upon them eager for blood. David and Bill got their first taste of the discomfort of jungle operations.

Dave had been able to avoid Bill's company during the journey by travelling in the Bedford's cab but now the cameraman sought him out and sat down beside him.

'Is it okay to smoke Dave?' he asked in a hushed voice, 'or could there be any bandits around?'

'Could be, you can never tell where they are, he exaggerated, 'if we knew where they were we'd have the war won.'

'Yeah,' he stared nervously into the blackness.

Dave heard him unscrew his water bottle and the unmistakable smell of whiskey intruded on the stench of rotting vegetation and rubber. He felt a tap on his shoulder.

'Here,' Bill said, 'bit of a livener.'

Dave took the bottle and instead of sampling the contents as he was meant he emptied the amber liquid onto the floor and then handed it back to the stunned Scot, 'You'd better fill that with water at the first stream.' No protest came from the newspaper man and until the end of the exercise he only spoke to Dave when the job necessitated him doing so.

David Baum was glad to move when the time came though he had dreaded the prospect of carrying the heavy pack that contained his food and shelter. The cold and the fervent attention of the mosquitoes made that dread less formidable.

It was uphill from the start and the difficulty of the ascent increased as soon as they left the plantation and entered the barely penetrable mass that was secondary jungle. Roots tripped him, vines and branches snagged his pack impeding his progress and thorns tore his clothes and flesh. The cold he had endured earlier was now remembered with affection as the sweat ran into his eyes and drenched his shirt, this was an assignment that he had been pleased and excited to be given but now he fervently wished that he was back on the cold wet streets of Bolton. David was a not particularly strong or fit but fear kept him in touch with the soldier in front, the thought of losing contact with him filled him with dread. Fortunately signals repeatedly came from the rear to halt; it seemed that his cameraman's physical problems were even greater than his own.

Simon was glad of this short patrol to test his fitness and despite the training he had done, whilst at the rehabilitation unit in the Cameron's, he soon realised that he was not fully back to operational fitness. He

201

had not appreciated just how fit he had become before being hospitalised. Even so, this constant halting was beginning to irritate him, they had barely covered a thousand yards, and it had taken them almost an hour. A message had been passed from Dave Snell informing him of the cause of their delays and suggesting that the newsman be sent to the front.

Bill took ten minutes to arrive and Simon was grateful that he seemed to have lost the power of speech. His drawn face was almost as grey as his hair; his mouth hung open with exhaustion and his eyes stared blankly at Simon.

Simon was worried; the man looked close to death, 'Are you all right?' he asked truly concerned, Bill looked as close to dying as anybody could be and still standing.

In answer Bill vomited and leaned his forearm on his forehead against a tree. Simon watched as column of red ants, having had their path blocked, swarmed over his arm and into his sweat plastered hair. Before Simon could react to warn the sad photographer of the danger, the aggressive horde attacked.

There could not have been a more effective cure for Bill's hangover and exhaustion. To say that he became a man possessed of demons would have been gross understatement. For a split second his body went rigid and his eyes opened wide in shocked and silent agony, but then his vocal chords made known his pain, and spinning like an ecstatic dervish he scrapped at his head and face as his tiny attackers extended the area of their assault.

The only people, close enough to visually witness this display of an exaggerated form of highland dancing, were Simon, Andy Barton, the leading scout and an intrigued Iban tracker, Ambau.

'Soft bugger,' Andy disparagingly observed without a grain of compassion, 'he'd have reason to shout if they were bloody hornets.'

It was as if Andy had secretly called on a malicious spirit for in his violent contortions Bill came into contact with a thick vine the movement of which dislodged an inverted tear drop shaped ball that hit the ground and seemed to emit an unmistakable buzz of great anger.

'Hornets,' Andy screamed.

All tactical procedure was abandoned. That single word was instantly followed by the sound of bodies departing the area through thick vegetation at high velocity; it had greater effect on a patrol than any enemy contact. The sting of the hornet was excruciatingly painful, and made even the toughest, roughest, jungle fighter quail, and renounces all claims to fortitude.

When the furious insects considered that enough chastisement had been administered, and the platoon had regrouped fifty yards away, Simon and Ambau cautiously returned to the site of the attack as Bill was the only one missing. Ambau followed the tracks and found him sat on his pack sporting a face that looked like a Ranger fan who had been foolish enough to drink in a Celtic supporters club. It was swollen to the size and shape of a football and his eyes mere slits.

When he saw them he rummaged in his pack and handed Simon his camera, 'Take ma' photo,' he mumbled through lips that resembled a couple of pork sausages. Simon did as he was bid admiring newspaperman's determination to get the right picture despite his agony.

*

Ben felt obliged to continue the search even though he held out little hope of coming across worthwhile signs of the CT he had set out to catch. They had cast for an hour and a half after first light but neither the dogs nor the Iban's could detect scent or sign of the CT.

He sensed that Goat, the Australian private, was taking some pleasure from their lack of success but it was difficult to tell, as he appeared always to wear a rather supercilious smirk. Ben had wanted to point out that the turmoil left at the scene of the ambush had seriously handicapped their task, but had seen this as making excuses and excuses were something that he did not deal in.

'Boggy' had done the job for him with his usual northern tact, 'Your lot might as well have ploughed the bloody area,' he grumbled, 'couldn't have found bleeding elephant tracks back there.'

They pushed on north it being the most likely direction a desperate quarry would take, to the east and west lay cultivated areas but to the north was a colossal hinterland.

Ben took post immediately behind the leading tracker, Emau, and following him were the two Australians. As they crossed a small stream Ben heard a low whistle behind him he stopped and turned, Sergeant Murphy was signalling him back to where Goat was crouched inspecting the ground.

'What is it?' Ben asked.

'Goat 'ere thinks he's found something,' the big sergeant said.

Ben squatted, 'What?'

Goat pointed to a half buried stone the size and shape of a large pear. It was dry, but along the edge where it entered the ground, there was a tiny strip of wet mud

'Looks like it's been stood on and slightly tipped over,' Goat explained.

203

'Could have been one us?' Ben felt the adrenaline awakening.

'Naw, it's too much to the right of our path.'

Emau joined them and when he saw the object of their attention he became excited patting Goat on the back and exposing a collection of gold teeth in a wide grin.

'You Iban,' he beamed.

'Naw, mate, me Abo.'

'Abo good tracker,' Emau went on his enthusiasm undiminished.

'How long ago?' Ben asked impatiently.

Emau spread the fingers of his right twice and look at Goat who nodded.

'Ten minutes?' Ben could not believe their luck, 'which way are they going?

Emau cast quickly about and then pointed half right, 'One man.'

He must have crossed their path only minutes before and was on a course that would almost be running parallel. Was he aware of their presence? Emau seemed read his thoughts and mimicked a slow steady walk like that of a tired man.

'He doesn't know we're here?' Ben asked hopefully.

Both Emau and Goat shook their heads, 'He'd be moving a bloody sight quicker if he did,' Goat observed.

Ben called 'Boggy' forward and held a hurried O Group. He decided to continue with just the Australians and Emau leaving the remainder to follow their tracks after a period of ten minutes.

'Boggy' felt aggrieved at be left out in favour of the Australians, 'You're getting close to the end of our operational area, sir,' he pointed out 'another thousand metres and you'll even be off this map.'

'We'll have caught the bugger by then,' Ben heaved his pack onto his shoulders and indicated for Emau to lead off.

*

Despite the fact that they had only arrived back at Sandes after three in the morning John and Ken made it to breakfast which was served until ten. The dining room was open on three sides and a cool breeze drifted comfortably in from the Singapore Straits.

Ken was already eating when John arrived at the buffet bar, and after he had filled his plate with eggs and bacon, he joined his friend, 'No sodding beans for me,' he plonked his loaded plate on the table, 'we get enough of the bloody things back there,' he went and got himself a mug of tea.

They ate in silence for a while.

'You're quiet, Johnno,' Ken observed, 'last night at that party you didn't even crack any jokes.'

John sighed, 'I wish I hadn't come, mate.'

'Why, it's bloody great here. You can just do as you like, get pissed, eat, get pissed, swim, get...'

'I know,' John put his knife and fork down and sighed again, 'but we'd planned and booked this with Keith. He should have been here, he should have been getting pissed with us, and laughing, and joking, and having a good time,' he watched a group of servicemen larking about round the pool for a moment. 'But instead he's six feet under thanks to some fucking slope 'ead who wasn't fit to tie his boots. He'll never see his home again, or his mum and sister's.'

He went quiet again and Ken could not think of anything appropriate to say that would ease his friend's pain. They had all been mates but John and Keith had been friends longer and although they were chalk and cheese there was a closeness about them that had been deepened by the hardships of operations together.

It was John who eventually broke the awkward silence, 'I wrote to his sister,' he said quietly still watching the group by the pool.

'He had two didn't he?'

'Yeah, Ann, whose married, and Joyce.'

'And who did you write to?'

'Joyce,' he turned to Ken a worried look on his inharmonious features, 'she's only just fifteen, am I cradle snatching, Ken?'

'Give over, you're only writing to her,' Ken drained his mug, 'did she reply?'

'I only sent it a couple of days ago; I hope it doesn't upset her.'

'Why should it, he was your mate?'

'Yeah,' John felt a little better; it had taken him the weeks since Keith's death to gather up the nerve. He wanted to comfort the family and in light of what Alan had told him he had come to the conclusion that Joyce would be the best medium. Writing to Ann could bring the wrath of her violent husband down upon her head and his mother was probably beyond any succour for weeks, if not years to come. So he had chosen Joyce. He had picked his words carefully not wanting there to be any misinterpretation of his intentions. Five times he completed the letter only to screw it up and start again. The letter was something of an achievement as he had only written two letters to his own family since leaving England.

He had written: *Dear Joyce, I hope you don't mind me writing this letter to you but I wanted Keith's family to know how well we all thought of him in One platoon and what a good mate he was. I know you will all miss him more than us and that must be terrible because we all feel like we have lost one of our family.*

When I was at depot with Keith we had a lecture by an officer who told us that the regiment was like a family, Keith laughed and said it was BS (I'll let you work out what that means). But I can tell you that officer was right I feel like I have lost a brother in fact it's more than a brother because he was my best mate and even when I am with the rest of the lads I feel lonely without him.

I am going on leave to Singapore in a couple of days but I don't really want to go because we had arranged it with Keith. But you have got to act tough and I don't want the others to know just how upset I am so I will go. Perhaps they are just doing the same.

If me writing bothers you just chuck it away and pretend you never got it. Best wishes, John Cantrill.

*

Immediately they set out on the trail of the lone CT Emau spotted droplets of blood that became increasingly frequent. He concluded, from some of the drops, that the wounded man was bleeding from the upper part of his body.

After ten minutes the Iban sank to one knee and brought his rifle into the aim. Ben quickly covered the three yards that separated him from his tracker and adopted a similar posture slipping the change lever on his Sterling to automatic.

He heard their quarry before he saw him through the green tangle, a rasping desperate struggle for air. He was a round faced Malay sunk down in the giant roots of a great teak tree no more than five yards away, and seemingly oblivious of their presence. The front of his khaki shirt was black with blood and a blood soaked rag was inadequately wrapped around his neck.

There was no visible weapon, Ben signalled Emau to apply his safety catch, he then stood up and quickly closed on the wounded man who had his eyes closed.

Ben stopped at his side and placed the muzzle of the SMG at the man's temple. '*Jangan tergerak,*' (don't move), he said softly.

The man's eyes opened quickly, full of fear but the fear swiftly turned too relief. Despite Ben's command not to move he half raised a hand as if in a form greeting and the hint of a smile began to form on his pain ridden face. He tried to speak but the words were no more than a gurgling sound.

Ben heard the two Australians move up behind him, it was Goat who spoke.

'Got the bastard,' the click of the safety catch on his FN was clearly audible and out of the corner of his eye Ben saw the movement as the rifle was brought into the aim.

'What the hell d'you think you're doing,' Ben snarled as he pushed the rifle away.

'That bastard killed one of our mates,' Goat hissed, 'I'm gonna blow his fucking head off.'

'Get a bloody grip of this man, sergeant,' Ben snapped at the Australian NCO, 'we're not in a bloody Hollywood film, we're fighting a war. This man's a sight more use to us alive than dead any damn fool would know that.'

'Pack it in, Goat, the captain's right.'

'Emau,' Ben waved an arm in the direction they had been travelling, 'see if there are any more tracks' and then to Goat, 'go with him.'

The wounded CT placed a hand on Ben's arm, the grip was feeble and his hand quickly dropped away. He tried to speak again but again the words remained unformed, lost in a liquid bubbling. The message was clear, he was asking for help.

'He's not got long, Cap',' Sergeant Murphy started removing the sodden rag around the man's neck exposing and entry wound just under his chin and a larger exit wound at the base of his skull, 'it's a bloody miracle he got this far,' Spud tore open his field dressing and placed the pad over the exit wound and wrapped the long bandage around his neck and secured it, 'he's hardly bleeding at all, he must have lost a lot.'

Emau and Goat returned just as the prisoner slipped sideways and died.

'You might as well as let me do for him in the first place,' Goat stared down at the sad form without any emotion.

'Well that would have been a waste of a bullet then, wouldn't it?' Ben retorted as be began to search the blood soaked pockets of the dead man, 'Anymore tracks Emau?'

Emau shook his head, 'No Tuan.'

The man had few possessions apart from a small amount of tobacco, ten rounds of .38 inch ammunition and a three faded photographs. Two of them showed a family in a Malay Kampong, a more interesting one showed a large group of CT posing in what looked like a well organised and large camp. Behind them a window in the trees indicated the camp was on high ground and an expanse of water was visible in the far distance. In his waistband was a poorly maintained Smith and Wesson, the cylinder held six empty cases so he had not had chance to reload since it had last been fired.

It was his right canvass boot that exposed the most interesting item. Ben noticed that the tongue felt thicker than that on the left one, and after closer attention, and the assistance of a knife, he discovered three sheets of rice paper which in themselves revealed little, as they were filled with Chinese characters but the fact that so much care had been taken to conceal them spoke volumes.

Sergeant Murphy was clearly impressed, 'No stone unturned ay?'

'You'll get to know their ways, sergeant,' Ben replied smugly.

Nothing else was found and when the rest of the team arrived 'Boggy' produced a camera and photographed the dead man.

'So that special branch can identify him,' Ben explained to the Australian, 'Get him buried, 'Boggy'.'

*

The mid afternoon heat lay like a hot wet blanket on the verdant gloom. Flora and fauna had sought relief in their own ways. No bird called, no insect or creature, prey or predator, scurried through the undergrowth, no breeze disturbed leaf or vine and the ponderous silence rang in their ears.

Ray felt his eyelids pricking and the desire to close them for just a few seconds was hard to resist but he knew that could prove disastrous and sleep, brief though it may be, could easily take over. He looked at the black dial of his issue Omega watch and saw that it was ten minutes past three, their relief was late and that did not please him. He gave the communication vine a sharp tug, at the same time he felt a slight tap on his ankle and he turned to look across at Bill Cliffe.

The two men lay at forty-five degrees to each other with their feet touching so that they could easily attract each other's attention with the minimum of movement and noise. Bill was staring intently at a spot on the top of the opposite bank his head bobbing and weaving slightly in order to see through the foliage.

Ray tapped his foot but Bill's attention remained fixed on the far side of the stream. At last he turned his head slightly towards Ray, gave him a thumbs-down, a slight shrug, and touched his ear, meaning he was not sure if he had heard something. Both men directed their full attention to the area ears and eyes straining, Ray's fatigue was now forgotten.

Ray heard nothing; it must have been movement that caught his eye for when he turned his head back to look at stream the man was crouching to drink, an American M1 Carbine in the crook of his arm. Instead of the normal CT cap he wore a security forces bush hat but the normal khaki uniform. Somebody on the bank, and out of their vision, spoke to the man very softly, he turned and answered and then got to his feet and retreated out of sight and the jungle was seemingly empty again and just as still and quiet as though there had been no intrusion.

At that moment Frank and Dan crawled forward to relieve them looking rather sheepish, 'Sorry, Ray,' Dan began, 'I was well away.'

'It's okay mate,' he whispered, 'it's a good job you weren't on time we've had visitors.'

'Charlie?' Frank asked eager for some action after three days staring at the greenery.

'Charlie,' Ray confirmed, 'at least two. I think they're a recce coming to see if the camp's been compromised.'

Leaving Frank and Dan to carry on with the OP, Ray and Bill warily crossed the stream and followed in the path of their recent callers. Between the OP and the camp they did not see a single footprint, damaged leaf or disturbed stone, the men were clearly expert in their environment. They spent an hour observing the camp from different positions but there was no sign of occupation and the crushing silence persisted.

As they were returning to the OP the faint sound of a mob of gibbon's uttering their hooting racket of protest reached them. Ray took a bearing on the noise, figuring that humans had caused the disturbance.

*

The patrol that Simon had planned was as much to test himself as to entertain the reporters. They had set out north from their camp, a long uphill drag through primary jungle with reasonable visibility. They were with Alan Bakers section and Simon was leaving the navigation to the experienced corporal while he kept a watch over the newsmen, and made sure they did not get lost or cause anybody else to.

It was a tough first hour as they patrolled to the three thousand-foot ridge. It took them two hours to cover a little over a mile and by any standard it had been a stiff climb, and again Bill Donald looked close to expiring but his condition did not prevent him from being a nuisance and constantly taking photographs.

For another hour they followed the ridge west and began the descent back down towards the stream on which they were camped. At noon they found a flat piece of ground, put out sentries and brewed up. Bill was beginning to feel better now that the going was easier and his irritating self-assurance escalated. He seated himself next to Simon clutching his mug of tea and brimming with his own importance.

'I was wondering if we could get our friend over there,' he nodded towards Ambau who, like most of his fellow tribesmen, could quickly fall asleep when his services were not required and was dozing with his jungle hat over his face, 'could be persuaded to act like a corpse for a photograph?'

'Act like a corpse, what d'you mean?' Simon knew what was coming but acted dumb.

'Just in case we don't kill any of these CT's, the people back home wouldn't be able tell the difference, and it would give a little colour to David's report.'

Simon was not sure how to re act and was even less certain of how Ambau would take the suggestion, or even if he could explain what was required of him, Ambau's English was quite basic, and Simons Malay was not even that good.

Alan Baker was sitting a few yards away and overheard what had been said; he unobtrusively moved over to Ambau and had a quiet conversation with him. Alan had always got on well with all of the Iban's and had spent a lot of time in their lines back at camp acquiring a smattering of their tongue.

'I heard what you were saying to Pearly before,' he said to Bill when Simon had gone off to relieve himself a little distance from where they had rested, 'and if I was you I wouldn't ask, just do it, cos there's no way that he'd agree to it. Iban's are very superstitious about having their photos taken.'

'Are they?' Bill looked surprised, 'why's that?'

Alan shrugged, 'Who knows they were still head-hunters twenty years ago, probably think it damages their soul or something.'

'Oh, pity,' Bill gazed disappointedly at the sleeping tracker.

'I'll tell you what,' Alan said as though he had just had a bright idea, Bill looked at him expectantly, 'they sleep like bloody logs; you could take it now without him ever knowing.'

Bill looked doubtful, 'Is that a good idea?'

'You want the photo, pal, and we're not likely to bump any bandits on this patrol,' Bill still hesitated and Alan continued, 'I'll go and take his hat away and put his rifle as though he's dropped it and Bob's your uncle, the photo's yours,'

Bill was convinced, 'Okay, let's do it.'

With exaggerated caution Alan slowly removed Ambau's hat from his face and with equal wariness took his carbine from his side and laid it as though it had been dropped, then he gave Bill a thumbs-up.

As the camera clicked the trackers eye's snapped open as if operated by the same button and he let out a hiss of rage, leaping to his feet and whipping his parang from its wooden sheath.

'Oh my god,' Alan sounded terrified and the attitude of the erstwhile head-hunter was conveyed in magnified form to Bill who stood petrified. Alan placed himself 'courageously' between the one wide eyed with rage, and the other wide eyed in horror. Alan, his arms spread in a gallant attempt to fend off the enraged savage, spoke rapidly in

210

what sounded like Malay as the two men swayed looking for an opening. Ambau jabbered back, his face contorted with malice.

'What's he saying, what's he saying?' Bill mimicked Alan's movements to keep him between himself and the wild man from Borneo.

'He says,' Alan replied breathlessly, 'you must pay for his soul.'

'Yes, yes,' the Scot produced his wallet and took out a ten-dollar note, 'will ten dollars do the trick?'

Alan 'interpreted' and despite Ambau making no apparent reply said urgently, 'No, no he's insulted.'

'Twenty,' Bill drew another ten from his wallet.

'Bloody hell man you're gonna get us both killed,' Alan and Ambau's darting and dodging became more demented, 'I can't chance insulting him again,' Ambau's parang gleamed and hissed as he slashed to and fro, 'how much have you got,' Alan was becoming hysterical.

'I don't know, take it all,' with sweating hand he dragged all the money from his wallet and thrust it at Alan.

Slowly, Alan knelt and reaching forward placed the notes on the floor in front of the now calmer Iban, who, with equal ceremony, bent down and picked it up.

Making the most of the re-instated calm Bill withdrew to a safe distance, content in the knowledge that he had the photograph he had wanted but a little disappointed that he had not had the presence of mind or courage to photograph the bizarre negotiations.

Simon returned, 'What the hell's been going on, corporal,' he demanded.

'It's alright, sir everything's under control,' he winked at Simon, 'I'll debrief you later.'

As they prepared to continue the patrol with Ambau leading, ahead of Alan, Alan muttered, 'You owe me half of the money, ragarse.'

Ambau grinned, 'Okay, wagarse.'

'There must have been over fifty dollars there,' Alan checked his compass and indicated their direction to Ambau, 'it's more than you get in a month.'

'Plenty good,' Ambau replied and set off back into the deep valley.

Later that evening Bill had his growing suspicions confirmed. They had finished their evening meal and in the dusk as they waited for stand- to, he said to Dave Snell.

'That young Baker speaks good Malay, Dave has he been out here long?'

'Al?' Dave asked.

'Yeah, the corporal.'

Well, he can speak it a little,' he lit a cigarette, 'and he's matey with the Iban's but he doesn't speak their lingo much better than anyone else.'

Inwardly, Bill cringed.

*

The clamour of Bugis Street epitomised the East and all of its excitement, glamour and mystery, providing stimulation to all of the senses. The noise was almost suffocating. The cacophony of brash Chinese music blending uneasily with the subtle, sensuous rhythm of Malay and Indian melodies and the brash unsophisticated racket of the latest Western pop hit jarred with everything. There were beautiful girls, Malays in brightly coloured sarongs coy and timid, Chinese seductive and willowy in tight cheongsams, and the Indian's shyer and coyer even than the Malay's, unsmiling, with large sad eyes. Hundreds of food stall's cooking and serving their wares in the street, filled the air with exotic aromas and tastes that intrigued even the most conservative palate.

Beggars and cripples shared the walkways with rich merchants, wealthy miners, and plantation owners, and at times this diverse mix of humanity even ate at the same stalls. Class was not a consideration in Bugis Street but money most certainly was. Even the poor, underpaid, British National Serviceman had enough money to be of interest to the traders, beggars and working girls.

As the four made their way along the bustling street they ignored the entreaties of the heavily made up girls reeking of cheap perfume and calling to them from brightly lit doorways.

'You want good time Johnny,' a small Chinese of doubtful age took hold of Brian's arm.

'Yeah I do love but I don't want a dose of the clap,' he released himself from her grip.

'This is it then,' Ken stopped in front an opened fronted bar, 'The Girlie Club.'

'Looks alright,' John surveyed the occupants, 'not many squaddies though.'

'Some gorgeous looking birds though,' Brian pointed out and Sam agreed eagerly leering at the girls lining the bar.

'Yeah, but that bloke at Sandes said it was the best bar in town,' John was hesitant, 'so you'd think that it would be packed with squaddies.'

'So, we'll find out,' Ken followed Sam into the bar.

They found an empty table and ordered their drinks from a rather effeminate Chinese waiter.

212

'He's a bloody 'queer', look at the way he walks,' Sam almost shouted, the man looked over his shoulder and tossed his head.

'Shut up, Sam, you don't have to tell the whole bloody bar,' Brian remonstrated.

'What's yer problem, Largy,' Sam replied as he took a cigarette, 'anyone who couldn't see that he was a raving poofter must be blind.'

The waiter must have been mortally offended for a girl brought their drinks, she was stunningly beautiful and the slit in her cheongsam almost reached her hip

'You want girl come and sit with you?' she asked with a sweet smile as she placed their beers on the table.

'And how much will that cost us love'? Brian asked ever cautious.

'You just buy 'em drinks,' she said.

'Forget it,' Ken butted in, 'that's how they fleece you. Just leave it love,' the girl departed the smile replaced with a pout.

'Look at some of them,' Sam was ecstatic, 'there like bloody film stars.'

'Sam grow up,' Ken took a mouthful of the cold beer, 'they'll order the most expensive drinks, champagne, cocktails anything that they can rip you off over, and you end up with a bill for a hundred dollars.'

'And sometimes they're only drinking coloured water,' John added.

'You're miserable shower of buggers you lot,' Sam turned to get a better view of the wares, 'what have we come here for if it's not for the birds?'

'It looks too expensive us, Sam,' John said.

'Well we've not tried to find out, 'ave we?' Sam responded.

'Sam,' Brian put in, 'd'you think birds as gorgeous as these are gonna charge less than a hundred dollars?'

'Well I'm gonna find out,' Sam got to his feet.

John pointed a warning finger, 'You pick up one of them, Sam, and you drink on your own, we're not get involved with a bill for hundreds of dollars.'

Sam sat down, 'You are such a load of bloody whimps, how are we gonna have any fun if we're too scared to take a risk.'

'It's not a risk, Sam,' Brian pointed out, 'it's a bloody certainty you'll get ripped off.'

'Who told you about this place, Ken?' Sam asked.

'A lad at the centre.'

'Well what did he say about the birds?' Sam pursued his point.

Ken shrugged, 'He just said there were loads of fabulous women.'

'Did he get off with one?'

Ken shrugged again, 'Didn't say.'

213

A subdued Sam reluctantly contented himself with just ogling the girls from a distance.

After a another drink it was agreed that the bar had nothing special to offer apart from the girls who were clearly out of their financial reach and they would seek a hostelry with a more common touch.

'Just one more round then,' Sam got to his feet, 'it's my round.'

'Call the waitress,' Ken advised.

'I'm going for a leak anyway,' Sam said, 'I'll get 'em on the way back.'

'Make sure you wash your hands,' John called after him, Sam signalled his reply with two fingers.

When he returned with the drinks he was grinning broadly and in the company of a tall exquisite looking slim girl who was wearing a black cheongsam and had her, raven, glossy hair piled on her head adding ten inches to her height.

'Meet Lola lads,' he put the tray down, there was an extra glass filled with an amber liquid, 'she's having a drink with us.'

'She's having a drink with you, Sam,' John reached forward to take his glass and Lola placed a slim elegant hand on his arm,

'Don't be an old misery,' her voice was husky and her English was good, 'don't you like have pretty girls around?'

'I do girl, but not at the prices here.'

'What's money for, if not spending on good time,' she sat down and crossed her legs exposing an expanse of thigh. Sam dragged a chair across from an adjacent table and sat next to her but she immediately stood up and took Sam by the hand, 'You dance, Sam.'

Sam turned and leered at them as he followed her to the small area that served as a dance floor.

'Look at the soft bastard, Brian laughed, 'he only comes up to her chin.'

'Hey,' John put his already half empty glass down, 'I've had enough of this place, there's a lot of weird looking buggers here now.'

Although some of the males were European, few appeared to be of military age apart from two, sat with two girls, a couple of tables away. One, a chubby individual of about thirty and the other, younger tall and dark haired, with hair that appeared too long for him to be a serviceman

'Hey pal,' John called across; the dark one looked his way, 'are you forces?'

'Why,' he had a soft Scots accent and there was nothing friendly in his attitude or voice.

John bridled, 'No need to get stroppy, pal I only wanted to ask you something.'

214

The man raised an eyebrow, 'Ask away.'

'Doesn't necessarily mean that you'll get an answer though,' the fatter one said, and laughed at his own wit.

'Just ignore the soft sods, John,' Ken could see his friend's anger rising. John raised his voice and continued, 'We just wanted to know what the score was in here.'

'Score, it's not a bloody football match,' the fat man replied. Ken was sure from their accents that they were officers, 'and yes we are forces, Intelligence Corps.'

'So you're nothing to do with the army then,' John grinned.

The tall Scot stood up and brushed his hair from his face, 'I'll have you know that you are addressing commissioned officers,' his masculinity a little doubtful as he stood, hand on hip.

'Leave it lad's, leave it,' Ken turned to look for Sam, 'let's get out of here,' he waved urgently at Sam to join them but his back was towards them and had the girl in a tight clinch barely moving to the music. They all got to their feet.

'I'll go and get him, you two just leave,' Ken turned away and as he did so they heard a shout. The words were incomprehensible but it clearly embodied rage, disappointment, and disgust. At the same time the two that purported to be officers were also on their feet demanding the identity and units of the three RWL's. John was about to decline their request in a forthright manner when Sam's shout brought all conversation to a halt. All eyes were directed towards the small dance floor in time to see Sam plant his fist squarely in the girl's face; the punch sent her staggering the five yards that separated her from the bar, where she crumpled to the floor semi-conscious, with blood pouring from her nose.

Flushed with anger Sam pointed at the distressed damsel, 'She's a fucking fellah,' he bawled.

Somebody at the far side of the room began to laugh, and soon the entire bar had joined in. They exited the bar at top speed before the mood changed. They could still hear the laughter when they were fifty yards down the road. Once they rounded the corner off Bugis Street, they slowed to a walk.

'You do get us into some shite, Andrews,' John wiped the sweat from his face.

'Wasn't my bloody fault,' Sam objected loudly, 'you didn't know he was a bloody bloke.'

'None of us did,' Ken agreed, 'but it had to be you that found out, and plant him.'

'You certainly made a mess of his makeup, Sam,' Brian handed round his tin of cigarettes.

'Which toilets will he go to powder his nose,' John pondered, they began to laugh.

'Hey, hang on,' Ken stopped, 'I bet there were no sodding women in there, I bet all those birds were men,' he looked aghast and the laughing stopped, 'we've been to a bloody queer's bar,' his alarm turned to anger, 'I'll batter that little bastard who set us up.'

'Come on,' John set off along the street, 'I need a beer, and I'm picking the bar.'

'If this gets out at battalion we'll never hear the bloody end of it.' Brian warned and then to Sam, 'How did you find out it was a bloke Sam?'

Sam hesitated.

'Come on Sam how did you twig,' John grinned anticipating the reply.

'I stuck me hand up her...his dress,' he admitted sheepishly, 'and got more than I bargained for.'

Chapter Twenty Four

Linda was surprised when she arrived at work to find John Sankey already in his office. The door was closed, and she could hear a number of different voices so she knew it must be quite an important meeting to have been called at such an early hour.

She put the envelope that contained her resignation on her desk and went to collect the mail from the central post room. The post room manager, Bijal Atal, a Hindu, who saw his position as being one of power, power that he wielded unreservedly at each mail collection by the way he treated those unfortunate enough to be delegated with the task of collecting it. All of the departments sent a junior clerk for their mail twice a day. Bijal treated them all with the same disdain that he had probably been exposed to back in Hyderabad in the days of the British Raj when he was an office boy in the Indian Civil Service.

A straight line had to be formed outside the Post Room, and irrespective of the order in which the juniors arrived he would call them forward by department as he thought fit. Special Branch had no junior and therefore the lot invariably fell to Linda. Mr Atal was an Indian version of Uriah Heap, the moment anybody higher than the office junior appeared at his door he became sickeningly obsequious and as a consequence Linda never had to wait with the poor, benighted, office minions. It made her feel uncomfortable to be allowed to bypass the Atal system, some of the girls, and youths could have been waiting for as much as half an hour. It was his fawning attitude that disturbed her most of all.

'Oh Miss Linda, Special Branch,' he greeted her with an exaggerated Salaam, 'it is always a pleasure to have such a lovely lady visit my humble office.'

'I've only come to collect the mail, Mr Atal,' she had to suffer the greeting every time she came, and it irritated her.

'And here it is all ready for you, Miss Linda, I always make sure that yours is ready first and...'

His sentence was cut short by Irene passing the office.

'Linda, see you in the café, I have something to tell you. I'm in a bit of hurry we're just moving an SEP into a safe house and the arrangements have landed with me to carry out the move. I've put the details on your desk. I'll to have dash, see you later.'

When she arrived back at her office the meeting was over and John Sankey was in her office.

'I hope this isn't what I think it is,' he held the envelope.

'I'm sorry,' she replied, 'it's my notice; I have to leave for personal reasons.'

'Have to?'

'Yes, I have to,' she began attending to the paperwork on her desk finding the conversation difficult.

'You don't want to talk about it?' he persisted.

She sighed, 'I don't want to seem rude, but it really is something that I don't want to talk about.'

'Very well, Linda, I'll respect your wishes,' he said, 'you realise that we don't allow people to work a notice, you would have to leave immediately.'

She nodded, 'Yes, that's okay.'

As she began to tidy her desk she saw the papers that Irene had left on the desk concerning the SEP who was being moved to a safe house and her heart stopped when she saw the name.

Irene had already reached the front of the queue in the canteen when Linda arrived so she went and found a table near an open window.

'I got you a cake,' Irene put the tray on the table and took the seat opposite, 'I've got a posting,' she was almost squirming with excitement.

'I take from your happiness that it's in Perak,' Linda smiled.

'Taiping'!

'Lovely, that's only an hour from Sungei Siput isn't it?'

'Well really he's mostly at Kuala Kangsar,' Irene beamed, 'and that's even closer.'

Linda reached across the table and took Irene's hand, 'I am really pleased for you, Irene, but I think it's about time he married you.'

'In time,' she replied, 'we both have careers and I'm not giving mine up to have a family.'

'I also have some news,' Linda said quietly as she stirred her coffee.

'Is it bad,' Irene looked worried.

'In a way, I've resigned.'

'What on earth for. I thought you were happy here?'

'I was, I am,' Linda stared at her cup and then looked up her eyes full of tears, 'Please don't ask me why or what I'm going to do....'

'You're not pregnant?' Irene interrupted.

'No!'

'What does Roger say?'

'He doesn't know I don't seem to have seen him for ages.'

Irene felt all of her happiness slip away, 'Why can't you tell me Linda,' she pleaded, 'we've been friends since school.'

'All I can say is that you know I have always wanted to teach, and I have an opportunity do something about it and I'm going to take that opportunity.'

'Where is this?'

'I can't say.'

'But you can't just walk away, leave and not tell me where you're going. We've been friends for so long, what's all the secrecy.'

'I have to Irene; I want to start a new life.'

'But what is wrong with the life you have, and what about Roger, I thought you loved him, what does he say?'

'I said I haven't told him yet, he's away. Nothing can come of our relationship, we're two different cultures, and I am sure that when the time comes for him to return home I would be forgotten.'

'I think he loves you and would want to take you back to England.'

'But would I want to go? I won't forget you Irene and promise that I will get in touch as soon as circumstances allow.'

*

The apprehension that had been with him since first being told that he was to be afforded a degree of freedom gradually dissolved as he walked alone through the busy streets of Kuala Lumpur. The air still retained some of the freshness left by the mid-morning downpour. Steam rose from the wet roads as the hot tropical sun soaked up the moisture.

The streets were busy, and the shops overflowed with goods. Lau went from shop to shop looking, touching, examining, but never buying. It all seemed too good to be true. He had money in his pocket,

218

more money than he had ever possessed before in his life, but he was scared to buy anything. He felt that his secret would be revealed the moment he handed over any of the blood money that he had received for betraying his comrades.

Even when he plucked up the courage to order food at a vendor's stall the man seemed to examine the five-dollar bill as if seeking a clue from whence it came. Sitting in the shade, eating his bowl of noodles and vegetables and watching the passing people his confidence grew when he realised that nobody spared him a glance, he was anonymous.

It was difficult to believe that in the countryside, a mere three miles away, a savage and bloody contest was being fought out in the jungle and cultivation, and country people were subject to a curfew and locked in their villages every night, guarded by armed men.

From where he sat he could see the block where he had been allocated a small flat and a wave of satisfaction swept over him. The life he had been leading a few months earlier was another life, another person living it. The fear, the danger, the hunger and discomfort were like a bad dream it was surprising how just a few weeks of civilised living could purge the memory. By the time he returned to his new home his anxieties had been greatly diminished.

*

Although he had only been back with the battalion for a fortnight, and could not recall a single event by which he could have blotted his record, Simon felt a shiver of apprehension when the company clerk informed him that the adjutant wanted to see him instantly. Leaving Sergeant Snell to complete the inspection of the platoon's weapons he made his way to Battalion HQ and Nigel Smith-Parr's office.

'Come on in, Simon,' Smith – Parr called when Simon tapped tentatively on the open door. Not a bad start he thought, his Christian name being used did not bode too much ill.

'Shut the door there's a good chap, and have seat,'

The mystery deepened, for a change it was Smith-Parr who appeared nervous. He cleared his throat, 'The colonel has asked, nay, told me to have a chat with you about something, well, er, a little sensitive.'

Simon's heart sank, was this bad news from home, had one of parents met with an accident or died?

'Cigarette,' Nigel held out a silver cigarette case, and then lit their cigarettes. He blew out a cloud of smoke, 'I really should give this foul habit up you know, I have tried a few times but without success. Have you ever tried, Simon? Bloody difficult I can tell you.'

Simon grasped the nettle, 'Sir could we get to why I'm here, is there a problem at home…?'

'Sorry, sorry, good Lord no, don't want to alarm you in that respect. No it's er, umm,' he seemed push aside his uneasiness and his mode changed back to the super-efficient scourge of subalterns, 'It has come to the attention of the commanding officer that you are having a liaison with a woman,' he corrected himself, 'a widow who is somewhat senior to you in years. Is that true?'

'Well yes,' Simon was astounded as well as relieved, 'I've not tried to hide it. In fact we both had dinner with the brigadier's wife, Jenny.'

Nigel held up a hand, 'Subalterns do not refer to the brigade commander's wife by her Christian name.'

'The evening that I spent with her she insisted that I did so, sir.'

'No matter, the CO does not think it appropriate that you continue seeing Mrs Blackburn. She has a position to uphold in her role with the WVS, and it is felt that this position would be undermined should the rank and file get to hear of this relationship.' Simon made to speak, Nigel held up a hand, 'Let me put the CO's view and then you can comment. He also feels that it is not very gentlemanly to take advantage of a lady in her position her being a widow and exposed to scandal. The colonel is a man of the world Simon but is saddened that an officer of the Royal West Lancashire's is behaving in such a despicable and caddish manner.'

Simon felt shocked and struggled to find a reply, 'Sir,' he began, 'we're friends, we enjoy each other's company, and neither of us is seeking any commitment from the other. I cannot see the problem...'

'I have explained the CO's feelings to you on this matter. Marriage would be out of the question, as you would need the CO's consent, as you know.'

'We have no intention of marrying,' Simon laughed, 'the idea is preposterous.'

'So you're just using this lady for your own sexual gratification?'

Nigel was showing signs of annoyance, 'There is no question of anyone using anyone; we just enjoy each other's company.'

The adjutant stood, marking the end of the interview, 'I expect you to do the right thing, Mr Gates.'

'Am I being ordered not to see Susan, Mrs Blackburn again, sir?'

'You know the colonel's opinion, Mr Gates and I expect you to respect that opinion.'

Simon stood his ground; he could hardly believe he was being so headstrong, 'Am I being forbidden to see the lady again, sir?' he insisted.

'Mr Gates,' Nigel was almost shouting, 'you know the commanding officers view; we shall leave it at that.'

Ray had left his OP at first light, and with Stan, had descended to where the rest of the troop was carrying out surveillance patrols on the jungle edge rather than being extracted and bringing their presence to the attention of the locals.

It had been agreed, with control, to remain for another forty-eight hours. But they had run out of rations and a platoon of the 10ᵗʰGhurkha's was on the way to re-supply, they were expected to arrive during the early part of the morning.

When Ray had given Pete and Roger a fuller account of the visit by the CT patrol, Pete said, 'Did you have a look at the camp again this morning?' He asked as he handed Ray a mug of tea.

'No, I thought it best to stay away. The more we enter the area the more chance there is that we'll leave a sign that we're about.'

Roger nodded in agreement, 'Yeah, but I'd lay odds that they'll be back in the next twenty-four hours. They'll be confident that if there's no sign of security forces in the area now then we don't know about the camp.'

'They didn't seem nervous?' Pete asked.

'No,' Ray handed the mug to Stan, 'they were on the ball, but didn't seem jumpy.'

'And you're still not sure how many there were?' Pete pressed.

'Two for sure, could have been three or four. As I said they were pretty switched on and left no tracks that I could detect.'

There was a slight commotion and some muted conversation then a grinning Gurkha entered the small clearing bearing a pack that was almost as big as he was. A portly figure followed close behind, his round face flushed with the effort of the climb.

'Hello chaps, your rations courtesy of 'B' Company Princess Mary's Own Gurkha Rifles, the 10ᵗʰ for short,' he shook hands with all present. 'Willie Ashton,' he introduced himself, 'Who's in charge?'

'I am,' Roger took his hand, 'Roger Howard.'

'Squadron Commander?'

'Troop,' Roger replied.

'We'll have a brew here,' Willie said, 'we've got a long trek out it'll take us at least two hours. These little buggers could probably do it in a sight less but I've just got out of dock, and the old fitness ain't what it should be...'

'Boss,' Rob Coupe, Rogers's signaller interrupted, his face tense, 'One Eight Delta are on the net.' The faint irregular buzz of Morse leaked from his headset; everyone waited watching the signaller scribbling quickly the incoming message on his pad. The sound of the transmission stopped and Rob handed the pad to Roger.

'Two Charlie Tango used Whisky Papa, figure's five minutes ago.' he read out aloud.

'The buggers are back,' Ray's face lit with anticipation.

The information was immediately relayed to KL, and it was decided that Ray should return and establish if the camp had been re-occupied, and if it was, then the OP was to be withdrawn.

*

When Simon left the adjutants office his emotions were in turmoil. Rage struggled with sorrow, and indignation with trepidation. He had been so delighted to be back with the regiment, and the homecoming had been comfortable and welcoming. He had slipped back into his role within 'A' Company like a veteran without any of the doubts that had haunted him in those first days in the BMH.

Now all had turned to dust, if he chose to ignore the warning he would be finished in the regiment, and if he did not then he would have to end his relationship with Susan. It seemed so unfair.

If he had been involved with a married woman or a lady of dubious character then he could have understood the CO's concern, but Susan was a cultured, educated and respectable widow who was liked and respected by the men who met her in her role as a WVS officer. Plus, she was beautiful and sexy. He smiled to himself as he headed back to the company lines.

The weapons inspection was completed when he got back and Sergeant Snell had the men stripping their magazines to give them a thorough cleaning.

'Just to fill in till lunchtime, sir, they're on sports this afternoon. Corporal Chester has arranged a football match with the signals platoon.'

'Very good!'

'Are you all right, sir?' Dave squinted at him, 'you look as though you've had a bit of a shock.'

Simon felt the desire to pour his heart out but knew this was something that he must bear alone, 'No I'm fine, thank you sergeant.'

'A visit to the adjutant can be a bit of a bummer.'

'No, no, that was er,' his voice trailed away and he changed the subject rather than invent a reason for his visit, 'there was nothing untoward,' he lied and then added. 'Is the match on the pitch behind the NAAFI?'

'Yes, are going over to support them? In fact if you fancied a game I'm sure Corporal Chester would find a place for you in the team.'

'No, no,' Simon replied quickly, 'I don't think my leg is quite up to a game of soccer yet,' he rubbed his leg to add conviction to his excuse, 'but I'll pop over to support the lads.'

*

Sam had not been completely ostracised but he had had it made clear to him that his behaviour had to change.

'If you don't stop thinking with your dick, Andrews, you can drink on your own tonight,' John informed him diplomatically, 'I'm pissed off with getting into fight's half way through the night and having to leg it before we get lynched.'

'Aw, come on, Johnno we've only had one scrap,' Sam protested.

'This time,' John agreed, 'but you got us into a punch up the first time we came here from Kota Tinggi.'

'Johnno's right, Sam,' Brian agreed, 'you've been a pain in the arse, and we've only had one decent night out since we got here.'

John had not finished, he jabbed a finger, 'Get into a scrap tonight and you're on your bloody own.'

Sam, undeterred put his arm round his friends broad shoulders, 'You wouldn't leave your old mate Sammy to get battered would you, Johnno.'

John pushed him away forcing himself not to grin, 'If he causes us anymore bloody trouble I'll batter him myself.'

They had walked down to the main road from the leave centre, as there were no taxis by the main gate. At the bottom of the hill there sat a small open fronted bar that had seen better days.

'Shall have one in here,' Ken suggested, 'we can watch for a taxi.'

A waitress with the build and eyes of an English Bull Terrier came to their table.

'Wha' you wan?' she asked not really wanting to know.

'Four bottles of Tiger, darling,' Brian told her.

She shuffled away with the rolling gait peculiar to Chinese wearing flip-flops and with nowhere in particular to go. She returned shortly with the order and put the bottles and glasses on the table.

'Four, twenty,' she stood waiting, her narrow black eyes fixed on something distant.

Sam handed her a five-dollar note, 'If you were a friendly girl I'd tell you to keep the change.'

'Wha' you say?' she raised her chin in question still scowling as she counted out the eighty cents change.

223

Sam grinned seeing a challenge, 'I said I'd let you keep the change,' he tapped the pile of change to make his point. Ignoring him she shuffled away talking in her native tongue to the barman, whom from his build, must have been related to her.

'Miserable cow,' Sam called after her.

'Sam, cut it out,' Ken warned.

'Well she bloody is,' he objected, 'I was only trying to be friendly.'

'Sam,' Brian put his glass down, 'promise not to be friendly to anyone at all tonight, and that way we might stay out of trouble.'

Sam shook his head, 'You're supposed to be my mates.'

Two more people they recognised as being from the leave centre came into the bar and sat at the next table.

Ken looked across, 'I've been waiting to see you, you bastard,' he pointed at one of the two men.

The accused youth put on an air of innocence, 'What about?'

'You know bloody well,' Ken grinned, 'I'm laughing now but if I'd seen you that night' I'd have given you a smack. This is the bugger,' he explained to the others, 'who gave us the name of that den of queer's.'

'We nearly got battered cos of you,' Sam complained.

'No Sam,' Brian shook his head, 'we nearly got battered because of you.'

John turned to face the newcomers, 'Perhaps you boys like going there and that's why you recommended it.'

'Yes,' Ken agreed, 'he was the one in the blue dress with those officers.'

They both laughed, 'Our secrets out. I owe you a beer for that but tell us what happened,' the waitress arrived, 'Six Tiger's, honey.'

They related the night's events while they waited for their drinks.

'Worse than that happened to one of our bombardiers,' the youth said when they had finished, 'I'm Roy by the way and this is Les, we're in the artillery, 26th Field Regiment in Seremban. Anyway, this bombardier of ours went there and this gorgeous looking bird took him upstairs, it's a knocking shop upstairs, and he'd stripped of ready for action when he found she was a he.' The beer arrived and he paused to pay, 'Said it had real tits though,' as he took his money from his pocket some change fell onto the floor.

The waitress assisted in the recovery of the coins, she bent over to retrieve a couple of dollar pieces. Unfortunately she was wearing a wide flouncy skirt that only descended to her knee, consequently, when she bent over her rear exposure was quite expansive and within reach of Sam. His reaction was instantaneous and smoothly executed. Without moving from his chair he threw the skirt over her back and slapped her ample posterior hard.

She screamed, turned, and punched Sam full in the face bursting his nose, and causing him to fall backwards of his chair. Her male double shouted and came from behind the bar with an agility that was frightening for someone of his build.

'Stop him,' John shouted to Brian and Ken. He stepped nimbly round the table as Sam scrambled to his feet and dropped him again with a fist to the side of the jaw, 'I bloody warned you, you daft bastard.'

Muscular and fit as he was Ken, had his work cut out restraining the irate barmen even with the help of Brian.

'There's a taxi here, let's go,' John shouted, and then, 'Oh fuck!' as a Military Police Land Rover pulled up behind it.

Chapter Twenty Five

Harry Woodhouse had received the news in silence. Jenny had said she would not telephone from the hospital; she wanted to give him the news, good or bad, in person. He had gone out the helicopter pad to greet her, and although they did not speak of the results until they reached the privacy of his office he knew from her demeanour that the news was not good.

She had announced the outcome calmly and with only the slightest catch in her voice, 'They've given me six months,' she said quietly and took a deep breath, 'possibly a year.'

They clung to each other in silence, and she was conscious of his slight, hard, body shaking as he sobbed quietly into her shoulder. Eventually he stopped, only a slight redness around his eye's told of his weeping.

'I shall get a signal of to FARELF HQ and request an immediate replacement,' he went to press the buzzer on his desk that would summon his aide.

'No Harry,' she touched his arm, 'I don't want any fuss.'

'It isn't fuss, darling, it's essential. We need to spend every minute that we can together.'

She shook her head, 'No, I don't want any changes to our normal routine. In fact, I don't want anybody to know how bad it is. I cannot handle sympathy, you know that.'

'But I can't carry on as though nothing is wrong,' he protested.

'If I can you can,' she placed a finger on his lips, 'you've got a big operation in the offing...'

'Damn the bloody operation,' he cut in, 'I've got first class subordinates who can handle things without my interference....'

'No, no Harry,' she smiled, 'if you want to make my final days happy, please let us carry on as normal. Don't you see I have always been happy with our life as it is, and that's the way I want it to finish. The same routine, it's what I am happiest and most comfortable with, don't let anything change, please.'

He took her in his arms again. 'You're so brave and sensible my dearest, Jenny, but you must promise me one thing.'

'I will if I can.'

'Oh you can. I will do exactly as you desire providing that we immediately take a month's leave in the UK once this operation is over.'

Her steadfastness slipped slightly and her green eyes filled, 'Yes, that's a lovely thought. It would be nice to see the old country again before, before...' she cried and he held her tight determinedly fighting off his own need to join in.

*

After spending ten minutes exposed to the crippling rays of the afternoon sun, watching his platoon engaged in violent activity from which the natives sensibly abstain during the day, Simon sought out Susan in the relative cool of the WVS room.

She listened to his encounter with the adjutant with a look of increasing incredulity on her face, 'I can't believe what you have just told me, Simon.'

'I swear every word is true,' Simon threw a furtive look at a couple of soldiers playing chess at table by the window, 'can we go into your office?'

'Simon this is just unbelievable,' her amazement was obvious on her face and he was somewhat puzzled that she displayed so sign of being upset, just bewilderment.

'I need a cigarette,' Simon took a pack from his shirt pocket, 'I promise that I won't let this go unchallenged,' he said after he had lit their cigarettes, 'even if I have to apply for an interview with the brigadier.'

Susan waved a hand to dismiss the idea, 'There's really no need, Simon.'

'No I insist,' he said forcefully, 'I'm National Service I don't have career prospects to consider.'

'Simon stop it,' she kissed him on the mouth, 'listen to me instead of charging the windmills.' When she saw that she had his attention she went on, 'It isn't your CO that's delivering this edict, it's Smith – Parr.'

'No,' Simon shook his head, 'he said it was the colonel, he wouldn't dare....'

'Nigel Smith – Parr was an absolute pain in the bum for the first year after I was posted here. Then, he was a platoon commander and he made my life very uncomfortable. So much so that I had to ask Jenny Woodhouse to help, I didn't want to get him into trouble with the regiment. Anyway, one quiet word from Jenny did the trick and he hasn't spoken to me since.'

'What was he doing?'

'Simon, don't be so obtuse, he was pestering me to go out with him of course. You look surprised.'

'Well, Simon shrugged, 'he's quite good looking, what was the problem.'

'Are looks so important?'

'Well no, but they help.'

She sighed, 'Yes, your right, but you only see him as a fellow officer, another man. But I can tell you, as a woman, that he's a slimy lascivious individual and Jenny came to the same conclusion without any prompting from me.'

'Does the brigadier know about it?'

'No, neither does your CO.'

'Well that's a relief,' he said.

'Why?'

'Well he can't do anything officially, in fact he's at a disadvantage.'

'Taking the CO's name in vain?'

'Indeed,' he paused, 'but he must have known I would mention it to you.'

'Well he's probably hoping that you will still believe that it has come from the CO despite what I tell you and you won't take the risk of ignoring your colonel's directive.'

'Hmm, possibly, but I tell you, if I get extra duties for non-compliance then I will take it higher.'

Susan kissed him lightly on the cheek, 'But not without discussing it with me first, promise?'

He hesitated, 'Okay, promise.'

*

When Ray had returned to his OP, Frank gave him greater detail of the sighting.

'They must definitely be back in the camp, Ray,' the lanky Irishman said, 'there were four of them, and they filled big palm oil cans with water so they wouldn't be taking them far.'

After a cautious and lengthy recce Ray estimated that it must be an advance party as he could only identify ten people present but knew there must be others out as sentries but he was only able to find one of these. From the actions of those in the camp it could be easily presumed that they were preparing the camp for a larger number.

'It seems,' Roger told them when they met up just before dusk and Ray had reported his findings and conclusions, 'the Aussie's had a contact a couple of days ago, and on the follow up they found a wounded CT who had intelligence on him that relates to the camp you were watching, and as a result of this info we've been told to do a covert extraction.'

*

May Ling was not sentimental about leaving nor was the thought of parting with all of her possessions an anathema to her, materialism was something she detested, it was a sickness of the affluent and she scorned their dependence on ownership. However, getting used to her new appearance would take a little time, and her reflection in the window as she walked to the door startled her. She went to the mirror that hung on the wall by the door and experienced a twinge of regret. Her long waist-length hair was gone and the crude short cut of village girl had replaced it. The positive side was its practicality and that it made her look younger.

She took a last look round the flat, switched off the light and closed the door feeling a pang of guilt at the caress of sadness and regret that suddenly stirred within her. She was leaving many friends behind, friends that she had become fond of and knew that they were equally fond of her even if they held opposing views. Shrugging off these feelings of remorse and sorrow she picked up her small case, set her mind on the future, and went down the narrow stairs and out into the wet night.

*

It was hot in the cell; the only window was small and high in the wall. In the door was a hole about two inches in diameter under which a previous occupant had penned the words, *Please do not lean out of the window*. No air circulated and John's shirt was not only soiled from the afternoon's events but was as wet as if he had lifted it from a bucket of water.

Despite protests from Ken and Brian, and the so-called victim, Sam, he had been bundled into the back of the Military Police Land Rover and brought to Provost Company HQ. At 1700 he had been given a very acceptable meal of much higher quality than was served back at battalion.

An hour later a RMP lance-corporal took to him to an interview room where another RMP, a full corporal, was seated at a desk, 'Sit down,' he said. He wore his cap, and the severe peak hid his eyes, 'You're in trouble, Cantrill, aren't you?'

'If you say so, but it was just a fight between mates,' John said defiantly.

'Well, your mate, as you put it, has had four stitches to the back of his head, and he's got a broken tooth. Some mate.'

'Well I only punched him once so I don't know how...'

'Banged his head on the edge the walk way, and that was as a result of your punch,' the MP's eyes narrowed 'so it was your fault.'

'He asked for it,' John shrugged.

'Scouser, aren't you, Cantrill?'

'Was, last time I looked.'

'Don't get lippy with me, lad,' the corporal warned, 'I eat Scouser's.'

'That's probably why you're such a big fellah,' John leaned back in his chair awaiting the storm.

Slowly a smile spread across the MP's face and John heard a suppressed laugh from the lance-corporal who was stood behind him.

'Go on, piss off,' the corporal said.

John was shocked, 'I can go, no charge?'

'I'll charge you for the room and your meal if you hang around any longer.'

John got to his feet, 'How do I get to Sandes from here, I don't know where I am?'

'You're mates are waiting outside in a taxi, now bugger off.'

Half dozen Land Rovers were parked outside the busy duty room, and at the back of the line a black, beat up, Mercedes taxi stood. Ken was standing by the front passenger door.

'Come on, Cantrill,' he shouted, 'you've wasted enough drinking time.'

'How's Sam,' John asked as he neared the taxi.

'He's fucking great you bastard,' Sam's ruddy head shot out of the rear window, his wide grin showing off his broken tooth.

'Shit Andrews, you're uglier than ever,' John opened the door, 'push up.'

'Look at the back of me bloody head, they've shaved it,' he turned his head to display a two inch square of shaved scalp the colour of iodine, 'it bloody hurt.'

'The MP's said you'd cracked the kerb,' John got into the cab.

'I didn't know I'd split me head,' he grabbed John's hand and gripped it, 'No hard feelings mate.'

John ruffled his hair, 'You're a gobshite, Sam but we love him, don't we fellah's?'

'Change the love to, put up with,' Brian suggested.

*

Irene had intended to catch an earlier train but the CID had held a little surprise party for her leaving, but as she had booked earlier it did not really create a great problem. Bo thought that she was catching the three thirty five but he was going on an operation so he would not be able to meet her. She had an Aunt who lived in Kampong Simpang, and the duty inspector at Taiping had agreed that a police vehicle could take her there, as the curfew would be in force when she arrived.

It was the night train to Georgetown and there were plenty of seats in the second class as most of the Europeans had sleepers, and the bar had closed. She found an empty table in the restaurant car and ordered a coffee, then settled down with the Agatha Christie thriller that she was reading.

She looked up as two armed Malay soldiers entered the compartment and occupied the seat by the door. The large clock on the platform showed 22.28, they would be leaving in two minutes and her new life was about to begin, a thrill of excitement ran through her body. The book was forgotten for a moment as she gazed out of the window watching the late comers hurrying, flustered, down the platform. A Tamil family, mother and five young children, the eldest being no more than ten, were being herded along the platform by the irate father, his face shining with sweat.

Suddenly, another traveller, a female, caught her eye; late as she was she seemed unperturbed by the urgency surrounding her, and casually progressed along the platform looking neither left nor right. She wore the ubiquitous pyjama suit like so many Chinese and a large straw had that partially hid her face. She carried a well-worn case that for its size appeared light. Irene could not see the woman's face but she sensed that she somehow knew her and there was something different about her. That was it; she did not have the shuffling gait that was normal among the class of people to which she probably belonged.

She watched the girl until she was out of sight but was unable to identify why she seemed to know her. She considered going along to third class to see if she could find her but decided against the idea. In her job as a policewoman she knew hundreds of people that she met only briefly but in memorable situations and this girl could be one such person.

*

Susan's story about Nigel Smith-Parr being the author of the warning over their relationship was proved correct that same evening. They had gone to the Garrison AKC to see Singing in the Rain, and as they were leaving Simon heard a familiar voice speak his name.

'Enjoy the film, Simon?'

Simon turned and his heart stopped, there stood Lt Colonel Crawson and his wife, 'Oh, er, yes sir very much, I um…'

'Hello, Susan,' Mrs Crawson beamed at Susan, 'it's nice to see you out enjoying yourself, we were afraid you were becoming a hermit.'

'Mrs Blackburn,' the CO acknowledged her, 'you're the garrison WVS lady?'

'That's right, sir', Susan smiled.

'Jerry, please.'

'Thank you, Jerry,' Susan responded.

'And how are things on the WVS front,' he asked amiably.

'Excellent.'

'Good, good,' then Simon's heart sank when he added, 'Forgive my bad manners Mrs Blackburn...'

'Susan, please.'

'Yes, Susan, if you would just excuse Simon and me for a moment, a little military matter.'

Simon saw the look of alarm on Susan's face as the CO led him a few steps away from the ladies.

'I've been called to an emergency briefing at brigade on Monday so you can be certain it is something very hot concerning Operation Clive. Your company, Simon, is ear marked for an important role; do you feel up to it?'

Relief, pride and excitement washed over him with equal intensity. Relief that he was not being censured over his relationship with Susan, pride that the CO thought enough about him to show this concern, and excitement at the chance to be involved in some certain action again but this time having some control.

'Yes of course, sir.'

'The leg's up to it then?'

'No trouble at all on this last op, sir.'

'Good show. Well I'll not keep you away from the lovely Mrs Blackburn. Goodnight Mrs Blackburn,' he called across to Susan, 'Er, Susan. Come along my dear,' he took his wife's arm.

'Goodnight, Jerry,' Susan called after him and then to Simon, 'so, what was all that about.'

'Something big is blowing up and as 'A' Company will be involved he was enquiring if I considered myself fit enough.'

'What a relief,' she grinned, 'I was beginning to think I'd got it wrong about NSP.'

'NSP'?

'Nigel Smith-Parr, dummy. Come on I need a drink.'

*

The final leg of the journey had not only been physically difficult but also harrowing. Tanjong Rambutan, although a friendly village towards the MRLA, was dangerous for that very reason. The security forces were equally aware of the village's sympathies and it was therefore a regular target for their attention. This attention came in many forms but predominately night ambushes in the cultivated areas that surrounded the village.

Lam Ten had made a wide detour of the village from north to south and had then swung back north-east through the cultivation to head back to the south side of the village. He had left the jungle edge at last light when the workers had gone from the fields and the security forces would have been moving to any ambush site that they may have planned. He was confident that he would see or hear them before they would be aware of his presence but once darkness had fallen he could bump into them anywhere, well almost anywhere.

Ambushes could only be reliably placed on tracks, bridges or track junctions and such like. To site them in the middle of tapioca or rubber would be too haphazard, so tracks, where it was easier and quieter to move, were the most sensible positions for an ambush to be laid. A man of Lam's skill and experience stayed away from these hazards and apart from having to cross the odd track he kept to large areas of cultivation.

Even so it was quite nerve wracking, alone, in the dark, and with the possibility of stumbling into a well-armed body of men whose one intention was to kill any human who crossed their path. He moved slowly and with great care stopping frequently for long periods to listen. No matter how well trained and proficient troops were few could stay completely motionless for more than ten minutes at a time and the alert listener would hear the slightest sound of movement.

The raucous nocturnal melody was a double edged sword, for it not only covered any careless noise that he made but it would also muffle the impatient shifting of the aching foot or limb numbed by remaining too long in one position, of those who may be lying in wait with violent intent.

He was getting close to the village and the security lights that it wore like a bright necklace lit the immediate area of the perimeter fence for fifty yards into the surrounding tapioca field, throwing long shadows away from each bush.

He found a mature tapioca bush and settled himself beneath it to wait for the dawn, it would be a long night and the mosquitoes, as ever, were active. From inside his shirt he took a folded banana leaf that held the only sustenance he would have until he returned to the camp ten miles away on the other side of the four thousand feet Korbu ridge. When he had eaten the rice and the few vegetables his thoughts were nagged by the desire to smoke but he was used to resisting the urge and settled himself down to sleep.

As he dozed he could clearly hear music from the village and the odd shout of greeting or peel of laughter. It crossed his mind that the villager's lives were, in the main, quite pleasant. The government had provided them with a small amount of land and the materials to build their homes, and during the hours of darkness they had protection and peaceful rest. The conditions were far removed from the life that he had led prior to the Japanese invasion in 1941. Most of the Chinese were squatters who lived in ramshackle communities on the fringe of the jungle. His father had built the family home with anything he could lay his hands on; woven atap, cardboard, planks of wood and the greatest treasure of all, sheets of corrugated tin. He and his three brothers and two sisters had shared the single room with their parents and the half dozen chickens that the family owned.

He must have drifted off because he did not hear the trucks arrive. The first he was aware of their presence was the slamming of doors and raised English voices. Two large army trucks and a Land Rover were parked a little way along the road from the main gate, and just visible, at the edge of the light, stood an armoured car.

As he lay watching the scene and wondering about the significance of their presence he heard the distinctive sound of a group of men moving quickly and with little fear of danger. To his right he could make out the shadowy figures of men moving easily and briskly towards the main gate. It was clear from their posture and shape that they were security forces, and from their size, probably British. They passed within twenty feet of where he lay, close enough for him to smell the sour odour of Europeans who had spent a number of days in the jungle sweating and not bathing. He counted eighteen figures silhouetted against the lights of the village and in no time they were out of view over a low brow. Ten minutes later they re-appeared by the trucks. This gave Lam confidence that there would be no further possibility of meeting the enemy again that night, and it also meant that there would be no others in the vicinity for his return journey the following day.

Chapter Twenty Six

Harry Woodhouse was a professional soldier in a long line of career soldiers. He had been born and raised in a garrison town, and only during his years at boarding school was he out of the sound of the barrack square. His father, and grandfather had commanded the Northumberland Fusiliers, and he had lived in the warmth of a northeast community whether it be in Africa, Egypt or India. When Harry took up his military career, at the age of eighteen, he had chosen the Royal Engineers much to the displeasure of his father. But academically he had done well at Wellington and he had considered that he could have the best of both worlds by making this choice. In 1940 he had been excited by the formation of the commandos and had volunteered for a unit where his knowledge and skill with explosives could be put to good use. He had ended the war as a member of the Parachute Regiment, but returned briefly to his parent regiment before being posted to the War Office in a staff job.

He had known the instant that he had received the news about the intelligence found on a dying CT, that his promise to Jenny to take a long leave in the UK would have to be postponed. She had taken the news like any good army wife with a resigned shrug and a smile.

'It can't be helped dear,' she pecked him lightly on his cheek. 'Dienst ist dienst und schnapps ist schnapps. We'll find time when this operations over.'

The brigade major, Allen Doyle, brought the gathering to a sitting attention as Harry strode into the room, mounted the dais and turned to face them.

'Relax gentlemen,' he placed his cap on a table beside the lectern. 'You will be happy to hear that I will have little to say at this briefing,' this was met with polite and predictable laughter, 'suffice to say that I consider that we are now in a position to strike a blow against the CT in Northern Malaya from which they will not recover,' he turned to Allen Doyle, 'Allen.'

The BM took his place at the lectern with a pointer in his hand, 'A mixture of hard work and good fortune has come together to provide us with new intelligence and confirm some things that we already knew.' He turned and pointed to the hills North of Lasah, 'Three days ago the 3rd Australians had their first incident with CT when one of their patrols bumped a group of at least five. In the exchange of fire the Australians lost one killed and one wounded. The RWL's tracking team was despatched to the site and the following day tracked down a badly wounded CT, who we now know to be, Najib Awang a branch committee member from Kelantan. He died shortly after being captured so we were unable to glean any intelligence other than from what he was carrying.' He faced his audience, 'In his possession was found a letter signed by Chin Peng informing his SCM's of a meeting to be held at the camp we having been searching for in the area of Gunong Besar.' He returned to the large wall map. 'A week ago an Auster returning from a reconnaissance flight at dusk, spotted a fire here,' he pointed at the map, 'and two days later, acting on this intelligence, a troop from D Squadron SAS discovered an abandoned camp at that spot. Grid references are included in your briefing notes that will be handed out later. The camp was in good order and, in the opinion of the NCO who led the patrol, it had only recently been evacuated.' At the lectern again he continued, 'The sequence of subsequent events shows that the camp was deserted because of the Auster's low flight over the camp which was caused by the pilot avoiding bad weather. It was decided to watch the camp for a period, and an OP was set up on a likely water point as the camp was so well sited that it proved difficult to keep it under surveillance. Two days later a lone CT was seen at the water point but subsequently tracks were found for at least three. We consider they were a recce to establish whether or not security forces had been around as a result of the aircraft. After another two days the patience of the OP was rewarded, and about a dozen CT returned to the camp. It was apparent from their behaviour that they were an advance party preparing for re-occupation. The OP has now been withdrawn as trying to keep it supplied would have been tempting fate too far. Gentlemen, as the Brigadier said in his opening remarks, success will prove devastating for the MRLA but the task before us is both difficult and dangerous. This is a camp capable of housing two hundred bodies,' a murmur of surprise ran through the audience, 'and conventional tactics would demand a force of at least six hundred to attack it.' He waited for silence to take hold, 'What is more, it is, as I pointed out previously, well sited and has bunkers that are estimated to be able to withstand air and artillery attack,' he looked across at Harry, 'Sir.'

Harry took the stand, 'There we are gentlemen, we know where they are, can we cut the mustard?' he paused and looked round the room; his question was met with nods and determined expressions, 'Before we continue I would like to express my thanks and admiration for the excellent work carried out by your chaps, Jack,' he addressed his words at Major Hooper.

'Thank you sir,' Jack replied and indicated Roger, 'it was Captain Howard's troop that deserve the praise.'

'Yes,' Harry continued, 'well done, Roger, please pass on my congratulations to your men. Now, how do we go about this task?'

*

Lam knew that it was a woman that he was to meet and escort back to the camp of 5 Company. The camp was a three day march distant at the northern end of the Korbu range. His instructions were to watch the buses that arrived at the village throughout the morning and look for an individual carrying red parasol which would be open regardless of the weather. The owner would then take the Tanah Hitam road and at the bridge that crossed a small river she would wait for him to approach her.

She was sitting on a large rock out of view of the road but she had left the parasol in sight for anybody who was looking for her. Lam put his hand inside his shirt and grasped the Nambu pistol that was tucked into his waistband; he always approached any new meeting prepared for the worst. The girl turned as he drew near and sight of her made him start.

'May Ling!' he said, shocked.

She looked equally surprised, 'We're not going to Beng Kim,' she began, 'I was told...'

'No, no,' he reassured her, 'Beng is on the move, we are going to 5 Company but it's a long march.'

She stood, 'That doesn't worry me; we'd better start straight away.'

'Right, but we will have to try to get some food at Tanah Hitam, I have nothing.'

She picked up a small pack, 'I have enough for both of us,' she shook her head when he tried to take it from her, 'I can manage.'

'Did you hear about Lau? He asked as they followed the stream towards the ulu.

'You mean his treachery?'

She was walking behind him and he could not see her face but the bitterness of the words told him of her feelings, 'Yes' he replied, 'but he had good reason, Beng treated him badly.'

'That is not reason enough to betray the cause,' her anger caused her to raise her voice and he turned and hushed her. She lowered her voice, 'I'm sorry, but there can be no excuse for what he did.'

They walked in silence for a few minutes; her next words made his blood turn cold,

'But he will pay, he will pay dearly.'

*

Roger had hoped to get a few days free to visit Linda in KL but the recent events meant that he had to stay in Ipoh with his troop as they

237

were on a four hour standby; even a drink was out of the question. He knew that Linda would not be pleased with the situation, he had seen very little of her for the past few weeks, and although it was not her way to complain he knew that events must be sorely testing her patience. He phoned her office from the Garrison Officers mess where he was temporarily billeted.

'Miss Tang no longer works here, sir,' the voice said at the other end of the line.

'Doesn't work there, what d'you mean? Of course she works there. She's in Inspector Sankey's office.'

'I now work for Inspector Sankey,' the girl said, 'Miss Tang left a few days ago.'

Roger was momentarily lost for words, 'Let me speak to Inspector Sankey please.'

'The inspector's away, sir,' the voice was bland and uninterested in his dilemma.

'Well where is he?' he snapped.

'I cannot give you that information.'

'Well can you put me through to, Sergeant Irene Larek, in CID?'

The phone went quiet for a moment.

'CID,' a voice informed him.

'Can I speak to Sergeant Larek please?'

'Sergeant Larek no longer works from this office,' came the reply.

'What's going on here? Well can you put me through to the office where she does work?' He struggled to suppress his frustration.

'That will not be possible,' the man said.

'Why not'? Roger was beginning to seethe.

'She has been posted out of the State.'

'And I suppose you can't tell me where?

'Sorry,'

Roger slammed the receiver down, went into the bar, and treated himself to a double scotch despite the stand-by.

*

Lau was pleased and surprised how quickly he had adapted to the normality of freedom. His earlier fears and loneliness had diminished until he only had the odd, mild attack of either condition.

The single event that had had the greatest influence on this feeling of wellbeing had been at the bank. When he had visited the branch to complete the opening of the account, which had been set up by some anonymous sole from either the government or the police, he had almost given his real name but as the words *Lau Fong* had all but formed he replaced them quickly.

'Tan Chen,' and then as if to convince himself, and her, repeated the name, 'Tan Chen.'

The statement had been passed across the counter and when he had seen his new name at the top of the sheet and the balance of $10,000 he had used the large mahogany counter to support himself.

He had been determined not spend more than he needed even though a similar amount would be paid to him in twelve months time. His confidence was further boosted by having made a friend at the tea bar where went for his breakfast each morning. Low Kow was more of an acquaintance than a friend but Lau was convinced that a friendship would develop. His suspicion of strangers had still been acute when he first met Low but the manner of their meeting could have only been down to chance. He had seen the short, fat, man every day for the past week in the tea bar but they had never spoken, although they would nod to each other. The previous day they had both been reading the Straits Times; this was unique in itself as all of the other customers, like most Chinese, were reading papers in their own language.

That morning, as was his habit, Lau was attempting to solve the crossword when he heard a sigh of frustration and looked up and saw Low at an adjoining table. He too appeared to be doing the crossword and his exasperated expression suggested that it was he who had emitted the sigh.

Lau smiled, 'I am out of practice,' he admitted.

'I've never been very good even with practice,' Low laughed. He stretched out and offered his hand, 'Low Kow, I own the jewellers across the road.'

'Tan Chen,' Lau was pleased that his new name came without hesitation.

'And what business are you in, Tan?' Low asked.

'I teach English privately,' he continued with the cover.

The rest of the week they chatted and confronted the crossword together. Lau was beginning to feel that he was on the verge of a new life. He had been looking forward to Saturday evening all week; Kow had invited him to his house for a meal and to meet his family.

The Lows lived on the south side of the city in an area called Pudu, it was about three miles away, and still retaining a lot of his frugality Lau had decided to walk there. When he had set off a rainstorm had just ended and the evening was hot and more humid than normal. To avoid arriving with a shirt that was limp with sweat he walked slowly and took in the sights and sounds of a city as it stirred itself for the exciting, evening night-life.

Since his surrender it had been a continual mystification as to why he had ever subjected himself to that period of fear, starvation, humiliation and discomfort. Had he just matured or had he become selfish and uncaring?

It was half past six when he arrived in Pudu. It was a pleasant leafy suburb from what he could see in the dark. The street light was sparse but effective enough for an area that verged on the rural. He stood under a lamp and studied the address that Low had given him. A man who had been walking behind him drew closer.

'Excuse me friend,' Lau smiled at the man, 'do you come from these parts?'

'I live nearby,' he stopped.

'Could you tell me where Rapat Grove is?'

'I know it, I am passing there I can show you.'

Grateful of the stranger's kindness he set off with him.

'We can cut through here,' the man said as he turned off the path and entered a grassed area dotted with bushes and palm trees. Lau immediately sensed danger and turned to head back to the path but found himself face to face with another man who must have been following them.

The punch to his upper ribs took his breath away and strangled his cry for help. As he turned away from his attacker he saw the first man with his right arm raised and saw too late the parang in his hand. The blow was delivered with such force that blade bit deeply the base of his neck severing the scalene muscle, rupturing the subclavian artery, fracturing his clavicle, and numbing the left side of his body. Lau sagged to the floor with a jet of blood spurting from the fatal wound. The knife, that he had felt as a punch to his chest, had entered his heart, and he was dead before his fall ended.

*

'Missy Blackburn outside,' Susan's Amah opened the door.

'Thank you, Didi,' Simon put his wide brimmed hat on the chair in the hall.

'You wan' nice cold drink, Mr Simon?' she called after him as he passed through the lounge, 'or you wan' tea?'

'A beer....' Simon began

'Bring him lemonade, Didi,' Susan called from the verandah.

'Why can't I have a beer?' Simon bent down and kissed her on the forehead

She looked up at him and smiled, 'Because, Mr Gates I'm taking you out somewhere special for lunch and I don't want you half sloshed before we get there.'

'Oh,' he took the lounger next to her, 'I'm regularly pissed am I?'

'You're not a hardened drinker, Simon and it only takes a couple for you to start slurring your words.'

'I do not,' he protested, 'Thank you,' he took the glass of lemonade from Didi.

Susan giggled, 'You do Simon, you probably aren't aware that you're doing it but you've often introduced me as Mishush Blackburn after a couple of Tiger's.'

'I don't believe you. Anyway,' he said changing the subject, 'what's the special occasion, and where's the special venue'? Before she could reply he went on, 'I was hoping that we were going to spend the day in lustful pursuits.'

She slapped him gently of the arm, 'I've got tickets for the Ipoh Turf Club with lunch included. Have you ever been to the races?'

'No,' he replied impressed, 'how did you wangle those?'

She half turned to him and peered over the top of her sunglasses, 'I have many admirers, Mr Gates,' she perceived a fleeting look of concern; she reached across and took his hand, 'but only one lover.'

The Ipoh Turf Club stood between the muddy waters of the Perak River and the Batu Gajah road amid vast swathes of neatly cropped but yellowing grass. Clumps of palm and bright green Tualong trees provided welcome patches of cool shade, and the white fencing that marked out the course dazzled in the searing afternoon sun. Brilliantly coloured parasols and wide brimmed hats protected the ladies from the worst of the effects of the sun's rays.

The bulk of the crowd was European, the larger part of them being services, but most wore civilian clothes the white shirts reflecting the fierce light. Hussar officers were mainly in uniform, stiffly starched bush jackets with painfully tight trousers that ended at highly polished boots and gleaming spurs, their epaulette's of chain mail and cherry red service caps all added colour to the scene.

Simon felt a little like a male Cinderella in a plain white shirt and lightweight twill slacks but Susan made up for his dour appearance. She wore a, wide brimmed, white hat, and yellow dress of a flimsy material that looked both cool and elegant.

'First thing I want is a nice cold drink,' she said, when they arrived, 'the first race isn't until two so we have plenty of time to place a bet.'

The bar was a large marquee beside the parade ring so that the punters could examine the mounts from the comfort of its shade. At one end there were tables and chairs but they all appeared to be occupied.

'Wait here and I'll join the scrum,' Simon told her, 'what would you like?'

'A long cold whisky and ginger please.'

When he returned with their drinks she was grinning widely,

'Guess who I've just seen?' and she nodded towards the area of tables.

Simon scanned the tables looking for a familiar face but failed to seen anyone, 'Who, I can't see anyone?'

'There,' she pointed, 'the table near the end of the bar.'

His heart sank, 'Smith-Parr.'

'And can you see who he's with?

'No he's hidden by that large couple,' he moved to his right to get sight of Smith-Parr's companion, 'Is it the colonel?' the fat couple finished their drinks and moved away, 'Oh, bloody hell it's Jenny.'

'And Harry,' she pointed out.

'Harry?' the third person was still screened by the bar.

She grinned wickedly at him, 'Harry Woodhouse, Jenny's husband.'

'The Brigadier?'

'Come on,' she took his hand.

He pulled back, 'I'm not going over there.'

For the first time he saw the anger of which she was capable, 'Why not for goodness sake, Smith-Parr needs to be bloody well embarrassed.'

'He's my adjutant,' the despair was in his voice and in his eyes, 'I'm the one who'll be embarrassed....'

'Don't be such a wimp, Simon,' she pulled him towards the group, his resistance was in vain for at that moment the group got to their feet and made to leave the marquee, the course they chose brought them in his direction.

'Susan,' Jenny saw them first, they hugged, 'Hello, Simon. Harry,' she turned to the brigadier, 'this is the young man that I met at Frasers Hill, Simon Gates; he was wounded in the ambush a couple of months ago.'

'Damn unlucky there, Simon, but it could have been a lot worse,' Harry shook his hand firmly. 'How are you feeling now, leg wound wasn't it?'

'And his poor face,' Susan touched the scar on his cheek.

'Susan my dear,' Harry kissed her, 'you've been neglecting us young lady when did you last come round to see us, must be at least six months.'

'Nonsense, Harry,' Jenny corrected him, 'Susan was round a couple of days ago for coffee.'

'Don't come to see me though do you?' Harry took Susan's hand. 'Well you're damn well going to spend the day with us today,' as he led her away he turned. 'Sorry to pinch your lady, Simon, but I'm pulling rank, and you'll just have to put up with the competition.'

'Well I've got two handsome young men of my own,' Jenny linked arms with Simon and Nigel.

Simon looked across at Smith-Parr and smiled, the response was a sickly, embarrassed, grin.

*

'Home sweet home,' John dumped his case on the floor and dropped onto his bed.

'Did you have a good leave, Scouse?' Alan was sat at the table in the middle of the room writing a letter.

'Good leave, good leave?' he half raised himself on his elbow, 'ask him,' Sam had just entered the door at the far end of the basha, 'Sam, did we have a good leave?'

'Smashing,' Sam unlocked his locker.

'He's a lying bastard,' John moaned, 'I tell you, Al, he's a fucking nutter.'

'I'm a nutter,' Sam protested and went over to the table, 'look what he's done to my good looks, Al, smacked me in the mouth and broke me tooth. I've a good mind to sue,' he returned to his bed space and started to unpack his bag.

Alan laughed, 'What the hell have you two been up to.'

'Al,' Brian entered, 'don't ask, I went for a week's rest and I've come back looking forward to the next op just to get some quiet time. That mad bugger,' he nodded at Sam, 'could get into a fight in an empty room.'

'Oh that's right pick on Sam. You're all pissed off because I got me leg over and you didn't.'

'In a knocking shop I suppose?' Alan said.

'No, no Al,' Sam returned to the table, 'no, no, wife of an airman, who was on duty.'

'You rotten sod, Sam, having it off with a bloke's wife while he was on duty,' Alan chided.

'All's fair in love and war, Al,' Sam went back to unpacking his holdall.

'There's mail for you lads, in the company office,' Alan told them.

John got to his feet re-energised, 'Is anyone up there now?

'Harrison should be,' Alan replied.

Harrison, the company clerk, mixed very little with the rest of the company. He slept in a space behind a curtain at the back of the office, and rarely visited the NAAFI and always arranged either late or early meals in the cookhouse.

It was always his way to act as though every request made of him by the men was a great trial but after an amount of huffing and puffing he usually conformed to what was asked of him. After complaining that he never really got a day free from his responsibilities he unlocked the ammunition box by his desk, and handed over a half dozen letters. There were two for John. After giving the other three theirs he lay on his bed and opened the first. It was from his mother, this he knew from the hand writing; it was a single page that re assured him as to the families health and urged him to take care of himself.

Slowly and carefully he opened the second and smiled, the address at the top of the first page told him it was from Joyce, Keith's sister;

Dear John, You'll never know how grateful my mother and I were to read what you had to say about Keith, we both cried. Although I miss him terribly it is far worse for my poor mother who has now lost the two men in her life to war. I was too young to know my dad and Keith was the dad I never knew and now he has gone too, I still can't believe it, and sometimes I think I see him across the fields or walking through the village. People say that time heals but I don't believe that, I don't think this pain will ever leave me.

I do hope you and your mates had a good leave, Keith would have wanted you to and I am sure you deserved it.

Please write again if you have the time, you and Alan are our last connection with Keith, you saw him more recently than us. Do you have any photographs of him? He did send us a couple while he was on the ship going out there, you were on one of them, he wrote the names on the back, you were all lying on the deck sunbathing.

My mother sends her thanks for the letter, and thanks again from me. I do hope you will keep in touch.

Keep safe and we'll pray for you, Joyce.

*

As the light began to fade they stopped, and while Lam prepared a shelter May Ling cooked some rice and placed it onto a couple of large leaves with some dried fish.

They had said little throughout the day and he could tell that she was struggling. He had slowed the pace but was confident that her fitness would improve daily so long as he did not tire her too much to begin with.

The day before their meeting he had managed to get to a 'letterbox' and had read the message and then destroyed it. The suspicion of his contact was probably correct but he could not imagine how he could now get in touch. This journey was taking him away from his normal area and it would not now be possible pass on any information. He

244

knew that once he had delivered the girl he would be moving with 5 Company to the camp in the north, the camp he had only visited on the one occasion, and it was the camp his controller wanted to know about. It was only a matter of time before they found it and he did not want to be there when they did. It was in a difficult situation, perhaps the time had come for him to follow the example of his friend Lau and return to the outside world.

'I have enough for only two more days.' May was examining the food from her pack.

The words startled him, he had almost forgotten that she was there, 'That will be enough,' he assured her.

She looked at him with dark eyes that seem to search his mind, 'My cousin greatly angered and disgraced me,' she said after a long silence.

The darkness closed quickly around and they sought the shelter of the small basha that he had made. It was unavoidable that their bodies touched as they lay under the small shelter and in the night he thought he heard her crying softly and her slight body shook a little with her suppressed sobs.

Chapter Twenty Seven

Insertion was to be in the same manner as their recent extraction but at greater distance from the target so as to maintain the highest security; it called for a two-day march in carrying a week's rations, resulting in their packs weighing at least sixty pounds. The mission was to confirm that the camp was fully occupied and then pass the information back to brigade with a suggested plan of attack.

Brigadier Woodhouse knew that an effective plan could not be formulated at brigade HQ, the men on the ground, especially the SAS, would be able to take all the circumstances into account and come up with the tactics most likely to succeed. Protests, by senior officers at brigade, carefully phrased, had been numerous and well-presented and he had listened patiently to the all with an open mind. But none of the arguments put forward made him doubt for a moment that he was wrong in his decision.

As a consequence of the brigade commanders judgement, George Elloy, the commanding officer of 22 Special Air Service Regiment, had decided that D Squadron Commander, Johnny Hooper, should accompany the recce.

'I have every faith in your ability, as a troop commander, Roger,' he had explained at the briefing, 'if I hadn't you wouldn't be here. But this sounds as though it could be a two company attack and that needs to be planned by somebody who has staff training.' He held a match to the bowl of his pipe and when he had generated sufficient smoke, 'You're in command of the recce, Johnny will respect that, but he will make the plan for brigade.'

Roger was glad to be occupied, his failure to find Linda or even a clue as to where or why she had gone had troubled him, and with nothing else to occupy his mind he had begun to imagine all manner of scenarios. Now he would be fully occupied and he would allow nothing to get in the way of the difficult task that faced them.

The plan was simple but demanding, especially for the close observation team. The troop would establish a base a mile from the camp, which was now code named Market Drayton, and remain insitu purely as a back-up and quick response for the OP. This would be a trying and tiring part of the operation, just sitting, waiting and remaining undetected. The close observation team would be a four-man brick commanded by Ray because of his intimate knowledge of the immediate vicinity of the camp. His team was to consist of; Jerry, Pete and Tom Parnell as signaller. It had been decided to use NCO's because they needed to know the ground. They would have to live on cold rations for the duration and exist without hot drinks or cigarettes. They would use Ray's old site as a hide but spend some time lying up closer to the camp; the prevailing situation would dictate when this could take place.

Roger was uneasy about having his squadron commander along in the role of a trooper, until his expertise was needed, and he voiced his concern to his troop sergeant.

'Don't let it bother you, boss,' Pete advised as they sat outside the armoury filling magazines, 'The old man's got the instinct of a wild animal; when there's nothing to do he'll stay in his basha and sleep.'

'Oh I can see that,' Roger scoffed, 'the man is tireless, he bounces round camp like a rubber ball.'

'Believe me,' Pete insisted, 'when he's operational he can kip for England until the action starts and then he's pure adrenaline. I've never seen anyone like him, it's as though he can be switched on and off. But as soon as he's in his basha he's asleep; me, I never get a decent kip the night before an op, I really envy him.'

The de-bus went to plan and the truck was at a halt for barely a minute, as the other two kept moving slowly so that their engine pitch disguised the fact that one had come to a halt. In the jungle edge they waited twenty minutes until it was light enough to move and in that short stay Roger witnessed what Pete had told him; Major Hooper adopted the foetal position and went instantly to sleep.

*

They reached the top of the ridge a little after midday where they took their first rest since starting out at first light six hours ago. May Ling sank to the ground amazed that she had come this far but not at all certain she could continue at this pace for much longer. She knew Lam was not travelling at his normal speed for the distance between them continually widened and he had reduced the pace when he noticed this.

'You have done very well for somebody who has been living on the outside,' he handed her his water bottle and hoped that he did not sound patronising. She took a mouthful and passed the bottle back. 'Drink as much as you want,' he pushed her hand away, 'there is a stream in the valley and we can fill it there.'

She gratefully drank deeper, 'I had forgotten how high some of these hills can be,' she said and smiled for the first time since they met.

'We have a very steep descent now,' he took the banana she offered, 'and then I'm afraid we have another climb, steeper this time, but not as far.'

They sat in silence for about ten minutes and he thought that she had gone to sleep. He took out his tobacco and began rolling a cigarette.

'May I have one?'

'Yes, I didn't know..'

'A bad habit I picked up on the outside.'

After one puff of the coarse tobacco she had a coughing fit and handed the cigarette back shaking her head, 'I can see why I didn't smoke until I got out,' she rummaged in her pack and took out a tin of Players, 'Would you like one of these?

Lam's eye lit up, 'I've not had an English cigarette for years,' he smoked for a few minute's inhaling deeply, 'You should not be too hard on Lau....' he began but she held up her hand and stopped him.

'Do not foul the air with that traitor's name in my presence again,' she snapped her voice and eyes full of hatred.

*

Five miles to the north the four men lay a few yards from the chosen hide frustrated by the unexpected presence of a sentry. It was something that should have been anticipated, if they had considered it a good site to observe a likely water point then it was reasonable to think that the enemy would have regarded it a favourable spot to protect the water point. Even if they managed to get into the hide the man was positioned too close for them not to have eventually been detected.

They had arrived at the same time that he was posted, and it was only Ray's vigilance that saved them from being compromised, had he got into position before them then they would probably not have spotted him, but he would definitely become aware of their presence as they entered the hide.

Major Hooper was one of the group, the previous night, he had 'suggested' that it would be beneficial to the planning if he could get a good look at the camp instead of having to rely on sketches and reports. Nobody could really argue with his reasoning and he did carry the rank. Jerry Singleton was the only member who put forward any real opposition as he was the one who had to give up his place, and he was not a man to avoid action or be reticent about voicing his opinion on any matter.

They had lain no more than ten yards from the man for an hour to verify that he was a permanent sentry and then Ray had decided, as commander, to withdraw to a safer distance so that they could make new plans. Painfully slowly they withdrew up towards the summit of Besar, in twos covering each other, until it was considered safe to move more overtly. After thirty minutes they stopped and ate some cold rations as they discussed their next move.

'Let Troop know we're moving our position, Tom,' Ray said to Tom Parnell.

'I'll go and do a close recce, boss,' Ray said to Johnny, 'we can find another site and then move in at first light.'

'If you find one soon enough we could move in at last light,' Pete suggested.

'I wouldn't bank on that, Pete,' the major warned, 'Corporal Pell's right, 'the recce is going to have to be very cautious there could be a fair amount of activity around the camp.'

'We can always hope,' Pete defended his suggestion, 'I'll come with you Ray,' he added and then saw the look on the major's face, 'I suppose you wanna go, boss?' he grinned.

'Corporal Pell's in charge,' the OC said placing Ray on the spot. Ray chose his squadron commander, not for sycophantic reasons, but because he considered it would assist the major in his planning.

The major and Ray slipped off their Bergen's, ensured that they had a day's rations in their belt kit, and silently disappeared into the greenery.

Special Forces first task, on covert operations, is to establish the positions of sentries, once that is done they know that they can get on with their mission whether it be intelligence gathering or aggressive action. With this in mind, and knowing where one guard was, Ray took a line to the left of their withdrawal route so that they should end up with the camp on their right.

With regular stops to watch, and listen, they made slow progress down off the ridge and after about half an hour changed direction slightly until Ray estimated they were heading towards the camp. Visibility was good and they could see about five yards in each direction, which was helpful but meant that they could also be seen from that distance.

Ray froze as he was about to step over a large branch that lay in his path, a warning click of the tongue came from behind him, he went into a crouch and looked over his shoulder, the major was tapping his ear, a sign that he heard something.

Ray mouthed, 'What?'

The major motioned a chopping action and pointed slightly to the right and ahead. They listened crouching in the heavy jungle silence, not even a slight rustle of leaf or creak of branch could be heard in the still hot air. Then, very faint and far away, the unmistakable sound of metal blade on hard wood. The sound continued for about a minute, stopped and then began again. They continued with even greater caution guided by the sound. Again Ray heard the warning click; annoyed that he missed something he turned round, Johnny pointed briefly at something on the ground that Ray had missed. The indentation in the soft jungle floor, just to the right of their line of march, was so slight that the major had to outline it with his finger.

Ray did not feel that he failed in any way. He had taken the tracking course at the JTC and achieved a high rating but it was common knowledge, in the regiment, that the man with him had achieved the highest rating by any European; it was higher than many Iban's.

He changed direction slightly so that he was following the direction of the imprint and within a few yards spotted minute disturbance of the earth. He pointed to it; Johnny came closer and nodded.

They're erasing their tracks as they go,' he whispered, Ray nodded, 'there must be a number of them.' Johnny added then took a bearing on the direction from which they appeared to have come from. They did not see any more spoor but the signs that they had seen were nevertheless dangerous errors in the otherwise expert track eradication.

The chopping had long ago ceased and the suffocating heat was lessening, a sign that evening was approaching. It was certain they would not get back to the rest of the brick that night and if it rained it would be uncomfortably cold at this altitude as they carried no material to construct a basha.

Ray's concentration must have lapsed through tiredness or carelessness but he did not see the man until he was about five yards from him. He was sat side on to them looking to their left. Slowly Ray sank to a crouch by the large roots of a tree bringing his rifle into the aim as he did so and slipping his rifle's safety catch off. He knew that the major would have followed suit so he did not take his eyes off the man.

Making no sudden move, and certain he had not been seen, he slowly looked left and right for any companions that the man may have with him, or was he another sentry?. No, there was a pack just visible on the far side of him and it was not likely that a sentry would have a pack. A slight but sudden movement caught Ray's eye and to the right of the man was another getting to his feet. Ray saw them exchange a few words but heard nothing.

On their feet now, and with their packs on, the two men laughed quietly at something one of them said and it was clear from their stance and demeanour that they were having quiet exchanges with others who were out of sight.

Ray felt a touch on his shoulder he turned slightly keeping one eye on the group; the major mouthed, 'How many'?

Ray grimaced and mouthed back, 'Five or six?'

When he gave his full attention back to the enemy patrol the last man was just disappearing from view into the greenery without the slightest sound. No twig snapped, no leaf rustled, and no equipment creaked or rubbed.

They waited for five minutes and then Ray said, 'I reckon they're of course a bit if they're heading for the camp,' he indicated a line a little to the left of the direction they had taken with the edge of his hand, 'I think the camp's more over there.'

Johnny took a bearing on the line they had taken and then another on Ray's estimation, 'Okay but let's follow them.'

'I think that's dodgy, boss,' Ray disagreed confidently.

'Why?'

'They're good, they're not leaving a clear track and we could easily bump them if they stop again.'

'How far do you estimate the camp is?' Johnny asked.

'Two thousand yards, maybe less,' Ray checked the map, which was not particularly informative.

'An hour'? Johnny suggested.

Ray nodded, 'Yeah, we should have time to find it and have butchers round before dark.'

'Let's go then,' the major got to his feet.

*

After the shock of the last two days, physical and psychological effort, May Ling was happy to lie down to sleep in the secure surroundings of the 5 Company base. In a well-constructed shelter and ringed by more than fifty armed men and with sufficient food inside her, she lay contentedly on her back staring at the invisible roof of the basha.

It had been like a homecoming. Many times, on the two days journey with Lam, she had struggled with the doubts that assailed her. Had she lost the revolutionary zeal, had her ideals been contaminated by the false, easy, life that she had led for so many months? No, she concluded, it had been the extreme fatigue that had lowered her moral and made her question her decision and dedication to the cause.

Lah Leo, the commander of 5 Company, had greeted her like a daughter. He was an old friend of her father when they were both members Malayan Peoples Anti-Japanese Army, fighting alongside the British against the Japanese. Unlike Lah, her father had not survived the war and had died carrying out an ambush on a Japanese convoy near Segemat. In the two years of peace that separated the two conflicts she had met Lah on a couple of occasions when her brother took her to meetings of the Malayan Communist Party, MCP, when she was only nine.

She knew that another arduous journey still lay before her. She was accompanying Lah to the great camp on the border where an important meeting was to take place in a few days time. But now she had no misgivings about the journey or her ability to keep pace she was feeling so much fitter and for the past two nights she had only achieved fitful bouts of sleep. This night she would sleep soundly and wake fitter and more able to cope with the physical side of life inside.

*

The night had covered them with a suddenness that still amazed even after years of service in the country. As dusk had threatened they had pulled back from the camp so as not to be compromised by an early morning clearance patrol. The spot they had chosen to lie up proved ideal through chance rather than selection. Now, higher than the camp, they found they had a window in the jungle and as the moon rose there was a magical view out across the treetops on the lower slopes. In the far distance, the waters of Lake Temengor, two miles away four and thousand feet below them, reflected the brilliance of the moon.

If there was any noise from the camp it was masked by the swelling nocturnal symphony that, when at its height, masked any noise they made even from each other. The tension and physical effort of the day's close contact with a large number of the enemy had the right effect on Ray, and as soon as they had eaten their cold rations he sank into a deep restful sleep.

It was cold when he was reluctantly dragged from his slumber. Deep in the clump of bamboo they were perfectly safe from discovery and people rarely moved through jungle at night, it was too dark, so his normal, instinctive, alertness was suppressed and he resisted the hand that shook his shoulder.

'Ray,' the major's voice brought him swiftly to consciousness, 'look.'

At first Ray thought he was having a firefly pointed out but then realised that the light being indicated to him was stationary and a deep orange unlike the greenish small lights that flitted close by.

'Cheeky buggers,' Ray muttered.

'They must be very confident,' the major whispered.

'Well if, as we think, they vacated because the Auster flew over the other night,' Ray said as much to himself as to his companion, 'why are they pushing their luck now.'

'Nobody's flying this time of night,' Johnny pointed out, 'and if they were it would be heard in plenty of time to put it out.'

Ray lifted the cover on his watch and saw that it was only ten o'clock. He sensed the major settling into a more comfortable position and followed suit.

Chapter Twenty Eight

As he lifted the mug to his lips Bob Gill saw the girl reach out to a small sapling and pull herself up the steep slope. She was a mere ten yards away and passing in front of him, right to left.

His Remington shotgun lay across his thighs, without lowering the mug he slowly raised his right knee bringing the muzzle of the deadly weapon roughly in line with the girl who had now turned slightly away from him. It was apparent that she was oblivious to his presence. He was well screened from her view by a low tree palm, and remaining motionless was additional camouflage. She paused momentarily as if regaining her breath before passing from his view.

He felt safe enough now to move sufficiently to tug the vine that would warn the rest of the troop that enemy was close by. Slowly he placed his mug on the ground and took a firm grip on his shotgun. The girl, who was strikingly pretty, had come and gone without a sound.

Bill heard a slight movement behind him just as another CT moved into view following the girl, he urgently signalled for whoever was approaching from the camp to stop. In the next ten minutes he counted sixteen people pass by, all armed and all wearing the uniform of the MRLA. After waiting another five minutes to make sure there were no more, he turned and saw Roger crouching four feet behind him.

'Alright?' he mouthed Bill nodded and waved him forward.

Bill put his head close to Roger's, 'Sixteen of the bugger's,' he said, 'all armed and I think I might have missed a couple.'

'Why?'

'Well there was an unarmed girl leading and that's not likely,' he explained, 'so some must have passed a bit further away.'

'Which way were they heading?' Roger asked, Bill indicated and Roger took a bearing, 'They seem to be heading for the big pow-wow. I hope Ray and the Boss are on the ball.'

*

Ray had decided, and the major had agreed, to have another close look at the camp, this time from the north. This would mean a wide swing to the west and would take a couple of hours. They had plenty of time now and Ray was becoming very familiar with the area. The previous day's recce had confirmed that, although the camp was by no means full, the numbers had increased significantly and they estimated that there were at least fifty people now occupying the camp.

The defences were so well camouflaged that Ray had to point many of them out to Johnny as they skirted the camp using the plan that Ray had sketched on his first visit. They also discovered crude but effective booby traps in front of many of the bunkers, holes filled with sharpened bamboo, the points hardened with fire and contaminated with human excrement. The whole time Johnny made notes of things he would need to take into account when he made the plan of attack.

The north side proved just as well defended but had the additional obstacle of a steep ascent in some parts, although there were plenty of rocky outcrops hidden within the vegetation that an attacking force could utilise to give fire support.

They saw no activity outside the camp apart from three sentry posts that they had identified the previous day, but on the return trip to the remainder of the brick, they were forced to hide, when, on one occasion they heard voices and on another saw the a number of CT, fleetingly, in a gap in the dense foliage that filled a small valley.

By three o'clock Ray was beginning to get worried, they had been unable to find the spot where they had left Pete and Tom and then he saw a fallen tree that he recognised and knew he was in the right area. It was distinctive in that it was a recent fall and lay at an angle of forty-five degrees, supported by its neighbours and the vines in its foliage still clung to the canopy above.

'We've passed them,' he said, 'there over in that direction.'

'Yes,' the major agreed, 'I remember now, we passed this soon after leaving them.'

Fifteen minutes later as they shared a mug of tea with Tom and Pete, Ray brought them up to date with what he and the major had seen and discovered on the recce. He indicated a spot on the map, 'There's a decent hide among some rocks on the north side of the camp, it's not ideal because there's a limited view from it, but it's the best that we saw. Don't you think so, boss?'

The OC arched his back and stretched before answering, everybody could tell that he was reluctant to agree, 'It is, without doubt, the only decent place we saw but I'm not so sure that we should go back'

'I thought that was what we were supposed to be doing,' Pete grimaced to emphasise his confusion and disagreement.

'I know,' the major leaned forward and supported his elbows on his knees, 'our task is to gather intelligence; numbers, state of readiness, quality of enemy personnel all the usual stuff, agreed?' They all nodded, 'Alright, Corporal Pell, what do we still need to find out?'

'We're not certain about their strength...' Ray began.

'Fifty and mounting,' the major cut in, 'would you agree?'

Ray nodded, 'Yeah, I see what you're getting at, boss but you're planning the attack don't you want a better idea of the real strength?'

'I cannot see that we would ever get an exact figure, and planning a large scale attack in jungle has to be concentrated to maintain control, so, whether there's fifty or a hundred, it would not make much difference to the size of the attacking force needed..'

The soft static that was emitting from Tom's headset stopped, and the urgent sound of rapid Morse ended the conversation, all eyes watched as the signaller translated the dots and dashes into words on his pad.

Tom looked up and lifted one ear piece, 'Delta One Two had a sighting of at least sixteen Charlie Tango's heading north past their location at 1505 hours today,' he handed the pad to Major Hooper who handed it to Ray.

'It's your decision, Ray,' he said, 'you know my opinion.'

'Pete?' Ray looked at his troop sergeant.

'I can see the bosses point, Ray, but you've seen the area more than any of us, d'you think we will get any more worthwhile intelligence?'

'Well you can never have too much,' Ray shrugged, 'Tom, what d'you think?'

'I think you've been damn lucky not to have been compromised already with so many of 'em on the move,' he pushed his bush hat to the back of his head and scratched his head, 'I think we could cock it up if we go back, there's too many of 'em swanning around and we'll end up leaving signs.'

They all looked at each other and nodded, it was the consensus that further movement around the camp was too risky and would add little to the intelligence already gained.

*

When John Sankey was informed of Lau Fong's death he was attending an update briefing on Operation Clive at 28 Commonwealth brigade HQ in Ipoh, and he was unable to return immediately to KL.

He called KL CID at once and spoke with the DI in charge of the murder enquiry, DI Wood. Dennis Wood was a portly middle aged man with an enormous amount of experience, who had, like many of his colleagues, transferred over from the Palestine Police in 1950. He was familiar with the guerrilla environment and the brutality that went with it having spent a number of years hunting the vicious Stern gang.

Both men knew that witnesses would be hard to find even if it had taken place in broad daylight and at the main railway station. The people who had carried out the brutal killing would undoubtedly be members of the MRLA and would have been back in their jungle base hours after the event.

'At least one of them could have been a local man,' Dennis Wood pointed out, 'because the place they selected was quite remote, and secluded, and you would have had to have local knowledge to know that it existed.'

'What I can't understand is why he was in such a place,' John said, 'he knew that he was at great risk. Is there anything to indicate why he was there?'

'Nothing,' Dennis replied, 'but he must have felt secure enough to have gone there.'

'Could he have been taken there against his will?'

'There's nothing to indicate that,' Dennis said, 'the only injuries were those that caused his death. No rope marks, no signs of a beating. No I'm certain he went there of his own free will.'

'It's academic,' John replied, 'it's a revenge killing and the killers are well out of the area, what's more important to me is how they found him? He was in a safe house that we've used many times in the past without any problem.' He paused and Dennis was about to ask if he was still on the line, when he continued. 'There are only about half a dozen people who could have known and they're all in my department, perhaps you should make some enquiries there.'

'I already have,' Dennis confessed, 'it's a murder enquiry and it was a course I had to take,' he cleared his throat, 'I have a suspect.'

John asked 'Who, Linda?'

'A Miss Tang, she worked for you.'

'That's right, Linda!' he paused, 'Yes she's...'

'Do you know why she resigned?'

'No, she wouldn't tell me when I asked.'

'I assume that she was planted on you?'

'I suspected as much for when we ran a check on her there was a period in her past that was a bit short in detail which could have indicated she had been inside with the terrorists. I am pretty certain that she was related to the dead man and because of this I thought that I would be able to use her.'

'Did you unearth anything to support that?' Dennis asked.

'No, but I made sure that she didn't know of Lau's whereabouts but somehow she must have...'

'Well she seems to have disappeared from the area,' Dennis paused but John did not respond. He went on, 'She told a colleague that she was taking up teaching but wouldn't say where, and this colleague was the CID officer who organised the victims move into a 'safe' house.' when there was more silence he continued, 'I have notified all forces and put out a description but it would help if we had a photograph, I assume there is one in existence if she worked for you.'

'There is, but if my guess is right she will have gone inside by now, she'll know that she will be a suspect even though I don't think she had any idea that we were on to her.'

'I have arranged to speak again with the CID officer who arranged the move and I'll let you know if anything comes of it.'

*

Jack Winslow met the CO outside the orderly room and they drove over to brigade together.

'The brigade major wouldn't say much on the telephone,' the colonel told him as they travelled the two miles to Brigade HQ, 'but he did hint that this was something pretty hot.'

'I take it that it's concerning Operation Clive,' Big Jack asked of the back of the colonel's head as he held onto his cap in the rear of the open topped Land Rover.

'Undoubtedly,' the CO nodded and grabbed his own cap as the vehicle speeded up.

The conference room was filling quickly when they arrived and from the diverse gathering of arms and other agencies it was clear that there was a flap was on.

'Gentlemen,' Harry Woodhouse began when they were all seated and the doors closed, 'I cannot emphasise enough the secrecy that you must attach to the intelligence that will be imparted at this briefing. We are on the verge of dealing a crippling blow to the enemy that could bring the Emergency to an end, Allen!'

Major Doyle launched into his briefing, 'The camp that we suspected was located in the region of Gunong Besar was discovered on the twenty-third of last month, as you already know. The SAS have been back into the area and confirmed that the camp is being re occupied and by the time they thought it prudent to depart, the patrol estimated that there were already fifty people in the camp. We intend to attack the camp in four days' time.'

A flurry of unintentional noise filled the room as people shifted position, put down pens, opened notebooks and generally prepared for the detail.

'Detailed briefings will follow but here is a general outline of the overall plan. The day after tomorrow, Wednesday, 'A' Company of the RWL's will move to a position about here and create a base camp,' he pointed to the southern slope of the gunong, 'At the same time, 'B' Company 10th Gurkha's will do the same here,' he now indicated the western side, 'and 'D' Company the 2nd Gurkha's will move into ambush positions along the Lasah - Jenera road. Two batteries, of 25th Field Regiment Royal Artillery, will be sited in the cultivation on the western side of the ridge to deter escape in that direction once the attack begins, and the Kings Hussars will be located throughout the operational area to be utilised as required on the roads.' He took a sip of water, 'Each infantry company will have a detachment of SAS attached, as well as people from the Malayan Police Jungle Team. The troop of SAS that has carried out all of the legwork so far will be with the RWL's. On the evening of the following day, Thursday, they will move up to the camp, the SAS that is, and place a number of para flares which will be set detonate that night marking the camp site for a squadron of Lincoln bombers of the RAAF, who will each deliver sticks of ten, four thousand pound, bombs at 1930 hours. At first light on Friday the RWL's will enter the camp from the north, and deal with any CT remaining there, and at the same time 10th Gurkha's will close to a line, a thousand yards to the south, and remain there,' he turned to Harry, 'Sir.'

The brigadier went to the lectern, 'Now, that is the general strategic outline gentlemen. Every unit's detailed briefing will be attended by all company commanders, RAF, gunners, Hussars and police to ensure we all know what every other units is doing. I don't have to tell experienced commanders like you, that major operations like this, in jungle, will be difficult if not impossible to control. Your men, especially yours Jeremy, will find themselves involved in their own personal battles, so success is going to depend, largely, on the initiative and guts of your individual riflemen,' he thumped the lectern, 'Your briefings will be critical in painting as clear a picture as you can of the lead up, the action, and the mopping up. The commanders with most influence on this operation are going to be your non-commissioned officers, you, and even your platoon commanders, will find yourselves in the terrifying position, of not knowing what the hell's going at times.' He paused and looked round the room, 'Does anybody want to comment on the overall plan? Yes Willie.'

Major Ashton got to his feet, 'You haven't mentioned the 3rd RAR sir, yet I see we have a major here from that regiment.'

'Yes, thank you, Willie. The 3rd RAR will provide security for the gunners and supply a number of ambushes in that area,' he directed his next words to the Australian, 'Not the most glamorous of roles, Tim, but an essential one nonetheless. Now gentlemen we will break for coffee and then begins a period of intensive and demanding briefings, I suspect that we shall be burning the mid-night oil'.

*

'Has the dhobi wallah brought my kit back?' Sam bustled into the room.

'It's on your bed,' Brian told him, 'and the boot boy's done your boots, they're under your bed.'

Alan followed him into the billet, 'Good man, Lucknow,' he smiled up at his starched uniform on a coat hanger suspended from the beam above his bed.

'That's bloody favouritism,' Sam cursed, 'mine's just folded up with me towels and ulu kit, wait till I see that bloody enamel Tamil.'

'Not favouritism Sam,' Alan pointed out, 'it's an extra fifty cents.'

'Well you bloody corporals get more than us poor NS men.'

'Sign on,' Brian suggested.

Sam expostulated, 'Sign on and spend another year in this shit hole. You sign on, Largy.'

'I'm not complaining about the money.'

'How long have you got to do, Bri? John called across.

'Five months and three days, Johnno, just five months and three days.'

'When you lads go who will I go on the bevy with?' It was a scenario that John had not given much thought to and it frightened him.

'Ken will still be here,' Brian pointed out sympathetically.

'He's not in 'A' Company, he doesn't do ops.'

'Hey Cantrill,' Tom Duffy, a short stocky miner of low intellect entered the hut, 'have you seen detail?'

'I didn't know it was up yet,' John sat up, 'I haven't caught a guard have I?'

'You've only been made up, Lance fucking corporal Cantrill,' Duffy guffawed, 'really scrapping the barrel, eh lads.'

'Are taking the piss, Duffy?' John was on his feet and heading for the door.

'No, honest, I've just seen it.'

'Who read it to yer, Duffy,' Sam called down the room.

'Fuck off, Andrews.'

'If you're taking the piss, Duffy,' John left the billet and took the path that led to Company HQ. Five minutes later he returned in a mild state of shock.

'He's right, I'm a bloody lance-jack,' a cheer of derision filled the room. He shook his head in disbelief and sought the sanctuary of his bed, 'I don't have to take it do I, Al?'

Alan went across and shook his hand, 'Well done, Johnno, you deserve it,' he sat down beside the reluctant NCO, 'You can refuse it pal but you're an idiot if you do.'

'I don't want to lose all me mates,' he bemoaned.

259

Alan spread his hands, 'Have I got mates?'

'No you're a bastard,' Sam volunteered but was ignored.

'Yeah, but it's different for you Al, you're genned up, the lads respect you, I know bugger all.'

'Don't be bloody stupid, Johnno,' Alan punched him lightly on the shoulder and went back to preparing himself for guard mounting.

'You've been in two serious contacts, and you must have impressed Dave Snell and Pearly.' He brushed his beret as he returned to where John sat, 'And I'll tell you this,' he emphasised his point with the brush he held, 'nobody bamboozles Dave Snell he can judge a man better than anyone I know, he wouldn't have recommended you unless he was absolutely sure you were up to it.' He returned to his own bed space continuing his haranguing, 'Have you seen some of the shite that's got tapes in this mob, I wouldn't let 'em lead a dog let alone a section, why some of 'em get lost going to the NAAFI,' he breathed on the gleaming toe caps of his boot and gave them a final rub.

'Take it, John,' Brian encouraged him, 'Al's right you can do it.'

Alan returned to the attack, 'What did you think of your instructors at Depot?'

'We had some good un's, they knew their kit,' John replied.

'Gimme a name,' Alan demanded.

'Well there was Sergeant...'

'Not sergeants,' Alan cut in, 'corporals'

'Corporal Edwards, Corporal Barlow...'

'Stop there,' Alan interrupted again, 'I know 'em both. Barlow was a good skin but he'd never been out of the depot, never fired a gun in anger. And as for that shit Edwards, he wouldn't last five minutes in battalion. They were both training manual soldiers, never done the real thing, but decent instructors, well Barlow was. But you can be taught that, and as a lance jack out here you're not needed as an instructor you're needed to lead. Don't you let me and Snelly down, Johnno; we know you can do it,' he rummaged in his locker, 'Here, I've still got a wrist band with one tape on it,' he handed John a green cloth wrist band that bore a single stripe that had once been white, and was worn by NCO's to denote their rank when in bare buff order, 'Now get your shirts over to the tailor and get your tapes up.'

'I'm broke,' was his lame excuse.

'He'll do it on tick,' Alan said.

'Come on, Cantrill, Lance-corporal Cantrill,' Brian grinned, 'I'll lend you the money till pay day.'

*

260

During a break in the proceedings, Lt Col Crawson telephoned his adjutant and instructed him make sure that all of A Company's platoon commanders and sergeants were assembled in the IO's office by 2000 hours. He was also instructed that indents be prepared for enough rations and ammunition for a week's operation, plus enough transport to move a company.

At five o'clock Simon went into the mess for a cold beer before going to shower and change. 'A' Company had spent the morning on the 50 yard range at the back of MT lines, zeroing their weapons and expending all of the ammunition that they had carried on the last operation. While the men cleaned their weapons in the afternoon the subalterns had the arduous and boring task of bringing all of their platoons shooting records up to date.

He was looking forward to an evening with Susan wallowing in the luxury of air conditioning at the Cathay cinema and a few drinks in its comfortable bar.

'Pint of Anchor, Tan,' he called to the jovial Chinese barman who was wiping glasses at the far end of the bar.

'Make that two, Simon,' James Gavin stood outside on the verandah in dirty jungle greens and sporting four days growth of beard.

'When did you get back?' Simon called across after he had done his friends bidding.

He took the glass that Simon offered, 'Thanks old chap. Are you sitting out here with me?'

'Of course,' Simon settled himself at the nearest table.

'I'm getting legless tonight, Si, are you going to join me?'

'Sorry, James, I've made other arrangements.'

'Your sexy WVS lady, I bet,' James half emptied his glass, 'God, I needed that.'

'Rough op'? Simon asked.

'Only in so far as we've been up to our necks in bloody swamp for three days, no sign of Charlie, he's got more bloody sense than offer himself as sustenance for the bloody leeches. Big as cigars they were, Si.' He handed Simon his glass, 'Afraid you'll have to do the honours again old chap being temporarily excluded because of my attire and all that.'

'I think that it's permissible for your money to be taken in,' Simon suggested.

James patted his pockets, 'Don't carry money on ops, Si, you know that.'

Simon took the glass, 'Can you move down wind by the time I get back,' Simon asked.

261

'Do I pong a bit?'

'More than a bit, James, more than a bit,' he held his nose to make his point.

A few more members were in the bar now and he saw 'A' company's new platoon commander, Neville Tibbs, sitting with the Padre, Captain 'Holy' Walter. As Simon made his way across to greet them Smith-Parr came in from the foyer.

'Mr Gates.'

Simon turned and faced him motionless and unsmiling.

'Ah, you're here also, Neville. You are both to report to the IO's at 2000 hours,' he looked directly at Simon, 'Don't be late,' before Simon could respond Smith-Parr spotted James Gavin on the verandah, 'James, better get yourself cleaned up old chap you're on this briefing too.'

'What bloody briefing's that,' James got to his feet and stood by the door, 'I've only just got back.'

'Have you been de-briefed?' Nigel ignored his question.

'Yes I bloody well have, I'm not wet behind the ears, Nigel.' James was a regular and one of the senior subalterns in the regiment and having passed through Sandhurst with Nigel he was a little more relaxed in his attitude towards the adjutant, 'I say again, what bloody briefing?' his resentment was undisguised.

'You're in the army, Mr Gavin,' Nigel bridled, 'not a nine to five office job, so you will be in IO's office by 2000 as the commanding officer has ordered, ' he turned and addressed the room in general, 'Has anybody seen Captain Whitely?'

'He was in his room ten minutes ago,' Captain Hogan, the MO told him.

*

Activity had been kept to a minimum, some appreciated the quiet seeing it as the calm before the storm but others fretted, their pent up energy denying them rest. The urge to be physically and mentally stretched made some of them irritable but none of them unprofessional; they bore their restraint with fortitude.

Alertness could not be allowed to slacken with so many of the enemy close at hand. Through the hours of daylight three, well concealed, sentry posts gave the rest of them protection from being compromised or attacked without some warning. To keep the sentry's relatively fresh, in the soporific afternoon heat, they were changed every hour instead of the usual two. Everybody took a stag regardless of rank. For the sake of moral, Pete had suggested to Roger that the troop be allowed to brew up but the heating food was still forbidden.

Roger was finding this undemanding period of the operation as hard to bear as any of them. Try as he might to resist turning over in his mind the mystery of Linda's disappearance, it was constantly on his mind and he worried that his concentration might be affected. A sentry had to be alert to every noise, movement of foliage, smell, and sound. The slightest variation in sound, smell or the swaying of a branch had to be identified quickly and skilfully if one was to have the upper hand in a jungle encounter.

He sat crossed legged, backed under a dense growth of atap that reached fifteen feet above him, disguising his shape and colour in its dense, black, shadow. The position faced south, towards the CT camp that was their reason for being there. They were over five thousand yards away from it so no sound marked its existence.

The major and Ray had left the previous day to brief brigade and advise the planners, but Roger knew that Johnny Hooper would not take the role of a mere adviser when the regiment was to play a major role in the coming attack.

Their current function was pleasing no one, and even the most relaxed members of the troop were finding the inactivity difficult to cope with. He determined that on the next scheduled radio exchange, with control, he would seek permission to take out a recce in order to update their intelligence. Two of Corporal Pell's brick were still with them, and they would have good knowledge of the area. Not as detailed as the big corporal, who had spent more time in close vicinity to the camp than anybody, but certainly enough to circumnavigate the area without any great risk of being discovered. Pete had voiced his objection to this idea.

'If they've got some of their top men in that camp,' he had said firmly, 'then they're going to be in a state of very high alertness, and could even have a screen of small patrols out.'

'Things could have changed that we should know about,' Roger argued feebly knowing that his troop sergeant was right.

'That's always the way, boss, the old adage about a plan never withstanding contact with the enemy is true, purely on the grounds that your intelligence is always out of date, it has to be. Anyway,' he added to put an end to the debate, 'we all agreed, before the OC left, that the chance of compromising the whole operation with anymore patrols was too great,' he shook his head, 'and I believe that's still the case.' Roger had said nothing, knowing that his troop sergeant was adamant and his agreement was important to Roger.

'Whatever's planned and by whom, we'll have to do recce's then so why take the chance of cocking it up now?'

'So you're admitting that there could be a cock up then,' Roger contended weakly.

'That's always possible,' Pete agreed, 'but all the necessary forces will be in position then and we'll able to react quickly and effectively.'

Roger had given up the fight, his thoughts reluctantly returned to Linda, and he guiltily realised that his main reason for arguing for more positive action was to take his mind of his private affairs. He was relieved that he had lost the debate.

Chapter Twenty Nine

John felt self-conscious over the small wristband that told of his recent elevation. He felt that it could not have been more conspicuous if it had been in flashing neon. But apart from a word of congratulation, from both Sergeant Snell and Pearly, it hardly raised comment.

He was not sure which he feared most, a form of ceremonial duty such as a main gate guard or an operational excursion. He did not have to ponder the choice for long. As muster parade came to an end Dave Snell told the platoon to gather in closer.

'So that I don't have to raise my voice,' he explained, 'and anything that you're told from here on in must not be discussed in front of NAAFI staff, char wallah's, dhobi wallah's, shit house wallah's or shirt collars,' he looked round the faces serious with concern, 'is that clearly understood?' they all nodded, 'Andrews?'

There was general laughter.

'What you picking on me for, sarge?' Sam asked trying to suppress a grin.

'What are you picking on me for sarge,' Dave mimicked, 'because you're a bloody liability sometimes, Andrews, try not to be one for the next couple of weeks,' he looked at his watch, 'Draw weapons now and be back on parade by 09.30. Full complement of magazines.' Dave consulted the mill board that he was carrying, 'Corporal Baker, take a couple of men and a one tonner down to the ammo store and draw the allocation of ammo that's been set aside for the whole company.'

Corporal 'Busty' Cain was already at the store when they arrived. Both he and his store-man were sweating profusely in the windowless bunker.

'All of that stack to the right of the door, Corporal Baker,' Busty wiped the sweat from his heavy jowls. Charlie Cain was rather older than most junior NCO's at thirty-eight and was grossly overweight for an infantryman, he bordered on obese. Busty was a bachelor who had filled a series of cushy numbers throughout his service due to good luck and engineered circumstances. His pomposity was flagrantly misplaced and he was merely tolerated by his contemporaries.

The stack of boxes seemed too much for a day on the range.

'All this, are you sure, Busty? Alan asked.

'I don't make mistakes, Corporal Baker.' Busty thrust an indent in front of Alan, 'check it and sign it,' he snapped haughtily

'There are times when I think you're a complete arsehole, Busty,' Alan began checking the boxes against the list, 'and then there's other times when I know you are.'

'You're addressing the senior corporal in the battalion,' Busty huffed, 'and I could put you on a charge for insubordination.'

'Bollocks,' Alan finished the count, signed the indent and handed it to Busty with a grin, 'Come on lads, let's get it loaded.'

The remainder of the morning was spent with the rest of A Company test firing and zeroing their personal weapons and after lunch, which consisted of haversack rations, the company commander addressed them as they gathered on the hundred yard firing point.

'That the whole company has been united for some commonplace range work may have come as a surprise to you, and the observant among you will have noticed that we have an excessive amount of ammunition with us.' He looked around the hundred young faces, 'Tomorrow morning this company will embark on an operation which is probably the most important since this war began, and if successful could wipe out the entire high command of the MRLA and many of its most experienced and effective troops.' He paused again as a surge of excitement rippled through the seated troops.

'Quiet!' Jimmy Raven bawled.

'Secrecy is vital,' the OC continued, 'that is why all of the preparation will take place out here on the range away from prying eyes. Immediately after I have finished speaking you will clean your weapons and receive your compliment of ammunition. You will then split into your platoons to be briefed and before we leave the range the CQMS will arrive with your rations for the operation,' he spread his large hands, 'and thus it will not be apparent to anyone that this company is preparing for a major action.' Jack Winslow put on his most menacing look, 'You will not discuss, with any of your chums in other companies, what you hear today, and I am sure that you will all realise that on no account are civilian workers within the camp to get a sniff of what is pending. Is that clear to everybody?' He was satisfied to see that the seriousness of the situation was evident on everyone's face, 'Right, platoon commanders, they are all yours. I want everybody gathered back here again at 1600 hours.'

Number 3 platoon found themselves faced with not only Simon but a gaunt looking middle aged man wearing jungle greens but showing no badges of rank, and a large muscular, younger, man who displayed two stripes but no other insignia. Both of them wore maroon berets that bore the badge of the Special Air Service Regiment.

A model of the area of operation had been created in great detail in a patch of sandy ground.

'Before I begin the briefing,' Simon began, 'I just want to introduce Major Hooper and Corporal Pell who will be accompanying us for part of our task,' the two men nodded and Simon continued. 'A large enemy camp has been discovered in the region of Gunong Besar which is outside our normal operational area, but 'A' company have been tasked with its destruction on the grounds that we have more experience than the 3rd RAR in whose area it is. We depart at 2230 hours tomorrow evening and travel by road to a drop off point a day's march from our start line which will also be our company base.'

He went on to itemise the kit to be carried and confirmed the platoon's formation. He gave details of attachments, which included an SAS Troop and two personnel from the Malayan Police Jungle Squad and a member of special branch.

'Once we have made a company base camp, elements of the attached personnel will carry out recce's to establish the occupancy of the enemy camp and confirm the physical state of the defences and positions of sentries. Three platoon will then move out to form our own base about five hundred yards from our target. Again, recces' will go forward and this time place a number of para flares around the camp with delayed fuses set to ignite an hour after dark. This will coincide with the arrival of a squadron of Lincoln bombers of the RAAF who will then drop over a hundred and ten thousand pounds of high explosive onto the camp.' As Simon spoke he used the model to illustrate more clearly what he was saying, 'To the north, about here, there will be a company of Gurkha's, and behind us along this road will be another company of Gurkha's manning a number of ambushes. Here, in this cultivated area, will be the 3rd RAR and two batteries of artillery to deny escape to the west. Okay so far?' The only response was nodding heads, He went on, 'I am now going to hand over to Corporal Pell who has spent a considerable amount of time around the camp and is only one of two people who have actually been into the camp, corporal.'

'Make no mistake gents,' Ray began, 'this is a really tough job that lies ahead. Not only is it a big camp, capable of housing two hundred,' there was an audible gasp from the platoon, 'but it's extremely well defended with well-constructed bunkers that are expertly placed to give each other support.' He pointed to the trees behind them, 'We've had one built on the same lines, so after this briefing you'll be able to inspect it.' He turned and pointed to a patch of abandoned rubber at the back of the range, 'and over there we've tried to give you an idea of the size and layout of the camp, that's where you'll practice the assault, sir!'

Simon took over the reins of the briefing again, 'Thank you corporal. As Corporal Pell has said, he and Major Hooper will take us over both the bunker and camp layout and train us in the tactics to

267

overcome them. Very little time I must admit, but we can be grateful that we have a couple of experts to assist us.'

Simon was beginning to feel that the task ahead was beyond his abilities as a leader, he was still feeling a little stunned from the news that the OC had given him earlier.

'Only one platoon will carry out the initial attack,' Jack Winslow had opened his briefing to his company officers and senior NCO's, 'The aim is to puncture their defences at a narrow point and breakout into the heart of the camp. Jungle warfare and night attacks are ideal for this tactic gentleman. The Japanese used it to good effect at the start of the war and it was used extensively in covert night raids by Special Forces'. He fixed Simon with his sharp, eagle, eyes, '3 Platoon will be the leading unit, Simon, Two Platoon on the left, James and yours on the right, Neville', he turned to his 2i/c, 'I would like you to accompany One Platoon Chris.'

'I'd like a word before you go, Simon,' the OC called across the room as the briefing broke up, and he crossed the room and indicated that Simon should follow him out onto the verandah, 'I know that you would not question an order, Simon,' he began.

'Certainly not, sir,' Simon agreed.

'But I feel duty bound to explain why you drew the short straw, particularly in light of your recent and major contact.' He placed a fatherly hand on Simons shoulder, 'James' platoon has just returned from an operation that proved arduous and Neville has no experience, so I must use you for this task. Furthermore, I genuinely believe that yours is the best platoon in the company and I am sure that you are diplomatic enough not to let my opinion be known to the other platoon commanders.'

'Of course, sir, and thank you,' Simon was not sure if this compliment was merely a tool to soften the blow.

'If fact,' Big Jack added, 'I consider that you have one of the best platoons in the battalion, Simon, and I think that the CO shares that view.'

Simon felt himself reddening at this unexpected praise which he now believed to be sincere. It was a bit of a shock, a pleasant shock but still a shock. He had always felt that no matter how great his effort it only produced results that were satisfactory at best.

The major produced a silver cigarette case and offered the open case; Simon took one and got out his lighter and lit their cigarettes.

'You've got some first rate NCO's,' the OC continued, 'and it goes without saying that Sergeant Snell is worth his weight in gold.' Simon's ego, so recently inflated began to seep air with an almost audible hiss.

268

'But most importantly, Simon, your men like and respect you and you have all undergone the baptism of fire, together, with great success. Nothing, absolutely nothing, can weld a unit so well and give it that espirit de corp so vital to forming a good fighting force, than being exposed to combat. You and your men have done it, you have suffered the baptism of fire and you are now comrades in arms.' He looked at his watch, 'You and I will now go over to the Gurkha's ranges where the SAS have prepared a layout of our target.'

Simon tried not to show his disappointment at having another rendezvous with Susan ruined. On the short journey across town in the Land Rover Big Jack gave Simon more detail, 'Major Hooper of the SAS is in overall charge of the actual attack, and a troop of his men will be part of the vanguard along with a section of your chaps. We shall have a butchers at what they've prepared, and then after you've briefed your platoon the major and his men will rehearse you in the initial attack.'

After inspecting the bunker the platoon filed into the abandoned patch of rubber trees which was now used by the 6th Gurkha's as a training area. DZ landing panels of florescent yellow and red had been used to denote the sites of bunkers and stood out clearly, as was intended.

'This side, where we are standing, is the highest point on the camps perimeter,' Ray explained, 'and you will see from the panels it only has four bunkers. We think that this is because the entire side of this slope is protected by thick bamboo and carpeted with dry fronds that are impossible to cross with any degree of stealth, so they are confident that the camp cannot be approached from that side without plenty of warning.' He stopped and grinned, 'The morning after the air raid it won't matter a toss. Those that are left won't be in any great shape to put up much of a fight,' he saw the relief in many of the faces, so he added, 'but don't take that for granted, the cornered rat can be the most dangerous.'

Ray turned and faced the 'camp', 'Your task is to fight through these bunkers and secure the centre of the camp, the two other platoons will take care of the west and eastern sides of the camp but remain outside the perimeter, so anything inside the camp is yours,' he stopped, turned to face them and let the significance of his words sink in, 'But,' he cautioned, 'expect anything. You don't need me to tell you that in combat, especially in such close country, it can be a bit chaotic. Right,' he faced the 'camp' again, 'now what's the best way to take out one of these babies'?'

For the next two hours they practised attacks on the bunkers. Number 3 Section were given the role of attacking the two centre bunkers while 1 and 2 sections laid covering fire on the flanking defences. The two centre bunkers would be engaged by the gun team of 2 section, and four riflemen, while Alan and two more riflemen would close on one bunker and post Mills 36 grenades.

'It is essential,' Simon told them during a short break in the rehearsals, 'that only those who have had experience with grenades carry them, so that means that most of you NCO's are going to be very active during this attack.'

'And remember you chaps who have the responsibility,' Ray added, 'these are four second fuses, not the normal eight.'

After a last rehearsal the platoons gathered together for a final word from their company commander.

'When you normally go on operations,' Major Winslow began, 'you are usually relying on second or third hand intelligence evaluated by people who spend their entire service sat on their arses behind a desk and who have no comprehension of what life is like in the ulu. This operation is markedly different in that the information on which we will rely has been supplied by people who gathered it first hand and that is the best, nay, the only intelligence on which you can rely with any confidence.' He turned to Major Hooper who stood beside him, 'Our thanks to you and your men, Johnny,' the major nodded slightly and smiled. 'Despite this wonderful benefit, intelligence is only up to date at the time it was gathered; it changes constantly, and although it will be updated courtesy of the SAS, still be prepared for the unexpected.' Big Jack pondered briefly on the youth of his command; ten years earlier he had gone into battle with men whose average age was in their late twenties, now the average age of 'A' Company was nineteen. 'Those poor souls who were engaged in the battle of the Somme were told by their leaders that after the extensive and massive artillery bombardment, that preceded their advance, there would be no enemy left to oppose them, how wrong they were. When you hear the attack on this camp by the RAAF don't be tempted to think the same; as my old grandmother always wisely observed when confronted with a major problem; hope for the best but expect the worst.' He paused a moment, 'Battle is a lonely place,' he went on, 'your mates may be within touching distance but you engage the enemy as an individual. Battle is confusion, and there is no battle more confusing than in jungle where you cannot see more than a couple of yards in any direction, but the battle rages around you. Some of you have experienced a jungle contact and others have yet to experience that baptism, but this is going to be bigger than anything you have previously encountered.' He intertwined his fingers and slowly pumped his clenched hands up and down to emphasise his words, 'Remember this, it is fact; you are better trained than your enemy, you are better armed than your enemy, and no matter how afraid you are, and we are all afraid I can assure you, but he is more afraid than you are, I promise you. Now this is probably the last time I will be able to speak to you as a company, so I will take this opportunity to wish you all good luck, and when the chips are down, and you feel unsure of what you are about, remember your training, and trust in your own ability.'

*

May Ling had not been aware that Beng Kim had arrived in the camp. She knew that as a state committee member he would attend but had not been conscious of his arrival. The evening meal was just being served when a dozen, tired looking comrades, carrying large loads, appeared on the open Padang and waited patiently in line while their leader, Beng, conversed with another SCM. Even though he was twenty yards away she could just make out his piercing voice and a shiver ran down her spine. Despite being surrounded by so many people senior to him, she still felt threatened.

After the evening lecture he had sought her out as she sat discussing the talk with three other female members.

'So,' he sneered, 'you have not followed in the footsteps of your relative and betrayed us.'

She got to her feet and in as calm a voice as she could manage, 'Lau will pay the price.'

'He has already done so,' he spread his hands to embrace the camp, 'so we are all now safe from his treachery?'

A cold hand gripped her heart and although she knew that it had been inevitable the news was a shock. Without replying she stood and went to the large basha that served as the women's quarters, then alone in the gathering dusk, cast more tears for her cousin.

*

That morning they had received a signal to send two men to check on the latest situation in the area of the camp and to gather as much intelligence as they could without compromising the operation. Because of their knowledge, Dan Cullis and Bill Cliffe were given the job.

'Take no chances,' Roger warned, 'if we cock this up the old man will have our balls.'

'It's best to come back with nothing,' Pete added, 'than risking a fuck up now.'

271

Pete knew that Dan, a quiet unassuming Lancastrian in his late twenties, who had served in Burma with Royal Marines for the final year of the Second World War, was experienced and reliable.

'I know that, boss,' he remonstrated mildly as he checked his belt kit, 'How long d'you want us out there?'

'Return as soon as you've got something of interest, Roger replied, 'but get back by 1700 in any case so that we can include your report in the sitrep.'

'Will do,' the two men silently left glad to have something to do.

Roger realised that his concern must have been apparent when Pete joined him under his basha as the first drops of rain found their way through the dense jungle canopy.

'You've nothing to worry about with those two, boss, neither of 'em are Audie Murphy's, they've got their heads screwed on.'

'I know that, Pete,' Roger handed him his mug of tea.

Pete took a mouthful then passed it back and grimaced, 'You make tea like cats piss.'

'I'm just a bit bothered about this girl I was seeing,' the moment the words were out Roger regretted them. It was not good form to have personal problems when on operations, and if you had them, you kept them to yourself.

'What's the problem?' Pete asked.

There was no going back for Roger but he tried to cut it short, 'I don't suppose it's anything more than she's had enough of me, but she's just disappeared.'

'Is this the Chinese bird?'

'Yes.'

'You don't want to get seriously involved, love 'em and leave em,' Pete advised, 'don't lose any sleep over it.'

'I don't,' Roger lied, thinking that if that was the most sympathetic hearing that he was going to get, he should have kept it to himself.

Dan and Bill returned at 1430, Dan, grinning broadly, gave a thumbs-up as they entered the camp. They both sat down to be debriefed. Bob Gill was dozing in the next basha and Pete poked him with his foot.

'Make these two brew, Bob.'

Bob lifted his jungle hat from his face, 'Bloody Naafi girl now, am I?'

'Just get on with it,' Pete poked him again.

'Right,' Dan began, 'all the sentries are in the same positions and although we laid up in three different places we couldn't get a better idea of numbers but there's a lot of them in there.'

'Did you see any movement that would suggest people are still arriving?' Pete asked.

Bill answered, 'Nothing at all, nobody was moving about,' he turned to Dan, 'but they were making a fair bit of noise weren't they?'

'What sort of noise?' Roger asked.

Dan shrugged, 'Voices and the odd pan banging, but mostly voices.'

'They've moved their water point about twenty yards downstream where there's a bit of a pool,' Bill grinned, 'We stayed a while cos' a couple of birds turned up, we thought they might strip off for a bath.'

'Did they?' Pete asked.

'No such luck,' Dan replied, 'just filled a couple cans and pissed off. One of 'em was a right little doll even in that bloody awful uniform.'

'Armed?' Pete enquired.

'Yeah,' Bill looked at Dan, 'one definitely had an American M1 and I reckon the other had a Smith and Wesson, but you think it was an Enfield don't you?'

'It was an Enfield, I'm sure,' Dan replied confidently, 'I think they should call the strike as soon as possible. We think they're all there that are coming but we don't know for how long they'll stay.'

'I agree,' Pete said, 'Hey Gill, where's that bloody tea?'

'Coming, mighty, Tuan, coming.'

Chapter Thirty

Bo had been planning a weekend with Irene although he knew he was on standby for this major operation. As he pulled the straps tight on his 44-pattern pack he sadly eyed the holdall that he had packed that morning ready for their trip to Penang.

'All ready, Bo?' Bob Smith stood in the doorway fully kitted with his M1 tucked under his arm.

Bo's eyes shone, the disappointment of having to cancel with Irene was more than made up for by excitement of what lay ahead, 'Yes,' he replied eagerly slinging the pack onto his back and picking up his semi automatic shotgun.

The urgency of the call out was validated by the sound of a helicopter landing in the small police compound. As they left the building dust and debris thrown up by the Sycamores sixteen feet rotors caused them to pull the brims of their hats over their faces.

Gradually the blades slowed and the pilot waved them forward signalling that should approach from the rear of the aircraft. As soon as they had thrown their kit in and scrambled in after it, the sound of the 550 horse powered Alvis engine increased in volume, the wheels jerked from the ground, and with the door still open they were airborne.

*

John Sankey was dropped at the RWL's officer's mess in time for breakfast, and was pleased to see that there did not appear to be any unusual activity going on that would betray the onset of a major operation.

'Inspector Sankey?' the CO was just on his way into breakfast having remained in camp overnight to oversee preparations, 'I recall you from the brigade briefings, welcome.'

'Thank you, sir.'

'Will you join me for breakfast?' the colonel offered.

'That would be very welcome.'

Breakfast in the RWL's was always presented as a buffet and the members helped themselves.

'Ah, there's Major Winslow, he is company commander of 'A' Company to whom you'll be attached. Jack, may we join you?'

'Colonel,' Jack Winslow half stood.

'Have you met Inspector Sankey of special branch?' the CO asked.

'We've been at briefings together,' Jack said, 'but we haven't actually been introduced. How, d'you do, inspector,' he took John's hand.

'When are you having your briefing, sir' John asked.

'Oh we're all briefed and ready for the off,' Major Winslow said, 'but I'll arrange for you to meet the platoon commanders concerned and then you and I can meet at lunch and I'll give you the overview.'

*

Simon went to his platoon lines to take muster, which was a casual affair, the men parading in shorts and flip-flops.

'As soon as you fall out I want you to break off into sections and talk through your roles for the coming op,' he told them, 'but for goodness sake make sure that there are no locals within earshot. Discuss your individual tasks in depth and raise with each other any problems you may envisage,' he looked at his watch. 'After NAAFI break Sergeant Snell and I will return and answer any questions and listen to any ideas that you might have come up with,' he looked at his watch again, 'So you've got an hour and a half, fill the time usefully. Okay, section commanders take your chaps away, keep notes and we'll discuss the individual roles as a platoon.'

Sam did not need any encouragement to get the discussion started, 'I reckon we've got the shitty end of the stick,' they had gathered at one end of their long billet and he dropped onto a handy bed.

'Get up, Sam and treat this seriously,' Alan snapped.

Sam sat up, 'I am being bloody serious, and we have been given the crap job.'

'If that's all you've got to contribute then you can sit by the door and make sure no wogs are in earshot,' Sam remained sitting on the bed. Alan's voice rose a decibel, and his frown deepened, 'Come on move your arse, get by the door,'

Sam got up and went the nearest door, 'I'm supposed to be part of this you know'.

'You can hear what's going on and you've obviously got fuck all useful to say so you can just listen.'

When Alan faced the rest of the section there was no anger on his face and he winked at them.

'Can we smoke, Al?' Brian asked.

'You can burst into flames if you like Bri'. Right, let's just talk through the need to be able to react to the unexpected because you can bet your life it ain't gonna go as planned.'

*

Simon had phoned Susan from the mess. She was at work and he was on a public phone so their conversation was a little constrained.

'It's alright, Simon,' Susan said when he began to apologise for yet another broken date, 'I spoke with Jenny last night so I got the impression something rather special was going on.'

'She didn't tell you what exactly, did she?' He sounded shocked that after all the effort that was being made for secrecy the brigadier's wife would be talking freely about the operation.

Susan laughed, 'Don't be silly. If Jenny knew anything she would never discuss it with anyone. And anyway, Harry only tells her about things after the event, it's a policy that they always had. She prefers it that way, it neutralises a lot of worry.'

'How is she anyway?' Simon felt a little foolish for thinking so badly of her.

'Jenny's a soldier's wife,' she replied, 'stiff upper lip and all that,' her mood changed, 'I know this is something big, Simon, do take care.'

He was touched by her concern, 'Don't worry about me, Sue, they had one go at me and didn't do the job properly, I'll be alright.'

There was a short silence, and then she said, 'I'll pray for you every day and I'll light a candle for you in church on Sunday.'

'Thank you,' was all he could say, and then, 'I'll have to go, I've to meet Sergeant Snell outside in a couple of minutes.'

'When do you leave?' she asked.

He quickly looked round the foyer, 'I'm not supposed to say, but we won't see dawn in Ipoh.'

*

There were no streetlights in the camp, but a bright Oriental moon, assisted by a million brilliant stars, provided almost sufficient light to read by. Yellow light fell from the row of atap billets and radios spread the British Forces Network through the warm night.

Distant mountain ranges momentarily sprang into view as sheet lightening lit them, like malfunctioning searchlights, and the distant rumble of thunder was just audible above the radios and the singing of drunks returning to camp.

The hundred plus men in untidy lines, some sitting on their packs others standing and leaning on their rifles, were strangely quiet. When they spoke they had already slipped into their jungle voices but they had little to say and only answered each other in monosyllables. It was as though a cocoon of silence surrounded them, the noise from the camp was in another dimension.

In the block of tawny light that emanated from the open arms kote door, Jack Winslow stood surveying his company, and was happy with what he saw. There was an air of professionalism about these young men who were, by any criteria, mere amateurs. It was their training, their camaraderie, and their desire not to let down their section, their platoon, their company, that gave them the ambience of competence. It was a warm night and the young faces shone with sweat and supreme good health, their extreme youth was veiled by the moonlight.

The sound of trucks warming up on the MT Park changed note as the convoy of three-ton Bedford's, Ferret armoured cars and Land Rovers moved off to travel the two hundred yards to 'A' Company lines.

They arrived in the order that they would travel, a Ferret armoured car in the lead and another bringing up the rear. The vehicles stopped in a line with their engines ticking, over filling the scented air with petrol fumes.

'Get your men on board platoon sergeants,' CSM Raven broke the silence.

The night was suddenly busy as heavy packs were thrown up into the trucks and organised into rows down the middle of the cargo area, and men settled themselves on the hard wooden seats for the long journey. Two men were detailed as sentries on each truck, but most would doze fitfully as the night grew cold and seats became harder with each mile.

After five minutes the bustle and noise ceased and a hundred-armed men were seated, the only sound from the convoy came from the truck's engines. The driver of the leading armoured car engaged first gear noisily, and as the convoy began to move Big Jacks Land Rover overtook the armoured car and led the convoy out of the camp.

*

Lam had not spoken to May Ling since they had arrived at the camp, he had been kept busy carrying out repairs to basha roofs and defences during the mornings, and attending political talks and training sessions in the afternoons and evenings.

She had been rather distant during the journey to 5 Company when they were alone, and once they had arrived at their destination she became lost in the crowd and duty demands were made on them both. Now that they were in the big camp the crowd was even larger and the demands lessened.

He suspected that she had intentionally taken steps to avoid him and when they did briefly meet she was polite but never friendly. In retrospect she had never really been anything else even in the days when they had all served together. It therefore came as a surprise; when, after the evening lecture, she came and sat beside him on a log where there was a narrow view of a brilliantly moonlit valley.

'I thought you might like one of these,' she offered him a perfectly tailored Players cigarette.

'You don't have to waste them on me,' he protested mildly, pleased at her kindness.

'Why will it be wasted?' she asked with the hint of a frown.

'Well, I can smoke anything,' he explained, 'but you don't know when you will get hold of any of these again.'

She pushed the cigarette closer, 'Take it, as soon as they've all gone I shall stop smoking.'

They smoked in silence for a while hypnotised by the beauty of the moonlight and the peace that surrounded them.

'I know that you were a good friend of Lau,' she said softly, not wanting to be overheard, 'and he meant so much to me, he was like my big brother.' Lam thought he detected a catch in her voice. She went on, 'It all came as such a shock; I never believed that he would break faith. I thought that he believed in the cause and would die for it if he had to.' She drew on her cigarette and in the crimson glow he saw a tear on her cheek.

'He was driven to it,' Lam stared at the moon, 'Beng Kim hated him because he was educated. He did all that he could to humiliate him.' He turned and looked at her, 'Lau once told me that he thought that Beng's hatred of him was also because you had escaped his attention, and he was taking it out on Lau.'

'Oh no!' she covered face with her hands, 'I never considered that.'

He touched her shoulder in a futile effort to console her, 'But I think that it was Beng's savagery and persecution that drove him to do what he did.'

'Was Beng violent towards him'?

'Quite often'

'And did Lau just accept it?'

Lam shrugged, 'What else could he do, it would have meant death to strike back.'

May Ling, shook her head, 'How bad was it?'

'I think he could have put up with the violence in itself, it was the humiliation that caused the deepest wounds,' he put his cigarette out, 'If you don't mind I'll save this for later,' he put the stub in his shirt pocket.

'Give me an example,' she said softly.

'He would be struck in front of women and new recruits, he would be given all of the menial tasks, and not many months ago he was ordered to rape a young girl.'

The sharp intake of breath was loud in the still night, 'Did he?'

'Fortunately the security forces were spotted,' he laughed shortly, 'well so Lau said,' he smiled at her, 'Looking back that could have been a ruse, I hope it was.'

'So he didn't do it?'

'No.'

'If the army hadn't turned up, do you think that he would have?

He shrugged again and spread his hands, 'I can't know for sure, May Ling, but he would have died if he hadn't.'

The silence lasted a little longer this time, and then she surprised him again. She took his hand and kissed it, 'I'm glad that we've spoken of this, Lam. I am no longer ashamed of my poor cousin; I am now ashamed of myself.'

She stood, handed him another cigarette, and disappeared into the shadows.

*

The wait for first light was going to be a long one. Normally operations began in the early hours of the morning, so that once they arrived at the drop off point there was usually little more than an hour to wait before they could begin the march in.

Simon looked at his watch as the trucks drove off; it was 0230, nearly four hours to first light. The first priority was to get the platoon and all its attachments into the cover of the jungle. But the pressure, much to his relief, was not on him. His company commander and an SAS major were among the attachments, and he would be little more than their mouthpiece.

In fact it was a junior NCO who took command of the situation. He heard his name being called softly from the line of huddled figures along the edge of the road.

'Mr Gates?' the large form of Corporal Pell loomed and beside him was a smaller man who had the distinct smell of somebody who had been in the jungle for some time.

'Yes, here.'

'This is Trooper Gill; he will lead your platoon in to a spot where we can lie up until dawn.'

Trooper Gill shoved his unshaven face close to Simon's and his pungency was almost breath taking, 'Stay close together it's blacker than Zulu's arse in there,'

He went down the road for a few of yards and then lithely jumped up the bank and was immediately lost in the short span of undergrowth that preceded the jungle proper.

Simon followed the trooper more by the small amount of noise he made than by sight, and when he entered the trees the blackness, though he was expecting it, overwhelmed him and the panic of losing contact with his guide gripped him. He should have known better, the trooper was not only experienced but was a man who had passed the most extreme test that any regiment in the world had to undergo, that not only tried ones fitness but also intelligence and military gumption.

A hand touched him and he was once more conscious of the operational smell of sweat soaked clothes that had dried on the body a score of times,.

'Okay?' the disembodied voice hissed.

Fifteen minutes later the platoon and its attached personnel were all sitting in a close packed group in defiance of their training but necessitated by the situation.

Simon heard movement to his right and whispered words; he was about the order the miscreant to be quiet when he recognised Big Jack's deep voice.

'Where's Mr Gates?' The question was followed by 'don't knows.'

'I'm here, sir.'

'Ah good, everything okay Simon?'

'So far, sir,' Simon tried to sound confident and convincing.

'It all seems a bit vague doesn't it?' the OC chuckled quietly, 'Tell your chaps they can take their packs off and get some kip.'

'Righto, sir!'

'One sentry per section and I'm afraid there can't be any smoking or brew ups until we make base, which I'm informed is about two hours away and a pretty hard climb too, I imagine.'

'The map gives that impression,' Simon said hoping he did not sound too cocksure.

'Yes, quite.'

Simon willed him to go but he stayed close by, though not visible, 'These SAS chappie's have done a damn fine job so far don't you think?'

'They have indeed, sir. I'm sure the buggers can see in the dark, the chap that guided us in was uncanny.'

'I know,' Big Jack agreed, 'and there were two behind us covering the tracks we made.' There was another short silence, 'Righto, Simon I'll leave you to organise your sentries and get some shut eye. See you in a few hours.'

When the major had gone Simon turned to the man nearest, 'Who's that?'

'Barton, sir.'

'D'you know where Corporal Baker is?'

'No Sir, but Corporal Cantrill is next to me.'

'Ha, Corporal Cantrill.'

'Sir,' John's heart missed a beat, was he going to be sent on a patrol or ordered to do something as an NCO that was beyond his knowledge or ability.

'Detail someone to stay awake in your section and then tell your chaps to get their heads down.'

'Okay, sir,' John replied, relieved at the simplicity of his task.

'And pass that on to the other section commanders,' Simon added.

Sam was sat next to John, 'Pass that on Sam, each section to keep one man awake and the rest can get their heads down and tell Al I'll stay awake for us,' he leaned back on his pack hugging his rifle to his chest.

It was unfortunate that this operation had occurred so soon after his promotion, under other circumstances he would have attended a Junior NCO's Cadre for two weeks held by the Training Platoon, and could therefore have approached this operation with a little more confidence. He took some comfort that he was 2i/c to Alan who would help him as much as anyone would.

He hadn't even had the chance to write home about his elevation, it was something to tell Joyce in his next letter. The thought of her gave him some comfort. He had wanted to ask Alan what she looked like but couldn't bring himself to do so, it sounded a little shallow. He determined to ask her for a photograph in his next letter and to make it easier he would send her one; a nice jungley one. He nudged Sam, 'Have you got your camera with you?'

'Yeah, why?' Sam sounded as though he had been almost asleep.

'Just, asking.'

Suddenly a little patch of the jungle was filled with a flickering yellow light as somebody lit a cigarette.

'Put that fucking fag out,' it wasn't a shout but the menace in Sergeant Snell's voice had the desired effect and the cigarette extinguished in a tiny explosion of sparks and a muttered admonishment from an unknown voice, 'I bloody told yer.'

Chapter Thirty One

Pete left the troop's base a little after first light. After quick brew and an oat block, he led his brick up the hill towards the spot they had selected for the base camp for the RWL platoon, the base camp that 12 Troop would share with them for the next few days. The site had been selected with care, as it had to meet specific criteria. It had to be far enough away from the CT camp so that it would not be hit by stray bombs when the air attack was launched, but it had to be close enough for them to be able to attack the camp soon after first light and it had to be as secure from discovery as possible.

The position selected was in a small depression a hundred yards below the summit and a mere six hundred yards from their target. Pete hoped that the Aussie bomb aimers would not be consuming their normal intake of Tiger beer on the evening of the raid. The biggest drawback with the camp was the lack of water, the nearest source was over two hundred yards away but that could not be helped, the troops would have to cope.

Pete and his brick were returning to the site to ensure that there were no signs that any CT had been in the area. Dick Holt, Danny James and Jack Stone accompanied him. After an hour, the bearing on which they were navigating brought them straight to the depression.

'We'll put ourselves on the side facing the camp,' Pete told Dick who would be acting as a guide, 'They'll outnumber us two to one and then they've got two police and a special branch bod.'

'They'll have Iban's and tracker dogs,' Dick said more as a question.

'They've got Iban's, but I don't think they've got dogs, their tracking team is coming in tomorrow and they'll be at our present....' the sound of a far off shot stopped him mid-sentence.

'That was shot,' Danny said unnecessarily looking over his shoulder at Pete. Pete nodded and signalled for silence the four stood stock-still, heads cocked. Two more shots followed in quick succession.

'A pistol?' Dick looked at Pete.

'I think so, it wasn't a rifle.'

'A Sten,' Danny suggested.

'Could have been,' Pete agreed.

'Are we gonna have a butchers, boss?' Dick asked eagerly, glad of some possible action after days of inertia.

'No,' he said and took a compass bearing, 'it's come from the camp. We'll wait here for a while and see if anything else happens. They could have just been shooting something for the pot.'

'So close to their camp?' Jack Stone asked in disbelief.

'Why not, they don't know we're here,' Pete replied, 'We'll give it thirty minutes to see if anything else happens, but we ain't going any closer to the camp.'

'Could be an execution,' Danny suggested.

'They wouldn't have shot `em,' Jack Stone observed leaning on his rifle, 'too much noise, they just cut their throats.'

*

Beng Kim left the camp at almost the same time every morning to attend to his ablutions, and this morning was no exception. He tucked his Colt 45 into his belt, took a small shovel and set off to find a quiet spot not too far distant, but away from the prying eyes of a sentry. The spot he chose was no more than seventy yards from the camp at the side of a large fallen tree. He dug a small hole, placed his pistol on the trunk of the tree, lowered his trousers and squatted over the hole.

The movement was slight but enough to have him reaching up for the Colt, but before his hand could close over the butt it was whipped away from under his hand and he felt a fleeting contact with human flesh. In a millisecond he was upright with his trousers still around his ankles and not daring to reach down to rectify his nakedness.

May Ling was standing on the far side of the fallen tree with Beng's pistol in her left hand which was hanging by her side. It crossed Beng's mind that she had also been answering the call of nature and had stumble across him by accident, but this idea was quickly dispelled when he saw that in her right hand she held a Smith and Wesson. Slowly she raised it until the muzzle was pointing squarely at his stomach.

'What...' he began.

She cut him short, 'I have always despised you, Beng Kim,' she spoke quietly but her voice was full of venom, 'you have always abused those beneath you, people who were willing to risk their lives for the cause, especially we women. If I had not had friends I would have been used by you also, but I would have rather died.' Beng made to retrieve his trousers, 'Don't move,' she jerked her revolver towards him to emphasise her determination.

'But my...' he indicated his state of undress.

'Leave them,' she said, 'you can suffer some of the humiliation that you've poured on others. There will always be people like you, Beng Kim; the world is full of your sort. I could have put you out of my mind as you have been out of my sight but you drove Lau to defect, you caused his treachery and his death, and that I cannot put that out of my mind, nor do I want to.'

'You are being stupid woman, if you kill me you will surely...' his sentence was cut short by a tremendous blow to the stomach that threw him backwards, and he distantly heard the report of a shot. May Ling was now standing immediately over him and the muzzle was directed at his face.

'I wanted to say more to you,' her eyes were pitiless. 'I wanted to hear you begging for mercy, mercy that you have never shown to others. Now, I just want you to suffer pain before you die.'

Beng experienced warmth, that he knew was blood, over his exposed limbs and he felt as though his stomach was on fire. He opened his mouth and uttered a scream that was a mixture of anger, frustration and most of all pain.

May Ling leaned forward with the muzzle of her pistol only a couple of feet from Beng's head. Behind her she could hear people approaching stealthily, she pulled the trigger twice. Beng's face was awash with blood and gore, and his legs thrashed in his death throes.

*

Trooper Gill led the column at what he considered a reasonable pace, but it was a gait that others found a little extreme and he had to reduce it for the rest of them to stay in touch and able to move with a degree of stealth.

The climb was steep and constant and the estimated two hours became three. When they reached the site, where they were to make camp, basha positions were indicated and the platoon placed their packs at the allocated places and waited whilst the SAS carried out a clearance patrol.

Roger and Pete briefed the two majors on the morning's events and it was agreed that the shots that had been heard by Pete and his men had no significance to the operation but it was decided to bring the attack forward by twenty four hours. As soon as the clearance patrols returned Ray, Pete, Dan Cullis and Johnny Hooper left to set up the flares.

John was sharing a basha with Andy Barton and in the adjacent shelter were the Bren gun team, Tom Fitch and Roy Powell. When he was called to an O group with the rest of the NCO's in the platoon he quickly consulted Alan.

'What the bloody hell d'you do at an O group?' he enquired, concern etched on his face.

'Bugger all to worry about,' Alan delved into his pack and handed John a small note book, 'have you got a pencil?' he asked. John shook his head, 'here,' Alan broke his own pencil in half.

'Are you not gonna sharpen it for me?' John grinned.

'Piss of,' Alan backed out of his basha and stood, 'this isn't going to be a briefing for the main job.'

'How d'you know?' John sharpened the pencil stub with his parang.

'Cos those SAS lads are still out, things may change.'

'Oh yeah, so what's it going to be about?' John's nervousness diminished a little.

'Just camp admin.'

'So what do I need these for?' he held out the writing implements.

Alan shook his head, 'I'm not gonna answer, Johnno, what the bloody hell d'you think. Come on all the others are there.'

The six NCO's sat around Dave's basha a few yards away the OC was in deep discussion with Simon and Roger.

'Sentries,' Dave began, 'Corporal Murray, 1 Section will provide water point and 3 will be responsible for the latrines Corporal Rigby, and 2 will provide night sentries, Corporal Baker. Get rosters sorted and give me copies. Until further notice there will be no cooking but you can brew up. Clean weapons by half section as soon as this briefings over and I don't have to tell you, not to have all Bren's stripped at the same time,' he paused, 'Any questions?'

'Are the SAS lot not helping out with the sentry's sarge?' Rigby asked.

'They've already been here for about a week, Corporal Rigby and have already done a fair whack, but if you feel that they should help then you can discuss it with them.'

The others subdued their laughter.

'Go on Rigger,' 'Ruby' Murray urged with a grin, 'go and have a word and I'll get the first aid pack. '

Bo was having some difficulty in getting the fuel block to catch light.

'You've spent too long behind a desk, lieutenant.'

Startled, Bo spun round and towering above him saw Roger grinning down at him, 'Roger,' he smiled and got his feet, 'I knew some of these chaps were SAS but didn't for one minute think that you were here.

'I've been here for some time, Bo old chap,' Roger squatted down by the cooker.

Bo sniffed, 'So I can smell.'

'Come on, let's get this lit, then you can make me a brew.'

'So it was you who found this camp?' Bo asked with a hint of awe.

'Not me personally, but some of my chaps did.'

'They've done a fabulous job,' Bo poured water into his mess tin and placed it on the flame.

'I'd heard you'd been dragged away from KL,' Roger said as he slipped another fuel block on the cooker to speed things up, 'and I believe Irene's gone too.'

'Yes,' Bo agreed, 'she got a posting to Sungei Siput but I've not seen much of her, there's been too much going on.'

Roger's first thought when he had spotted the little Malay policeman squatting by his fire was that here was a possible link to Linda. With a fair degree of trepidation he asked.

'Bo, have you any idea where Linda's gone?'

Bo looked surprised, 'You don't know?'

Roger laughed shortly and shook his head, 'No, I just know that she's left her job.'

'Well I thought you may know more than us. All Irene and I know is that she has decided to take up teaching, but we don't know where, she wouldn't tell Irene.'

'Oh well,' Roger looked a little sad, 'Get the tea in, it's beginning to boil.'

Bo appeared equally sad, 'She hasn't been in touch?'

'She couldn't really,' Roger replied, 'I've been up here and in Ipoh for the past few weeks.'

'Perhaps there's a letter waiting for you back in KL.'

'Perhaps,' Roger agreed, but in his heart he knew different.

*

The ferocious anger had gone but the guilt that had helped fuel that devastating rage still remained as crippling as ever. It was not guilt associated with crime that she had just perpetrated, she felt not the least regret in that, it was the guilt of her own betrayal, the betrayal of Lau. Without her information he would still be alive today, he would never have been found.

Sadly she realised that she no longer hated the bloodied figure at her feet, he was no longer recognisable as the vicious bully Beng Kim. The two bullets in his face had destroyed his identity, he was now just the harmless remains of a man that had been.

They approached cautiously from behind anticipating an attack by security forces. Lam was one of the two who were the first to reach her. Despite the horrendous injuries to the face he knew instantly who the dead man was.

'Did he attack you?' Lam asked, she shook her head but remained silent.

'He attacked you,' this time it was not a question. He glanced at his companion, a man he did not know, to learn his reaction but he was paying no attention. He was a worn, thin man of late middle age, he had moved slightly forward of them and was scanning the undergrowth for signs of a possible enemy.

Lam gripped her shoulder and made her look into his face, 'He attacked you,' she stared at him blankly. He shook her, as one would wake a sleeping person, 'May Ling,' he spoke softly and urgently, 'you must say that he attacked you,' he shook her a little harder, 'May Ling,' she still did not respond.

They were in a throng of armed men; someone stepped forward and removed the two handguns from her limp grasp.

*

Two para flares were to be set at each corner of an imaginary square, two hundred yards by two hundred yards. Each flare provided 80,000 candlepower but only lasted for 30 seconds hence two at each corner, the second to be ignited as the light from the first faded giving the pilots a full minute of light to identify the target.

After some discussion, before leaving their base, they had decided that electrical detonation would carry too many risks although it would be the most reliable, and they therefore had to rely on time delayed fuses attached to the top plate of the flares.

For half an hour the four lay near the old water point, there was no activity and no sound to testify to the camps existence. Once they were satisfied that there was nobody around they set the first two flares below a significant gap in the overhead canopy. On the northeast corner the placing of the flares was easier as there was a steep drop and they were able to see the lake shimmering in the afternoon heat two miles away. Aircraft approaching would have an excellent view of the two flares on this side of the camp. As they were moving towards the final position to rig up the last two flares they distinctly heard the sound of raised voices. Thinking they had been spotted they froze in attitudes of readiness to either fight or flee.

Ray, who was leading, turned and exchanged a look of bewilderment with his OC who signalled him to wait, watch and listen. For ten minutes they listened to voices, angry voices much of the time, but not loud or distinct enough to know what was being said.

After an exchange of signals and a few whispered words, Pete and Dan remained where they were and Ray, followed by the major, moved closer to the sound of voices. It took them fifteen minutes before, after rounding a large mound, they could see the main square of the camp, and discovered the mound was the front of a bunker.

The loud voices had ceased ten minutes earlier. The area that they could see was empty except for a bundle that lay by a large basha on the far side of the space. In the basha a group of five people could be seen in discussion. To the left of the group, a figure of small build, probably a female, was sitting cross legged and she appeared to have her arms bound to her side.

After ten minutes Johnny signalled to Ray that it was time to withdraw. When they reached the other two they had a quick whispered de brief.

'That package could have been a body,' Johnny suggested.

'That's what I thought,' Ray agreed, 'and did you see the guy outside the hut, he looked as though he was tied.'

'I think that was woman,' Johnny said.

'If there's a body that could explain the shots this morning,' Pete said.

'An execution,' Ray suggested.

'Whatever it was I don't think we should let it alter our task,' Johnny ended the speculation, 'let's get this job done.'

*

Inspector Sankey had to possess a ruthless streak in his makeup; the nature of the job demanded it. An operative had to form friendships to gain peoples trust but they were merely a means to an end. The moment that an agent had outgrown his or her usefulness their fate was irrelevant. John felt a little differently about the Blind Man. For one thing they had worked together for a two of years and his worth had been enormous. In addition he was brave and had taken great risks on the behalf of the security forces. It was not just heat of the moment heroism; he had the same constant, cold, courage of a bomb disposal officer. But Blind Man did not only have to sit for a few hours in front of an unpredictable explosive device, he had to live cheek by jowl, for months at a time, with a savage and cruel killer, Beng Kim, a state committee member renowned for his brutality.

John had a plan in place to pull Blind Man out if he knew he was about to be compromised. He had organised for messages to be left at all of his regular 'letter boxes' in the last twenty four hours, warning him that the time had come to get out and give himself up. He hoped fervently that he was not in this camp; if he were he would not have received the warning. He tried to push the thought from his mind that less than half a mile away sat one of his best agents who, in all probability, would be dead before twelve hours had passed and there was not a thing that he could do about it.

*

At 1635 hours the SAS team returned to the base and at 1700 Major Winslow gave the final briefing to all of officers and NCO's.

288

'At 1930 eight Lincoln bombers, of the RAAF, will be overhead to deposit their loads of HE on the enemy who are situated about seven hundred yards to the north of us just over the ridge. We will be in touch with the squadron leader throughout the attack and will therefore know of their approach. The ridge should protect us from the worst effects of the blast, but with the amount of HE that is being used, and its proximity, there is sure to be some, so it would be advisable that everybody is in the prone position during the raid.' He paused and consulted a notebook, 'Five minutes after the last bomb has fallen, the artillery will commence firing on the western slopes to deter any escape in that direction and hopefully drive them towards the Gurkha's who have stop groups along the road and on the northern slopes. This barrage will continue until 0600 hours and that gentlemen will be our cue.' He gazed round the faces confident in their ability and eagerness to get on with the task. He went on, 'There are no changes to any of the plans you have been briefed on and rehearsed. Initiative will play a great part in the degree of our success and in minimising our own casualties. I have every confidence that each and every one of you will do your duty to the very best of your abilities.' Once more the large major allowed time for them to digest his words. 'Each section will have an SAS guide so that section commanders won't have the headache of navigation, and will arrive at the start line without mishap. We will move off carrying only belt order, packs will be left here with the rear-guard, we will be using this base for the rest of the operation.' He drew a sheet of bright red paper from his shirt pocket and held it aloft, 'The last plane in the formation will also drop ten thousand of these as well as its bomb load.' He waved the paper above his head, 'Safe-conduct leaflets, telling the survivors that they are surrounded and that their lives will be spared if they are unarmed and showing one of these. They are to be allowed to surrender. Now I know that I can trust in your inherent British decency and depend on you showing mercy. Because some poor bugger has not been able to acquire one of these does not mean he should be shot out of hand. If he is acting in a manner that you consider not to be aggressive, then take their surrender, if they are indicating that is their intent. But, and this is a big but, don't take any risks, err on the side of caution, I'd much rather one of those buggers be shot in error than one of you killed because you were being merciful. One final thought, impress on tonight's sentries that those fleeing the camp could possibly come this way so they need to be doubly alert.'

'The old mans a good skin,' John said as he and Alan went back to the section.

'Big Jack's alright,' Alan agreed, 'he's one of the lads when he's on ops.'

'Anything new, Al?' Andy asked.

'No, things are just as we've planned but you can all gather round.' Al waved his section to close in.

'I've just put me brew on,' Tom Fitch complained.

'Well you know what they say in the Mexican army, Fitch, el tuffo shito, get yer arse over here.'

'Nothing's changed,' he said when they had closed in, 'we leave here at first light, belt order, us leading and we'll have a lad from the SAS with us. Also the last bomber will be dropping a load of 'surrender' leaflet, you've all seen them in the past, these are red and any CT wanting to surrender has to be allowed to...'

As he spoke Dan Cullis and Jerry Singleton came and stood by his basha.

'Are you Corporal Baker?' Jerry asked.

'Yeah.'

Jerry offered his hand, 'I'm Jerry and this is Dan, we'll be leading you in tomorrow morning.'

'Which part of Liverpool are you from, mate?' John asked.

'How did you know I was a Scouser,' Jerry asked grinning.

'Just a slight accent,' John replied, 'I'm from Aigburth.'

'We're near neighbours, I come from Garston, we'll have to have a chat later and see if we drank in the same pubs,' he turned his attention back to Alan, 'What's your first name, corporal?'

'Alan, everyone calls me Al.'

'Right, Al,' Jerry squatted beside him, 'Dan here has been around the camp and he's been in it.'

'He's been in it?'

'When it was unoccupied,' he explained, 'so what we'd like to do, if it's okay with you that is, as we've both seen the defensive positions and the camp layout, we could take out the first bunker for you.'

Alan wanted to agree but his pride and that of the regiment made him oppose the idea, 'Thanks Jerry, but we've seen a mock-up of a bunker and a layout of the camp and I appreciate your offer but we have been tasked with the job,' he shrugged, 'and I just feel that we should do it.'

'Fine,' Jerry got to his feet 'but we'll be there if you want to use us. See you later lads,' the two men left.

'Are you after a fucking medal, Al?' Sam's disbelief was tinged with anger, 'they volunteered to do the toughest bit and you refuse.'

Alan reply was delivered with equal anger, 'Shut up Andrews, I'm running this section and I'm not passing the buck. If one of those guys copped it, it would be on my head, we've been given the job and we'll do it.'

'So it's alright if one of us cop's it?' Sam was not deterred, 'they're bloody regulars they...'

'Sam,' Alan cut in 'if you haven't got the bottle for it then I'll put you with the fire team and somebody else can go up front with me.'

Though Sam seethed, inwardly, at the implication of cowardice he held his peace and said no more.

When Alan had finished his O group and the section had returned to their basha's to make their final kit and weapon checks, John Cantrill stayed.

'Bit hard on old Sam, Al,' he said quietly as he wrote out the section's names in his notebook to make out a sentry list.

'I know,' Alan admitted.

'For all Sam's faults he's not lacking in bottle, brain yeah but not bottle,' John handed Alan the list.

'He just pissed me off,' he took the list and looked at it, 'he's always bloody moaning.'

'Well we all do our share,' John pointed out.

'Don't bother with a stag list, Johnno,' Alan screwed up the list and put it in his gash bag, 'I don't think any of us will sleep much tonight.' He looked at John and grinned, 'You're gonna make a good NCO, John, you care about the lads.'

'Yeah, I just know fuck all.'

Simon lay in his basha giving the impression that he was studying his map and the sketch of the camp, but in reality he was going over all that could go wrong on the morrow. The OC had already stated that the success would lie in the hands of each individual and how they reacted to each unique situation that would face them. This did not sit easy with Simon; he knew his platoon and knew that some of them were devoid of any glimmer of initiative and if success was going to be dependent on them then failure could be staring them in the face.

But then, when he surveyed them in a more positive light, there were those whom he could not fault. Most of his NCO's and a good number of the private soldiers, both conscripts and regulars, were reliable and effective soldiers. He realised that it was himself that he had most qualms about. He had come through that awful ambush more by good fortune than his ability as a leader or his skills as a soldier. He was still dumbfounded as to why his seniors seemed to regard him in such a favourable light. He had had no control whatsoever over those events, if it had not been for Sergeant Snell's calmness, know-how and courage, the platoon could easily have been wiped out.

At least now they had the initiative, or did they? The air raid and the shelling would be indication enough of an inevitable ground attack. Would they stay or would they run when the air raid had ended? The CT had been fighting this war for eight years now and would realise that security forces would be close by after an air attack; would they run or stand and fight? If he were commanding them what would he do? By running they would have to scatter and could be picked off by the patrols and ambushes, but some, probably most, would escape. The SAS estimated that the bunkers would withstand anything but a direct hit and their numbers would make them tough nuts too crack in such a well-constructed defensive position. He came to no conclusion as the arrival of Dave Snell cut short his deliberations.

'I think it's time to call stand-to, sir,' the interruption startled him; Dave Snell was crouching at the entrance of the basha.

Simon slid out dragging his SMG with him, 'Thank you, sergeant, will you pass the word.'

As the last shreds of light departed the green gloom the night creatures began their harsh, disharmonious hymn to the approaching night. Simon, accompanied by the OC and Sergeant Snell, dispensed the rum ration, circumnavigating the camp, checking the men and offering words of reassurance and encouragement.

When the tangible velvet blackness had enfolded them and the men had settled in their basha's to wait rather than sleep, the hiss of static from the radio joined the nocturnal clatter. It was too soon for the black humour that men indulge in when waiting to face danger and possible death. They lay in their basha's confronting their fears, some praying some simply hoping, but all of them alert and straining to catch the first sound of the bombers.

'Those poor bastards don't what's about to hit them,' John said more to himself than to Hodge, 'some of them will go to sleep and never wake up.'

'Not a bad way to go,' Hodge observed sleepily.

'S'pose not,' John agreed.

He lay on his back and stared at the blackness, thankful that the altitude meant that there were no mosquitoes. He wondered what Joyce would be doing now. The luminous dial of his watch read 1820, it would be around lunchtime back home. It was Sunday and he could almost smell the roast in the oven and Family Favourites would be on the radio with half the population listening as record requests were sent and received by servicemen and their families across the world. He promised himself that if he survived tomorrow he would send Joyce a request and he began to consider the record that he would choose.

*

As the night slowly enveloped them Lam could no longer make out the slight form of May Ling through the open side of the hut. She had lain there all afternoon, bound and silent, her face expressionless. Had Osman Chang and Hor Lin not been due to arrive at the camp the following day her trial would have been over by now and she would have probably already been dead. The other SCM's had agreed that it would wiser to let these two senior comrades have a say in deciding her fate.

He discovered, on questioning one of the women guarding her, that she had taken no food all day and only accepted a drink on one occasion. There was still a fragile ray of hope for she had not spoken since the deed so, if she chose to, she could accept Lam's advice and claim that Beng had attacked her. He had to find a way to speak with her and persuade her to take that course. He had no plan other than waiting for the cloak of darkness, then watch for any opportunity that may present itself.

Sentries were dispensed with during the hours of darkness; it was difficult enough moving silently through jungle by day and impossible at night, so there was little risk that security forces could approach them unawares. One fire remained lit in the kitchen area, surrounded by low atap screens and a roof, of the same material, to protect it from rain or any passing aircraft. Until recently they had felt secure enough, in their remote camp, to have a fire in the middle of the parade ground as a boost to morale, but a spotter plane had flown low over the camp a few weeks earlier causing enough alarm to abandon the camp for a period. They had not returned until they were sure that ground forces had not been sent to find them.

In the lecture hut a group of about ten men were engaged in a political quiz. As no lights, other than the fire, were permitted, it was the only entertainment available to them. Lam went and sat with his back to one of the poles that supported the roof, it was only a few feet away from where May Ling was being held, and here his presence would not appear suspicious. From where he sat the small amount of light from the fire, which seeped through the grass wall, was enough for him to distinguish the shadowy forms of May and the women in the basha with her.

He knew that these quizzes could go on for most of the night which suited his purpose, if it ended and the men dispersed to their respective sleeping quarters then his presence would become suspect. His patience

293

was going to be severely tested, as were his powers of observation, to identify the slightest chance of exchanging words with May. A guffaw of laughter rose from the quiz and attracted a severe voice of admonished from the darkness causing Lam's heart to race; the last thing he needed was for the quiz to be halted.

The diversion that Lam needed came from an unexpected and deadly source. It began with a low ominous drone that gradually grew into a recognisable, but still distant, grumble. Lam got to his feet and stepped clear of the roof and looked skyward but saw nothing other than black, not a single star cut a path through the dense canopy. He was now able to identify the direction from which the noise came; it was coming from the north, from the great lake. He knew that if he went to the far end of the parade ground there was a gap in the trees that offered a view of the lake in daylight. He was lucky; a bright tropical moon silhouetted a far off mountain range and shimmered ghostlike on the water of Temengor. The huge distant valley and lake were washed in a soothing light that softened the landscape with its placid radiance.

The beauty of the scene momentarily filled him with a great sense of peace, but even as he experienced the wave of serenity he was conscious that it was only ephemeral and there was the prospect of great danger closing in on them.

The noise was not only a little louder but much clearer, it was definitely an aircraft, not a helicopter or even a light spotter plane; it was something much larger. Lam was not unduly concerned, 'voice' aircraft often flew at night booming out their propaganda and dropping leaflets to substantiate the message. Then, he saw a single light as the invisible aircraft changed course and headed south towards him. His heart missed a beat as another light became visible and then another and another until he could count eight separate lights, in formation, bearing down on the hill. The adrenaline surged through his veins; they were about to be bombed. As he turned to shout a warning to the camp he heard a number of muffled reports and the camp was flooded in light as bright as the sunniest day. Lam sprinted to the shelter where May Ling lay.

*

Fireflies flecked the velvet night with tiny florescent bubbles of greenish yellow lights, and the nocturnal noise had reduced to the occasional call of predator and prey. The red glow of cigarettes mingled with the radiant insects but did not imitate their constant, erratic, motion.

The camp was silent but everybody knew that all of his companions were awake and straining to hear the first sounds that would announce the attack was imminent. The heavy air was taut with expectancy.

John felt someone touch his booted foot.

'Are you awake Johnno,' it was Alan.

'You bloody kidding?' John asked.

'Pass it on to the next basha,' Alan whispered, 'that everyone's has to remain lying down during the raid. They should be here any minute.'

'I make it five minutes,' John said as he slid out of his basha. He groped his way to the next basha and the message flowed round the camp. When he got back Alan was still there.

'D 'you want a smoke?' Alan pushed the tin onto Johns hand and with cupped hands lit their cigarettes.

'I'll be glad when we're on our way,' John exhaled and then blew on the cigarette causing the glow to increase, 'this waiting's bloody awful.'

'That's soldiering,' Alan's disembodied voice told him, 'ninety percent boredom and the other ten percent shitting yourself.'

John laughed, 'Do you get scared, Al?'

'Too bloody true, everybody does, don't you?'

'And how.'

'If anyone ever tells you they're not scared then they are either liars or nutters, so avoid both,' Alan advised.

'I don't think those bloody SAS wallah's show much fear,' John argued.

'Yeah, but they are nutters,' Alan laughed, 'But that's not true, I remember when I was on guard one night at the depot and we had this sergeant who was in transit on his way back to his parent regiment. He had just completed a tour with the Malayan Scouts, they were the forerunners of the SAS, and he got caught for guard commander. He was telling us jungle stories, scared the pants off us, cos it was really bad in the early days. Anyway, he said something I've always remembered; he said courage was overcoming your fear. He put it like this, he said some people had no fear of parachuting but that did not mean that they were brave, the brave bugger was the one who is shitting himself but still jumps.'

'Yeah I see what you mean,' John mused. 'Well just remember if I'm still with you when the shit starts flying, I'm a real brave bastard.'

'Shhh!' Alan hissed, 'd'you hear them.'

'Hell, yeah!'

The drone of the approaching aircraft dragged him back to his childhood in Liverpool, he half expected to hear the wail of the air raid siren that alerted the population and sent them scurrying for the damp shelters that reeked like open toilets.

'This is it, Johnno, I just hope those Aussie pilots haven't been on the piss.'

There was no evidence that the flares had ignited but the sound and blast wave of the bombs hit them simultaneously. A mighty rush of wind passed over their heads causing small branches and leaves to shower down on the camp. The crash of the high explosives and hurricane lasted for a full four minutes, and when it had passed the sound of the eight bombers were once more a distant hum and a silence descended on the breathless group of men.

An anonymous voice spoke for all of them in tones loud enough for the whole camp to hear, 'Now that's what I call a fart.'

In the distance artillery shells could be faintly heard, bursting in the west.

*

The first stick of bombs failed to hit the camp but the blast from them flattened all of the huts and basha's, throwing those, running for cover, against trees breaking bones and tearing muscles. The screams of fear and pain and futile, bellowed, orders were lost in the uproar of ear splitting explosions that could scarcely be distinguished one from the other. It became a continuous, thundering roar. Lethal chunks of shrapnel scythed through the night air felling small trees and humans alike. The light from the flares began to fade but the camp was lit by flashes from dozens of crippling explosions that gave the place an appearance of what hell could be, blackness continually scorched by blinding eruptions of orange and red flame.

Lam's slight advantage, of seeing the attack coming, stood him in good stead, and by the time the first bomb exploded he was dragging the trussed May Ling into the closest bunker where they cowered throughout the few minutes that death and destruction rained down on the jungle. As he freed her from the ropes he could feel her slight body trembling with fear. The cool ground that gave them shelter shook with each explosion and damp earth rained down threatening to bury them.

When the bedlam finally ended he groped his way to the entrance over the piles of earth that had been loosened from the roof. Fortunately the stout logs had provided the protection for which they had been intended. He felt her close behind him as they emerged from the earth like two subterranean creatures. All was blackness again but almost at once torches began to be switched on thrusting fingers of light into the dust filled night.

From various parts of the camp the moans and sobs of the injured could be heard and orders were being given by those in charge who had survived the holocaust. The sounds that he could hear seemed distant and full of echo and his ears still rang from the uproar that had just passed.

Lam was suddenly aware that there was light other than the dozens of torches that flickered eerily and when he looked up he could see the moon. The jungle around them had been cruelly destroyed; the jungle canopy no longer existed.

Taking May's hand he led her through the massed tangle of vegetation and fallen trees, south, to the part of the wilderness that was home to him and where he had many 'letterboxes' through which he could make contact with his controller. He knew that the air raid was just part of what they could expect, there would be patrols and ambushes, and he realised that it would be safer to meet security forces in the open rather than encounter them close to the camp and in jungle.

To the west he heard the artillery shells beginning to land and knew that he had taken the right course. He could also hear the sound of intermittent pistol shots. A shiver ran down his spine, for he knew that this signified the severely wounded being dispatched rather than allowing them to fall into the hands of the British or waste scarce medical supplies on the hopeless cases. He was confident that they would not be confronted by patrols until first light but he had to be careful not to stumble onto a camp or ambush.

His hearing had still not recovered from the bombardment and he picked his way slowly through the expanse of mutilated forest, still holding May's hand. They had not exchanged a word throughout. Lam's emotions were running riot. He felt a combination of emotions; relief that they had survived thus far and that he had been able to rescue May, fear that came from the reality that they were not yet safe but over riding all was the sense of betrayal. He had not been warned of the attack, the inspector had sacrificed him. He knew that he had to give his thoughts fully to their survival and he must put all else out of his mind including his anger.

As they crossed a small-dishevelled clearing that had been caused by a stray bomb, the moonlight showed a shower, of what appeared to be large leaves, fluttering to the ground. He paused and retrieved one. The moonlight was enough for him to see that it was a safe conduct leaflet encouraging surrender. He could not make out the detail but he knew that it could be their salvation as they must have been dropped at the time of the raid and the one purpose could only be that surrenders were being encouraged and would therefore be accepted.

Lam decided that before they reached the jungle edge he would discard his rifle, an unarmed man walking into an ambush was more likely to be arrested than shot. He recovered another leaflet and handed it to May

'Keep this; if we get separated show this to any soldiers that you meet,' she stared at him blankly, 'you know what it's for?' She nodded.

*

Jenny heard the staff car pull up, the doors open and muffled words exchanged. The car drew away and she heard Harry talking with his batman in the hall and then the sound of his footstep on the marble stairscase.

'At last,' she said to Susan.

The two women sat by the open window that looked out over the glittering lights of Ipoh. When they had moved into the official residence, an Edwardian house of great elegance in colonial style, Jenny had turned a large bedroom that boasted a generous, covered, balcony into a lounge. It was a room that afforded views over the town and across the Kinta valley. To the right were hills, behind Kampong Durian, over which there was almost a nightly display of, riotous multi coloured lightening and the town, half a mile distant, spread glittering two hundred feet below.

Susan looked at her watch, 'Almost nine, I'll leave you to have some time with Harry.'

'Don't go, please,' Jenny begged, 'Harry always likes to see you, and he does prefer company when there's something big brewing; it takes his mind off things that he can no longer have any control over.'

'Ah, Susan what a nice surprise,' Harry entered looking dapper despite having been at Brigade HQ since seven am, 'what are you girls drinking?' He picked up Jenny's glass and sniffed it, 'G and T, I think I'll join you,' he went the cherry-wood cocktail cabinet and poured three generous measures of gin, 'You are joining me?' it was more of a statement than a question.

'I shouldn't really,' Susan protested mildly, 'I'm driving.'

The brigadier tutted, 'What an excuse, I'll get Watkins to drive you home if you get tiddly,' he handed them their glasses and kissed Jenny on the forehead, 'And what have you been up to today, old girl?'

'I've had a very pleasant day,' Jenny replied, 'I had lunch at the Swiss Hotel with Fiona Slaughter and then went to Whiteway's to look at some warmer outfits for when we go home.'

'Slaughter, Fiona Slaughter, do I know her?' Harry wrinkled his brow.

'The new judges' wife,' she explained.

298

'Ah yes, bit, Margaret Rutherford as I recall.'

'She's a very nice lady,' Jenny laughed, 'but your right; she's very Home Counties.'

'What a bloody name for a judge,' Harry went on, 'Slaughter, I ask you.'

'Seems quite appropriate,' Susan sipped her drink, 'and it would be a perfect name for a soldier wouldn't it?' Harry grimaced.

'Did everything go smoothly today,' Jenny asked.

'So far, but we won't know the results until a little after dawn.' Harry put his glass down, took out his pipe and went onto the balcony.

'Is this something big, Harry?' Susan asked as they followed him.

'It is indeed,' he pressed tobacco into the bowl of his pipe and then tested it for draw, 'probably the biggest since this all started.'

'I know that I shouldn't ask,' Susan said, 'but are the RWL's involved?'

'No harm in your knowing now my dear girl,' Harry blew out a cloud of aromatic smoke, 'it's no secret anymore now that we've kicked off. Yes, a company of RWL will be playing a major part early tomorrow morning. Why are you so interested?'

'God, Harry, you are getting so damned absent minded,' Jenny scolded gently, 'we spent the day with Susan and her young man at the races, Simon Gates, a platoon commander in the West Lancs.'

'Of course,' he tamped the tobacco in his pipe, 'Jerry Crawson has a very high opinion of him,'

'His CO?'

'Yes, in fact, and I really shouldn't tell you this so it does not go beyond these four walls, but he has put him forward for an award.'

Susan put her drink down, and winked at Jenny, 'For his part in the ambush.'

'Yes.'

Susan laughed, 'But poor Simon considers himself a bit of a failure in that event.'

'Glad to hear it,' he drained his glass, 'it's when young subalterns think that they are God's gift to the army that I have concerns. I'm having another and then I'm going to get my head down for a few hours. Are you girls joining me, in the snifter that is?'

Chapter Thirty Two

The platoon was ready and stood-to thirty minutes before first light. There had been no need to rouse the camp, the artillery had shelled intermittently all night, but it had not been the far off crump of the twenty-five pounders that had kept them awake, their nerves had denied them their sleep.

Slowly the pitch black became diluted by the advancing dawn and gradually the nearest bushes and trees became detached from the blackness. There was a stirring in the centre of the camp. Low voices of authority were making last minute checks of orders and equipment.

A soft voice at his side startled John; he had not heard its owner approach, 'Corporal Baker?'

He recognised the Liverpool accent of the SAS guide, 'Next basha along,' John whispered.

Two ghostly forms passed by him with barely a sound and a few seconds later the signal came to move off. In single file the platoon left the camp and began the climb to the top of the ridge. After fifteen minutes they stopped. It was almost daylight. A signal came down the line for John and his gun team to go forward.

By an outcrop of small rocks he found Alan with Simon and the two SAS guides, the jungle around them had been decimated. What trees remained standing had been stripped of their foliage and most of their branches, a mass of shattered tree trunks and craters spread before them for two hundred yards in a tangle of impenetrable vegetation. The devastation was appalling. The bombing had been accurate and it was hard for him to imagine that any living thing could have survived such a storm of high explosive.

'Fucking hell,' was all he could say.

'Right, Corporal Cantrill,' Simon tried to keep his voice calm, his mouth was dry and his heart raced, 'd'you see the bunker, there,' he pointed and when John did not respond immediately he went on, 'about twenty yards to your front, there's a fallen tree with a split trunk lying across the top of it.'

'Seen,' they were slightly higher than the bunker and it was angled to their left. As he looked he began to identify other defensive positions in the confusion of broken trees; none showed any signs of occupation.

'That will be our point of attack,' Simon went on, 'to the right and a little to the rear, is another and that appears to be the only one that can support it.

'Right, sir.'

'The signaller will stay with you. Corporal Baker, Andrews and I will drop down to the left under the cover of that banking. When we get to that crater in front of the bunker I'll give you a thumbs-up and you will put a fire into the slit as we close on it. When we get up to it switch your fire to the other bunker even if there has been no fire from there. Okay?'

'Okay, sir.'

Then they were gone, the two SAS soldiers with them, five minutes later they reappeared in the crater. Simon raised his thumb and the ominous peace of the morning was shattered as the attack began by Hodge emptying thirty rounds of .303inch ball and tracer into the black, narrow opening, obscuring the slit in a shower of dirt, the tracer scything visibly into the opening. Hodge slickly whipped off the empty magazine and Fitch, with equal dexterity, clicked a charged one in its place and Hodge opened fire again.

John felt something touch his boot and rolled over with his SMG poised to find the OC and the SAS major knelt behind him.

'There are enemy in the foliage on top of the bunker,' Big jack shouted and he and the SAS major blasted the area with their SMG's, 'you keep the bunker engaged, corporal.'

*

As soon as the planes had passed and before the last, undulating, echo of the final explosion had died away, those who had survived scattered in groups and singly, into the safety of the darkness.

So Ying, the Branch Committee Member for North Perak, was responsible for the day to day defence of the camp with his forty men, he therefore still saw it as his duty to remain behind to defend the camp against the inevitable attack that would come with the new day.

Like most other senior ranks in the MRLA, So, had fought alongside the British against the Japanese. A man of slight stature and quiet manner he was nevertheless feared and respected by his subordinates. When he smiled he displayed a set of teeth that resembled a vandalised cemetery but he smiled rarely. He had been selected by Chin Peng to command this important camp because of his courage, his loyalty and his determination.

So, was, by any criteria a cripple, nearly ten years ago a Japanese machine gunner had stitched a line of six bullets across his right hip, but despite a severe limp he was able to keep pace with the quickest and cover distances that seemed extreme even to the ablest of his men.

He had only been able to rally twenty-three of his command and he assumed that the remainder were casualties. If that was not the case then he would make sure that they paid the price for their infidelity. He did not have enough men to protect the entire perimeter but knew that it was unlikely that any attack would come from the west because the artillery seemed to be concentrating their fire on that side of the ridge. Also, it was harder to attack uphill so that they were not liable to come from the north. Therefore, he concentrated his defending forces on the south and eastern sides of the camp.

Most of the bunkers had been rendered ineffective, not from bomb damage; fallen trees had obliterated their arcs of fire. Two on the south side and one on the east still retained a reasonable field of fire and were accessible. It was in one of the bunkers, on the south side of the camp, that Goh found himself in that fateful morning. Clutching a Japanese 6.5mm rifle, a weapon that he had never fired, and peering through the narrow fire hole at the tangle of branches and leaves he fearfully awaited the inevitable storm.

There were only three of them in the bunker but the dense green mess above them concealed another seven men. It was their fate to defend this side of the camp. In the bunker with him was Tan Chen, an experienced fighter, with an ancient Bren and four magazines of ammunition and Ah Loy, a youth of eighteen, who it was rumoured, had only joined the cause to escape the Taiping police who wanted him for a number of petty crimes.

As the light increased so did the tension in the bunker and as the coolness of the morning faded the space, the three men occupied, became suffocating.

'How do we know the rest have not left us here?' the boy hissed.

'Quiet fool,' Tan snapped as he scanned the depression and rise to their front.

'He's right,' Goh said nervously, 'we can't....'

His sentence was cut short as So stuck his head in the entrance.

'They're here,' he whispered urgently, 'get ready.'

Before he had withdrawn his head a machine gun opened fire filling the slit with dust and wood splinters and forcing them all below the parapet.

*

The two SAS soldiers had moved to the left and forward of Simon's position, so that when he leapt to his feet they were able to put fire down onto the target as he ran forward with Alan and Sam. Simon had his eyes fixed on the slit; his Sterling slung round his neck and a 36 Mills grenade in his hand. There did not appear to be any movement in the bunker but he was aware that a lot of shooting had started; somehow it seemed far away and unconnected. It was only when he heard the vicious zip and crack of passing bullets and heard someone close by shout out, in alarm or pain, that he realised that he was being fired at.

Out of the corner of his eye he saw Alan Baker keeping pace with him and firing his SMG as he ran. The twenty yards seemed like a hundred, he was running, and weaving as hard as the mess of vegetation allowed but for what seemed a long time the bunker did not appear to get any closer. The front of the bunker was still being churned up by his supporting fire team and it flashed through his mind that they might not switch their fire in time for him to post his grenade. Suddenly he was up against the pile of tree trunks that formed the front wall and was frozen by the sight of the unmistakable shape of a Bren's flash eliminator being depressed in his direction. Corporal Baker was quickly at his side with the barrel of his SMG in the opening and blazing a full magazine into the interior. As he ducked down to change magazines Simon raised himself and posted the grenade, he heard a scream of horror, and in the four seconds before it went off, a lot of scuffling and incomprehensible shouting.

*

Everything that could go wrong went wrong, and in the fire fights that were won and lost, luck played a significant part. When the firing stopped and they were able to see out of the slit again Goh saw three men racing towards their position, he fired and saw one of them drop and in that split second his confidence grew, but was all too brief. The bolt on his rifle jammed as he tried to slide another round into the chamber. He ducked down to try and free the action. As he struggled with the rifle's bolt he was dimly aware of what was happening with his comrades. Ha was frantically pulling his trigger but only creating a clicking sound and Tan was cursing and trying to manoeuvre the machine gun to engage the swiftly closing enemy. Goh did not see the muzzle of the SMG appear in the slit, he only heard the deafening racket. Tan dropped, his head shot away and Ha sank screaming to the floor. Then something hard bounced off the back wall and Goh was staring at a grenade lying menacingly by his feet. For someone so ill forged for athletic movement he moved with great speed for the exit reaching it at the same time as Ah. Both men died struggling to get out of the narrow opening, cursing each other with their final breaths.

*

Jerry saw that from where the two men were in front of the bunker they were not in the line of fire from the defenders in the fallen trees but nor would they be able to engage them.

'Stay where you are,' he bawled, 'stay where you are.'

He could see Major Hooper crouching by the gun team that was laying heavy fire onto the area above the bunker and knew that if he moved forward the major would realise his intention.

'Come on,' he shouted to Dan. and the two of them dashed across to the left of the bunker.

The defender's positions were made apparent by the way the foliage was gyrating from the blast of their weapons. By keeping well to the left Jerry and Dan were able to stay out of their line of sight. As they passed the bunker Simon and Alan stood, and each fired a burst into the mess of fallen trees before ducking down again. It was only as Alan was changing his magazine that he saw Sam, a few yards away, crawling towards the protection of the stout limb of a fallen tree. Fountains of earth danced around him as the CT above the bunker tried to finish the job.

'Sam's been hit,' he shouted at Simon, 'cover me.'

At the moment he levered himself away from the bunker wall at a running crouch, Simon put another magazine of 9mm into the enemy's position. It was only a distance of about ten yards to where Sam now lay, partially under cover; Alan fell beside him and dragged him into shelter.

'Where are you hit?'

'In the guts,' Sam groaned.

Alan rolled him onto his back, unbuckled his belt and tore open his blood stained shirt. Sam's stomach was bleeding but it did not seem severe. Alan groped into Sam's left-hand shirt pocket and pulled out his field dressing.

'It's not bad, Sam,' he reassured him as he tore open the dressing. He placed the thick pad over the source of the bleeding, 'Just hold this in place; someone'll be with you soon. I've got to get back to Pearly he's out there on his own.'

As he poised ready to dash across the open ground the rate off fire from above the bunker increased dramatically but it was not coming his way and he could now hear intensive fire from the direction of 2 platoon. He noticed that Simon was no longer in front of the bunker. He spotted a movement on his right and saw his gun team run across the open ground towards the right of the bunker. Big Jack was with them and he signalled Alan to stay where he was, he turned back to Sam.

'How are you feeling mate?'

Sam looked pale, 'I'm alright Al, but it fucking hurts.'

'Let's have a proper look at it then,' he lifted the dressing, 'Bloody hell I can see the bullet, it hasn't gone right in,' he laughed, 'this is where your belt would've been. Yeah, look,' he showed Sam the belt with a ragged hole through the webbing, 'you lucky bastard, Andrews, it must have been a duff round, your belt's almost stopped it.'

*

Without trying to get a visual of the enemy Jerry and Dan blasted the foliage, Jerry emptied a magazine and as he clipped on a new one Dan blazed five slugs of heavy load 12 bore into the same area. The sound of quickly departing bodies was partially drowned by a scream of pain.

Simon scrambled up the bank behind them, 'We'd best not follow,' he suggested, reluctant to give a direct order to men of the calibre of these two, 'we'll be straying into 1 platoon's arc.'

In answer he received a withering look from Jerry who crawled to the edge of bunker's roof and signalled his SC, who was still with Major Winslow and John's gun team, waving them forward. The group arrived sweating and went into defensive fire positions. Jack Winslow, crouching, crossed to where Simon was trying to attract the attention of Alan Baker and patted him on the back.

'Text-book stuff, Simon, bloody well done,' he beamed

'Thank you, sir,' Simon realised that he was shaking with the excitement of the past ten minutes but he felt elated.

'You've got a casualty,' Jack pointed out, 'but I think Corporal Baker's got it under control,' he called across to John, 'Corporal Cantrill.'

'Sir,'

'Take a man and check the bunker.'

'Sir,'

Firing was continuing over to the right but with less ferocity.

John took Fitch and led the way down to the bunker's entrance. 'We've got a shit job, Fitchy,' he muttered.

The entrance to the bunker was a small trench big enough to allow one person at time to access the opening to the bunker itself. From the outside the entrance was visible, only if the observer crouched. Together, John and Fitch slowly crouched and peered cautiously into the opening. They fired simultaneously at the figures that appeared to be coming out and it was immediately obvious, when neither flinched, that they were shooting dead men.

With some trepidation John dropped into the hole and, with the barrel of his weapon, pushed the bodies back into the bunker. It took great effort as the blast from the grenade had wedged them into the narrow opening. As they slowly fell backwards he instinctively loosed off another burst at a figure crouching in the far corner but again he was shooting a corpse, the man's face had been shot away.

John climbed out, 'All clear, sir, three dead CT's', he shouted, then he turned away and, to his shame, vomited.

*

Roger fumed, the distant firing meant that a significant contact was been played out no more than two hundred yards away. His troop had worked hard and long to find the camp and here he was with half his command leaving the area of conflict to rendezvous with the RWL's tracking team.

Major Hooper had sympathised, 'There's nothing that I can do about it Roger,' he shook his head, 'the brigadier has insisted that it is to be an RWL responsibility. I've managed to find a way to get half of your troop involved but that's the best that I can do.' When Roger made to protest further, he went on, 'And Harry Woodhouse is right, our role is primarily intelligence gathering and that is what we've done, and I might add, with great élan and I commend you and your chaps on the job you've done.' He tried to assuage Roger's disappointment, 'I would lay odds that you'll get as much action with a follow up as you'll get in the camp.'

With just half of his troop he met up with the RWL's at mid morning. They were already at the RV eager to be on the trail and looking relatively fresh and clean compared to Roger's stinking and tattered band.

Ben got up from his pack where he was sitting studying his map. 'Who's in command?' he asked.

'I am,' Roger did not like his brusque manner, 'Captain Howard, 12 troop.'

'Ben Murphy,' Ben introduced himself, 'I've had control on the radio telling us to head off on a bearing of 75 degrees,' he held the map so that Roger could see it, 'We have the area to ourselves as far as Easting 102 and then we will have to be on the lookout for the Gurkha's.'

'I suppose that it's better than sitting here on our arses,' Roger mused.

'That's for sure,' Ben said, 'we will dissect any tracks going east which, with the shelling, is their most likely escape route.'

'Well they could come this way or go north but I suppose it would be a bit risky not to comply.'

'Well,' Ben said with finality as he closed his map case, 'not complying is out of the question as far as I'm concerned,' he looked at his watch, 'we'll be moving off in ten minutes; unless your chaps want a rest for a while.'

Roger sensed that he was being provoked but he resisted reacting negatively but he could not entirely keep the scorn out of his voice, 'It's considerate of you but I think they will be keen to see a bit of the action.'

Ben grinned, 'So I would expect, I was regiment until a year ago, just a little leg pull.' The tension eased, 'How many are you?'

'Eight.'

'We're going to be a little cumbersome,' Ben said, 'but it can't be helped, if we split...'

His words were cut short by an outburst of furious small arms fire close by, brief and savage; it was followed by the murmur of voices.

Ben and Roger discovered one of Bens team, Rob Eaton, knelt by a diminutive form in CT uniform and the sound of bodies moving cautiously towards them caused the two officers to raise their weapons.

Rob held up a hand of caution, 'It's Emau and Pangau searching for the other one,'

'Just, two of them?' Roger asked.

'I think so,' Rob looked pale and shaken.

'Are you all right, Eaton?' Ben asked.

Rob jabbed the barrel of his shotgun at the body, 'It's a bloody women I've shot.' he sounded angry and wretched.

'If you hadn't she'd have shot you,' Ben dismissed his leading scouts concern and disappeared into the undergrowth.

Roger looked down at the body. She was small, no more than five feet tall. She must have been close when Eaton had fired for the charge had not had time to spread and she had taken the full charge to the bottom half of her face and throat totally destroying it below her eyes which were now closed.

Roger's heart sank; he detected a slight rising of her chest. He sank quickly to his knees and checked her heart, 'She's still alive.'

'Oh, shit,' Rob dropped beside him, 'she can't be, the poor little cow.'

At that moment a low, almost undetectable moan emitted from the destroyed face.

'She'll die,' Roger lay his hand on her chest and felt for her heart again, 'but how long will she suffer?' he felt for her pulse in her wrist, 'very faint,' he said.

'Can't we help her,' there was desperation in Rob's voice.

'There's only one way we can help her,' Roger said looking directly into Rob's eyes. They understood each other without speaking the awful words, 'Who else has seen her?' Roger asked.

'Emau saw her go down but only you and Captain Murphy saw her lying here,' there was hope in his voice.

'Can I trust you?' Roger asked. Rob nodded fervently, 'this stays between you and I,' again Rob's head bobbed vigorously. Roger switched the change lever on his SMG to single shots, 'Fire two rounds off in the air,' he commanded and pointed his gun at the girls heart. As Rob's first shot crashed out Roger pulled the trigger and the small body jerked and then lay still.

Roger knelt again and went through her pockets; all he found was a surrender leaflet and a Players cigarette packet with two cigarettes remaining. Roger studied them, 'I wonder how she got these.'

'Have you seen something,' Ben re-appeared with an excited Emau in tow.

'We were mistaken,' Roger lied 'we thought we saw something.'

Ben did not reply immediately, his eyes running over the shattered body and the two men's faces. He nodded slowly and the single word. 'Okay,' provided agreement and understanding.

*

May Ling did not hear the shot that felled her or see the man who fired it. She had followed Lam in a trance not knowing where they were going or how far they had travelled.

Suddenly the world went black and she was aware that she was lying on the ground. She could taste blood, but was unable to see or move. Somewhere, far away, she could hear shooting but it did not worry her, nothing seemed to matter.

Pain suddenly enveloped her entire being, a pain beyond belief or description, a pain so great that she dared not cry out. Then like a balm she heard his voice. The pity and tenderness in Roger's voice washed over her like an anaesthetic. She tried to speak his name but she could not make her mouth form the words.

She felt a hand placed gently on her heart and knew his touch. Then his hand closed over hers and held her wrist for a moment, she tried to speak his name again, but again found it impossible.

She heard another voice and Roger replied. Fear overcame the pain; somehow she knew they were talking about her although she could not distinguish the words. Regret and sorrow pushed the agony aside as her recent life flashed by. There was a short silence, she tensed herself. She heard the sudden thunder of a shot close by, and then Linda was at rest.

*

Lam saw May Ling thrown backwards by the force of the shot and he felt the blast. Years of being hunted and numerous scraps ignited his instinctive response. Without having to think to consider all the

308

probabilities he knew this was not a situation in which to try and surrender. With a speed that was created by the intrinsic will to live he was gone from the scene as swift and as silent as a passing thought.

As soon as he was out of immediate danger he slowed to a pace that allowed him to cover his tracks, care rather than haste would be his greatest protection. The greatest danger was dogs and in the commotion he was certain that he had heard one barking. He needed to find a stream or swamp to cover his scent but this was strange country and he would have to use his knowledge of the jungle to know where to find where a stream would naturally form.

He felt a failure, not only was he failing as an agent but he had failed May Ling, after having already saved her from certain death for the killing of Beng Kim, fate was so cruel. When the bombing had occurred he thought that good fortune was with them, he had been able to rescue her and they had survived the rain of death only to accidentally walk blindly into the very people they were seeking to help them, to provide them with sanctuary. It was pointless trying to reason and explain your intentions to men engaged in a fire-fight in jungle, so much depended on sound rather than sight. He could have called out that he wanted to surrender but in what language? His adversaries could have been English speaking or Indian, or Chinese, or Malay. No, he had done the right thing and fled the area.

The safest opportunity to surrender would be when he hit the Lasah road; he could be out in the open with his hands raised and the safe conduct pass visible. He patted his shirt pocket to make sure that he had not lost it. He could hear the sound of running water ahead and he increased his pace without forfeiting caution and tried to push May Ling from his mind.

*

Jack Winslow was well satisfied with the performance of his company though a little disappointed with the body count. 3 Section had accounted for three in the bunker that they had attacked and another one in the defenders outside. 2 Section had killed another three when the defenders engaging 3 Section had withdrawn. On a search of the camp area another sixteen bodies had been discovered, the CT had clearly finished off casualties of the bombing raid as some of them had gunshot wounds to the head.

Sadly, Private Jolly, a rather slow-witted youth from Chorley, and Lance corporal Walsh from 2 platoon had both been killed in a fire-fight with the withdrawing CT. It had been a very close quarter action steeped in confusion and the platoon had been lucky not to have sustained greater casualties.

'Not a bad tally at all,' John Hooper observed as the two majors sat on top of a bunker that they now designated as their HQ. While they talked Big Jack's batman crouched over his stove preparing a brew of tea.

'How's the chap who was wounded in the assault?' John asked.

Jack laughed, 'That bugger, Andrews, would come up covered in gold if he fell in a sewer. Not only did it seem to be a faulty round, but it hit his web belt and only just penetrated it giving him the slightest of wounds.' He spotted Alan placing his section in defensive positions on the south side of the camp, 'Corporal Baker,' he called and waved him over.

'Sir,' Alan came to the base of the bunker.

'How's our wounded hero, Andrews?'

Alan grinned, 'I've had worse leech bites sir,' he squatted down in front of the two majors, 'It bled quite a lot and you can just see the base of the slug but I think he should be casevaced if we're staying on in here.'

'Well it's going to be at least a two day hike out; we're going to sweep the western slopes of the ridge in case any of them chanced their arms down there in spite the shelling.' In the distance the sound of artillery fire could still be heard. Major Winslow waved a hand in the direction of the sporadic shelling, 'That will go on until first light tomorrow. In fact we can have an O group in an hour's time,' he turned to face Dave Snell who was checking his platoon's ammunition state, 'Where's Mr Gates, Sergeant Snell?'

'He's doing a search of the camp with some of the SAS lads and the police, sir.'

'Okay, get a message to him that there's to be an O group,' he looked at his watch, 'at thirteen hundred,' Big Jack took the mug of tea his batman offered. 'Has your medic looked at Andrew's yet, Corporal Baker?'

'One of the SAS medics cleaned him up and changed his dressing sir.'

'Good,' he looked up at the great hole in the jungle canopy, 'D'you think the Brylcreem Boys would risk bringing a chopper in if we cleaned it up a bit?'

'For your badly wounded casualty?' Johnny Hooper grinned, Jack Winslow nodded, 'No need to,' Major Hooper continued, 'if his wounds not that bad he could be winched out.'

Twenty minutes later Alan watched, greatly amused, as Jerry Singleton secured the harness under Sam's arms and round his chest. Sam's normal ruddy complexion had turned chalky white. Alan took a

310

step closer and shouted into Sam's ear above the racket of the Whirlwind that hovered a fifty feet above.

'You look sacred, Sam,' Sam shook his head vigorously; 'well you've gone white.'

'Loss of blood,' Sam yelled back unconvincingly.

Further exchange was abruptly ended as Jerry took a step back and gave a thumbs-up to the winch-man who was sitting in the open door. The pitch of the 700-horse power Wright's Cyclone engine rose, as the big machine ascended and at the same time the winch man reeled in his anxious catch. The downdraft and turbulence gradually decreased and the helicopter disappeared from view with Sam still dangling beneath it.

'I don't think your mate enjoyed that,' Jerry observed with a wry smile,

'You can say that again,' Alan agreed, 'I think shitting himself would better describe it.'

*

Control had insisted, that as the dead girl's face was so badly disfigured, a photograph of her would not suffice for identification and her body would have to be carried to the nearest LZ, or out to transport.

'I don't know of any old LZ's around here,' Roger said, 'the best place is the camp or down to the Lasah road.'

'Well this is new territory to us,' Ben pointed out, 'so I'll go with your recommendation on this, but we only need a small party, she's only going to be light.'

They wrapped the girl's body in a plastic sheet and then tied her to a pole seven feet long. Two, of the four men detailed, lifted the pole to their shoulders and Private Coupe led the small party of four RWL's back towards the spot that May Ling had escaped from only a matter of hours ago.

As Roger watched them set off up the slope he suddenly experienced a sensation of great sorrow and was amazed to hear himself saying, 'Treat her gently, fellah's.'

Chapter Thirty Three

Jenny favoured native dress when working in the garden. She wore a Chinese peasant straw-hat that offered complete protection from the burning rays of the sun and a Malay sarong with a loose blouse for coolness.

She found the more mundane horticultural chores therapeutic and their execution did not cause any distress to Lim Sang, their gardener. Anything other than weeding, or hoeing, brought him tutting and clucking like an old hen; shaking his head and hovering close by, his black eyes boring holes in her back. Lim was a bony Hokkien, with ears like jug handles, Harry's batman always referred to the wiry gardener as the wing commander.

This morning she was hoeing the beds of purple Bougainvillaea and yellow Hibiscus and Frangipani. She was beginning to feel tired, it was almost ten thirty and she had been in the garden since before eight. Harry had already left the house when she rose at seven and she had breakfasted on the terrace enjoying the brief cool of early morning. Susan had phoned to see how she was and they had arranged to meet for lunch at the Ipoh Cricket Club.

She rested on her hoe and looked out across the lush green of the large garden towards the distant hills that crouched untamed beyond the fertile Kinta valley. The cultivated valley was a patchwork of light green padi fields and regimented forests of grey leafed rubber trees. To the right, the town of Ipoh spread north to the banks of the Perak River. Regret welled within her; she would soon leave this beautiful country for the last time, with its languid, shady Malayan Kampong's and its urgent, energetic Chinese villages. Its violent sun and savage storms, storms that left town, village and jungle refreshed, revitalised and expurgated, smelling of damp fecund earth and hot drying dust.

Most of her life had been spent in the Far Eastern reaches of the Empire. She had been born into an army family at Naini Tal in the Himalayan foothills where her father commanded a company of the 2nd Battalion of the 1st Gurkha's. She had not seen England until the age of ten. When she was five her father disappeared from her world at the outbreak of the Great War and did not return until she was nine. The horrors of that war passed by Jenny and her two brothers, they spent the four years in a world that had barely changed since Victoria's reign.

After the war the regiment moved to Lahore and then Burma and in 1931 to Singapore. It was here that she met Harry Woodhouse a young, ambitious, subaltern who was attached to a sister regiment, the 6th

Gurkha's. Three years later they were married and honeymooned in Hong Kong.

After a two year posting home to England, where Harry served as an Instructor at the RMA Sandhurst, they re-joined his regiment, which was stationed in Delhi, and there they remained until the outbreak of the Second World War.

Now she would soon be going to a country she had always referred to as home, but where she had spent so little of her life, it was 'home' purely through her blood line, her spiritual home was here in the East.

'Brigadiers on the phone, ma'am,' Watkins South Welsh lilt startled her, 'he'd like a word if it's convenient.'

'Darling,' Harry sounded cheerful, 'start packing for a long trip all this should be over in a couple of more days so we'll be free to do as we please come Saturday.'

'I take it that things have gone well?'

'Wonderful, tell you all about it at dinner.'

'Shall we eat out?'

'Probably be best thing old girl, but don't make it before eight thirty.'

When he had hung up Jenny sat on the large dolphin chair in the hall and cried.

*

Lam lay in the undergrowth on a slight rise that afforded a view of the road in both directions. To the right, it disappeared in a gentle left hand bend after about a hundred yards, and to the left the distance in view was less as the road dropped steeply down fifty yards away and was lost from sight.

He lay in the belukar for an hour trying to spot the slightest movement that would give away an ambush position. Nothing stirred, not even a bird or inquisitive monkey, no creature called, the silence and heat were equally oppressive, and a storm was approaching. As the thought entered his head he heard the distant drum roll of thunder.

If there were security forces around then they were of the highest calibre for in the space of an hour he would have expected to spot or hear some indication of their presence. He had to conclude that they were around, it would have been bad tactics not to have sealed this escape route and in the main the British did not make such errors. So, if there were stop groups about then they were experienced soldiers. That could be in his favour, for they were not likely to open fire prematurely the moment he stepped into view. They would hold their fire waiting for more enemy to appear, assuming that he was the leading man of a group. This would give him the opportunity to hold his safe conduct pass aloft and show his intention to surrender.

Lam took a deep breath, pushed his rifle under a clump of fern and slowly got to his feet. Holding the red leaflet above his head he stepped out onto the hot tarmac.

*

Abdul was not sure where he was going but cared little providing it was taking him away from the shattered camp and danger. Sek Fu was a branch committee member whom he had known for a number of years, and who commanded 11 platoon of number 5 Regiment that operated on the east of the Ipoh, KL road. As a result of Beng's death he had been given temporary command of the regiment and his aim was to get back to his own territory where he would feel safer. In the confusion and the dark he had been unable to rally any of his own men but knew they would head 'home'.

Sek knew of Abdul's slow wittedness but his company was preferable to being alone despite his lack of brainpower, furthermore he was armed and he was experienced. At the road they waited watching and listening and after a half an hour, when they had niether heard nor seen any sign of the running dogs, Sek decided they would dash for the other side. But he had a dilemma; should they make the dash together or singly? Should he send Abdul first, in order to draw the fire of any waiting ambush or should he go first? He remembered from his days of fighting alongside the British against the Japanese that they would normally hold their fire until they had a number of their prey in the killing zone. If he sent Abdul first and he moved quickly, would it forewarn any watcher who was alert for the second man to cross? However, the first to cross could be shot and in that case the one who remained behind would escape. After a few moments Sek decided that if he sent Abdul first and he got across safely, then Sek would move down the edge of the jungle a few yards and wait ten minutes before he followed. That way he would exit from a different place and they would probably have thought that Abdul was alone, if the time span were long enough.

He signalled to Abdul to make the dash. As the stocky Malay rose to his feet Sek quickly grabbed his arm and dragged him back undercover. A figure had appeared on the road in the uniform of the MRLA, unarmed and with his hands raised, in his right hand he held a sheet of red paper that Sek instantly recognised as a surrender leaflet.

'Lam Ten,' Abdul hissed.

'You know him?' Sek asked.

Abdul nodded, 'He is in our group.'

314

Lam did not hear the shot that killed him; he felt a mighty blow at the back of his head and was thrown face down onto the road where he lay twitching in his death throes. The rain storm began with a sudden ferocity, almost drowning out the final shots, and diluting Lam's blood that flowed from his dozen wounds. It was as if the gods were both angry and weeping.

*

After Special Branch had photographed those killed, 2 Platoon set too digging shallow graves in which to bury them. It was not an easy task when the only digging implements that they had were their personal entrenching tools. While 2 Platoon sweated over their distasteful task 3 Platoon hefted their packs and left the scene of destruction to search the side of the ridge that had supposedly been denied to the enemy by the gunners.

'We're splitting into sections,' Simon had briefed his platoon, 'I will be with two section, Sergeant Snell with you Corporal Baker, and you will have Yau with you Corporal Murray.' He gave them their respective compass bearings, 'We will all RV at GR109540 tomorrow afternoon.' Simon had his doubts about the usefulness of this part of the exercise; three sections dissecting a fifty square mile patch of jungle as it dropped down to the upper Sungei Perak would cover an insignificant part of the wilderness but it was too large an area to do a full sweep.

'You will see that the RV is a cross roads outside the village of Ayer Kala, but once you hit the cultivation, which I believe is tapioca and pineapple, there will be a lot of security activity in the shape of our colonial friends, the Aussies. They are aware that we are on our way but be on your guard, we don't want any accidents with mistaken identity at this stage of the operation. Any questions?'

The going proved easy for 3 Section, they were in primary jungle with sparse undergrowth and it was downhill. On only three occasions did they come upon areas that showed signs of shell-fire. Compared to the devastation caused by the bombs dropped on the camp, the damage was unimpressive.

'I can't believe those buggers were firing all night we've hardly seen any damage,' John said when they had camped for the night. He sat with Alan outside Dave's basha drinking mugs of scalding tea and smoking.

They had camped at 1630 on the side of a re-entrant above a stream. Nobody had got much sleep the previous night and the energy sapping excitement of the day had crept up on them, so Dave had elected to give the section a decent rest and had them make camp earlier than normal.

'Don't pig out,' he had warned them, 'we could be spending another night out; I think Mister Gates may have underestimated the distance and the terrain.'

'Make out a night sentry roster, Johnno,' Alan told his 2i/c, 'start it from 2100 that'll give 'em an hour apiece. I'll organise weapon cleaning.'

By half past five, as the light was beginning to fade, all the routine tasks had been completed; sentries informed of their stags, weapons cleaned and most important evening meals consumed. The jungle slipped into the peace that preceded the nightly evening chorus. The light began a gradual softening; darkness would be upon them in less than half an hour.

'We better get them stood-to,' Dave stood up and picked up his belt kit.

'HALT,' the shout startled them; it came from the direction of the stream where Andy Barton was sentry. And then, '*Berhenti.* (Halt)'

Dave grabbed his FN, 'Come with me, Johnno, stay here Al.'

The water point was twenty yards away and Andy was situated on the far side of the stream. He was out of cover, kneeling, and aiming his shotgun at a target out of their vision. He caught sight of Dave's approach out of the corner of his eye and swung the gun in his direction.

'It's me, Barton, what's the problem?'

'There's two of 'em here, sarge, they seem to be unarmed.'

Dave and John moved quickly forward until they could see the two CT's. They stood knee deep in the stream, their hands raised and clutching safe conduct leaflets. They were an incongruous pair. The man was young, in his late teens or early twenties, tall, with delicate features and quite out of place in such an untamed environment. The female was squat with a broad face and short thick hair. She could have passed for a man had it not been for her enormous bosom.

'*Mari sini,* (Come here)' Dave said and motioned them to come towards him, 'Keep watch, Barton. Cover them, Johnno; make sure you're on single shot. *Bercakap Inggeris?*' (Do you speak English?)

'A little, Tuan,' the women said smiling, bowing slightly and waving the leaflet.

'Sarge,' John said, 'the lads wounded.' A piece of shrapnel the size a cigarette tin lid was embedded in his left thigh.

'*Kamu sendiri?*' (are you alone) Dave asked, the women nodded,

'*Ada kamusenapang?* (are you armed)' again it was the women who responded

'No, Tuan we, we...' she could not find the English and she waved her hand back the way they had come.

316

Back in the camp, after stand-to, Dave allowed the rules to be broken, 'Someone make these two a brew, and I'm going to need two field dressings.'

While John got a mess tin full of water on the boil Dave dressed the man's wound by packing a dressing each side of the shrapnel and then wrapping a third round his thigh to hold them in place.

After they had drunk their tea, which the women did with audible relish, their feet and hands tied with parachute cord and they were placed in the centre of the camp beside the night sentry. In minutes the woman was snoring loudly.

'Bloody hell,' Alan said, 'why did it take us so long to find that bloody camp. I bet they can hear her in Ipoh.'

*

Sek had left the area at great speed after he had killed Lam; he knew that he could have possibly stirred up a hornets nest. Had he been able to choose his travelling companion it would have not been Abdul. Like most Chinese he did not hold the Malays in high regard, he considered them lazy and lacking in ambition or aggression. Abdul compensated somewhat for these defects through his congenital brutality but his movements were ponderous and slow and speed and silence were now essential.

*

Rifleman Sing Thapa was the leading scout of a four-man patrol under the command of Corporal Lal Rai. Their task was to cover the half a mile between two of the dozens of ambushes that were spread along the Lasha road. 'B' and 'C' Companies had been allocated five miles of the road and it would have been impossible to secure it solely with ambushes therefore, large stretches were the responsibility of small patrols to deny the ground to any escaping CT.

It had not required a signal from Sing; they had all heard the distant shots, despite the teeming rain. All the four Gurkha's sank to a crouch, their keen almond eyes scanning their arcs and with ears straining to detect human presence above the downpour that hissed and rattled on the foliage. Thunder crashed immediately overhead and lightening briefly touched the gloom that had descended over the dense belukar.

The four men waited, drenched, but oblivious to the cold in their expectation of a welcome contact with the enemy.

Lal was an experienced NCO who had served for almost five years in the jungle. He went close to Sing, 'We will go forward slowly side by side,' he whispered, 'take off your safety catch.'

Sing pressed the button at the front of the trigger guard of his Winchester shotgun, as Lal slowly drew the cocking handle back on his

317

Sterling, the breechblock settled home behind the seer with a slight, metallic click.

Lal leaned close to Sing, 'Go slowly and carefully, my son,' he whispered, 'they are close I can smell them.'

Sing signalled the patrol forward, he and Lal, almost rubbing shoulders, their heads swinging and dipping as they tried to look through the undergrowth, seeking a gap that would reveal the enemy.

It was Sing who saw them; although at first the sighting did not register. The patch of sand coloured cap could easily have passed for a dead leaf still clinging to a branch, but when the wearer moved his head the red star on his cap denounced him. Abdul died taking the full load of shot under his left arm demolishing his ribs and bursting his heart. As Sing let off a second round at sounds in the undergrowth, he saw Lal disappear, falling backwards and he was conscious that bullets were cracking about him. As he moved forward he saw a CT struggling to remove a magazine from a Tommy gun, he could hear him cursing in a language he did not understand. He fired and his heart stopped when the only sound from his shotgun was an audible click. Sek also heard the click of a misfire and leapt forward, throwing down his empty Thompson, he grabbed the M1 that had fallen from Abdul's lifeless hands. Sing dropped the Winchester and his right hand reached behind his kidney pouch. Sek's hand closed over the wooden stock of the carbine just as the razor sharp blade of a kukri bit into the side of his neck.

Sing crouched by the almost headless body covered in his victim's warm blood; there was no sound other than the teeming rain.

'Well done little brother,' Corporal Rai stood grinning down on him, his shirt bloodied at the shoulder, 'you have killed as many of these dogs in one minute as I have done in five years.'

When the four had taken up all round defence and dressed Lal's wounded shoulder, the signaller relayed the news of their successful contact to control and requested a casualty evacuation.

*

Harry was pleased with way Operation Clive had gone so far. The kills had been in the low twenties with only two fatalities among the attacking force and just as he was about to leave his office he was informed that the Gurkha's had accounted for another two. He knew from experience that surrenders would follow after such a devastating blow to the enemy's moral and security.

The smile with which he was greeted did not deceive him for a minute; he knew instantly that it masked deep sorrow.

'How is it going?' Jenny asked as she poured him a gin.

318

'Damn well,' he took the glass, put his arm round her slim waist and led her out into the relative cool on the verandah. Lights twinkled over the town and the inevitable lightening over distant mountains heralded the equally inevitable approaching storm.

'Just another day old girl and then we'll be off to....'

'I'm not sure that I want to go 'home', Harry,' she cut in.

'No?'

'No. We've spent so little time there; all of our happy memories are in the places in which we've served,' she looked up at him, 'aren't they?'

Harry gave a great sigh, 'True, but that's where our wider family resides and at a time like this,' he looked away towards the mountains to hide the pain in his eyes, 'it is probably best to be with family.'

'But the army has been our closest and immediate family, darling,' she lay her head on his shoulder as they took in the familiar night scene, 'apart from Peter and Roger,' she spoke of their two sons, 'and they're soldiers now and spend precious little time in England.'

'So you want to stay?' He removed his arm from her shoulders and produced his pipe from the pocket of his bush shirt.

'Just so long as we're together, I'm happy if you want to have some time in England?'

'I had a long chat on the phone with Frank Fielding, the GOC, this morning, and persuaded him that I wouldn't be missed for a few months. Convinced him that Jerry Crawson could cover for me and of course he could, he's more than capable'

'I know that you are prepared to make great sacrifices for me, darling, but I would prefer things to remain as normal as possible. I don't want to say good bye to my dearest friends and then go and wait for the inevitable, in what would be a foreign land, among vague acquaintances from my youth.'

'That's where the best treatment is old girl.'

'Well,' she replied thoughtfully, 'let's be honest, there's little to be done and I would rather have a happy year than a lonely and boring two.'

'My brave, sensible, Jenny,' he kissed her forehead. He forced his mood to lighten, 'But I'll tell you what, old girl, you and I are going to have a rip roaring month in Europe. Paris, Venice, London and a final week at home in Evesham. I'll get back onto Frank first thing and withdraw my request for a home posting and instead ask for an extended leave,' he put his arm round her shoulders and steered her through the drawing room, 'I'm bloody starving let's go and eat and make plans.'

Chapter Thirty Four

Dave gave the male SEP a shot of morphine. He had clearly suffered through the night but to carry him would be too difficult, he would have to keep pace and the painkiller would help. They did not want to spend another night in the jungle, as the majority of men had used most of their rations and barely had enough to keep them going on the long march that lay ahead. There had been a few, subdued, grumblings when he had ordered that all rations be pooled.

'It's the greedy bugger's who've scoffed everything that'll be best off,' Barton complained.

'You've only got a tin of sausage and beans,' Alan said as he placed the tin on the meagre pile.

'It's better than nowt. Anyway here's a teabag as well.'

'Won't we get back tonight, sarge?' Fitch asked as he handed over two oatmeal blocks and three teabags.

'We should,' Dave replied, 'but if this wounded guy slows us down we won't.'

'Why don't we just dump him,' Fitch suggested nonchalantly, 'if he really wants to surrender, he will.'

Dave looked at Fitch and shook his head, 'Apart from the military need for intelligence, Fitch, that's a pretty inhumane thing to say even in jest.'

'I wasn't joking,' Fitch looked mildly surprised at his platoon sergeants reaction, 'he's fucking enemy, would he have looked after one of us if the boot was on t'other foot.'

'Probably not, he'd have probably cut your balls off and left you to die, but we're in the British army and we do the decent thing where we can. Now piss off.'

Dave heaved his pack onto his shoulder, 'Let's get going'

The section, led by Barton, set off down the slope with the distant rushing sound of rain in their ears and within ten minutes the tropical rainstorm burst through the canopy two hundred feet above and drenched them again.

Whu Bing, the wounded SEP, kept pace with the section despite his wound but found it difficult to maintain his balance on the greasy slope and was soon covered in mud from his constant falls.

'Keep a close eye them, Corporal Cantrill,' Dave had warned, 'even though they seem harmless enough now, never take the enemy for a fool, they are still enemy,' he grinned and winked, nodding at the strange pair, 'But if they were all like this pair the war should have been over years ago.'

Brian winced every time Whu hit the ground but the slight Chinese never uttered a sound, bearing his pain in silence. The woman tried to support him with her squat frame but the terrain defeated her and in the main she had to be content with helping him to his feet, urging him to greater effort with unintelligible whispers that were unmistakable in their purpose.

Early in the afternoon they hit an area of flatter jungle and Dave signalled for a halt. They were still in primary forest and the pouring rain intensified the natural gloom. Dave squatted and studied his map with some difficulty, having to continuously wipe the water from the protective plastic.

He signalled Alan to close on him, 'I reckon we're about here,' he touched a wide gap on the contours about half way down the western side of the ridge.

'Bloody hell we'll be lucky to make it tonight,' Alan studied his own map. 'I think we're further on than that. If you remember, we crossed a pretty wide stream about an hour ago and then a few minutes later another smaller one that turned sharply west,' he pointed to an area much closer to the cultivation, 'I know there's loads of stream that aren't marked but if I'm right that wide stream could be this one and there's the smaller one with the sharp bend.'

'You could be right, Al, I hope you are, that'd be much better news.' Dave signalled Barton to go on.

Alan had judged correctly, for twenty minutes later they found themselves in swamp, waist deep in slime and mud, and the map showed there to be swamp close to the jungle edge. The pace became painfully slow dragging already tired legs from the sucking mire. After an hour and thirty minutes, to every ones relief, they hit firmer ground and the undergrowth grew denser.

A further twenty minutes elapsed and then Barton turned and grinned, raising a thumb, 'We're out,' he mouthed.

It was only when they stepped out into the warm sunlight that they realised it had stopped raining and that the sodden canopy had continued the effect of steady, depressing rain. They were in a belt of pineapple, hundreds of sparse, spiky leafed bushes spread before them, each holding a single fruit in its centre. About a half a mile away glimpses of the Sungei Chenderon could be seen in the bottom of the valley as it wound its way through a taller patch of palm oil bushes. The section sat in a spaced line, steaming, as the sun dried their sopping clothes.

'You can make a brew and eat the remaining rations or we can push on to meet the transport,' Dave told them.

The decision was unanimous and instantaneous; carry on.

'Sarge,' John moved up the line, 'this lad can't keep going much longer; his leg's a right mess.'

'Let's have butchers at him,' Dave crouched beside Whu. His face was greyish white, not the jungle pallor that they all displayed, but the complexion of a sick man. 'Changing his dressing won't improve things,' Dave mused, 'it's the walking that's giving him the problem.'

'We could carry him, there's fuck all of him,' John suggested, 'now we're out of the ulu it'll be a piece of cake.'

'I'm not carrying no fucking CT,' Fitch objected.

'You'll do what I say, Fitch,' Dave snapped, 'and if you shoot your mouth off again you'll be carrying her,' he jerked his thumb at the stocky women who was attempting to clean the mud from Whu's leg with the sleeve of her shirt.

As dusk approached they could see, in the distance, a group of military vehicles at the end of the red laterite road that dissected the plantation, a score or so men, in clean uniforms, milled around the parked vehicles. As the section got closer they could make out a dozen or so shabby individuals lying on the grass at the side of the track.

Simon stood up to greet them, 'Well done,' he said with a smile but then his face dropped when he saw the makeshift stretcher and lightened again when he realised the casualty was not one of his own men.

The 3 RAR had supplied the trucks and ambulance and a CQMS doled out welcome stew and mugs of hot sweet tea. Dave briefed Simon on the events of the last twenty-four hours and just before darkness fell, when de leeching was in progress, 'Ruby' Murray's bedraggled section appeared out of the gloom and 3 Platoon was re-united.

*

'You're quiet boss,' Pete observed as the three tonner trundle through the muggy evening.

'Must be beginning to feel my age, Pete,' he lied.

'Bloody hell, boss when you get to my age you'll be for the knackers' yard,' Pete retorted.

'Is that where you're going when we get back, sarge?' a voice asked from the front of the truck.

'You do try to get yourself in favour don't you, Gilly' Pete laughed, 'but I'll not be swayed by your crawling.'

The banter continued unheard by Roger whose thoughts dwelt on the girl and what he had done. At the time it had seemed the kindest thing. She was going to die, even if they had been able to get her to a hospital, but it would have been a long and agonising death for her, and for those

322

with her. He speculated on whether there had been a chance of her surviving her terrible injuries. If he had dosed her heavily with morphine would it have dulled the pain enough for a trek to the LZ and the flight to Taiping? Even if that were the case she would have been hideously disfigured, would a young woman have wanted to live the rest of her life with such mutilation? She had not had the choice; he had made the decision for her, he had played God.

A shiver ran down his spine so violent that Ray, who was sat beside him, was conscious of it.

'Have you got a fever, boss?'

'No, I'm fine.'

'I thought I felt you shivering.'

'Someone must have walked over my grave,' Roger said and tore his thoughts away from the dead girl and addressed his other concern, the whereabouts of Linda. This would be his first opportunity to find out what had happened to her. He suddenly realised just how concerned he was. For the past weeks he had put her to the back of his mind whilst he got on with the task in hand, the question was now of enormous proportions and he was really finding it disheartening to think that he may not see her again.

*

Bo and John Sankey had stayed at the site of the camp until the two remaining platoons of the RWL's had carried out the noxious task of burying the dead, who were already beginning to emanate the stench of putrefaction. Before they had been interred the two police officers had photographed the bodies and taken the fingerprints of two that were so disfigured that a photograph would have been of little use.

John was relieved that his agent, Blind Man, was not among the dead but his relief only lasted until he returned to 28 Brigade HQ when the results of the actions carried out in the Gurkha's area revealed Lam's death. John took some comfort from the fact that he had been murdered by his own and not killed by security forces. Guilt still lay heavily upon him and he knew that the trust of his other agents would be seriously reduced when they learned of the manner of Lam's demise.

The party stood with heads bowed as Major Winslow said a short prayer over the two rows of unmarked graves. As it was not likely that many of the occupants were Christians Jack had instructed that the crude wooden crosses, that his troops had started to put in place, be removed.

As Jack surveyed his fifty or so, sweat stained and tired troops, standing in the battle torn clearing, bare heads bowed in the rain. His mind went back twelve years to a similar scene, when, as a young subaltern in the 13ᵗʰ Battalion the Kings Liverpool Regiment, they hurriedly buried a number of their comrades as they fled from the surrounding Japanese. That had been the first and last time that he shed a tear in public. Although they were burying their enemies now he still found it a moving occasion and from the expressions on the faces of the men lined up before him he could detect that these young men were experiencing similar emotions.

'I can't put my finger on it,' Bo said as they cooked their evening meal, 'but there was something disturbingly familiar about that girl who had been shot in the face.'

John looked up from stirring a curry that simmered while they waited for the rice to cook, a look of alarm on his face.

'I felt that,' he said fearfully.

They stared at each other silently for a moment; Bo broke the silence.

'We must be mistaken, even if you'd known somebody all of your life it would have almost impossible to recognise them with such horrific injuries.'

'You're right,' John replied quickly and gratefully, 'is that rice ready yet?'

*

Relief, pride, remorse and fatigue filled the long barrack-room as the 3 Platoon unpacked their grimy webbing and deposited their stinking uniforms on the floor for the dhobi wallah, Lucknow, to collect and return, freshly laundered the following evening.

'We'll just have time to get a bevvy, Bri,' John shouted across the room.

'You'll have to use the corporal's mess now, Johnno,' Arnie Hodge called from the other end of the room.

'Piss off, Hodge,' John began but further comment was cut short as Alan entered the basha still wearing his noisome jungle greens.

'Mail up,' he shouted.

John had a letter from Joyce. At first he determined to keep it until he could find time and quiet to enjoy it fully, but the desire to have a quick look was too great. He carefully tore it open. There was a photograph enclosed. The girl who smiled out at him shyly had short blonde hair, large eyes, a small but wide nose and full lips. Even though it was a black and white photo John knew that her eyes were blue and her complexion had the freshness of a country girl. She was slightly built and possessed an air of careful neatness.

'Get a move on, Cantrill,' Brian headed for the door a towel wrapped round his waist.

Chapter Thirty Five

Susan left while Simon was still asleep. Didi had made her toast and strong coffee and could be relied on to wake Simon in time for him to get back to camp for first parade.

The previous evening was their first together for some time and had been spent, after a splendid meal at the Swiss Hotel, in sensuous lovemaking made serene by the oppressive humidity. They had had little sleep for when not making love they had talked and shared a bottle of ice cold champagne. Simon had arrived in high spirits, lifted by the successful operation but as the night had worn on his mood became more serious, though not depressed, and instead of lauding the competence and courage of his platoon, he dwelt more on the horror of what he had seen without being too specific.

She remembered waking at half four and drawing a blanket over them to ward off the chill that had settled on their nakedness. The alarm clock dragged her back to consciousness at six o'clock.

The drive to the station had been cold and she was glad that she had had the sense to wear a cardigan. She parked her car at the front of the huge, pink and white marble Moorish styled, mausoleum that was Ipoh's railway station and went quickly into the cavernous interior, usually pleasantly cool but now uncomfortably chilly. After checking the information board she went to platform three where the train to Singapore was noisily preparing to depart. She spotted Watkins, Harry's batman, and then Harry in conversation with a rather nervous RTO and OC train. Harry saw her, waved, and then knocked on the carriage window.

'Oh, I'm so glad you made it,' Jenny said smiling as she stepped down onto the platform. She looked tired and drawn.

'Thank God,' Susan said breathlessly, 'I thought I might have missed you.'

'Thank you for making the effort,' Jenny winked, 'it must have been difficult to leave a warm bed,' she grinned knowingly.

'Are you alright?' Susan hugged her, trying not to let her concern show.

'I'm fine dear,' Jenny replied cheerily, 'just a little tired.'

Harry had concluded his conversation with the OC train and his eyes met Susan's over Jenny's shoulder. His expression was grim and he gave a slight shake of his head. A whistle shrilled and in answer the huge engine spat steam noisily.

'Better get aboard, old girl,' he took her elbow and helped her up the steps then turned back took Susan in his arms, 'Thank you for coming dear girl,' Susan detected catch in his voice and when he stepped back she saw tears in his clear grey eyes.

'What's the matter, Harry?' she whispered urgently, 'has something happened?'

Before he turned and mounted the steps he said softly, 'I don't think that we shall be coming back,' and then louder, 'Cheery bye, Susan, see you in a couple of months.'

The train lurched and more clouds of steam burst forth from the engine. Jenny held on tightly to the carriage verandah as the train began to move and waved the blue silk scarf that she had been wearing round her neck.

'Bye, Susan, thank you, I'll write,' she blew a kiss.

Susan stood waving until they were out of sight, tears streaming down her face, Harry's last words had crushed her, and she knew in her heart she would never see her friend again.

*

'Come on, Al,' John said when they had been dismissed, 'it's NAAFI break; I'll stand you an egg banjo at the char wallah's.'

'Hey, Al,' Tom Fitch was sitting on the floor outside the hut reading a newspaper, 'me mums sent me a copy of the Bolton News, you wanna read the shit that reporter's written,' he handed the paper to Alan.

For a while Alan read the double centre page article in silence despite the requests of those around him to tell them the detail.

'Listen to this crap,' he said in due course, '*Our reporter David Baum and his photographer Bill Donald, have just returned from a hair raising operation with some of our brave local lads who are doing their National Service fighting the ruthless Communist Terrorist's in the jungles of Malaya. Dave and Bill joined a fighting patrol of the Royal West Lancashire Regiment, in one of the most dangerous areas of the country, hunting for the most notorious gangs currently operating in North Perak. Carrying over fifty pound packs, our intrepid reporter and photographer, accompanied 3 Platoon of 'A' Company, on a ten mile hike through jungle covered mountains...* Ten miles?' Alan scoffed, 'it was about five thousand yards, the lying bastards,' he went on reading it to himself and treating them to the more bizarre claims '*..although contact was made on three occasions with the Communists they refused to stand and fight, instead, they melted quickly away into the dense under growth.....not only do our lads have the to fight a violent war against a merciless foe but they carry on a constant battle against the climate, the terrain, dozens of wild animals and hundreds of poisonous snakes some of which can kill a man in seconds.* This is utter bullshit.'

'Look at the photographs on the opposite page,' Tom said.

'Bloody hell,' two photographs of the photographer, Bill Donald, stared back him, one as he normally appeared and one after his confrontation with the hornets. The caption read; *Photographer Bill Donald was lucky that the snake that bit him in the neck did not prove fatal, but it resulted in an unexpected trip by helicopter to a military hospital.* '

Alan shook his head handed the paper back to Tom, 'I'll never believe anything I read in the papers again.

*

Roger did not know whether to be pleased or disappointed. His interview with George Elloy, his commanding officer, had been brief but earth shattering.

'You're going to Sennybridge to join the Directing Staff, Roger,' the CO looked up from filling his pipe when Roger did not answer, 'Nothing to say'

'Well, sir,' Roger began and then hesitated, 'do I really have the experience, I mean; I don't want to appear to be questioning your judgement.'

'Sit down,' Colonel Elloy waved his pipe to the chair in front of his desk, 'You're not questioning my judgement, Roger, but you are questioning the judgement of your squadron commander and even I would not make so bold.' The big colonel smiled,' Johnny has more experience than the rest of us put together and he was selecting the best men for the job back in the early days with David Stirling. If he had the slightest reservations about your qualifications you wouldn't be sat here.' He reached forward and picked up some papers from his desk and handed them to Roger, 'These are your movement orders; you'll be flying from Changi the day after tomorrow so you'll have the chance to have a farewell drink with your chaps at Nanto's.'

Roger left the CO's office in a state of shock and made his way through the morning deluge oblivious to the soaking. Unconsciously he sought out the father figure of Pete Thompson whom he tracked down in the squadron stores with a number of the troops exchanging unserviceable kit.

'Can you spare a minute, Pete?'

'You look like you've found a tanner and lost a shilling,' Pete responded and then to the SQMS Leathwaite, 'Four pairs of new socks and new jungle boots, Flapper,' he called.

'I have to have the u/s ones, Sergeant Thompson,' Flapper Leathwaite called from the gloomy depth of his lair.

'Well they're there on your counter,' he followed Roger down the verandah, 'What's up?'

'I've been posted,' Roger said still stunned.

'Where?' Pete asked.

'Sennybridge, on the DS.'

'Well that's good,' Pete said, 'that's an honour, they don't pick the idiots for DS.'

'I've only been with the troop a year, the lads have just about accepted me and now I'm posted,' the shock had changed to muted anger.

'That's called soldiering, boss,' Pete replied, 'you go where you're needed and when you're needed and do the best you can when you get there. If it was fucking easy then civilians would be able to do it.'

'It's leaving the chap's, and all of the friend's that I've made since being here. I'm happy now that people have enough confidence in me to give me this task but it's the troop I'm going to miss.'

'I've told you, that's soldiering. You've got to leave the regiment in eighteen months when you RTU so make the most of this it'll stand you in good stead if you decide to come back to the regiment. You'll always make new mates in the army, our way of life requires reliable friends not like the rat race out there where it's dog eat dog and no bastard can even spell loyalty.'

Roger nodded, 'You're right, Pete, but it doesn't make it any easier. Can we have a piss up tonight?'

'When d'you leave?

'Tomorrow morning.'

'Leave it to me, I'll sort it, you just be in Nanto's for 1900 hours.'

Roger stared out across the camp, 'You know,' he said thoughtfully, 'I was going out with a nice little Chinese girl who worked at the civvy police HQ...'

'You told me,' Pete interrupted, 'but we all knew'

Roger looked up a little surprised, 'Oh, did you?'

'Come on,' Pete laughed, 'd'you think you'd get anything like that past 12 Troop?'

'I suppose not,' he smiled, 'she just disappeared while we were up north and I've heard nothing of her again, even her closest friends don't know where she's gone.'

'She worked for the police?' Pete confirmed. Roger nodded, 'Maybe she's gone 'inside', maybe you've been sleeping with the enemy,' he joked.

Roger's heart went cold and the vision of the girl CT's shattered face flashed before his mind's eye.

*

British infantry regiments exist in a state of constant change and in the days of National Service this condition was magnified tenfold. Every two weeks a batch of these transient soldiers would depart the regiment and a new batch would arrive and have to be turned into effective members of the unit. Those arriving were milky white, nervous, quiet and wearing shapeless crumpled uniforms. Those leaving were ebullient, tanned and vociferous and had all the appearance of professionals. Thirty years on, only one National Serviceman in twenty thousand would say that he had not benefited from his two years with the colours, and derived a good deal of pleasure from the experience.

In addition to the flux caused by the comings and goings of NS men, there was also continual movement of the regulars within the battalion. Postings, courses, leave and the occasional transfer. But the changes taking place within the RWL's were more consequential than normal.

At the very top, Lieutenant Colonel Crawson had handed over command of the battalion to his second in command, Major Quigley, and had taken up temporary command of the brigade in Harry Woodhouse's absence. Adjutant, Nigel Smith-Parr, left on secondment to the Kings African Rifles, it was later rumoured that pressure had been applied from brigade because of ungentlemanly behaviour but nobody ever knew what this could have been. Simon suspected that Susan had let his bizarre conduct over their relationship be known to Jenny, but she would neither deny nor confirm his suspicion.

3 Platoon did not escape significant change, Sergeant Snell was moved back to Training Company, Alan was promoted in his place, John Cantrill departed briefly on a Junior NCO's Cadre and they lost four NS men with the experience of two years soldiering and received six new sprog's as replacements. The platoon, under Simon's command, never had another contact with Charlie Tango despite a further two operation's and numerous ambushes.

But Simon was to experience another major upheaval.

*

Didi opened the door to Simon, 'Missy Susan in shower, Tuan,' she informed him, 'you want beer?'

She brought the ice-cold glass of Carlsberg out to the verandah and disappeared silently back into the bungalow. The night was humid but the stars shone cold and diamond bright. He sank into one of bamboo easy chairs and stared up at the stars. The smell of cooking could be faintly detected on the blossom-laden air, somebody nearby was going to enjoy a nice meal, and he briefly envied them their domesticity.

Susan emerged from the living room smiling, and smelling of expensive perfume, she leaned over and kissed him on the forehead.

'I've asked Didi to cook us a meal, I hope you don't mind.'

He smiled up at her, 'Not at all, I was only thinking a moment ago how delicious it smelt, I thought it was a neighbours.' There was something in her expression that was different, that he could not identify, 'Is something wrong; is there a reason why you've changed our plans? You usually enjoy going to the Martajam for a meal.'

'I have something to tell you that I'd prefer we shared in private,' though said sweetly the words were foreboding. She took a glass of gin and lime that Didi brought to her and sat in the chair beside him.

Simon had had enough partings for one day, he met the problem head on and when he spoke he knew that there was a little defensive anger in his voice, 'Am I getting a verbal *Dear John*?'

She placed her hand on his arm, 'You knew we couldn't make something permanent of our relationship, Simon, you're too young to settle down you have your entire life before you and there's no way that I could....'

'Oh, it is a *Dear John*,' he said sadly.

She reached forward and took his hand, 'Simon do you really think our relationship was going to develop into something more permanent; marriage?'

He shrugged, 'I suppose not but I thought...I'm sorry, it's been day of people I like and respect leaving. Sergeant Snell has moved on, back to HQ, I lost four good men who've gone on release,' he paused and then became a little agitated again, 'and now you, but why?'

'I had a signal this afternoon asking me to take over things at 51st Division in Hong Kong.'

'Oh, and you're taking it?'

It was Susan's turn to show a little passion, 'Simon, in less than four months you'll be going home and I will be left here alone, just a memory, of course I took it. It's promotion; it's a fresh start. I won't have memories of you everywhere I go.'

He sighed and nodded, 'I'm being extremely selfish aren't I?'

'You are,' she smiled and touched his face, 'let's enjoy our remaining time together and just retain happy memories of our relationship.' She stood up and sat on his knee, 'I will always think fondly of you, I've enjoyed all we've shared.'

*

By the time the troop made their noisy departure from Nanto's Bar, Roger knew that he had had enough to drink but he also knew that there could be no excuse accepted for ducking out. He had only had eight cans of Carlsberg but he had been around his troop long enough to know that they would have been spiked with something a little more volatile.

At the Galloway Club they lined their stomachs with plates piled high with nasi-goring before embarking on a raucous bought of, liar dice. The night became more and more bizarre and the sixteen of them were soon alone as other drinkers moved into other rooms, or left altogether.

Roger found himself in the toilets unable to recall how he got there and inspecting his recently consumed meal in the urinal. He felt a little better now that he had parted with the food. His watch told him that it was almost 0200 and he groaned at the prospect of the train journey to Singapore that he was due to take in another six hours, providing that he made it to the station, but at least he would be able to sleep on the train.

'Here he is,' Bob Gill's grinning face appeared round the door, 'come on, boss, you've got drinks lined up.'

'Just coming, Gilly,' Roger realised that he was slurring his words as badly as Bob. He went to the sink and splashed cold water over his face and head.

Jimmy Powell, Bob's unkempt shadow had now joined them, 'Did you foind 'im?' He saw Roger at the sink and placed a huge arm around Roger's shoulders, 'Oi'll look after you, boss.'

An hour later Roger began to feel that he was sobering up despite the fact he was still being plied with unidentifiable drinks. Tom Parnell was standing on an upturned shell case that had been placed in the centre of the table. A length of parachute cord had been secured to the beam above him and the other end formed a noose round his neck, he was obviously the loser at liar dice. Jerry Singleton was passing him a fire bucket brimming with a cocktail of drink that would probably render a water buffalo unconscious or even cause its demise.

Roger shook his head in wonder as Tom slowly raised the heavy container to his lips, he was as drunk as any of them, and it was a miracle that he could even stand let alone balance on his precarious perch. The manager, who had clearly witnessed this sport in the past, hovered in the background with a vicious looking knife in his hand. Just as Tom got the bucket to his lips and was carefully tilting it, Ray Pell leaned across the table and gave the shell case a mighty push. The cheer failed to drown Tom's choked scream.

'Bastards!' He still held the bucket and was trying to drink but the contents poured over his head adding the possibility of drowning to strangulation. Pete nodded his assent and the little, tubby, manager scrambled quickly onto the table and cut the cord. Tom dropped with a clatter onto the table scattering glasses in every direction.

The troop had had a good night out.

Chapter Thirty Six

They stood on the platform looking like a crew of dangerous, dishevelled, pirates who had just disposed of the fleet's rum ration. Roger leaned out of the window; his grief sensitised by the drink and listening to their banter.

His kit had appeared, as if by magic, by the time the three overcrowded taxis had deposited them at the station and he was helped into a crisp pea green uniform behind the human screen of his troop. Then Pete Thompson thrust a No 5 carbine and ten rounds of .303 into his hands and he was unceremoniously shoved up the steps of the carriage. The RTO appeared at his side complete with clipboard and troubled expression.

'Captain Howard?' He enquired, nervously.

'No,' Pete answered for him.

The RTO's anxiety turned to confusion; he studied his list and Roger's shoulder titles and red beret. He tried again, 'You're not Captain R Howard 22 Special Air Service?'

Again it was Pete who answered, he beckoned the WO2 closer and the man obediently stepped down onto the platform.

'He is Captain Howard but he doesn't always know it,' he paused and watched the words shredding the man's nerves. He lowered his voice a little. 'He's been lost in the jungle for over twelve months and it's made him a little strange. Now he's going home to a special hospital.'

'Twelve months?' disbelief was written on his face.

'Twelve months,' Pete confirmed seriously.

'I didn't hear about that.'

Pete gave a snort, 'You don't think the SAS would let something as embarrassing as that get out do you?'

'And it's made him..,' he left the sentence unfinished and tapped the side of his head.

'And how,' Pete confirmed.

'Shouldn't he be under escort then?' He was becoming more alarmed.

'He'll be fine, he's been drugged.'

'Been drugged?' the RTO almost shouted the words.

'Don't worry about it,' Pete reassured him, 'the moment that the train starts to move he'll go to sleep and you'll probably have to wake him up when you get to Singapore,' he could see that the warrant officer was not completely convinced, 'It's a special type of drug that was developed during the Korean War; it has a delayed effect that is only triggered by the motion of a train or other vehicle.'

The guards whistle made further explanation unnecessary and the RTO climbed back onto the train muttering that he had Roger down as OC train and eyeing his rifle warily.

'Would you like me to look after your rifle, sir'?

'That's very kind of you sergeant major,' Roger handed him the rifle and true to Pete's word stretched himself out on a seat of the first class compartment and went instantly to sleep.

*

Roger dreamed that he was travelling on a train, with Linda, to Singapore but the scenery through which they travelled comprised of an English scene, green rolling hills with herds of cows and sheep grazing peacefully. This did not seem unnatural in his dream world.

He felt happy and content but was unsure of Linda's feelings and he was doing his best to put her at ease. She was smiling but her smile seemed fixed and feigned. As he pointed out things of interest to her he gradually began to realise that the countryside on one side of the carriage had all the pastoral representation of England but on the other side was thick jungle, so close that the foliage brushed the carriage windows.

Fear began to replace his joy and his concern for Linda's contentment increased. He considered asking her if she would like to go to the restaurant car, not really wanting to leave their seats in case they lost them. They were sat opposite each other and he turned to look out of the window and as he did so he sensed her lean forward and felt her touch his arm. He turned to look at her; his scream was a scream of terror and despairing wretchedness, her face was the shattered face of the girl he had shot to end her suffering.

'Are you alright sir?' a worried looking young soldier stood over him.

Roger sat up, his sweat cold on him, 'Yes, thank you,' he rubbed his face, 'did I call out?'

'You did,' the soldier replied.

Roger did not go to sleep again and although he could not have known it then, he was to be revisited by the same dream for many years to come.

*

Brigadier Woodhouse and his wife arrived at number one Beach Road Singapore, commonly known as Raffles, in time for late tiffin which they took in the Empire Café in peaceful solitude and luxurious air-conditioning.

'It would have been more sensible to have stayed at Changi,' Jenny said as she refilled their cups with refreshing Darjeeling tea.

'I know,' Harry agreed, 'it would have been sensible, but this month's leave isn't about being sensible, it's about enjoyment, it's about luxury, it's..,' he hesitated,'...it's about us,' he smiled encouragingly.

'Yes,' she reached across the table and placed her hand on his, 'we must make the most of this time.'

He grasped her fingers, 'Do I sense a touch of maudlin, eh? Well let me make it clear from the start, maudlin is forbidden, d'you hear? Totally forbidden,' he squeezed her hand.

She lifted his hand and kissed it, 'I agree.'

'Right!' Harry enthused and looked at his wristwatch with an exaggerated flourish, 'I think it's about time we had a snifter, what d'you say to a stiff G and T?' He stood up and offered her his hand, 'I think the Courtyard Bar would be just the place.'

Chapter Thirty Seven

During the next three months much changed in Simon's life. Susan left for Hong Kong, and as promised, wrote to him once a week. More changes took place in the platoon as people came to the end of their engagements and new additions arrived to carry on the fight against communism. Luckily his nucleus of NCO's remained fairly intact giving the unit consistency, but sadly for the platoon, Alan Baker chose to try for SAS selection and disappeared in the direction of the bleak landscape of the Brecon Beacons. For a few weeks Corporal Rigby filled in as acting platoon sergeant but without the third stripe or the increase in pay but then a replacement arrived in the shape of Sergeant 'Nobby' Bradley.

Simon's replacement, also arrived at the same time, a bespectacled fresh faced youth, named Geoffrey Appleton.

'Pleased to meet you, Geoffrey,' Simon took his hand, 'they're a damn good platoon even if I say so myself. Hopefully we'll get a couple of op's in together to give you chance to get used to their little foibles.'

'There'll be no more operations for you, Simon old chap,' the company commander told him the following day when Simon had enquired if there was anything on the cards for an operation.

'Why's that, sir?' Simon asked fearing the worse.

'You fly home next week.'

'But if I'm flying home why do I need to go next week? I still have almost another two months to serve.' Simon protested

Big Jack smiled and addressed his 2i/c, 'I think we might be able to persuade young Simon here to stay on, what d'you think, Chris?'

'Well he doesn't sound too pleased about going home,' the large Chris Whitely agreed.

'What about it then, Simon?' the OC urged, 'are you going to apply for a short service commission?'

'Sir,' Simon said sadly, 'this has been the greatest experience of my life and it will never be bettered, but my father needs me in the business and I will be the third generation, I can't let him down.'

'Well, Simon,' the OC stood and straightened his bush jacket, 'we'll chat again before you leave but I'll just say now, that you would have gone far in the Army,'

In one way he was glad to be going, since Susan's departure he had been too busy to miss her but he knew that he would be somewhat at a loss if he had too much free time on his hands. On the other hand he knew that civilian life was going to seem rather tame after the last year but he would get over that, his father's generation had after a much longer and more brutal war. It was leaving the men that would be the hardest to bear.

He had led a typical middle class existence prior to his call up, rarely mixing with those less fortunate. The odd village fete or concert brought him into contact with the working class but the country working class were nothing like their contemporaries from the big cities. His little command was made up of a mixture of town-dwellers and country folk; he had found them warm, loyal and caring of their immediate group. Their humour and fortitude had given him greater faith in humanity; beneath those tough exteriors were kind, gentle and caring men. Had he had the impertinence to voice this opinion in their presence he would have been howled down for a fool or a snob?

It had only been a little over a year but it had been the most important and remarkable year in his life. All of his previous years seemed alien, he felt comfortable and at home and closer to the thirty disparate beings, with whom he had shared so much suffering, sorrow, adventure and triumph, than to any other group in which he had been involved .

When he woke he was soaked in sweat and he could hear Retreat being played by the duty bugler over by the guardroom. It was poignant a call and on hearing it anybody outside had to stand to attention for its duration, as the Union Jack was slowly lowered to mark sunset and recall to barracks.

He had a terrible thirst and raging hunger; he grabbed a towel and went out and along the verandah to the showers.

Chapter Thirty Eight

The Comet 2 stood on the apron gleaming in the sunlight like a huge, silver cigar tube, a heat haze distorting the undercarriage giving the appearance that it was floating. The blistering heat bounced off the concrete magnified four times, and bright sunshine reflecting from the same concrete, made the approaching passengers squint.

Some, of the forty service personnel and families approaching the jet, who kept up with events taking place in Europe, harboured emotions ranging from trepidation to terror. Over the two previous years the Comet had developed a disagreeable habit of exploding in flight and as a consequence all of those owned by civil airlines had been grounded while the problem was being investigated.

The RAF on the other hand, either had not learned of the aircraft's propensity to detonate without warning or considered it a risk worth taking in light of the fact that they took risks in many other ways and this was just one more.

Simon found the interior surprisingly small but very modern and the seat comfortable. Two airmen directed people to their seats.

'Don't rate the 'air-hostesses' very highly,' the middle-aged man sat next to Simon observed. 'James Carr,' he shook Simon's hand, 'Royal Artillery, away home to a job as a desk driver in the bloody War Department surrounded by tight arsed, humourless, civil servants for the next three bloody years.'

'Simon Gates, RWL's I'm going on release.'

'National Service?'

'Yes.'

'Army life didn't tempt you then?'

'A bit, but not enough, though I must admit I've enjoyed every minute and I really did not expect to when I was called up.'

'In my opinion, anyone who does not get some pleasure from Army life is either a bloody queer or a mummy's boy,' James said.

For diplomatic reasons everybody had to travel in civilian clothes so Simon did not know his companions rank but from his manner of speech and the fact that he had a job in the WD he gauged that he must be at least a colonel.

The four powerful Avon engines increased their volume and the two airmen closed the fuselage door. From the window Simon could see the stairs being towed away, he was going home.

The take-off was dramatic, the acceleration pinned them back into their seats and the pilot virtually stood the aircraft on its tail. Altitude was swiftly gained with much ear popping and seat arm gripping.

Simon looked sideways at his companion to see his reaction; James Carr was busy with the crossword in the Straits Times.

They had taken off in an easterly direction and their first stop was to be Karachi in West Pakistan. The plane began to bank gently as it gradually turned north taking them over the southern state of Johore, where Simon had started his jungle life.

From five thousand feet the vastness of the jungle was breath-taking and frightening in its enormity, it was a wonder that they ever made contact with the CT. The medium sized town of Kluang appeared minute, it would be possible to hide the entire British army under that mass of green foliage and they would have been difficult to find.

His thoughts drifted back over the past week. On Wednesday he had been dined-out in the mess, a pleasurable if formal affair with good food, company and an abundance of drink. Towards the end of the evening the senior officers discreetly withdrew leaving the subalterns to indulge their high spirits until the early hours.

The following evening, before he was fully recovered, the platoon had arranged a farewell party for him, a little more unorthodox. Army etiquette forbade him using the OR's canteen and likewise OR's only entered the officers mess as servants. He had gone to their lines expecting to take taxi's to some bar in the town but was surprised to see that only a few of the platoon were there and some of them were wearing JG's.

'Are you not coming with us, Corporal Cantrill?' he asked.

'Bloody right I am, sir,'

'Are you,' he hesitated, 'aren't you going to wear civvies.'

John grinned, 'No, this is the best gear for where we're going.'

Instead of taking taxi's, they led him out in the fading light across the regiments sports field to the area of scrub that served as a small training area. In a clearing he found a group of basha's laid out like one of the jungle bases that they had shared on so many occasions but with one difference; a large, unlit, bonfire was in the middle. The entire platoon was present including Dave Snell and two Iban's, Yau and Lameh; the merrymaking had already begun. Two hay boxes, filled with bottles and cans of beer and lager and smothered with ice stood by the unlit fire. Shouts of welcome greeted him and a can of Carlsberg was thrust in his hand.

'Wow,' was all he could think to say, he could not have been dreamt off a better send off.

Their comradeship, their bond that held them closer than family, their knowledge of each other's strength and weaknesses, they had all been formed in settings such as this. They had shared the incommunicable experience of combat, something that civilians could never understand or appreciate; they were brothers in arms.

The drink flowed, memories of loss, endurance, danger and humour were shared and laughter filled the tropical night. The fire was lit, and he had consumed four cans before he noticed that there was somebody missing.

'Where's Sam Andrews?' he asked.

'You're best not knowing, sir,' Brian handed him another can. Before Simon could ask why, someone shouted.

'Here's the scran.'

Sam and Ossie, a cook, entered the ring of light staggering under the weight of another hay box. Mess tins and eating irons were produced and a meal of curry and rice was served.

Later, as the fired died down the atmosphere became a little more serious, Ruby Murray stood up and held a bottle of Tiger aloft, 'Let's drink to Al and wish him good luck on his selection course.'

They all repeated the toast.

'And to the lads who won't be going home,' Dave said, 'Keith, Mike Donaldson who wasn't with us long enough to get to know but was one of us just the same, Len Knowles the driver, Geoff Pratt, and Terito the Maori. They all paid the price and I'll tell you something lads, no matter how long you live you'll never forget any of them,' he lifted his bottle above his head, 'to lost mates.'

'To lost mates' they said in unison.

For a moment they sat in silence with their private thoughts of their dead friends and Simon once again laboured with the responsibility he still felt for the deaths of these young men. Images flashed to mind, of the cab interior and clanging of bullets as they smashed into the metal, the flying glass and the moment that he felt certain that he was about to die.

'Another toast,' Dave interrupted, they went quiet. He produced a water bottle, 'Issue rum,' he explained, 'the drink we've shared so many times.' He went round the clearing adding a tot to whatever they were drinking. When he had completed the task he went and stood in front of Simon. 'Simon, I know that I am speaking for everybody here when I say you've been a bloody good platoon commander,' there were shouts of agreement, 'you learned quickly, not only the operational skills but also, more importantly, the skills of leadership and again I am speaking for all when I say we felt that you were one with us. We are a good platoon, and it's mainly down to your leadership. We're sorry to see you go, Simon,' he looked around the clearing, 'Those of you who

340

are National Servicemen may be eager to get home and back to your normal lives.'

'You can say that again,' Sam shouted.

Dave went on, 'But I'll tell you this now; you will never have mates again like the mates you've got here, in 3 Platoon, never!' He paused and the total silence registered that his words were being taken seriously, 'When your old men and you're beginning to lose your marbles...'

'Sam, lost his sometime back,' it was John who interrupted this time to universal agreement.

Dave continued...'you'll remember everyone one of these ugly buggers and what you went through together, and you'll be proud and glad you were a member of this platoon, and this regiment. To you Simon, thank you for your friendship and the care you have shown for your charges and good luck in the years to come.'

The shout was unanimous, 'Good luck, Simon.'

Simon had struggled to respond, the emotion of the moment and the effect of the drink brought forth a few, stilted but heartfelt words. As the sun rose over rubber estate behind them, they sat exchanging memories of the time that they had shared.

The plane was now passing over the central spine of mountains that ran down the peninsula, and had gained more height. The great wilderness was spread like a map below them and his eyes filled with tears. He knew that an important chapter of his life was over, a chapter that had taught him more about friendship, sacrifice, loyalty and courage than most people would learn in a life time.

'Good bye chaps, good bye Charlie Tango,' Simon said softly.'

The End

Postscript

It was a year when a Socialist government was making *improvements* to the armed forces. The RAF was losing four squadrons of fighters, the Royal Navy were to mothball two destroyers and an aircraft carrier, and would now have more Admirals than fighting ships, and the Army was to *gain* by having a quarter of the infantry disbanded.

The cap badges of Northern Regiments who had done the dirty work for monarch and politicians for over three centuries, from Quebec to Basra were to disappear from the Army List. The Kings Liverpool, The Manchester's, The Kings Own Royal Regiment, The Border Regiment, The East Lancashire's, The South Lancashire's, the Loyal North Lancashire's and the Royal West Lancashire's were all to be represented by one cap badge and only three battalions.

Invitations to the amalgamation ceremony had been sent to all members of the Regimental Association's. Simon had joined his regiments association a few years after his release and regularly made donations. The crowd that had gathered at Fulwood Barracks was much bigger than the organisers had anticipated. Word had spread beyond the associations and from all over the North of England ex-members of the regiments, both regular and National Servicemen, flocked to the barracks in Preston.

A contingent from each of the surviving regiments formed a hollow square facing a dais on which stood a number of dignitaries including the GOC and the Minister of Defence, who had no military experience of his own, but wore an expression of hypocritical melancholy. Also on the dais was the Mayor of Preston be-robed and be-chained and beside him a small pink faced man with a head like a billiard ball. Simon thought that he recognised the bald man but could not put the face with a place.

The Rt. Hon Les Black MP gave a short speech in which he tried to convince those who knew better that the changes that he had made to the three services would improve the fighting efficiency of all arms. At this fraudulent claim a lone voice from the rear suggested he do what everybody else was thinking.

'Fuck off you lying bastard.'

'I know him,' Simon said excitedly to his grandson, Robert, 'I know that voice.'

'He's not very polite,' Robert grinned.

'Politeness was never one of Sam's failings as I recall,' his grandfather replied with a grin.

The crowd rocked with suppressed laughter and the disconcerted Minister brought his speech to a pre-emptive close.

'Mr Gates, MC?'

Simon turned to find himself looking at a face that was familiar but harder and more worn than he recalled.

'Baker,' he said at last, 'Alan Baker?'

'The very same,' his weathered brown face split in a grin, 'and how are you, sir?' Simon clutched the strong brown hand unable to speak, 'did you recognise that voice?' Alan asked.

Simon nodded blinking back the tears, 'Sam, Sam... I can't remember....'

'Andrews,' Alan supplied.

Their conversation halted as the Last Post was sounded. All around the square, tough looking men, of all ages struggled with their emotions and when the call ended and *Auld Lang Syne* was stuck up by the band, most gave way to their tears of anger and sorrow.

'Are all right, granddad?' Robert looked up at him concerned.

'I'm fine Bob,' he lied, feeling a great sadness.

Wearing the badge of the new regiment, the various contingents marched off as one, a much saddened regiment.

'There's somebody else here who you know,' Alan told him as the crowd began to disperse.

'Oh,' Simon said eagerly, he had not really expected to meet any of his old friends but he had hoped he might, 'who?'

Alan looked around, 'He was here a minute ago. There he is. Johnno,' he called.

This time Simon had no problem in identifying his former platoon member. John Cantrill had the type of face that changed little with the passing years; he had a rugged timeless look and always had.

'Alright, sir?' he was the same amicable Liverpudlian, the same impudent grin and powerful grip. The face was a little more lined and the thick mop of black hair salted with grey, 'Did yer hear that silly bugger Andrews,' he shook his head and laughed, 'he hasn't changed.'

A smart faired haired woman clung to his arm and without waiting for introductions she held out her hand.

'I'm Joyce, John's wife. We still have your letter,' she smiled.

'My letter?'

She nodded and tears filled her eyes, 'The one you wrote to my mother, I'm Keith Gardner's sister.'

343

Totally out of character, he wasn't a tactile person; Simon hugged her but could not speak.

'Will you have time for a drink before you leave, sir?' Alan asked.

'Can we drop the, sir; Simon, please,' Simon protested, 'or Pearly if you like. I would only be too pleased to share a drink with you but I'm afraid that it will have to non-alcoholic we've got a long drive ahead of us haven't we, Bob. This is my grandson Bob, by the way'

'We could use the sergeant's mess,' Alan said after he had greeted Robert.

'You can get access?' Simon asked.

'Alan became RSM of the battalion,' John told him.

'Wonderful! Wonderful!'

'Did you stay on, John?'

'No I did my three then left, married Joyce here and became a woolly back,' Simon looked puzzled, 'I went to be a farm worker.'

'Good grief,' Simon was beaming, 'I bet that was a bit different to Liverpool.'

'But I thought that you went to the SAS, Alan?'

'Yes I did, but after two tours with them I returned to the RWL's'

They headed towards the grey stone building at the head of the square.

'Tell me, John, but I think I know the answer,' Simon asked, 'was it you who deposited that young officer in the er... the toilet?'

John smiled and winked but before he could speak they were interrupted.

'I remember you,' the small bald man, who had earlier been stood beside the mayor, blocked their path wearing a supercilious smile on his shiny round face. Beside him, stood a hard faced woman who was a head taller than he.

Suddenly, Simon was back in the CT camp struggling with a man who had lost his nerve, 'Yes,' he said slowly, 'now I remember you. Hayes, isn't it?'

'Mr Hayes to you, I'm not in the army now, I have an important position in the council.'

John pushed between Simon and Barry and put his face close to Barry's, 'I don't swear in front of my wife, Hayes, but I'm going to make an exception in your case. I don't know who invited a cowardly little shit like you to a parade to honour brave men, but if you don't fuck off I'll give you the battering you deserved way back then.'

Barry Hayes ruddy complexion paled and his sour faced wife gasped, 'And I'll have you arrested,' he blustered.

'And that's just your style, Hayes,' John sneered, 'you're not man enough to stand up for yourself.'

'Barry,' said the woman, who could have only been his wife, 'ignore them they obviously don't know who you are.'

'Oh, we do missus,' John laughed mirthlessly, 'we know exactly who he is, he's the only coward that I met in the regiment.'

Hurriedly, the unsavoury couple turned to leave, and in doing so collided with a fat, red faced man who, grinning, slapped Hayes repeatedly on his head.

'Little baldy, Barry, how the fuck are you...wow,' he scrutinised the woman, 'so you married that ugly bird who yer had on yer locker door,' he slapped Barry's head again, 'Yer braver than I thought, Haysee.' He looked past the subject of his defamation, 'Bloody hell!' his grin widened, 'is this a reunion you didn't invite me too?' He shook his head, 'no it can't be cos' this shit,' he indicated Hayes, 'wouldn't be here.' The affronted couple, one, puce with indignation the other scarlet with humiliation, forced their way frantically through the throng watched with amusement the four men.

'Al, Johnno, Mr Gates MC,' Sam threw up an exaggerated salute, 'this is magic. I'm buying you all a drink, no argument.'

'You're not gonna touch us for the money are you, Sam?' John asked.

Sam laughed, 'You haven't changed have you, Scouse lad?'

'You haven't either from that comment that was directed at the minister of defence, 'Simon smiled.

'You heard me then?' Sam was pleased.

'I think everybody did,' Simon replied.

'So long as that slimy bastard did,' Sam looked over their heads to see if the Rt Hon Desmond Black was still within hearing.

'We're just off to the sergeant's mess,' Alan told him, 'if we take you will you behave yourself.'

Sam put on his hurt expression, 'Al, this your old mate Sammy, did I ever let you down?'

Laughing, the four old men turned away and walked off across the square, briefly brothers in arms once again.

During their hour together, in the crowded mess, Alan updated Simon on a few of the company members from the mid-fifties of whom he had knowledge.

'Dave Snell emigrated, with his family to New Zealand and I heard that he was working for a logging company.'

'What was your friend's name, John?' Simon asked, 'the quiet chap.'

'Brian, Brian Large' John supplied.

'That's him, nice chap does anyone know what happened to him?'

John and Alan shook their heads.

'I met him in St Helens about five years ago,' Sam said, 'he was a bobby, he'd joined the police.'

'Was he arresting you, Sam?' John grinned.

'Piss of Johnno, Brian was my mate, he wouldn't arrest me,' and then after a short pause, 'He had just put a parking ticket on my van though.'

'Big Jack Winslow died,' Alan told them 'very sad.'

'What happened?' Simon asked, glumly.

'He was on a railway station, I think it was Waterloo, and was crossing between platforms, in one of those tunnels, when a couple bloody blacks mugged him. If he'd handed over what they wanted he'd have probably been alright but could you imagine Big Jack backing down to a couple of coons, they gave him a right kicking and he died three days later.'

'Bloody hell, how old was he?' Simon was shocked.

'Not sure,' Alan replied, 'but he must have been close to ninety'

'The bastards,' Sam was flushed with anger, ' a bloody grand old soldier who'd survived all the battle's he'd been through, and then to get kicked to death in his own country by a couple of blacks who probably shouldn't have been here anyway.'

'Mustn't be racist, Sam,' John mocked.

'Racist my arse,' Sam growled.

Simon drove the ninety miles back to Shrewsbury on automatic pilot. Robert listened to his CD's on his personal player while Simon re lived those two most important years of his life. As he turned the Mercedes onto the gravel driveway of his eighteenth century house he concluded that the world had changed and not for the better.

Glossary

AFN	American Forces Network
Amah	Maid
Auster	Light reconnaissance aircraft
ACC	Army Catering Corps
AWF	Armed work force (a branch of MRLA)
Banjo	Sandwich
Baju	Malay dress
Basha	Shelter/hut
BCM	Branch Committee Member
Belukar	Secondary jungle/thick undergrowth
Bevvy	Beverage/drink
BMH	British Military Hospital
Bondook	Slang for rifle
Bren	Light machine gun
Brick	SAS four man team
Browning	9mm Semi auto pistol
Cadre	Training course
Casevac	Casualty evacuation
CC	Company Commander
Changol	Long handled spade
Cheong Sam	Chinese dress
CEP	Captured enemy personnel
CO	Commanding officer, usually a Lt Colonel
CSM	Company Sergeant Major
CT	Communist Terrorist (Charley Tango)
CQMS	Company quarter master Sergeant (Colour Sergeant)
DEP	Dead enemy personnel
DZ	Dropping zone
DS	Directing staff
Dingo	Small armoured car
Egyptian PT	Lying on a bed
FARELF	Far East Land Forces
Ferret	Small armoured car
FN	Semi automatic rifle 7.62mm
Gecko	Small lizard
GOC	General Officer Commanding
Gunong	Mountain
GR	Grid reference
HE	High explosive
IA	Immediate action (a practiced response)

Iban	Tribesman from Sarawak
IO	Intelligence officer
ID	Identity
JCLO	Junior Chinese Liaison Officer
JG/OG	Tropical uniform
JTC	Jungle Training Centre
Kote	Store
Kremlin	SAS planning team
Kris	Malay knife
Lalang	Tall, course grass up to ten feet high – elephant grass
LMG	Light machine gun
LZ	Landing zone
MI	Medical Inspection
Monkey's	Military Police
MO	Medical Officer
MRLA	Malayan Races Liberation Army
MRS	Medical Reception Station
MT	Motor transport
NAAFI	The services shop/canteen. Navy Army Air Force Institute
Nashie	Slang for National Serviceman
NCO	Non commissioned officer
OC	Officer Commanding
O Group	Orders meeting
OR	Other rank, all ranks excluding commissioned officers
OP	Observation post
Parang	Iban version of a machete
Paludrine	Foul tasting anti malarial tablet
PIAT	Anti tank rifle
Pippy	Slang for subaltern
Pom	Australian slang for British
PTI	Physical Training Instructor
QARANC	Queen Alexander's Royal Army Nursing Corps
QM	Quartermaster
QR's	Queens Regulations
RAAF	Royal Australian Air Force
RAMC	Royal Army Medical Corps
RAOC	Royal Army Ordnance Corps
RAPC	Royal Army Pay Corps
RAR	Royal Australian Regiment
RASC	Royal Army Service Corps
REME	Royal Electrical and Mechanical Engineers
RE	Royal Engineers

RIO	Regimental Intelligence Officer
RMP	Royal Military Police
RSM	Regimental Sergeant Major
RTO	Railway Transport Officer
RTU	Return to Unit
RV	Rendezvous
Running dog	Collaborator
Sambur	Small deer
SC	Squadron Commander
SCM	State Committee Member
Scran	Food
SEP	Surrendered enemy personnel
Sitrep	Situation report
Smith and Wesson	.38in revolver
SMG	Sub machine gum
Snowdrop	Air force police
Sonkok	Malay hat
Sten	Make of SMG
Sterling	Make of SMG
SSM	Squadron Sergeant Major
Stag	Period spent as sentry
Syce	Waiter
Tuan	Lord/Sir
Ulu	Jungle
Wilco	I will cooperate
WO	Warrant Officer

Made in the USA
Charleston, SC
12 September 2014